BROKEN
by desire

By Dani René

Copyright© 2016 Dani René
Published by Dani René

Print ISBN 978-0-620-68463-7
Epub ISBN 978-0-620-68189-6

All rights reserved, including the right to reproduce this book or portions thereof in any form whatsoever.

The following story contains mature themes, strong language, and sexual situations. It is intended for adult readers.

No part of this book may be reproduced or transmitted in any form or by any means, electronic or mechanical, including photocopying, recording, or by any information storage and retrieval system, without permission in writing. If you would like to share this book with another person, please purchase an additional copy for each recipient. If you're reading this book and did not purchase it, or it was not purchased for your enjoyment only, then please purchase your own copy. Thank you for respecting the hard work of this author.

This book is a work of fiction. Names, characters, places, and incidents either are products of the author's imagination or are used fictitiously. Any resemblance to actual events or locales or persons, living or dead, is entirely coincidental.

The author acknowledges the trademarked status and trademark owners of various products referenced in the work of fiction, which have been used without permission. The publication/use of these trademarks is not authorized, associated with, or sponsored by the trademark owner.

Printed by CreateSpace, An Amazon.com Company

Table of Contents

Prologue

Chapter One

Chapter Two

Chapter Three

Chapter Four

Chapter Five

Chapter Six

Chapter Seven

Chapter Eight

Chapter Nine

Chapter Ten

Chapter Eleven

Chapter Twelve

Chapter Thirteen

Chapter Fourteen

Chapter Fifteen

Chapter Sixteen

Chapter Seventeen

Chapter Eighteen

Chapter Nineteen

Chapter Twenty

Chapter Twenty-One

Chapter Twenty-Two

Chapter Twenty-Three

Chapter Twenty-Four

Chapter Twenty-Five

Chapter Twenty-Six

Chapter Twenty-Seven

Chapter Twenty-Eight

Chapter Twenty-Nine

Chapter Thirty

Epilogue

Playlist

Acknowledgements

About The Author

Other books by this author

Connect with Dani René

*"I loved her not for the way she danced with my angels,
but for the way her name could silence my demons."*
― *Christopher Poindexter*

PROLOGUE

"Kneel." His voice was raspy and deep. I complied and kneeled on the plush black carpet. The room was exquisite, with a large four poster king-size bed. The bedding was black and purple. A chest of drawers and the ornate chair were a deep charcoal. There was a full-length mirror in the corner next to the walk-in closet. With two large patio doors and a balcony just beyond where I was kneeling, you could see the city flickering in the dark. The moonlight shone through, illuminating the darkness. "Do you want to be here, sweetness?"

"Yes, Sir." I murmured, low and breathy, just how he liked it. I kept my gaze trained on the carpet, concentrating on the pattern of the dark woven wool. When he moved around the room, my body hummed in anticipation. A match strike sounded behind me, and my heart stuttered. This was the first time I was in this room. He called it the play room. There weren't any toys lying around, but I knew there were hidden mysteries in the chest of drawers behind me. The scent of lavender and rose filled the room, and I realized he lit some candles. The glow in the room was a soft romantic light. Such a contrast of what we were doing here. In the darkness there's always light. That's what he liked to say. I was his light. He was my darkness.

He asked for my acceptance of him, of his love of darker things. He asked also for my submission. There wasn't a question, of course, I would give it to him. I loved him. I wanted to please him, serve him. To be his girl, the only one. "Close your eyes." His gruff order had me shuddering. The heat between my thighs pulsed with need. For him to take me, rough, hard, and deep. The soft black blindfold covered my eyes, and I smiled in the darkness. My pulse skittered and my palms were sweaty. "What is your safe word?"

My smile deepened then. "Summer." I murmured the word that would make him smile too.

"Good girl." I could hear the amusement in his tone. "Stand. Slowly." I knew what he wanted to see. One leg at a time, then to push up with my feet. Bent over at the waist. My hands on my ankles, slowly stroking my legs as I straightened. My slick pussy, open to his hungry gaze behind me. As soon as I was upright, I heard the groan rumbling in his chest. I was naked. He had ripped my pink panties off earlier. My bra discarded on the floor somewhere. My skin was on fire and my need increased. The heat of his body surrounded me and I trembled. His gaze burned into me. "You're beautiful, lumiére." I started at his warm breath on my neck, his words had my core pulsing

"Thank you, Sir."

"Move your hands over your nipples. Make them hard for me." His command was low, restrained, and sexy. Instinctively my hands moved up, over my breasts. My nipples hardened at the contact. A low growl rumbled in his chest. He watched me play with them, tweaking, and tugging, until they were aching pebbles. He leaned in and flicked his tongue over the tight buds and I whimpered. "So perfect, little tigress. Are you hungry?" I nodded. "Tell me." He needed the words.

"Yes, Sir. I am hungry." His hands were on my shoulders then, the heat of his touch burning into my skin. With a soft push, I lowered to my knees. Once again I kneeled before him. With a whoosh the blindfold fell away, and I glanced up into intense mossy green eyes. A devilish smile curled his lips, and I knew what he wanted. The low slung sweatpants he wore tented, making my mouth water.

"It's yours, let's see how hungry my little kitty is." Without another word, I untied the string of his sweats, tugging them down his toned thighs. His erection stood proudly. A bead of arousal glistened on the crown and I flicked my tongue out to lick it. The salty musky taste of him was exquisite, and I needed more. My lips wrapped around the tip, and I sucked him into my mouth.

My tongue scraping the underside of his ten-inch cock. I savored every ridge and pulse. As soon as he was deep inside my throat, his hands fisted in my hair, holding me still. "Fuck." He hissed the word through his teeth. Slowly he pulled me off and then pushed back in. The man in control. Fucking my face. He took his pleasure from me. My slick sex dripping and the knot in my stomach tightened.

Pleasing him made every nerve in my body tingle. I realized I could come just by giving him pleasure. When his cock hit the back of my throat, I moaned around him, and his grip on my hair tightened. He tugged roughly. The bite of pain sent a jolt of pure pleasure straight to my throbbing clit. "Jesus, sweetness, your mouth on my cock feels like heaven." I peered up at him, my chocolate eyes, locked on the green glistening stare of him. He pulled me off suddenly. "Enough."

"Thank you, Sir." I bit my bottom lip to keep from smiling. His hands slid down my body, his fingertips left goose bumps in their wake and I shivered.

"On the bed. I want you on all fours. That sweet peach ass will be mine." The order made me gasp, but I didn't argue. The soft satin sheets felt cool against my fevered skin as I kneeled on them. I placed my hands on the bed in front of me, facing the window. The lights of the city twinkled below. "So fucking beautiful." He rasped from behind me. Suddenly a swat came down hard on my ass. I yelped in surprise. The tingle prickled my skin. Another swat came down on my other ass cheek. Then both his warm rough hands were on me, smoothing, massaging the tender flesh. "Is my little tigress wet for me?"

"Yes, Sir. Very wet." I moaned as his fingers slid down my ass and over my sopping bare cunt.

"You are. Do you like letting me have my dirty wicked way with you?" I nodded. A hard slap in between my thighs caught my pussy and my toes curled with the pained pleasure that shot through me.

"Fuck!" I cried out loud, and another swat came down hard on the apex between my thighs. My orgasm ripped through me, sending waves of pleasure splintering through my core.

"I think my dirty little kitty wants me to fuck her. Doesn't she?" I nodded. Quickly. There wasn't anything else I wanted more. The need to entice him fueled my actions, and I pushed my ass back towards him. I wanted him to make me purr. To make me come again, and again. He was quiet for a long moment, and I thought he would not do anything. "Do you really want to be mine, sweetness?"

"Please, yes! I want to be yours, please. Take me. Please?" He told me he would make me beg. This evening while we sat side by side at the dinner table in the posh restaurant. His words rang true in my ears. 'I will make you beg, and when you do, it will be for me to fuck you. When you submit to me, it will be because you need to, ache to, and that's a promise. And tomorrow, when you're walking into the office, you will feel me between your thighs.'

"Open those incredible legs, sweetness." My legs open as soon as the words leave his lips. His warm rough hand comes down and cups my bare lips. "This, is mine. Do you understand?"

"Yes, Sir." With a slow steady hand, he slides it up my slick folds, and suddenly plunges two fingers into me. The knot in my stomach tightens and I cry out as another orgasm shatters me. My arms buckle, and my core cinches around his fingers. Coating his fingers in my arousal. I hear his groan. Without another word, his fingers are replaced with his thick veiny shaft, sliding so deep inside, my whole body ripples with pleasure. I am so full, his cock hits deep, knocking the breath from me. With a firm grip on my hips, he slides out, almost all the way, then suddenly slams back into me. His primal groans send me teetering on the edge of another earth shattering orgasm. I realize I will not be able to hold myself up. My arms are shaky.

His relentless drives continue, the thick shaft twitches, and I know he's close. "Come for me, sweetness. Coat my cock in that sweet honey from your tight little cunt." His words are my undoing and my body obeys. My orgasm splinters me; my arms give way. His one arm bands around my waist, and the other grips my neck. Holding me up, my back flush with his chest, as he continues to pound into me.

His teeth tug at my earlobe. "Now I will mark you, ruin you, and possess you, so that no other man can have you." Before the words leave his mouth, his release shoots into me. The hold on my neck loosens and I fall forward, my hands come out to hold myself up as he pulls out and shoots his hot seed on my back. Marking me. Owning me. Possessing me. I am his.

Cassandra

I hugged Kenna at the airport and boarded my flight. She would join me in a few weeks, but it was never fun saying goodbye to your best friend. She would stay in New York while I found my way around LA. My decision to leave came after I got the call for an interview, with one of the most renowned magazine publishers in Los Angeles.

Luckily, I had a window seat, so I could watch the clouds move as I made my way to my new city. I have only ever spent holidays on the West Coast and now I would be living there. The excitement was taking over and I couldn't concentrate on the in-flight movie.

Once I landed, I would be busy. From furnishing my new apartment to finding an outfit for my interview, which would be in a week's time. The flight wasn't long, but I closed my eyes and let my mind drift into a dreamless sleep.

Walking into my new home was surreal. My dream of packing up and moving to California has finally come true. I had chosen to rent close to the offices that I would hopefully work in. Beachwood Canyon is iconic, I think the whole of Los Angeles is, but that's my opinion. As I walked through my one-bedroom apartment; I smiled, it was perfect. I loved the split-level layout and hardwood floors. Opening the sliding glass door, I looked over my private patio. That was the main reason I chose this one. The privacy it afforded me, is something I needed.

Before I unpacked, I needed to call Kenna. She was as excited as I was. We used to talk about living together in LA and making a name for ourselves. For us, it's been one of those magical cities, the one where your wildest dreams could come true. So it would make sense to be here, The City of Angels.

I woke up early Friday morning and decided to go for a run. I had only been in LA for 2 days and I wanted to explore. My interview was next week so I had time to get used to the area and my new neighborhood. It was easy to navigate and I found a coffee shop that would soon become my refuge. I walked in after my run and decided to try it out. Ordering a coffee, I took a seat at the table in the back. Watching the people come and go.

He caught my attention the moment he walked through the door. Holding my breath, I watched him. His face was almost angelic. I say almost because there was something in his eyes, something darker. No man that beautiful could be good news. He ordered his drink and I watched him move through the crowd. He took a seat at a table close to the window, not far from mine. He was magnetic. I licked my lips as my eyes followed the beads of sweat running down his perfectly sculpted biceps. His arms were works of art, I tried to see the tattoos, but he was too far away. It took a lot of effort to look away and even then, I could see him in my mind. It was like there was a magnetic pull I felt towards him.

I left New York to start fresh and a romance is definitely not what I needed. That didn't mean I couldn't drink him in with my eyes. He was definitely drinkable. I took in every inch of him. He was too perfect. There had to be something else wrong with him, mustn't there? Maybe he was married. Yes, he must be. I shook my head and made my way through the shop. As I passed his table, his scent hit me like a freight train. It was intoxicating, a mix of spice and sweat.

I ran home trying to clear my head, but it didn't work, as soon as I closed my eyes that night he was there. Those piercing green eyes. That spikey brown hair and those amazing lips. I dreamt about him that night.

I wasn't looking for anything remotely romantic in my life. After the tragedy that struck me, there was no room for anything like that in my heart. My life was about my career. I needed to heal from the pain. Kenna would disagree. She told me every day that I had the two years to recover. Although losing everyone close to you in the way I did is not something you just get over.

Of course, she was the only one who knew the whole story. She knew why I was so torn, broken. It was more than just losing someone you loved. There was so much more hanging on me, my decisions that night. I know it will haunt me forever. I doubt anyone would want someone like me. I mean, my demons are ugly bastards. I did this, it was all my fault.

Somehow, though, when I looked into those smoldering green eyes, it stilled my mind. He made me see past the demons in my own heart. Calm down Cassie, you don't even know him. Deep down, I wanted to know him. Even though I didn't want a relationship, I still found myself at the coffee shop every day. Just to look into those piercing green eyes. To still myself, my mind and to see the beauty that lies inside him.

Lucien

Running every morning gives my mind a break from the everyday mind-numbing business meetings. I got into this business to publish, not to sit in stuffy board meetings. Although, I know I have to. Taking over the business from my father is what I was meant to do. My life is perfect, I have a penthouse apartment, nice cars and a little black book of every hot model in LA.

Some call me the ultimate playboy, I call myself lucky. Love isn't something I want or need. So, I have fun. Being young and single allows me the freedom to fuck any girl who wants it and let us be honest, they all do. Since I turned sixteen, every girl I came across wanted in my pants. If it wasn't my money they were after, I would have probably settled down. Actually… Who am I kidding? Settling down wasn't in my vocabulary. After what happened with my ex, those words were blasphemy.

As soon as I reached the door of the coffee shop, I step inside and take in the early morning queue and the intoxicating smell of roasted coffee. The best smell ever. I order my usual and make my way up to the table. Glancing up, my breath stops and my cock twitches. She's fucking beautiful. Taking in her appearance, the first thing I look for is a ring. None that I can see. Which means she's single, perfect.

Sipping my coffee, I find myself wondering why she's sitting alone. I have never seen her here before and I wonder if she just moved here or if she's one of those girls that knows where I hang out and now she's waiting for an open. When her gaze falls on me, there isn't a hint of recognition. Maybe I was wrong.

Her brown curls are tied back, but there are a few that have escaped the clip and frame her beautiful face. Those mocha eyes seem to pierce through me. I imagine her looking up at me with those soft lips wrapped around my cock. Fuck. Her hands tremble around the mug of coffee and I know that's due to my intense gaze on her. I am confident about that.

Play it cool. She would look so good bound to my bed. Moaning with pleasure as I taste her. I bet she tastes like fucking honey. Taking another sip of coffee, I pull out my phone. With the steel erection in my sweats, I think I need to get out tonight, I message Jayce. This girl needs time. She's timid and nervous, just how I like them. I need to take my time with her. Then and there I decide I want her, but I am going to do this my way. Is there any other way?

I can see she's going to play right into my hands. When she rises from her chair, I watch her. The way her lithe body moves, to that tiny tank top that's hugging her torso. Her ass is tight and I imagine marking it with my hand. I know there's a tent in my sweats, but I don't care right now. The only thought I have is taking her and making her scream my fucking name. Her under me, my cock buried in that tiny little cunt. Yes, that's exactly what I want, and I always get what I want.

As soon as I walk into the office and hour later, my new assistant is at my heels. She's fucking annoying, but insanely good. Once I am at my desk, seated, she starts rambling off about the meetings I have set up for today. "Stacy. Just bring me a coffee. I need a moment." Her tirade of words stops dead and she nods. She spins on her heel and leaves me to my thoughts.

I close my eyes and sit back. The memory of the mysterious girl from the coffee shop has been invading my thoughts all morning. My shower was one of the best I had in a long time. When I open my eyes, I turn to face the city, the view from my office was incredible, but nothing could top those mocha eyes that seemed to stare a hole inside me this morning. "Sir?" I glance up and nod. Stacy places my coffee on the desk and takes a seat in one of the black leather wingback chairs opposite my desk. "There's a marketing meeting in thirty minutes, I have all the documents you need. Then you have the four-hour board meeting and your father will be here as well." I nod. "And then there's the interview on Monday with the new candidates for the publishing assistant. Victoria will head it up, but you should be there."

"Why?" I sit back. She looks dumbfounded that I should even ask her something like that. I don't see why I have to sit in an interview when I know Victoria can handle it.

"Well, sir, I mean—"

"Victoria can handle it," I say dismissively. "Call Jayce, tell him to be in that marketing meeting." I grab my coffee and take a long sip. Grabbing the paperwork, I rise and Stacy follows me.

"Meeting room four sir," she tells me as I make my way out of the office, turning left, walking down the hallway. As soon as I'm seated, the thoughts of her invade my mind again. Fuck this. I need to find her. I need to make her pussy come all over me. Fuck her out of my system, because that's all that it will ever be.

Chapter One

Cassandra

My feet pound the ground hard; it was a dismal morning with the threat of rain. The rhythm of the song urged the tired muscles in my legs forward. I run towards the modest cafe at the bottom of the hilltop, people were lining up for their daily fix of caffeine and it wasn't even 6:45 yet. I slow to a steady pace taking a deep breath, my legs throbbed from the exertion. I had run the normal six miles today but seemed more like sixty. Exhaustion creeping up on me, feeling it in my muscles. I hadn't been sleeping properly. I put it down to excitement for the interview on Monday, but also that I couldn't get a specific green-eyed man off my mind.

When I walked into the small coffee shop and waited in line, pulling my phone from the zipped pocket, I went through my email. As I glance up, I realize I am at the front of the queue. I turn off the music and step forward to place my order. "One black coffee, please? The Brazilian blend, no sugar."

The barista smiled and responded. "The usual then?" He takes the Styrofoam cup, turning to the machine. A few moments later, he hands me my order, and I find my usual table empty. I loved to watch people, and this table gave me the bird's-eye view of the whole café. With a slow sop of my coffee, I keep myself distracted on my phone. I notice his presence the instant he sauntered into the shop. My heart hammered in my chest and the butterflies came alive in my belly. Every morning without fail, he orders a large cappuccino. He wore grey sweats and a grey tank top. His ritual matching mine, a long jog and then a coffee.

His dark brown spikey hair wet from the soft drizzle outside, causing me to crave running my fingers through it. He takes a seat at this usual table neat the window, two from me. His deep green eyes examine the screen of his phone.

The realization hits me, I am blatantly staring, but I can't help it. I have never seen a more beautiful man. He has become the only reason I stop here after my run. To get my fill of him for the day. I wondered what he did? He must be in a band, or advertising? With those tattoos I doubt that his passion was anything, but creative.

I took in how his long lithe fingers gripped the phone and his thumbs move over the screen. It didn't take him long to finish the email or text message. When his eyes dart up, locking with mine for the first time and I am startled. The heat pools in my belly and my pulse quickens. A mischievous smirk curls on his amazing lips. I flush, biting my thumb to keep from smiling. His eyes narrow as he watches my reaction to him. I avert my attention to the damp morning. I can't let him know he's affected me.

There is no way I can get involved with anyone. Romance was a no go area. The only thing on my mind, besides this handsome stranger, was the interview later today. I had to make sure I landed the position. I couldn't go back to New York.

His heated gaze burned into me. I needed to go. Now. The last gulp of coffee is lukewarm, and I finish it quickly. I go to stand up. My legs are wobbly, but I make my way towards the exit. I sense his eyes on me, but I steel myself from turning to look at him. I am sure he will be here again tomorrow. Same time, same place. The door closes behind me, and I run into the deluge.

Lucien

  My run is consumed with her. I haven't spoken to her yet. I can't afford to scare her off, so I need to figure out how to approach her. She will be beneath me. Soon. I take what I want, especially to piss my stepmother off. This girl is new. I haven't seen her around before and I wonder what her story is. She has starred in my fantasies since the first day I saw her and now I find myself getting a coffee every morning to stare into those mocha colored eyes. She's sexy as hell and all I can think of is how she would look naked, writhing below me. I need to get that image out of my head, it won't be a good idea to walk into a busy coffee shop with a fucking hard on.

  When I reach the door, I push it open and step inside. My eyes dart around until they fall on her, but I don't dwell on her too long. I can't let her know that I spotted her, not yet. *Come on dude, she's just a girl, actually, she's a woman.* She has curves for days and that little tank top she's wearing does nothing to hide the beautiful set of tits on her. I want her.

  I grab my phone out of my pocket to distract myself, opening my emails I groan at the sheer number of them. Once I get my coffee, I grab a seat at the table close to hers. I don't want to make it obvious, but I need to be close enough to drink in every detail of her. Her long brown hair is tied back into a ponytail; her cheeks are flushed. I take in the curve of her lips, they are natural, soft and pink and they would look so good wrapped around my cock. *Fuck!* I glance down at my emails again, but I can't concentrate. I tap out a message to Jayce about the latest shoot, which is only a week away. It's the only thing I can do to keep my mind off her. The photo shoot this weekend will help; I can find a hot model eager to let me fuck her. Easy enough, they're all so brazen in their attempts to trap me, I find it laughable.

  I glance up, her eyes are on me and I'm awarded with those chocolate eyes drinking me in. She's staring. Giving her one of my signature smirks has her flushing and my effect on her doesn't go unnoticed.

  Why else would she come here every morning? Yea, the coffee is good, but not that good. When she glances out the window, I take in the profile of her soft features, the smooth skin, the way she glistens with sweat from the exertion of her early morning run. I bet I could make her sweat in more pleasurable ways. My mind completely focused on how her lips must taste. She rises and walks towards the exit, our time has come to an abrupt end, my stare doesn't leave her lean frame, the way her hips sway and how her ass looks in those sweats. My cock aching for attention and I tear my eyes away as the door closes behind her.

  This will be an incredible fuck. She must be so fucking tight. With my past, it's too risky for a relationship, but I wouldn't mind finding out what she tastes like, how sensitive her nipples are. The thought of her swallowing my cock is in the forefront of my mind now. Maybe I would see her tonight, Jayce and I plan to hit that bar down on Sunset. I glance at the emails again, apparently, there's an interview today. I know I should be there, but I am definitely not in the mood for it. Once they've hired a replacement, then I plan on meeting her. I specifically wanted them to hire a female, not for the reasons you're thinking. Mainly because she will manage my photo shoots and I didn't want more men around the models.

I finish my cappuccino and make my way to the door. It's started raining again. My eyes do a quick glance down the road, but she isn't there. Of course, she isn't! She left ages ago. I will have to just see her tomorrow morning. I look forward to seeing that blush on her cheeks again.

Cassandra

I walk into the offices of Verán Publishing fifteen minutes early. I have a fear of being late so I always tend to be too early. The white tiles and glass that surround the reception area were a severe contrast to the drab morning outside. I take in the impeccably furnished area. My nerves are getting the better of me and I shudder. A crimson and black splattered canvas hangs above the reception counter.

This is an important interview and tension tightens my shoulders. My iPod was on full blast, one of my favorite bands, Bullet for my Valentine, screamed in my ear. Funny enough they always seemed to calm me. I snagged the earphones from my ears and gave the receptionist a shaky smile. "Can I help you?" She asks glancing up with a flawless grin.

"I, um… Cassandra Winters, here for an interview with Ms. Richards?" She nods, pressing a few buttons on the base of the phone. Her headset remains perfectly in place. She talks into the mic announcing my arrival. I take in her polished appearance. I am sure it's a requirement to look good when you're basically the face of a publishing company.

"Have a seat, one of the human resource staff will get you in a minute." She beams and carries on typing and answering calls. I turn around and make my way to one of the wide sofas. I perch on the plush leather, my back to the revolving doors. Checking my phone repeatedly, no messages or emails this morning. I take a deep breath and hit play on the song.

I am calmer as the song ends. Suddenly a voice startles me. The timbre of this voice is like velvet being draped over my skin, warming my body and a knot in my stomach tightens. I whirl and glance into the intense green eyes I have seen every morning for the past four days. He acknowledges the receptionist as he confidently strides up to the counter. She blushes and flutters her perfect eyelashes. Flirting like her life depended on it. *I don't blame her! Look at him!* He turns on his heel, locking his gaze on me and I am floored. My face heats, my cheeks flush under his powerful stare. He smirks, giving me a slight nod. Turning and striding towards the elevators. I take in his departing form noting how his suit pants cling to his muscled thighs. His jacket just covering the tight ass I am drooling over. I had only ever seen him in sweats; I am breathless at how sexy he looks in a suit. So he works in an office. *My office!*

Green eyes emblazoned in my mind. *I wonder what he does here?* We work in the same building. That means I won't just see him in the mornings after our jog. The thought flip flops my belly and my nerves start up again. I can't let him affect me like this. I need to pull myself together. It was one thing seeing him every morning, and he featured every night in my dreams, but seeing him every day at the office? *Could I deal with that? I can, I am an adult, not a lovesick teenager.* I needed to make sure I remained far away from him.

Lucien

The hot shower does nothing to stop the thoughts of my mystery woman from playing in my mind. I have a long day ahead of me. With meetings back to back and a working lunch, I have to clear my head. Every day for me lately is long. I recall my morning coffee, it is the only thing pushing me through. Fuck, I needed to stop thinking about her. *Come on Luke, get a fucking grip. You can have any woman in LA or any other city for that matter. Why is she haunting me?* Tomorrow I will just go up to her, ask her to join me for dinner and once I fuck her, it will be fine. I need to fuck her out of my system. That's all. It's easy as that, no strings, no hearts, nothing oddly romantic about it.

I turn off the spray, stepping out of the shower, I grab a towel and make my way to the bedroom. My walk-in closet is filled with suits and shirts, ties and shoes, but I was always more comfortable in a pair of sweats and a tank top. Since taking over my father's publishing company I suppose I had to dress the part, never in my life did I imagine I would be a suit. Jayce gave me shit about it every day, telling me I looked like a high-powered executive, which I was far from. I decide on my charcoal Armani suit, crisp white shirt and the olive green tie. Jayce is the jeans and trainers type, he's lucky, being the photographer he doesn't have suit up every day. Maybe I should ask dad if I can become a photographer, looking at beautiful women all day would definitely be right up my street.

Grabbing my phone, I text Robert to be ready in five minutes. I am ready to kick ass today and tonight I will be inside some hot brunette or blonde. My mind flits back to my mystery woman. I pull on my pants and button up my shirt and start on my tie. I hate these things, like a fucking noose. With a shrug I slip on my jacket and tie the two buttons. The suit looks good, tailored to be a perfect fit. Those mocha eyes are still burned into my eyelids. *She's so fucking hot.* I grab my briefcase and make my way to the garage. Today I need to concentrate on work.

"Robert, how are you this morning?"

"Good Sir, thank you. And yourself?"

"Ready to get the day done. I would like you to drive Jayce and me tonight." He gives me a stiff nod. I have known him most of my teenage life. He's been my driver since I was sixteen and needed to get to school and back. Now that I am thirty, it's like he's part of the family. He's probably the only one besides Jay that knows me as well as anyone can.

Fifteen minutes later I step into the offices, and I feel calm. I shoot a glance at the reception desk and see the perky receptionist. She's brunette. That would be way too easy. As soon as she spots me her smile brightens, and she pushes out her chest. *It's like taking candy from a baby.*

"Good morning," I glance at her nametag, "Trisha." She offers me her best smile.

"Good morning, Sir." The words on her lips make my cock twitch. As I turn to walk away my glance falls on the people waiting on the sofas when I spot her. My heart hammers in my chest and I am sure it will stop. She looks up at me and my world spins. *Play it cool man! Just fucking relax. I give her a smirk and I see the blush spread across her cheeks. She's in my building. Fuck!* This will be interesting. I need to tear my eyes away from her. She's even more stunning all dressed up in those sexy heels. *I wouldn't mind having her wearing nothing but those heels. Luke, get a grip man!* Turning away was difficult, but I had a meeting and if I stared at her for much longer, I would have to sit through the day with a hard cock. Her hungry gaze burns a hole into my back as I walk away and a smile curls my lips. *Keep looking sweetheart, because I will be inside you, very soon.*

Cassandra

I step onto the sidewalk two hours later. My body was noticeably shaking. *I got it! I got the position!* The first thing I need to do is tell Kenna. I find her number and hit call. She will be so excited. On the second ring I hear my best friend. Almost as if she's poised with her phone in her hand, the excitement evident in her tone. "Tell me good news Cass?!" I giggle. I am walking on a cloud.

"It is excellent news, I got it!" Her shriek was so loud I had to hold the phone away from my ear. Once she's calmed down I speak again. "Kenna?"

"Sorry babe! I am so excited!" She shouts and I wince. "Okay, job sorted! Have you found any hot guys yet?" My mind latched on those haunting green eyes at once. I grinned but didn't answer right away. "Cassie!" I realize she will pick up on my hesitation.

"Well," I wasn't sure if I should mention Mr. Green Eyes. The thought of him had my belly in knots again. I ached to look at him in his sweaty tank top again. Although when I recall his impeccable suit from this morning and I wonder what turned me on more. I couldn't decide.

"Cass? Are you there?" Kenna's words pull me out of my naughty reverie of the hot man I would love to get closer to. I nod. "Tell me! Who is he?" She will not let me hear the end of this.

"Nothing, it's nothing. I have to go. Call you tonight. Okay?"

"Mmmm, you're hiding him from me, Cass! You know I will find out!! And if he is hot and you haven't talked to him yet, I will murder you!" I giggle at her threat, but she would kill me because he was hot. I decide to walk home. The sun is peeking through the clouds and I can't help smiling. It will be okay. This city will have my dreams coming true. I needed to focus on work and building my career. I wanted to make my parents proud. The thought of them tugs at my heart so much.

On the way back to my apartment, I stop at the small café on the corner. I grab a sandwich and water. "You're new around here?" The cashier is a young girl, with a pretty smile.

"Yes. Just moved here from New York."

"Really? That's great. Welcome." She scans the items. I pay and make my way out to the sidewalk, with a slow walk up the road to my apartment. When I get home I flop down on the sofa. It's only lunch time, but I am exhausted. The high from getting the job and seeing the handsome guy with the green eyes has been more excitement than I can handle in one day.

Lucien

I glance around the room, eight of my father's associates talking amongst themselves about the numbers, the bottom line and the online publications and all I can think of is that stunning brunette I left sitting in the reception area this morning.

My mind hasn't dwelled far from her most of the day. I glance at my watch and notice it's 11 am and I realize I should have wrapped this up ages ago. "Gentlemen, I have my marketing ladies working on the online publications. To be fair, they're the best in the business. I have faith they will get us the data on time. The print media will not stop production, we need to find a cost-effective printer, but I am not giving up on the quality. This company will keep to the standards that our clients are used to. Now if you will excuse me, gentlemen." I place my hands on the table, rising from my seat, they nod in agreement and we make our way out of the large boardroom.

When I reach my office, my assistant is hot on my heels. "Sir, you have a call from Veronica, she's found a replacement for when she leaves. The interview ended thirty minutes ago. She mentioned that you wanted to know?" I nod. She follows me into my office, placing the messages next to my computer. I round my desk, and sit down, taking in her appearance. It seems she's taken her time getting dressed this morning. Her tight pencil skirt hugs her hips; the soft pink blouse she's wearing accentuates her breasts. As much I would love to take her and bend her over my desk, there's another set of eyes burned into my mind. *Fuck it, Luke, you're going soft. Well, not in all areas, but you're turning into a pussy. You don't even know her name.*

"Thank you, Stacy, that will be it." She smiles and walks out of my office. Her hips sway just a little too much. I hate when women are so obvious. I need to learn about our newest recruit. When I pick up my desk phone, I dial Veronica. She's older than me by ten years, but she's always acted younger, full of life. After a few rings she answers.

"Lucien, how are you?"

"Veronica, I hear we have a new team member." Her laugh sounds carefree and I smile. Women are so easy. "Tell me about our newest lady?"

"Luke, she's lovely, her name is Cassandra Winters. She is actually here from New York, aspiring writer and she is absolutely stunning. I am sure you will love her." Veronica's words tug me from a daydream of the new girl. *Love? Ha, not likely darling. That word and me do not work well together. After what I did, there was no way I would love anyone again. And nobody would ever love me. Not with my fucking demons.*

"Thank you, Veronica. I think she can accompany me to the shoot this weekend. I look forward to meeting her. When does she start?"

"Tomorrow. I am sure she will enjoy being on location. She's eager to learn." A smirk curls my lips. *Oh, I am sure I would be happy to teach her anything she wants to know.*

"I will stop by tomorrow and say hello to Ms. Winters." *This should be interesting.*

The rest of the day goes by with ease. When Robert drops Jayce and me at the club, I make my way straight to the bar for a beer. "Dude, check out the brunette over there." Jayce motions to my right. I take a sip of my beer, set it down and turn. *She's hot. Curves in all the right places, the shortest fucking skirt I have ever seen and her tits are all but falling out of her top. Her long brown hair is dead straight and her blue eyes are piercing.* Turning back to my best friend, I shrug.

"Are you fucking serious?" His face is a picture. I know he's shocked that I don't even bat an eyelid at this girl. *Any other day I would, but she's not my mystery girl. This is ridiculous.* Even my best friend thinks so. After I gulp down the rest of my beer, I turn and walk towards her. Jayce is hot on my heels, probably because she has a cute blonde sitting with her.

"Ladies." My voice is low, and I see the flicker of desire on their faces. The obvious way they hold themselves is frustrating. It's not fun when they're pretty much laying on the table with their legs spread.

"Hi!" Even her voice is annoying. I slip into the booth and motion to the waiter to bring me another beer. This will need an extensive amount of alcohol. She slides closer to me and her blonde friend has her sights set on Jayce. He doesn't seem to mind, me, I don't think I have ever been so bored in my life.

After fifteen minutes of mindless chat about nothing in particular, I grab my beer. "I have to go Jayce. Catch you at the office tomorrow." I slide out of the booth. My best friend eyes me warily, but I am sure he won't mind having two girls for the night.

Robert drives me home, and as soon as I walk into the penthouse, I feel calmer. I need to see her again. Once I am ready for bed, I set my alarm. The thought of an early morning run isn't exactly filling me with excitement, it's the need to see her that's driving me absolutely fucking mental.

Cassandra

Since I opened my eyes I had been debating with myself if I should run to the coffee shop this morning or not? I wanted to see him; I ached to see him. My mind was absorbed by thoughts of him, even my dreams, he was there. I didn't understand what it was, but I couldn't get him out of my head. My feet struck the sidewalk hard as I made my way to the coffee shop. I couldn't stop myself, even if I tried. Even when I denied it mentally, my body ached to look at those magnificent green eyes.

I came to a stop at the large glass doors. Grabbing the frosty steel handle, I step into the air-conditioned shop. It was welcome after the run. I stood in line and pulled out my iPhone, texting Kenna to let her know I will call her later. Smiling at the barista, I didn't have to order. I turned into a regular within a few days; he handed me my usual, and I trudged up to my table. As soon as I slip into the chair, I stare at the door impatiently. My stomach in knots at the thought of seeing him. I started my new job today, the first day of my new life. I had two hours before I had to be there, so I relaxed and savored my coffee.

To distract myself I studied my phone, but it didn't work. Nerves and excitement sent shivers through me. The excitement to start on the projects waiting for me was fun. My job entails shadowing Veronica, the sub-editor to gain experience in the industry. Since I am effectively taking over from her, I needed to be on point today. I had two weeks before she left, and I am expected to learn everything I can from her. She said I would get the writing assignments, so that was valuable. I was so lost in my excitement, that I didn't notice him walk in and order his drink. When I heard a chair being pulled out on the tiled floor, I glanced up he was standing at his regular table, observing me. My heart leaped into my throat.

A devilish smirk curled his lips as he slid into the chair, his eyes locked on me. My stare on his fluid movements and I resisted the urge to lick my lips. *What the hell was wrong with me?* I chewed my lip to keep from smiling and averted my eyes. I couldn't believe he had such an effect on me. My whole body ached to drink him in with my eyes. The need flourished in my belly and the heat pooled between my thighs. He was bad news, and I wanted him. There was no denying it, not anymore. I looked up, and he had resumed typing on his phone. The butterflies in my stomach relaxed though the knot tightened and the flutter of yearning for this handsome stranger didn't subside.

I watched him for a few minutes longer, only because I could not tear my gaze away. Observing the veins in his hands pulse as he typed on his phone. His tongue flicked out licking his lips, and I longed to do the same. I needed to get home. Finishing my coffee, I got up and pushed my chair in quietly, hoping to leave without getting his attention. That was hopeless because as soon as I moved his head jerked up, and his eyes fell on me. His intense gaze burned into my back, but I resisted the impulse to turn. I didn't need to see those green eyes to know that he was watching me because my skin pricked with the heat of his gaze.

Lucien

Today is the day, I plan on making sure she knows I want her. As soon as I walk into the coffee shop, I spot her immediately. She looks breathtaking. Tendrils of dark curls frame her flushed face and her tiny purple sports bra is begging me to rip it off and taste her. I would be happy to oblige. She's concentrating on her phone and I wonder if she's texting a boyfriend. The thought sends a jealous tingle through me. I order my regular and grab my table, pulling the chair out, making enough noise for her to glance up. I am awarded when her mocha eyes lock on mine. My cock jumps to attention and I am thankful I wore tight briefs today. *Fuck, she's beautiful!* A smirk curls my lips and I flash her a tease of my dimples, apparently, women find it sexy. Her hands are trembling and an image of her tied to my bed, trembling while I drive into her pops into my head.

Slowly I slip into the seat, pull my phone out and text Jayce. I needed to tell someone about her. She was driving me insane. Her eyes are on me; my skin is prickling. She wants me, it's obvious. I need to think about something else. The new girl at work could be a welcome distraction, I type in the name Veronica gave me for our new girl in my browser. Cassandra Winters. Her Facebook profile pops up with the picture of the girl sitting across from me. My heart thuds in my chest. *It's her! Fucking hell!* This will be interesting. A weekend in Hawaii with one of the hottest and most beautiful girls I have ever laid my eyes on. My mind is whirling with ideas of what we can do on the beach, in the house. On every fucking surface. Excuse the pun.

When she moves, my eyes shoot up. She's leaving. *See you later, darling.* God, her ass is exquisite. My eyes bore a hole into her back. I drink in the last bit of her before she walks out of the shop.

I find my assistant's number and hit dial. "Stacy, get IT to bring a new MacBook Pro to my office, I will be there in ten minutes." Robert is waiting for me when I walk out of the coffee shop. Grateful for the shower at work and my emergency suits ready for me, we make our way to the office. This is going to be a good day. I can feel it. My plan is in motion when I walk into the office a few minutes later. As soon as I am showered and changed, I write the note and send it along with the shiny new laptop to be delivered to Miss Winter's desk. This will be easy, she's will want me, ache for me.

Walking back onto the sidewalk moments later, I wait for her to arrive. I glance around and spot her coming from the opposite direction. Perfect timing. The Gods' are in my favor today. My eyes rake over her appearance as she walks towards the building. Her hips sway in slow motion, and I picture my fingers gripping those hips as I drive my dick into her. I follow her in, keeping my distance. She gives the receptionist a smile. I take in her flawless appearance, sexy, yet smart. A black knee-length pencil skirt and a white button up blouse. Her black heels give her some height, but she's still much shorter than me. Those calves look incredible with every step she takes. Her curly hair is pinned up and a few stray curls have escaped. When she pushes the call button for the elevator, I take two strides and stand next to her. Watching her intently, she's realized I am here. Her lips part and I watch her lick them. *Fuck!* A sign of nerves. She doesn't turn to me which I don't mind, I take the opportunity to drink in her soft skin. I can't wait to make you speechless with my mouth.

While we wait for the elevator, my thoughts are driving me insane. Just standing beside her is intoxicating. She smells of lavender and hints of patchouli. It takes all my restraint not to press her against the wall and inhale her scent. *Soon, baby. I will have you. Lucien Verán always gets what he wants and guess what? You're the lucky girl I want. Once you've had me, you'll want no one else.*

Cassandra

I step into the office fifteen minutes early. The perky receptionist gave me a small smile as I passed by her desk. At the elevators, I push the call button. As I watch the lights for the floors count down, my skin prickled with certainty and I knew he was standing next to me. His intense gaze struck me like a tidal wave. With my attention locked forward, I don't turn. If I looked at him and saw that handsome face, I may have leaped up and ravaged him.

I giggle inwardly at my thoughts; I could imagine Kenna's reaction being the same if she laid eyes on him. The elevator doors open, and I step inside, pushing the tenth floor button. I make my way to the back and stand against the wall. Four other people followed me and then he strode inside pressing the button for the top floor. He moved towards me and settled so close heat radiated toward me from his body. I sensed the tension in the air; it was so thick you could cut it with a knife.

The elevator climbed, people stepped off onto their floors, until we were alone. "Welcome to the firm," his voice was serious, raspy and so inviting. His scent was intoxicating, a rich spicy cologne that surrounded me perfectly.

"Thank you." I murmur, unsure of myself. This was the first time he spoke to me, and the low timbre of his voice increased the pulse between my thighs. My body ached to step closer, the heat from him sending shivers over me. I drew a deep breath as I stared at the numbers, hoping for this to speed up and reach my floor.

As soon as ten lit up, I stepped forward. "Have a wonderful day, Ms. Winters," he said as the doors opened. I was speechless at the way my name rolled off his tongue. I walked out, turning to react, but the doors closed and his intense green gaze disappeared along with my words. The encounter had goose bumps rising over my skin. Turning back towards the office, I shook my head to get him off my mind. I hope I didn't run into him again today. When I got to my desk there was a brand new MacBook waiting for me with a short note.

Congratulations on your new position, Ms. Winters

I gazed at the elegant script wondering about the owner of it. "Ah Cassie, I am glad you're here early, come into my office let's chat!" Ms. Richards' bubbly voice pulled me from my reverie. It seemed I was getting right to it. I was pleased, needing a distraction.

Once I drop my bags and grab a notebook and pen, I follow her into the contemporary sea-view office. "Sit!" She gestured to one of the exquisite ornate suede armchairs. "I am thrilled you've joined us! Now, Cassie, I need to get you started on two major projects. I have two shoots you will be covering. You mentioned you would like to write editorials; this is a requirement for the shoot."

I nodded, delighted at the opportunity to be writing for Fire & Ice Magazine. "Thank you, Ms. Richards! I am thrilled for the opportunity!"

"Excellent! All your travel details including the brief are circulated through to your email, which IT will help you with setting up." She peeked over my shoulder and grinned. "It seems our IT staff are on it." I shifted to look behind me and saw a young guy sitting at my desk working on my new MacBook.

"That's perfect; I will print out all the information and make sure I am ready Ms. Richards." I beamed.

"And call me Veronica, I am not that old!" She chuckled. I smiled and nodded. "You should get a company mobile phone as well; I expect that will arrive after lunch. Mr. Verán has all his executive staff on the same network. He may even pop by to meet you." She winked. I glanced up at her shocked. *He knew who I was? The elegant scrawled note on my new laptop came to mind. Did he personally send me a laptop?* As if reading my mind, she responded, "Oh honey, he knows everyone who walks through that door in the morning. After the way his dad ran the business, he is quite the opposite, he is more hands on. His father runs the holdings' company and was always away on business. Lucien is only running the publishing company, so he is in the office every day." Her smile was sincere and I could see she regarded him with respect. I hadn't heard about him taking over the company. I must remember to Google it.

As soon as I am at my desk, I start on my communication with the photographer, editor and publicist for the first shoot which was taking place this weekend in Hawaii. Communication with the team I would work with got me comfortable with my new position. I worked most of the morning with no interruption. My thoughts didn't drift to a certain pair of green eyes either. That's a lie, I thought about him more than I should have. Just before midday I got a cup of coffee from the communal kitchen. Inhaling the deep flavors I took a minute to appreciate the aroma and made my way back to my desk.

Lucien

"Stacy, what meetings have I got today?" My mind is still on the lovely Ms. Winters when I walk into my office. I slip into my large office chair, I stare as Stacy fumbles with the notes and messages. When she glances up, a frown creases her brow. Normally I would be in a foul mood with her taking so long. However, I am in a good mood. And I know the reason for that.

"There's the meeting you have at three, other than that your day is free. I rescheduled the photography meeting for this weekend to 10 am tomorrow."

"Perfect, call the airfield and add another passenger to the flight details for this Friday. I think Ms. Winters needs to accompany me on location." My plan to take her to Hawaii will be the perfect opportunity to get her even more flustered than she was this morning. I want her, under me, writhing and begging me for release. Her nails digging into my back as I fuck her tight little body.

"Yes, sir. Anything else?"

"Coffee, please Stacy." She nods, leaving me alone.

I close my eyes for a moment, a picture of Cassandra flushed and nervous pops into my mind and I smile. Her scent still lingering, giving me an overpowering urge to take her. Own her. *What the fuck was that?* I need to fuck this girl, get her out of my head. I power on my laptop and go through the documents I needed to sign for today's meeting. When Stacy came back with my coffee, I glanced up and noticed her top had suddenly got tighter since her visit to the kitchen. I needed a new assistant. Preferably Ms. Winters. God that would be amazing. Would love to order her around, have her kneeling in front of me. Have her present herself. Naked. *Jesus, I need to work. Fuck.*

"Stacy, get IT to deliver Ms. Winter's her new mobile phone. Also, ask them to set up the mail accounts on it and send me the number, as soon as possible."

"Yes, sir." Fuck, I wish she would not call me that. There is only one woman I want calling me that and she's on the 10th floor. I need to see her again today. This is ridiculous, she's just an employee. Before midday, I decide to pay a quick visit downstairs. As I step out of the elevator, I can't help smirking. I walk down the corridor and find Veronica in her office.

"Hello, Veronica."

"Luke, how are you darling? Come in." I step inside noting that the reason I came down here isn't at her desk. "What can I do for you?" I don't sit because I need to officially meet Ms. Winters.

"I came to welcome the new member of our team."

"Great, I think she went to grab a coffee." My little coffee addict. I must find out what her favorite coffee is. At least I know the guys at the coffee shop that shouldn't be too hard.

I step out to her desk, there's not much on it. I suppose she hasn't had time to make it her own. The faint smell of her perfume hangs in the air and I inhale it like it's a drug. I perch myself on her desk, making conversation with Veronica about Hawaii. My skin suddenly tingles and I see Veronica's gaze flicker behind me. When I turn, my gaze meets that molten chocolate stare of Ms. Winters. She is delectable. I take in the slight curve of her hips, the legs that look like they go on for days. When my eyes get to her chest I notice her breathing is deep. *Perfect! She's turned on.* When she gets closer, I stand and offer her a smile. She's so fucking submissive. Perfect. The stirring of an erection in my pants starts. There's a light pink flush on her cheeks, she's impressive. *Yes, darling, I am your boss. You best obey my wishes. God, how I wish she would obey me.* Her eyes drop to the floor, and I drink her in. The soft smooth skin of her neck pulses as her heartbeat skitters.

Cassandra

As I round the corner, I almost drop my cup when my gaze lands on Mr. Green Eyes perched on the edge of my desk chatting to Veronica. Her eyes settle on me, causing him to turn my way. He rose as I neared them. "Ms. Winters, I assume you like our preference in coffee," he motioned at my mug. He would point that out since we had our early morning rendezvous 'together'. I hope he didn't see my trembling body. I smile, my voice evading me in his presence for the second time that day.

"Cassandra, meet, Mr. Verán," Veronica introduced him. *This was my employer!* He held out his hand. As I slipped mine in his, the jolts of electricity shot up my arm and it coursed through my body. His skin was soft, smooth and warm just as I had imagined. There was a familiar knot tightening in my stomach and heat blushed my cheeks. I averted my eyes from his stare and took in his elegant charcoal Armani suit, silver dress shirt and black tie. The dark colors bringing out the green of his eyes.

"Nice to meet you, Mr. Verán," I choked and smiled. He stepped forward, his eyes seared into me. My skin ignited at his nearness as I stood uncomfortably under his intense gaze. I glance up again, chewing my bottom lip to keep from smiling. His smile crinkled the corners of his eyes and I saw two deep dimples appearing in his cheeks. It was a boyish grin, and I stared, again.

His eyes twinkled with something. "Since we are spending the weekend together, I figured we should…" he looked me up and down, "… become acquainted." The word rolled off his tongue in a way that had my thighs squeezing together instinctively. I didn't like the way he had such command over me or my body. "We will travel together to the private airstrip on Friday at 16:00, the company plane should be ready to fly us to Hawaii and we start work." Surprise left me speechless. I didn't respond. I could just manage a nod.

He released my hand and turned to Veronica. "It's been a joy as ever, Veronica." He spun on his heel and sauntered down the corridor. All I could do was stare at his back and what a magnificent one it was. *Goddamnit stop it Cassie! He is your boss for crying out loud!*

Lucien

I walk into the coffee shop the next morning and my eyes immediately fall to her table. She's not here, she's late. I grab the barista and ask him about her. He knows exactly who I am talking about. The jealousy rages inside me that he noticed her. She's difficult to miss, though. When I ask about her coffee preference, he gives me the name and I buy a large bag of the same blend. I decide to wait; she could just be delayed. I sit at my normal table, my eyes trained on the door. After thirty minutes, she doesn't show. This is really frustrating. *Where is she? Is she avoiding me? We work together, it's not like she can avoid me forever. And why does it bother me so much if she is avoiding me?*

I get up to leave when my phone rings. "Verán."

"Son, you sound so formal, it's your old man, can you swing by the house? I need to give you paperwork." I give up on Cassie and make my way out of the coffee shop, my heart is heavy. I was looking forward to seeing her face. I need to see her. It's ridiculous, she's still just a stranger to me. My feelings can't have grown for her. There is no way in hell I can give her what she needs. Or deserves.

"Sure dad, I don't have any meetings this morning. I will be there in an hour."

I run home in record time. She's still on my mind. Maybe I should call one of the numbers from my little black book. That would certainly help this raging fucking hard on that doesn't want to go away. It's been too long and I need to get laid. I step into the shower, the hot spray beating down on me and the tension in my muscles relax, but as soon as I close my eyes her face haunts me. Her voice, the way she licked her lips constantly. *Didn't she ever hear of lip-gloss? It's fucking distracting, thinking about her tongue, having her lips on my cock.* I glance down, I am rock hard. There's only one thing I can do. I grip my dick and pump it in a slow up and down motion with thoughts of her swirling in my head. An image of her bound in my play room pops into my head and I shoot my release down the drain. *This is fucking ridiculous!*

Once I get to my Dad's, my mind is busy and we are talking about overheads and marketing and the next five shoots coming up. "Who's got you so wound up son?" I glance up at him in shock. *How does he see right through me?*

"No one, dad. Come on, I need to get these projections done." I need to change the subject. My old man will not let it go until I tell him, and to be honest, I don't know why I am so hung up on this girl.

"Lucien Verán, do not think I am stupid. It's etched all over your face. She's got you hasn't she?" I glance at my father; his face is one of amusement.

"Dad, drop it, please?" He nods, my pleading gaze obviously got to him.

"That's fine Luca, but I know you will bring her home. I can't wait to meet her." He gives me a sly wink as we work on the rest of the numbers.

"Dad, seriously. I am never getting into this with you."

"We'll see."

Cassandra

The previous two days had been uneventful, which is what I needed to prepare for the upcoming weekend with my boss. The prospect made me shiver. It was Friday, and I wander into the office with a packed bag, ready for my trip. I press the call button for the elevator, hoping I had just missed him. Thinking about a hot cup of coffee since my caffeine fix wasn't satiated yet. I didn't stop at the cafe this morning again; in case I saw him. *Yes, I was avoiding him!*

I didn't admit it till I stepped into the elevator with eight other staff and relaxed. With my back against the wall I watched the doors slide close, letting out a sigh of relief. Until a smooth soft hand blocked the doors, thick veins pulsed, and I craved to touch them. I knew exactly who that hand belonged to. The doors glide open and all the staff mumble a hello. Those green eyes will be the end of me, Mr. Verán, my sexy, distracting and so unattainable boss.

A smirk curls his full lips as he greets them and his gaze falls on me. He reached passed them to push the top floor button. He starts his approach to the back and stands next to me. "You didn't get your coffee this morning." It wasn't a question. He noticed I wasn't there, the thought sends butterflies fluttering in my belly. I glance up and offer him a small smile. "What makes you say that?"

"I didn't see you at the coffee shop today. Actually, you weren't there yesterday either." He spoke easily, like we were friends who met up every day. As the doors opened and closed, I noticed we were once again, alone in the elevator. My pulse raced, and the intense heat that emanated from his sculpted body made me tingle. He was close, too close.

"I missed my run this morning," I responded. "Had a trip to get ready for," I gestured at my little travel bag. *It was a lie. He didn't need to know that. Did he?*

His eyes narrowed as he pondered my reply. "Right, maybe when we're away we can run together? I would love to give you a solid workout. If you can keep up with me," his grin was dangerous. My whole body reacted to his words. As the doors opened on my floor, I stepped out and spun towards him, our eyes locked.

"There is no doubt I can…" I smiled, "… Mr. Verán," I said his name in a soft voice. His pupils dilated when his name escaped my lips. The last words were mine, his mouth opened and closed, saying nothing. I turned and reveled in the bit of satisfaction it offered me. Turning on my heel, with a satisfied smile on my face, I walk to my desk. The look of shock, desire, and danger on his handsome face has my belly in knots. There is something so sexy about him and my skin prickles with the thought of spending a weekend alone with him on an island.

It's been too long that I have been near a man who made me feel like he does. He looks at me as if I am something to be admired, desired, and utterly, thoroughly fucked.

That gaze was hungry. At my desk, I place my bags on the chair. It's time for caffeine. I think of coffee as liquid courage to get through the day until I need to be near him again. Another bundle of knots tightens in my belly and I can't help the yearning I have for him and my core pulses.

Lucien

As soon as the doors close, I am dumbfounded. The way my name slipped from her lips had my cock trying to escape my pants. It was a low, sexy, seductive tone she used and I know that she knew exactly what she was doing. Teasing me. *There's no way you'll get away with it, baby. That little cunt is getting fucked, by me, deep and hard.* The temptation to call her up to my office, bend her over my desk and spank her hard, taking her tight little body and making it mine overwhelms me. That's what she does to me. *Talk about a caveman.*

I needed this girl. There was something in her nature that made me want to own her. Mark her as mine. Something so animalistic and possessive it scared me. I couldn't give her a relationship, but maybe that's not what she wants. I wonder if she could be happy with a good fuck. A regular thing.

On my floor, I stalk to my office, not glancing at Stacy as I pass her desk. "Hold my calls." Once inside, slamming the door behind me, I slide into my black leather chair and lean back. I close my eyes and take a deep breath. *What the fuck was that? I mean, she just said my fucking name, but when the words left her lips the only thing I could think of was driving into her tight body and making her scream it out loud. Luke, man, you need to get her out of your system.* I grab my phone and dial Sasha. As soon as she answers, I regret it. "Luke?"

I don't answer and hang up before she can say anything more. Her words are ice water straight to my groin and my erection settles down. With my office chair facing the window, I take in the view. It never fails to calm me. I love the City of Angels. My decision hits me, I grab my phone, calling Robert. He will be able to help me.

"Mr. Verán."

"Robert, I need a background check on Ms. Cassandra Winters. She's from New York, but I want the dirt on her, if any." I hear him sigh and I wonder what has him so stressed by my request.

"Yes, sir. Is she the new girl?"

I consider not telling Robert about her, but he's known me all my life. I trust him more than I do anyone. "Yes, I might want to take her to dinner." *What? You just said no dating. Yes, no dating. Maybe dinner and then I can get her naked and taste that sweet little cunt.*

"I can get you the info by ten."

"Perfect." When I glance up, Stacy is in my doorway. "Later." I hang up before my assistant learns of my plans to get Cassandra in my bed.

"Mr. Verán, I brought your coffee and messages."

"Thanks." Once she leaves, I power up my laptop. With a quick scroll through my emails, there are a couple that I can reply to before I leave. The rest can wait till I get back. An alert pings on my online staff account and I open the window. There is a user searching for me. I click on the IP address it's showing me and find a smile curling my lips. Its seems our sweet and innocent Ms. Winters is looking for me. How intriguing. I decide to play a game with her. *Care to show me how interested you are Ms. Winters?*

I type out the carefully thought out email and wait for a reply. As soon as her email arrives in my inbox, I picture a soft pink blush on her cheeks. That smile of hers that knocks me for six curling her pink plump lips. My cock twitches at the images running through my mind.

This weekend will prove once and for all if she is Verán material. I will fuck her, and I will make her scream my name. If she can't handle a weekend of fun and then work alongside me then she can find work elsewhere. I am not here for love, I am here to work hard and play hard. I hope she's ready for me.

Cassandra

I get comfortable at my desk, ready to draft the press release for the swimsuit edition. My thoughts wander to Mr. Verán, it made sense he worked the shoot, all those beautiful models around him must be his idea of heaven. Curiosity instantly got the better of me and I wondered if there was any information on him online. An option would be to ask Veronica but I didn't want her to think I was interested or suspect anything untoward. Now I wanted to find out everything I could about him. Suddenly I realized I had access to the entire database of team files. I click on the online program and type in the search bar *Mr. Verán* and hit the enter key. I waited as the results appeared on my screen. It picks up his father's name, which pops up a few times on screen as the search engine did its job. Then, there it was. The name of the green eyes that's haunted me for so long.

Lucien Verán

I stare at the screen. A seductive name, fitting him perfectly. I want to click on his file, but I didn't want to get caught snooping. I close the search window and open the email program as an alert pinged with an incoming message.

From: *Lucien Verán*
To: *Cassandra Winters*
Date: *June 01, 2014 - 10:35*
Subject: *Research Material*

Ms. Winters,

It's great to see you making use of our company resources so soon into your employment.
I think researching information about your employer is possibly not applicable reading material for the event coming up. Perhaps you should consider our earlier editions of the swimsuit shoots?

If you would like any help in your pursuit of material about me, I would be more than delighted to help.

Personally.

Lucien Verán
Chief Executive Officer
Verán Publications

My heart raced. *Shit!* He was monitoring our computers. I blushed at being caught.

28

I should have known he would check staff use of resources. *How else would he run such a massive enterprise, Cassie?* I wasn't sure what to respond. My grin widened at his remark. I wanted to uncover more, but I wasn't convinced if that was such a wonderful idea.

From: *Cassandra Winters*
To: *Lucien Verán*
Date: *June 01, 2014 - 10:50*
Subject: *Knowledge is Power*

Mr. Verán,

I am well versed in the early issues of your swimsuit photo shoots, as I am positive you are. I didn't expect someone in your position had time to concern yourself with insignificant matters such as a lowly staff members' research on her current employer. Don't you consider knowledge to be power?

Thank you for the offer, but I believe my inquiry is complete.

Cassandra Winters
Marketing & Publishing Assistant
Verán Publications

    I sat back and hit send. My stomach was in knots as I waited for his response. I picture him sitting at his massive desk with views of the ocean. My cheeks heat with a blush as I think about how sexy he must look. Dominant and in charge, a powerful figure running his business. I didn't wait long till my inbox pinged with a response.

From: *Lucien Verán*
To: *Cassandra Winters*
Date: *June 01, 2014 - 11:05*
Subject: *Power comes with Responsibility*

Ms. Winters,

I consider knowledge is power, funny you should point it out, one of my choice quotes. I do not appreciate you referring to yourself as lowly, which you are not at all. I should reprimand you for saying something so outrageous!

Since you are so thoroughly versed in the company's photo shoots I assume you realize that you and I will be in close quarters for most of the weekend. I expect you can deal with the power and responsibility that comes with it.

Your inquiry is far from finished, Cassandra Winters, so far indeed.

Lucien Verán
Chief Executive Officer
Verán Publications

    My whole body was on fire and tingling from his words. I read and reread the email four times. "Cass?" I glance up startled at Veronica standing at my desk. With a quick click, I minimize my email program and grin.

"Sorry Veronica, I was…" glancing at my screen, "… doing research."

She smiled, "No problem, that's wonderful! Listen, I guess we should grab a quick lunch since you're leaving at four today? Say in about…" she glanced at the delicate silver watch on her wrist, "… ten minutes?" I nodded, and she went back into her office. Opening the email again, I hit reply. I enjoyed the mood he was in. The innocent flirting with him made me smile, and I knew Kenna would approve. She was the one who demanded that I move on from that past two years. Perhaps I was ready to move on from the past. Maybe, Mr. Verán was the one I could move on with? *Really Cassie? Your employer? Why not? He's hot, successful, and he is flirting with me!*

From: Cassandra Winters
To: Lucien Verán
Date: June 01, 2014 - 11:25
Subject: Close Encounters

Mr. Verán,

Thank you for the information. I can deal with anything that comes my way; I am a big girl and can take care of myself. Regarding dealing with power and responsibility, I fair remarkably well, I will have you know, Mr. Verán; of that, you can be certain.

Well, it seems we both have so much to learn.

Cassandra Winters
Marketing & Publishing Assistant
Verán Publications

I hit send and giggle, this back and forth banter pulled me out of a slump. That's all it was, and all it can ever be. I had no place in my heart for a relationship. *What was I considering? A few emails didn't mean he wanted to date me! Get a grip Cassie!* "Ready?" Veronica stopped at my desk and I nodded. I shut the lid on my laptop, grabbing my bag and follow her to the elevators.

Lucien

I push the button on the elevator and step inside. As it descends, my mind flits back to her again. When the ten lights up, my breathing stops and as the doors slide open, I see her. *God, she's beautiful!* "Ms. Winters," I take in her appearance, not missing the unmistakable blush on her cheeks. She's so perfect, I imagine her on my plush carpet, kneeling with her wrists bound behind her. *Does she realize I am the devil?* She shouldn't be here; I shouldn't bring her along on this trip. Against my better judgment, I am allowing her to come with me. Who am I to deny a beautiful submissive girl to train?

Her smile intoxicates me. Already I am in way over my head and I know it. "Are you looking forward to the trip?" I glance at her and smile.

"Yes, thank you, Mr. Verán." Her eyes peer up at me and I want to press her body against mine. To have her kneel in front of me, with those mocha eyes staring up while she swallows my cock. There's an animalistic feeling coursing through me when she says my name. Oblivious to my discomfort, she rambles on. "I have only ever been to LA and New York. Well, the last time I was in LA was when I was a teenager, but that was only for a vacation." She suddenly stops herself and my body is on fire. I rearrange myself, but her eyes cut down to my hand. *Fuck, she noticed it. How the fuck am I meant to spend the weekend with her and I can't even keep my erection down when she talks?* Although, I realize she's nervous, I can see her brain working overtime. She's trying to think of something to say to fill the silence. "Mr Verán?"

I can't help the agony on my face when she says my name, and she sees it. *How can she not understand how sexy she is?* Her soft murmur is like an aphrodisiac. All I want to do is pin her against the wall and… *Stop it! Don't freak her out!* "Call me Lucien, please?"

She gives me a small nod. The innocence on her face makes me think twice about wanting to do deliciously dirty things to her. Things that she would never even dream of. My mind needs to stop this. I have to stop this. Work. Talk about work. *How can she not have travelled?* I want to give her that. To show her all the places my father took me, I want to take her to Spain. *What? Luke, you're losing it. You can't take her there, she doesn't even know you. Fuck, you don't know her.*

"It's a shame you haven't travelled. I will make sure this position gives you plenty of freedom to do just that." Her sweet lavender perfume invades my senses again and I savor it. She turns a smile on me again and my heart rate spikes.

My phone interrupts the moment and I am frustrated beyond words. "Forgive me, Ms. Winters," I give her a grin and swipe the screen. "Verán." People don't do what I tell them to and the shit hits the fucking fan. Why is it so difficult for people to obey orders? As the financial director rambles on, my mind goes to the beautiful Ms. Winters standing next to me. I want her to obey my orders so much. Her gaze on me, prickles my skin and it sends blood straight to my crotch. If this guy doesn't stop going on about the numbers and do his fucking job, I will lose it. "I don't care what it takes, you need to fix it." The elevator doors slide open and we step out.

When she glances up at me, my fingers brush the small of her back and the electricity between us is unbelievable. A simple touch. Like we're magnets meant to be locked together. Robert is waiting at the car and I need to end this call. "I am away this weekend you know that." My eyes fall on her pert ass when she slides into the back seat and my cock strains against my zipper. I slip in next to her. "I do not care. I am sick of these excuses. Get it done." When I hang up, I take a deep breath, needing to calm down. When I offer her a smile, I notice her eyes flit to my lips and dimples.

"Sorry about that. Business." I shrug my phone back into my pocket and turn my attention to her. The pulse in her neck spikes and I can't help smiling. I affect her as much as she does me. This is perfect because I want her. Fuck the consequences. I can deal with those when they crop up. Relaxing back in the seat. Her soft trembling hands are in her lap, and I want to place mine on them so she can calm. She's so nervous. *You better be scared of me darling.* I reach over and press a small remote, Fall Out Boy wafts through the back of the SUV. Her face is a picture. Guess I have good taste in music. Somehow, the lyrics of the song are appropriate for how I am feeling about this girl.

I'll be as honest as you let me
I miss your early morning company
If you get me
You are my favorite "what if"
You are my best "I'll never know"

"So, have you been on a shoot before?" I wait for her to answer and she doesn't disappoint with her innocent rambling. Goose bumps rise on her smooth skin and I wonder how else I can make her tremble. So many possibilities. I can't believe how nervous she is, I haven't even begun to play my games with her and she's like a shaking leaf.

"No, I um… This is my first real job; I have… I just moved here." She doesn't meet my gaze, but the pink on her cheeks tells me she knows I am watching her.

"Cassandra…" Her name rolls off my tongue, low and serious. "Do I make you uneasy?" She smiles and mumbles something about me being her boss. She licks her lips again, her little nervous tick. I like it, the way her tongue darts out slowly, the way her lips glisten. *Fuck!* Immediately I avert my gaze; I can't do this in here. I am about ready to fucking pounce on her. The need to calm her down is coursing through my veins. She can't spend a whole weekend with me like this. "I don't want you to be nervous. I am just the person that goes jogging every morning." Her reaction to my statement is priceless. I watch her thighs squeeze together and that is more than enough for me to take full advantage. She wants this as much as I do. *Don't worry darling once I have made you come hard over my tongue you won't be so nervous anymore.*

"Yea, I need this position, so I need to make a good impression." *She's scared I would fire her? Why the fuck would I do that?* I reach out to her and touch her shoulder. *Fucking hell!* The electricity surging through me when we touch is incredible. *I need to run my fingers over her naked body right now! Verán, relax!* The need to calm her is unbearable. I have to think about the next words out of my mouth.

"Trust me, that's not something you need to concern yourself with. When I first saw you I realized you were perfect for…" I want to tell her for me, but it's too soon. I can't have her. There is no way I can keep her. She wouldn't even give me a chance if she learned about what I want. Her instinct would be to run for the hills if I even mention it, so I opt for the next best thing. "… Verán Industries." With a reassuring smile, I see her thighs squeeze together again and I am certain she knew the words I was too scared to say. Her mocha eyes fall to my mouth, her pupils dilate and I realize she's as turned on as me.

"Thank you, Mr. Ve… Lucien." When she replies it falters, but she remembers to call me by my first name only. As soon as my hand leaves her shoulder, I feel strange. The need I have to touch her is unbearable.

"Tell me, Cassandra, what appeals to you?" I steal a glance at her; the blush is permanently on her cheeks. *Has she never had a man's attention? Surely, she must have men falling over themselves to get to her.* I realize Jayce will like her. The thought doesn't sit well with me and I don't know why. It's not like she's mine.

"I, I read and music. I mean I read books and like music. Um, I suppose I don't have much that I do outside of work. Is that what you mean?" I nod. She's obviously completely oblivious to the effect she has on men, keeping her nose buried in a book. I am sure they're hot romance novels. Robert pulls up to the airfield and I get out. The sun was beating down; I am overdressed in my suit. I walk around the car as Robert opens her door. When she sees the plane, her reaction is exquisite as she breathes the word 'wow'. Her lips form a perfect O and there is only one thing on my mind. I love when her voice is low and breathy. *Jesus, Luke, sounds like you've been reading those fucking romance novels! Falling in love? No fucking way! I need to get into her panties. My black heart is on lockdown. Forever. No way some chick will get inside there.*

"It seems I have impressed you today. Come on, Robert will pick up our suitcases." We stroll together towards the plane; my hand once again finds the lower curve of her back, just above her pert little ass. *Why do I want to impress her? I should just show her my cock that will leave her speechless.* There's something about her that makes me want to show her more, impress her, but I can't. My heart suddenly constricts at the idea of just having her as a one-night stand, but with my demons, there's no space for a sweet girl like her. I can't give her anything more than that.

Once we board the plane, we slip into our seats. "I expect you are ready for an action packed weekend. No sleep and hard work. That's what these shoots are typically like."

"I can handle myself, I am not afraid of hard work." Her response is easy and relaxed, and I smile. She's sassy, I like that. The way she takes in every movement I make is adorable, it's like she's trying to assess me. *Nothing here to see darling, you won't find what you're looking for.*

"Mr. Verán, can I bring you both anything?" Miranda asks, she's been my flight attendant for several years. She's gorgeous, but she doesn't hold a flame to Cassie. I don't think any woman could.

I glance at Cassie. "Would you like something Ms. Winters?"

"A sparkling water would be good?" She asks and I nod.

"You heard the lady and please bring me the usual? Thank you." As soon as Miranda disappears to the rear of the plane, I turn back to Cassie. "You are more than welcome to have whatever you like, on the flight and over the weekend. Everything is compensated for by Verán Industries."

I wonder if she drinks alcohol. She can have anything, including me. *Where the fuck did that come from?*

"Thank you, Mr.… um, Lucien." She falters with my name again, suddenly I am too aware of the way my name rolls off her tongue. When she murmurs my last name it sends erotic shivers down my spine and into my cock. Thoughts of her screaming it out as I pound her whirl in my head and the need for that drink is overwhelming.

I open my laptop and work as soon as we're at cruising altitude. My eyes glance up while I work and I can't help noticing how lovely she looks. It's getting dark and I realize we will land quite late. She looks tired and I want to put her to bed, preferably my bed. I am certain she looks like an angel while she's sleeping.

Cassandra

Once we were airborne I got a few emails done that required urgent attention but left the others for tomorrow. Our flight to Hawaii was five hours and by the time we reached Hanalei it was dark. There was a car waiting for us and Lucien let me slip in first. I was drained and leaned my head back against the seat as we pulled off. It was too dark to see anything anyway so I couldn't take in the view.

"We should be there shortly. You look tired," his voice gentle, filled with concern.

"I am tired now. It's been a long day." My eyes cut to him, even in the dark, I see those vivid green eyes that draw me in. A smile curls his full lips and in my deliriously tired mind I wish I could kiss him. The idea vanishes as I turn to look out into the darkness. I can't allow myself to think like that about him. He was my boss, and I was absolutely not ready for any romance, it didn't matter what Kenna said. She wanted me to move on, that much was evident, but after the past two years, allowing myself the luxury is not an option. My heart couldn't deal with losing someone I love again. That pain is indescribable. Lucien seems to be a good person, and I can't tell him about the things I have done. There's too much darkness in my past to even fathom sharing it with someone.

"Cassandra," I open my eyes and blinked hard. It was still dark. I twist to see Lucien leaning over me, nudging me gently. "We're here, you fell asleep," he offered me a tender smile. His eyes crinkled at the corners and his dimples deepen. That smile would be the death of me. Emotions are running through me that I shouldn't have.

"Oh, right? I was so tired." I sat up and suddenly we were too close. His spicy scent, mixed with a clean manly smell enveloping me fully and I breathed him in. I licked my parched lips and his eyes focused on my mouth, his intense gaze was so fierce heat shot straight to my core. If I moved an inch further I would feel his lips on mine. The door opened abruptly, and he cleared his throat. Lucien moved back quickly, and the spell between us broke.

"Mr. Verán, I have put the luggage in the foyer." The driver's tone was sharp and rumbled through his chest. I am pulled from the dirty thoughts of Lucien's lips against mine. Or any other part of my body.

"Thank you, Robert." Lucien slipped out of the car, turning around he offered me his hand. As soon as I slid mine into his, the electric spark that coursed through my veins every time his skin was in contact with mine shot into my arm. "Let's go, Cassandra. You're in need of a bed." The way my name rolled off his tongue caused me to tremble.

I stared up at the mansion and gasped, it was magnificent. A double-story home, white slats, with wooden window frames. There were fairy lights along the pathway. The house had enormous windows with what would have to be a sea view.

Even though it was dark, you could tell that this was an incredible home. A dream house on an island.

"Did I impress you twice in one day?" Lucien asked pleased at my reaction to the house. All I could do was nod. "Well, I will give you a complete tour when you're not falling asleep. Let me show you to your suite and you can rest."

My suite, as Lucien suggested, was unbelievable. It was double the size of my apartment back in LA and as soon as I laid my head on the pillow, my dreams of Lucien's lips, hands and every other part of him took over.

Hours later, I groan at the incessant ringing next to my head. When I reach out to find the source and swipe the screen. "What?"

"Jesus, Cass! What's crept up your ass?" Kenna! I totally forgot to text her last night.

"Sorry babe, I am so tired. What's the time?"

"It's 6 am…" I grunted into the phone and she giggled, "… but I needed to talk to you!"

"At 6 am?" I questioned her incredulously.

"Yes! My paperwork came through from LA; I should be there in about three weeks. My contract is confirmed. They're giving me a minimum of 6 months with the opportunity to extend." She was very excited, but I was groggy with sleep.

"And you assumed 6 am would be the right time to tell me?" She chuckled at my grumpiness. Yes, I am always this evil before I have had my morning coffee.

She giggled again, "Well, I was impatient. Wait a minute missy! Why are you still asleep? Don't you typically go for your jog this early?"

"I do. Although I am not in LA. I am on location." I sat up and opened my eyes fully. "OMG!"

"What? Wait, where are you?" I didn't answer her, but rather took in the view from my bedroom. "What's going on? Cassie, spill it!"

"I am in Hawaii with my boss, on a shoot and I have the most un-fucking-believable view from my bedroom!" I got out of bed and stood at the massive sliding doors. The sun wasn't up yet but from where I stood I looked out at the clear blue ocean in the dawn light and the exquisite garden below.

"You're where?! With who?! OMG! Cassie! Is he hot?" Kenna was shouting now, and I had to keep the phone away from my ear. "Cassie!!"

"Yes, yes, hold your horses. I am in Hawaii. We're here for a shoot." I evaded her question about Lucien, but she wouldn't let up. This is why she's my best friend.

"You didn't answer my question!" She cried loudly, and I flinched.

"What Kenna?" I realized she wouldn't give this up till I responded.

"If you don't tell me I will Google him!" She warned, knowing I would give in and tell her. I shook my head, realizing I didn't have a choice.

"Yes, he's hot, okay!" I giggled. At that moment, I spun around and laid eyes on Lucien standing in my doorway with a mug of coffee and a wicked grin on his face. *Fuck! He heard me. Shit!* "I got to go!" I hung up before she could respond.

Lucien

Once I am at her door, I hear her talking. She must be on the phone. I turn the doorknob and see her standing in a tight white tank top and a pair of boy shorts. *Holy fuck!* Her pert little ass looks good enough to eat. *God, help me!* Her words catch me off guard. "Yes, he's hot, okay!" As she spins around, her startled gaze falls on me and I offer her a wicked grin. Her eyes roam over my body and I hope she doesn't notice the bulge in my pants, I can't help it, she looks so fucking good in those panties. "Hi…" Her voice is a low whisper and her body trembles with embarrassment. She stands in shock and stares at me. Her eyes drop to her attire and her cheeks pink. She reaches for her robe, pulling it on. *I have already seen your tight panties, darling.*

"Who's hot?" I tease her, a blush spreads across her cheeks once again. It was one of the sexiest things I ever saw.

"Um… The…" I contain the laugh that is begging to be let out, but the amusement is clear on my face. "I was just asking… telling my friend about… this place. It's hot, like nice… um…" She finally gives up and I let her off, just this one time.

"Mmmm, I guess it is hot." I set down the coffee on her nightstand. "I brought you coffee. Brazilian blend no milk or sugar." Her expression is worth everything, and I feel something tug at my cold heart. The thought of making her smile, has my heart filled with something. *Affection? No!*

"Thank you! How did you—"

"I know people." *Get out of this bedroom, now Luke!* I step back. "We need to leave in an hour, breakfast is made. Just come through to the kitchen when you are ready."

Without a backward glance I close the door behind me and make my way to my bedroom to get ready for work. A pair of faded jeans and a T-shirt would do. It's too hot on the island so there's no chance of my wearing a shirt. In the kitchen I set up the breakfast and put the bread in the toaster. Another pot of coffee is brewing. The image of Cassie in her panties is now engrained into my mind and I can't even think straight. All I want to do is rip her panties from her body, bend her over and ram my cock inside her. *I can't offer her love, but I can offer her a good time. I hope that will be good enough because I want her.* The ache in my chest is back and all I want is to make her smile.

Cassandra

I can't believe he caught me! I swipe my screen calling Kenna back.

"What the fuck? You hung up on me for your hot boss?"

"He heard me Kenna!" I hissed into the phone. With a loud whoop, she giggled. She would consider this to be amusing. She's been trying to set me up with guys for a few months, but I had never been interested. Until… I shook my head I couldn't think of that now.

"Well, I am glad he overheard you, maybe he will take the initiative and ask you out!" I thought about it, maybe it wouldn't be so bad to go to dinner with Lucien. "Cassie!"

"Huh?"

"If he asks you to dinner, promise me you'll go? Please?" She was serious now; the only time she got serious was when she wanted me to move on. It was just painful. After all the heartache, I wasn't sure I was even up to trying to make it work with someone. I needed to focus on my job. Then I would be fine.

"I will consider it. I need to go. Call you later?"

"Yea, unless you're out with Mr. Hot and Rich. Then you don't need to call!" She snickered and hung up. Her last comment made me shake my head. I picked up the coffee and took a small sip. It was the same blend from the coffee shop. I smiled, the barista must have mentioned it to him, but why would he even care?

Once I was dressed, I wander through the house to the kitchen. Lucien was on the phone again and he sounded furious. "I do not care! Did I not explain that to you yesterday? I am not backing you if this is what's going on!" He glanced up as I strolled in and smiled, his face softened a little. "I have to go, don't call me until you've solved it!" He turned as he hung up and placed the mobile on the table. "Good morning, how did you sleep?"

"Excellent, I didn't realize how tired I was. I missed my run." I glance up and am met by his handsome smile. He had changed into a pair of ripped blue jeans that hugged his hips and thighs in ways that made me want to peel them off. His white T-shirt was tight and showed off his athletic arms. *He is so delectable!* I blushed and studied the breakfast on the counter. *Would you settle down?*

"You could run tomorrow? With me?" He passed me a plate, and I grabbed toast. The prospect of running with him sounded incredible. I didn't think it would hurt going, so I nodded.

"Sure, sounds perfect."

"Fantastic! There's juice, or coffee. I can get you a refill?" It was weird seeing my boss waiting on me, but I needed more caffeine in my system if I had to make it through today.

"Please?" He busied himself with the coffee machine and grabbed two mugs. "So, is this your place?"

"Yea, my dad's actually, he owns Verán Industries. I am just taking over the publishing house from him. I always wanted to work in the field, so when he asked me if I would like the opportunity to be his successor, I jumped at it." I watched the muscles tense in his arms as he moved. Mesmerized. I took in all the tattoos that adorned his skin. The one on his bicep flexed when he moved, it looked like the tail end of a dragon. I would love the opportunity to trace the intricate design with my tongue. The slice of toast crunched as I bit into it and I imagined biting his shoulder…

"Cassandra?" Lucien pulled me from my dirty thoughts and I glanced at him. He had spun around and was staring me. "You okay?"

"Uh yea, sorry! I… The toast is great!" *You need to calm down Cass! But it's been so long since… Well you know!* This is the conversation I would have with myself every day if I was working with Lucien. He set my coffee down, and I clutched the mug. It was a welcome interruption, inhaling the incredible aroma. "Thank you."

"Glad you enjoyed the toast. It's from a local bakery, the bread is, and I made the toast." Those sexy dimples deepened when he smiled. "We can stop by tomorrow morning after our jog." He seemed to look forward to it and I found myself eager as well.

"Yes! I am sure the views are stunning!" I gestured to the window.

His gaze intensified as it wandered over my white tank top, up to my eyes, and then settled on my mouth as I sipped on my coffee. "Oh, the view is unbelievable." The devilish smirk that I have become accustomed to appeared on his face. Unsure that we were even talking about the same thing anymore. A serious expression passed over his features suddenly. "We should leave in 15 minutes, is that okay?"

"Yes, I am ready. Is there anything specific I need to bring?"

"Just your phone, if you want to take your laptop you can. You might find time for writing. Although I highly doubt it," he walked past me towards the bedrooms. His cologne washing over me causing my stomach to flutter. He was so intoxicating.

Lucien

As soon as I walk into my bedroom I close the door behind me. The barrier between us now calms me somewhat. Being so close to her is becoming more difficult. There's something about this girl and I am not sure it's a good idea that we're here together. I want her. There's a fucking ache in me for her and I can't stop it. Why does she affect me like this? It makes little sense.

I am a fucking playboy; I don't care about girls. A relationship is out of the question. I can't go down that road again. If she knew what I wanted, needed, she wouldn't be so willing. Her flirty smile, those tight panties. That fucking tank top that hugged her tits was driving me insane. My mind is swirling with thoughts of her. The need to have her, mark her, is driving me crazy. When she walked into the kitchen, she knocked me breathless. She is beautiful, but so fucking innocent. She would be perfect to train.

The idea for a run is perfect, to see how she handles me. I would love to get her sweaty. Since I first saw her at the coffee shop, I thought about running with her, then making her even more sweaty when we got home. *Yes, darling, I can't wait to get you sweaty.*

I realize I shared more about myself than I meant to. She doesn't need to know who I am; it's not like we're dating. For some inexplicable reason I want her to know who I am. This is such a bad idea. I will walk away from this, with my heart where it is, locked away.

My new hobby, teasing her, is something I want to do all day. When those cheeks turn pink it makes me want to grab her and kiss her. Bend her over and spank her ass until she's begging me to let her come. That tight white tank top she's wearing is so flimsy, I could shred it from her body and feast on her beautiful tits. God knows, I am dying to suck those nipples into my mouth and tug on them with my teeth. *Lucien, you need to go to work! I need to reign myself in, I don't know if she would say yes to being with me.*

My cock is rock hard again. I need to find some release or I will never get through the day. With a quick glance at the time, I realize there's still another twenty minutes. Perfect. I free myself from my jeans and fist it with the image of her soft hands gripping me spurs me on. When I picture her beautiful pink lips swallowing my dick, I come all over my stomach. *Fuck this. I will fuck it up, like I always do.*

Once I clean up the mess, I tug my briefs and jeans back up. She's too pure, too innocent. My soul and heart are too dark for her. I need to get hold of myself because there's no way I can be what she needs. As I make my way out of the bedroom I shut my door. With a deep breath, I steady myself for the day, because I will need the strength to get through this.

Lucien

I stop at her bedroom door and smile; she looks ravishing. She's slipping on her sandals, my eyes drink her in, and I lick my lips. We walk to the kitchen and I open the door. Noticing her expression when she sees the Jeep. "I decided to drive today, Robert will pick us up later for dinner." I open the door for her and let her slip in. Her tanned legs look so good. I needed to get her in my bed so bad. I needed to fuck her senseless so I can go on with my life. *What is it about her? Why is she different to the other girls?* I keep convincing myself once I have had her pussy I will be fine. That's all. Tonight, I plan on taking her, feeling her tighten around my cock, and making her come hard. *Shit, I need to work and doing it with a hard on will not be good.*

"Nice jeep, it definitely makes me feel like I am on an island." She smiles across at me as I slip into the driver's seat. Her hungry gaze burns into me and I can't help smiling.

"Yea, I always hire it when I am out here." Once I have pulled out onto the road, I take the turn to the beach. The island is small and the roads are quiet. My glance shifts to her.

"So, did you move to LA alone? I mean you have no... family there?" Might as well feign interest.

"I am alone yes. I mean I moved alone. I don't have family in LA." Her voice is so low. Glancing at her, I notice her swipe a tear from her eye. *Fuck! Did I upset her? God, I am such a fucking idiot!*

"I didn't mean to..." I glance at her again. "... be an ass and ask about anything personal." *This is interesting. What happened to her?* I need to know what made her move, but I can't ask her. There is a story hiding behind those chocolate eyes and now I want to learn more about Ms. Winters. "I say stupid things occasionally, I apologize, Cassandra." I decide the rest of the drive will be a quiet one.

"It's okay." She gives me a small smile, but it doesn't reach her eyes and I realize I messed up. Once we hit the beach, I park the jeep. I jump out and round the car, to open her door. Women like men who are gentlemen, it will make it easier to get into those tight white panties of hers. *They looked good; I bet I can get them all wet, just using my fingers. Fuck, I would love to stroke her sweet lips.* My cock seems to be hard every fucking moment since I met her, actually, since I first saw her in the coffee shop. When we walk into the tent, she takes in her surroundings. Everything is so new to her. *I am tempted to show her a lot more that will be new. Like tying her up in my play room and making her beg me to fuck her. Get yourself together man!*

"Come on Cassandra, I need to introduce you to our photographer. You will work with him a lot over the coming months. I would prefer to have you handle most of the shoots." When I place my hand at the small of her back, she trembles. "Jayce, let me disturb you." When his eyes land on Cassandra I can see his mind is already undressing her. *That fucking bothers me too much.* "This is our lovely Cassandra Winters; she's new to the company. She will supervise the shoots in future."

"Well, I am glad Lucien isn't keeping you to himself. It's a pleasure gorgeous!" He charms her with his fucking pretty blue eyes. A blush spreads over her cheeks, she's affected by him. *This is not good Verán; get her the fuck away from him! Now!*

"Okay Jayce, can you at least try to be professional!" When Jayce's gaze meets mine, I can see he's setting his sights a little too high. I give him that 'back-off' glare and I hope I am making myself heard loud and clear.

"Luke, chill, I was being friendly." Jayce's blue eyes fall on her again. "He can be a grouch, especially when he hasn't got any in a while," he laughs.

"Okay, that's enough!" I fix Jayce with a scowl. Turning to Cassie, I place a hand on her back. "Cassandra, I need you to give me some feedback on a thought I had." Guiding her onto the beach and away from Jayce. When we were out of earshot, I lean down and whisper in her ear, "Just be wary of Jayce, he is overly affectionate." I need to watch her with him; this is not a good sign if she's so affected by him. *Why the fuck do I care anyway? I want to get my cock wet. Once I am done, then he can try his luck, but she will never feel with anyone what I can make her feel.*

We're not in a relationship, but I want to protect her. I need her to be safe. The overwhelming urge to hide her from the world takes over and all I can think of doing is locking her in my apartment. Against my better judgment I want her. For some inexplicable reason all I need is for her to be mine. I want to own her. Possess her and make her take me deep inside her tight little body. She's so independent, she doesn't need me looking out for her and I know that, but it's in my nature. As I stand here glancing at her I decide that I want her. Enough fighting this urge, she will be mine, no one else deserves her.

We walk onto the beach and in the sunlight her hair shines with gold streaks in the chestnut brown. It's like she's glowing. "Lucien, I can handle myself, I do not need a bodyguard," she smiles, "but thank you for the concern." Her words feel like a blade to my heart.

"I am just," I hesitate. I need to stop acting like a pussy in front of her. *Fuck man, get a grip of your balls and dominate her.* "I mean, I… Never mind." With a shrug I turn to look ahead of us. "I was considering a few doing shots over there. This here…" I point to the abandoned log. "… would make an excellent shot." When my gaze lands on her, the smile she rewards me with is incredible and that knife in my heart disappears.

"Yes, that's an excellent idea. I think if you had a pose like, um…" Her words trail off as she struggles to describe what she means. *This is it, I want her to present herself to me. In so many fucking ways. Most of them naked. Do you like taking orders, darling? Show me.*

"Show me?" I stare at her, giving her a dark intense gaze, similar to one I would give her in the play room. "Come on! I need to have a visual, picturing it doesn't help." A wink and those cheeks pink instantly. She smiles and obeys me. *Perfect little sub. To have her hands pinned behind her, those beautiful tits pressing against my chest. I want to feast on her.* There is a list of orders I want to give her, to make her obey me and if she doesn't, my hand will mark her perfect ass. Seeing her posing in that little tank top makes me want to ram my cock between her perfect tits. I grab my phone and take snaps of her. The giggle that escapes her mouth has my cock throbbing inside my jeans.

"Hold on! That's it!" Clutching my phone, I point the lens at her and take a snap.

"What are you doing!?" She giggles again, but I don't stop.

"Just getting a visual," I chuckle and snap a second shot. All the tension about Jayce is forgotten and instantly we are both giggling.

"That's enough! I am a journalist, not a model!" She straightens and I step forward as she steps over the log, I notice her lose her footing and I reach out. My arms around her and she's clutching my biceps. Her small hands send sparks down my spine. *She's in my arms. God, she smells good.* Her heart is thrumming against her throat and I want to trace my tongue along the gentle curve of her ear.

"I got you…" Our eyes are locked and the desire in hers is evident. The tension between us makes me ache. Everything else falls away at that moment. Only us. Her body, her scent, her warm breath, everything has me intoxicated and turned on. My body welcomes her in ways I can't explain. The hammering of my heart is so loud, I wonder if she can hear it.

"I…" When she steps back, her absence leaves me cold. This can't be happening; I can't do this. I am no fucking good for her. Maybe she's better off with Jayce. He's a good guy, but the thought of any other man's hands on her rips into me. "I'm okay, thanks." She smiles. The tension is so thick in the sweltering temperature, the heat from her and the sun is too much. "We should…" She points to the tent behind us, "…get water, hydrate… You know?" She's rambling. I have no idea how to deal with the attraction I have for her.

"Yea, we should um… head back," I turn, and we walk in silence. It was so clear there was something between us, but pushing it away might be more difficult than giving in. Her phone beeps, she laughs out loud and I turn to see the stunning way her face lights up. I wonder if it's a boyfriend, but she said she had no one. "What's up?"

"Nothing, my friend, she's just joking around." I hope to God it's a female. This bothers me more than it should, but I can't help it anymore.

Cassandra

We wrap up with our day as the sun was sinking on the horizon when a stunning blonde strolls up to the tents. "Luke darling!" She pulls him into a passionate hug and the bite of jealousy hits me hard. I have no right to be, but I am. He's not mine, although I wish he was.

"Sasha, how are you?" His voice is cold and serious, but he returns the hug. He leans in and pecks her on the cheek. His eyes flit to me for a second. Then he turns his gaze on her.

"Magnificent! Thanks for offering me the cover. I am looking forward to it. Thought I would drop in and check out the location," she steps past the tents onto the beach. I watch as Lucien goes with her with a smile on his face. She clutched his arm, practically draping herself over him. Dismay and a bite of sadness tugs at me, he seemed so relaxed with her. Though with me he seemed on edge all the time. That was my cue to take a step back. I couldn't have my heart broken, my fascination with him needs to stop.

"Luke's ex, Sasha," I started at Jayce's voice behind me. When I turn around to look at him, I am not sure what the appropriate response should be. As far as he is concerned I am just an employee. "She's doing the cover for us. They broke up four months ago." This extra bit of information doesn't help the jealousy raging in my stomach.

"Oh, right…" I tear my eyes away from them.

"Hey, he's not with her anymore, thank God." When Jayce shakes his head, it looks like he's in agony.

"Why? What happened?" I turn to Jayce. My curiosity piqued, wanting to learn more about this man that seems to affect me so much more than I ever expected. Jayce could see my interest was more than that of a staff member.

"They have a sordid history, it's in the past, but they just don't fit together. When the time is right he should tell you." His voice trailed off for a second. When his eyes found mine again I could see there was something he didn't want to tell me. "So, if ever you and Mr. Grumpy get together, the story will have to come from him." I stared at him and nodded. He dropped the subject suddenly and moved on, chatting about the photographs from the day, but I was preoccupied by the two people on the beach.

An hour later, the sun was setting when Lucien joined Jayce and I at the workstations that had been set up. "Ready to go, Cassandra?" I turn to him, noting the blonde had disappeared.

"Yea, we were finishing up here. See you tomorrow Jayce?" I placed my hand on his shoulder and he winked. I realized he did it to rile Lucien up and that caused me to snicker.

"Of course gorgeous! When can I get you in a swimsuit?" A cheeky grin grew on his handsome face. I laughed and shook my head in disbelief at how often he worked to upset Lucien.

"Jayce, you realize that I can end your contract?" Lucien's tone a warning, a sensual one at that. The commanding manner in which he spoke had me trembling. *It's so Goddamn sexy!*

"Luke, you know me! I am just joking around." He chuckled, and I noticed there was more between the two men than they let on.

"Yes, I do, Jayce, that's the problem." There was wariness in his eyes and I realized something had taken place in their past. His focus shifted to me. "Cassandra," holding out his hand. I slipped mine in his and rose as he drew me to him. "Tomorrow, Jayce," he gave a slight nod and turned.

Once we were in the jeep, he visibly relaxed. I glanced over at him as he pulled out of the parking lot and onto the peaceful road back to the house. "How long have you known Jayce?" As quickly as the words were out of my mouth, I noted his shoulders tense.

"All my life," he responded in a clipped tone. I waited for more, but he didn't continue, so left it alone. I could always ask Jayce tomorrow. "Dinner isn't formal, so you can dress comfortably. It's a quaint Mediterranean place I like down on the other side of the island." His smile returning with earnest and I was relieved.

"Sounds great, thank you." His smile continued to floor me. *What can I say? I am a sucker for dimples.*

He pulled into the driveway and we retreated to our respective rooms to get ready for dinner. I opened my balcony doors to cool down. The view was impressive. The sun had set, and the moon was glowing brilliantly. I drew my phone out of my pocket. Swiped the screen, and scrolled to the message from Kenna, hitting reply.

Going to dinner with my boss. I haven't kissed him, yet! LOL

I didn't wait long for a response and I could imagine her sitting with the phone attached to her hand just to get all the juicy gossip. I realized she would be thrilled about this. To be honest, I was excited about having dinner with him.

I knew it! You like him! Well, you would be blind if you didn't! I want every detail!

I grinned, yes I liked Lucien. There was no longer a point in denying it. A weight lifted from my shoulders when I finally admitted it to myself. *Was it so awful to move on?*

Okay! Will chat later xo

Cassandra

I step into the shower and let the spray calm my nerves. For two years I was a hermit, not dating, being outside only when I needed to get to work. Now, here I am getting ready for my first date and suddenly it's like I am thirteen again. Lucien is different, there's something in his demeanor that calms me, but also unnerves me. My feelings for him are strong, and I fear that every day I spend with him, they will only grow.

I didn't want love. That's not why I moved across the country. Also, the thought of falling in love with my boss is ridiculous. *What if we didn't work?* I mean, wouldn't that be uncomfortable? As I step out of the shower, I shake my head. My thoughts are all over the place tonight. I need to concentrate on dinner. Just relax and enjoy it. There aren't any strings attached. *So why am I nervous?*

In the bedroom, I moisturize my skin with my lavender lotion, slip on the black bra and panty set. I chose a simple topaz skater dress with delicate straps. It had a narrow silver belt at the waist and ended mid-thigh. As I slip on my black sandals, I take one last glimpse in the mirror. I clipped my hair up leaving stray curls to settle around my neck and face.

My make-up was basic. I hated wearing any, especially in this hot weather. The clear lip-gloss I dab on my lips accentuates them and my thoughts are filled with his lips on mine. The heat of his body against mine. I hoped that he wasn't expecting a supermodel because I could never pass for any of those girls from today's shoot.

I walk out of my bedroom and leave the door ajar. Since I don't need my phone, I leave it laying on my bed. The only person who would call is Kenna, and I told her I was going out tonight. As I make my way into the living room, I hear Lucien's deep voice. He was on a call again. As I round the corner, my breath hitches. Dumbstruck would be putting it lightly. He looked incredible. Dressed in a pair of deep blue jeans and a black dress shirt. The first three buttons are undone, his smooth tanned skin peeking through, teasing me. When Lucien turns, his heated stare burns into me. Those olive eyes dim to their mossy hue as they drink in every detail of my appearance with a dark hunger. From my strappy sandals to my dark brown eyes.

He gives me a small smile, mouthing, *'be a minute'* and I nod. Still unable to pull my gaze away from him. His jeans tight on his muscled thighs and hugging his taut ass. I lick my lips as my eyes drift back up to his messy spikey hair. Kenna's voice echoes in my mind, convincing me to forget everything that happened and move on. With him… And how I crave to right now!

Lucien

I stare at my closet with the realization that tonight is more than just a dinner; Cassie is someone I want, with a fire that I never felt before. Yes, I want to be inside her, but there's something else there. To have her as mine is the only thing on my mind. As I pull my jeans on, fastening the button, I grab my black shirt. My phone buzzes and I see it's Jayce, I knew he would give me shit for today.

What the fuck was that man?

I smile at the screen, hitting reply.

Nothing, it was absolutely nothing. Why?

His reply is immediate.

That was not nothing. Does she have a magic pussy or something?

My blood boils when I read his message, he's joking, but they anger me more than they should. We've spoken about girls before, but the mention of Cassie in that way makes me angry. She's not just a random fuck that I found while on a night out. She's different. There's something about her. No, I can't explain it. All I want to do is be inside her. Make her smile, to see those mocha eyes sparkle. She's something special and I need to treat her like an angel. There is something inside her that's pulling me in deeper every day.

Drop it Jayce, I mean it. There's nothing to know

I button my shirt and pull on my boots. A last glance at my reflection, and I am ready to sweep her off her feet.

Yea, sure, you keep telling yourself that. Save some for me

He's really starting to piss me off. I need to end this conversation.

Jayce, I am serious lay off. Talk to you tomorrow

When I pass her room the door is still closed, so I make my way to the living room. My phone rings, thinking it's Jayce, but when I glance at the screen, I realize I have to answer this. I am so fucking sick of my accountants not doing what I say. "Verán," I listen to him complaining about the same figures we went over before I left. "Why don't you sort it out the way I told you to?" My skin prickles, and I realize she's near. Her perfume wafts over to me and I am drunk on the sweetness. I glance up at her and I have an instant fucking hard on. I mouth "be a minute", she offers me a small smile and a nod. My gaze is hungry when I take in her appearance, too aware of how short that dress is, how it hugs every sensuous curve of her.

Her stare matches mine, and a fire flares inside me. *Yes, gorgeous, you will get me tonight. I will make sure of that because I need to fucking bury myself inside you.* When I finally end the call my thoughts are far from what I just discussed, instead they're with Ms. Winters. I step towards her and her pulse riots in her neck.

"Sorry about that, I hate when people don't do what I instruct them to. It's frustrating." I take in her appearance again and the blush spreads across her cheeks.

"Are you used to getting people to do what you order them to?" There is so much I want to say to her, but I don't. Oh, darling if only you knew how I want to command you, and having you doing what I tell you to. Tonight though, you will be begging me to take you, that I promise.

I stand flush with her; the electric current between us is fucking insane. My voice is rough with desire. *Can she hear it?* I flash her a smile and her cheeks pink. "Yes, Cassandra, I am." I acknowledge that I love getting my own way. She needs to know that I will fuck her, and when I do, it will because she is begging me to. My gaze falls to her soft pink lips. I can just about taste them. They're glossy and I want to lick them, bite them and suck them into my mouth, until I hear her whimper.

"I can be…" Reaching for the stray strap of her dress, I replace it and goose bumps rise on her skin in the wake of my touch. "… demanding." I leave my fingers on her for a moment and she licks her lips, chewing on her lower lip and I can only imagine how wet she is right now. My eyes are locked on hers and her pupils dilate. "I guess we better leave. I am…" I step back and walk past her towards the kitchen, making sure we have the briefest contact as I do. "… hungry." Now that there is some distance between us, I take a deep breath. My phone and wallet are on the table, I grab both. At the door, I hold it open for her, flashing her another smile. *What do girls call it these days?* A panty-dropping smile, because I need her to drop those little panties. "Ready for dinner?"

"Yes, I am looking forward to it."

"Perfect. I think you will love the food. The company won't be too bad either," I chuckle.

"I suppose the company will be pretty enlightening," she glances at me. Her cheeky mouth makes me smile and I can't help flashing her my dimples. Robert has the car ready as we make our way outside. This is a date, and I am smiling from ear to ear. I haven't been on one in a long time, I can't wait to see what delights are in store for me and the lovely Ms. Winters.

Cassandra

We pulled up to the restaurant only a few minutes later. The sea view was breathtaking, and I spotted a narrow lane to the shore. Fire lit lamps dotted the garden which added to the island ambience of the diner. "Wow, this place is beautiful," I smiled. The sound of the waves crashing created a soothing atmosphere. Contemporary music played in the background creating a lovely, yet romantic location. The smell of food made my mouth water, and I realized I was starving.

"Let's go." Lucien's hand found the spot on my lower back as we strolled to the entrance. He stepped aside and let me enter first, as a waitress showed us to our table in the garden. Since it was still quiet, we got one of the best tables. The waitress brought our menus and retreated into the restaurant. "What would you prefer to drink?" Lucien's gaze fell on me, his eyes twinkled under the dim light of the lamps. His tanned skin was aglow and added to the allure of his handsome face. *How is this man so good looking?* He could have easily passed for a model with those chiseled features.

"I enjoy wine." He nodded. I peered down at the options for dinner, a mix of Lebanese, Greek, French, Italian, and even Spanish cuisine. The waitress returned with a candle putting it in the center of the table. The flame lit up my view of Lucien and I was ravenous. For him. *Cassie! Concentrate on your menu!* I reprimanded myself and stifled a giggle of girlish excitement. The heat from the night air or the way I felt when I looked at him. I was unsure which made me tingle more.

"I think a bottle of Sauvignon Blanc will pair perfectly with the meal." He set down the wine list and picked up his menu. I stole a glance at him, watching his glittering green eyes read the dinner options. I stared at him, drinking in every detail I could. "Ms. Winters, do you enjoy the view from your chair?" He asked in amusement. His gaze never moved, but I am sure he felt my heated stare. I flushed with embarrassment. *How did he even see me staring at him?*

"Yes, the ocean is incredible." He glanced up suddenly and a devilish smirk curved his full lips. With narrowed eyes, he stared at me as if weighing my answer to be true or not.

"I am confident it is," dropping his gaze as he folded his menu and set it on the table. He continued. "Since you've been gawking at your… menu, in such detail, do you have a thought of what you'd like to order?" My mouth parched, I wasn't even sure I saw what my options were. Nervously licking my lips. I skimmed the choices quickly hoping he didn't realize my stalling.

"Um…"

"Do you always do that when you're nervous?" His eyes darkening in the faint light and I could tell the mossy green was back.

"Do what?" My eyes locked with his gaze. I realized my hands were trembling, and I hope he didn't notice my menu shaking.

"With your mouth," he nodded towards me.

"I um… I suppose so," My belly was in knots as his molten stare fell to my mouth, in only what I could describe as a hungry lustful gaze.

Thankfully, the waitress came back, taking our order. I chose the Poke Du Jour. The menu described the dish as 'fresh fish of the day with soy sauce, red onions, sea salt & sesame seeds. Served with steamed rice.' Lucien got the lamb with pita bread, Tzatziki and quinoa. He also ordered a bottle of wine and sparkling water. Once the waitress walked off, I sensed the tension between us come back. It was magnetic and the knot in my stomach tightened.

"So, tell me about yourself Ms. Winters? I love to get to know my staff, specifically those that will be an essential part of my team." His gaze seared into me and I prayed the waitress would hurry with the water. Lucien played with the flame as he awaited my response. His index finger danced over it and through it. It was distracting as he slowly dipped his finger in the hot wax. He didn't even flinch at the heat. My mind once again drifting in another direction. Images of hot wax drizzling over his chest, those abs dipping into a prominent v. *Cassie, answer him! Shit! What did he ask? Oh yea, about me?*

"I um, well; I was raised just outside New York with my parents. I studied writing at Columbia and graduated 3 years ago." I glanced up at him again. I wasn't sure what else he needed to know.

"And why did you choose to come to LA? I mean there are publishing companies in New York?" The waitress came back with our drinks and I sat backward, Lucien gives the nod for her to pour the wine. She filled both glasses and set it down inside the ice bucket. When we were alone again, he picked up his glass. He didn't wait for my reply, instead he toasted. "I am delighted you've joined Verán Publishers." He clinked his glass on mine. "I need to trust the people I have on my team." His gaze intense. "Welcome to the company Ms. Winters."

"Thank you, Mr. Verán," realizing my mistake when his eyes darkened. It wasn't anger, this was darker, pure unadulterated lust. I squirmed in my seat. Lucien emanated sex from every pore of his magnificent body. The way his dress shirt clung to the planes of his chest. His shoulders looked good enough to hold onto while he pinned me against a wall. *Jesus Cassie, it's been way too long!* A shiver ran down my spine and I squeezed my thighs together. The desire inside me ignited to an unbelievable level.

"Lucien, please, Ms. Winters," his voice raspy. My body shuddered at his request. I nodded, taking a sip of my chilled wine. It didn't relieve the fire raging over my skin. *Cassie, keep it together! Deep breaths remember.* My inner dialogue was frenzied. "So, tell me, what made you move?"

"Lucien. Of course." My teeth chew on my bottom lip as my nerves took over. His gaze settled on my mouth. He raised his wine glass, his stare not wavering. His fingers gripped the stem so hard I expected it to shatter. My gaze fell on his perfect mouth on the rim of the glass as he sipped his drink. His calm, relaxed demeanor hid something darker that he seemed to struggle with. "I um…" Gulping as my heart raced, the tension just got heavier. "Decided to move to LA…" I licked my lips again. It felt like I was in a desert. "… because, I needed a change. A fresh start." He set his glass down. I hoped the change of topic would ease the hypnotic attraction between us, but it merely intensified.

I tore my eyes away from him then. "That's a healthy reason," his voice low. The music drifted through the air and I recognized Lana Del Rey, singing about Blue Jeans. I thought about Lucien's jeans and the heat rose to my face. My body on fire from the sexual tension. How was that even possible? "Tell me, Ms. Winters, are you in a relationship?"

My head jerked up and our eyes locked. "I…" shaking my head, "No… I um… I don't. I mean I'm not." Why am I such a klutz around him? I can't even form a coherent sentence.

He nodded, as if delighted with my response. The waitress served our dinner and as incredible as it looked my hunger was gone. All I could think of was Lucien, his lips, his hands and having them on me. *Cass! Calm down!* "I hope you enjoy dinner." Lucien smiled, his eyes returning to the shimmering olive green.

We both reached for the pepper and his fingertips brushed along my hand. The jolt of electricity shot through me, straight to the ball of fire blazing inside me. His touch so gentle, yet so intense. "You first," he grinned.

How could I work with him tomorrow? My mind and body betrayed me with thoughts of him hovering over me. *Cassie just use the pepper and calm down!* I wanted him, there was no longer a doubt about that, but it scared the hell out of me. Something niggled at my mind, something about him deep down. *Why would someone like him be single? It didn't make sense. Unless he was a serial killer? Cassie! Relax!*

"Cassandra?" His voice filled with concern.

"Yes? Sorry!" I handed him the pepper grinder. This time he deliberately brushed my hand with his fingers. *Fuck!* That sent an ache straight to the apex between my thighs. I craved those fingers. *Yes, I did! Okay Cassie, just play it cool, or try to!*

I picked up my fork and tried to focus on my dinner instead of gawking at my boss. As soon as I scoop a forkful into my mouth. Flavors assaulted my senses. *It was incredible!* "This is excellent!" I glanced up and found him looking at me.

"Yes, their food is wonderful." This is crazy. How can he be so calm and composed?

"So why did you get into publishing?" I needed to talk, to break the tension.

"My dad started the business before I was born. I recall growing up and visiting him at the office. It always seemed so glamorous, thrilling. I went on so many shoots with him and loved it. We spent time at New York Fashion week, and I fell in love with the concept of producing my own fashion magazine." His eyes twinkled with adoration and joy.

"That's fascinating! Did you grow up in LA?" He nodded. "And," my gaze dropped to the candle. *How do I ask him?* "A, um… girlfriend?"

"No," he continued eating, and I realized he had shut down. His expression serious, the mischievous smile was gone. I shouldn't have brought it up. Then he astounded me by carrying on, "I was… I don't…" He picked up his wine and took a mouthful. "I'm single." There it was he was available. *Yes, Cassie, he's single and interested in you! No way! He can't be! Can he?*

I finished my dinner, without disintegrating into my chair. The conversation was less intense after that. The waitress came back and asked if we would like dessert. "Maybe a coffee?" I suggested, he nodded and ordered two coffees.

"We can take a walk on the beach after I have paid the bill." It wasn't a question, but his hopeful gaze made me smile. I nodded.

"Okay, glad I wore sandals." I giggled. *OMG Cassie! A walk on the beach? At night? Alone? What if he kisses you? Well, that would be… I blushed at my wayward thoughts I hope he couldn't hear. OMG! What if he can read my mind? Don't be ridiculous Cass, he's just an ordinary guy. No, there's nothing ordinary about him!*

Lucien

The waitress brings the bill; this is the moment of truth. A romantic walk on the beach. Who said Lucien Verán doesn't do romantic? *Fuck you Jayce!* I chuckle inwardly, he is going to have a field day with me, but nothing mattered right now. As we walk onto the sand, I watch her slip her sandals off, her feet padding on the sand that I am guessing was still warm. My boots were not exactly beachwear, but I didn't care, as long as she gave me that smile, I would be happy doing or wearing anything. "So, Ms. Winters, tell me what excites you besides music and books?" Her quick glance has me wondering what ran through her mind when she looked at me.

"Well, I love trying different foods, I would love to travel. I enjoy my writing; it's been a passion of mine for a long time. I am a tomboy; my running is an obsession…" She trails off. I recall our early morning routine. Yes, that's right, she's the writer, so of course that would be her passion. I watch her talk; she's so animated talking about it. Everything about her fascinates me. Her dark brown curls frame her face and neck and I am jealous of their proximity to her skin. She has an obsession. I want to be her obsession, I want her to ache for me, as much as I crave her. When our eyes meet, the air is thick with sexual tension. *How the fuck can she feel like a tomboy? Has she looked in the mirror? My God, she's pure female perfection.*

"You definitely don't look like a tomboy. Especially not when you've been running." I step close to her, I need her. Now. Her body is warm and I need her warmth all around me.

"What do I look like then?" Her voice barely audible. We are both frozen in place; I can see her holding her breath. The intensity of the situation causing a tremble to travel over her body. Her pulse quickens and I can see it against her throat. Blood rushes through me and gathers in my cock. *Why the hell does she make me feel like this? I can't do it. Can I? Is there a possibility that I can own her? Would she be happy to submit that beautiful body, her mind, and heart to me? Do I even want her heart?* Her sweet hot breath fans over my face and it takes everything in me not to pin her down and devour her. Time to test the waters.

I lean in and murmur in her ear, "A very..." I lean in closer. "... breathtaking woman." Even in the dark, I can see the blush warm her cheeks and I step back. Her pulse riots in her throat and I want to lick it, to calm it with my tongue. There are so many other places on her body I would love to put my tongue.

"Let's walk." I turn to walk on, expecting her to follow me and she does. A submissive even though she doesn't know it. Yet. I let her walk into the surf and watch the water splash over her feet. The air is hot and I wonder if I can convince her to go swimming. I pull my boots and socks off, when I step forward, her body flush with mine. If I roll my hips my hard cock will brush her ass, it's so fucking tempting I almost do it. She can feel my breath on her neck as I whisper the question. "Did you want to swim?" She's quiet for a moment before she replies.

"I don't have anything to wear," she giggles.

"Who said you have to wear anything?" My teasing tone earns me a laugh, a beautiful sound. If only she knew I wasn't joking. To see her naked, in the ocean would be my ultimate fantasy.

"I doubt you should say that to a staff member." She turns with her reply and taunts me as she murmurs my name in the dark. "Mr. Verán." I drop my boots and reach for her, hauling her up against me, every soft curve of her body molds to mine and I know she can feel my erection. Her body wriggles in my grasp, only making me harder, as I walk into the water, she needs to be punished in the worst way and I am itching to give it to her.

"Lucien! Your jeans!" She squeals, making my cock throb, pushing against my jeans in a painful surge. There are so many fucking things I want to do to her right now.

"Ms. Winters, does it look like I care about getting soaked?" My reply is rough. I can't help it. I am beyond turned on now and if she keeps this up I was going to ram myself deep in her tight little cunt right here on the beach. My thoughts are so much darker than she could imagine.

I am about waist deep in water now and we're both soaked, but I don't give a fuck. I glance up at her and see the desire in her chocolate eyes. Her lust matched mine, and she was definitely going to get it tonight. I let her down in the most exquisite way, sliding her down my chest. Her hands come down on my body and every inch of my body is on fire for her.

"Now will you remember to call me Lucien? It's not a request. It's an order." My voice is firm, and she nods. When I turn back, walking back to get my boots, leaving her trailing behind me.

"Why?" When she challenges my order, I am vibrating with need to spank her pert little ass.

As I bend to pick up my boots, I don't face her when I reply. "Because, I can't handle you calling me that." I hope my answer will suffice, but she presses on.

"Why Lucien?" She walks out of the water towards me. *Fuck! She needs to stop right the fuck now!* I growl, it's a primal sound. She's goading me, and my body is not ready for this.

"Drop it, Cassandra." Her stubbornness is going to hurt us both.

I am about to fucking lose it when she taunts me again. "Lucien, you can't say that. It doesn't make sense. Everyone calls you Mr.—"

I spin around to face her, completely losing it. "Jesus, Cassandra just quit!" There! Now just fucking leave it alone. I am radiating emotion, but she doesn't back down. *So my little Cassie isn't scared of me? Well she ought to be!* I am a fuck up; I don't want to hurt her. She's not right for me. From the look on her face, I can tell she's excited, there's amusement behind her eyes and I am dying to know what she's thinking. *Do I scare her? Is she really into me?* I like her. I haven't liked anyone in such a long time. It scares the fuck out of me.

Chapter Six

Cassandra

"No! Tell me why?" I took two steps forward and stood in front of him. The tension between us was like a volcano about to erupt, and I shuddered. He looked like he was about to explode. I was trying to understand what was so bad in calling him by his name.

He dropped his boots then, clutching my shoulders, he stood flush with me. I was sure you could see bolts of lightning as our bodies touched. "You are so goddamn frustrating! Why can't you drop it!?"

"Because you make no sense!" We were both yelling, but all I could think of was his solid body against me. Heat radiated from him. I realized I sounded like a petulant teenager but I needed him to tell me what the hell was wrong. *What on earth could be so bad about calling him what everyone else calls him?* He dropped his hands at his sides, his body frozen against mine.

His expression changed, from frustration to resolution. "Fine, you demand to know why?" I nod, slowly. "I will show you." The words came out low and dangerous and it sent an exquisite shiver down my spine. I stood squirming in front of him. He was so close his scent filled my senses. I was aching for him now. He stole my breath, every time he was close to me. This isn't normal. "Close your eyes Cassandra." I obeyed. When his fingertips brushed the curls from my collar, I shivered. The spark between us was tangible. It had a life of its own. I couldn't not want him. "Stay perfectly still." His warm breath fanned over my neck. He gently traced a path from the spot behind my ear, down my neck, to my shoulder. His fingertips were hot and his touch sent sparks to every nerve in my body.

By this point I was completely at his mercy, my body aching for him. My panties soaked with desire, and my clit throbbed. I could literally see fireworks behind my eyelids from his touch. It was intense, and I couldn't stay still. This was killing me. A slight whimper escaped my lips. "You feel that?" I nod slowly. "This is what it does to me when you call me, Mr. Verán."

His fingers traced back up my neck and his lips found my ear. "It makes me crave you," I gasped, "makes me need to take you…" I quivered and his fist grasped the back of my neck. The roughness of his movement only ignited me further. I wanted him to kiss me, touch me, anything. He held me still as his lips teased my ear. The heat traveled down my neck, "tie you to my bed…" My breathing hitched at the images racing through my mind. *Yes, Lucien, do it! Please! Take me! Calm down Cassie!* "And punish you."

My eyes shot open and found his. Never have I been so turned on in my whole life, the need for him was unbearable. A minute passed before I recovered my voice and responded. "Then punish me," my tone a hoarse whisper, barely audible over the sound of the crashing waves. "Mr. Verán." His name rolled off my lips, with intent and desire. *OMG! Did I just do that? Shit! OMG Cassie!!*

He clutched me, pulling my body against him and his impressive erection pushing against my belly. His lips crashed onto mine, sealing my mouth with a deep lush kiss. His tongue licked into me, tasting me for the first time. I reached up and tangled my fingers in his spikey hair, tugging him into me. My body on fire and he was my gasoline. He lifted me, walking towards the ridge, pinning me against it. The steel of his body against mine, solid and hard and I moaned into the kiss.

His hands gripped my hips so hard, I was sure I would be bruised tomorrow, but I didn't care. I craved him, desired him. The ache so deep inside me, I didn't think I could ever rid myself of it. *Fuck!* I want this man so much. *He's your boss Cassie! I don't care!* Nothing else mattered right now. All I wanted was him. Suddenly Lucien broke the kiss, and stepped away, his eyes searching mine. We were both breathless. I was still shaking, my body on fire. "Cassandra," his voice a tense whisper. "We can't do this." He spun to face the ocean. He had winded me with his words. *What did he mean? Why was he turning away? Was I too normal for him!* Not a blonde supermodel.

"I get it Lucien. I am not your type. It's—"

He whirled around with a pained look on his face. Then he took a step towards me. With a hand either side of my head he leaned in. I thought he was about to kiss me again, but then he spoke. In a strained hushed tone. "No. That's not it." He stared at me. I am tempted to reach out and touch him. To run my hand through his messy hair. "Cassie, I am not…" His voice dropped further and I could just about hear him. "I will hurt you… I will fuck this up."

"Why? What are you talking about?" He dropped his hands, but didn't turn away this time. His gaze dropped to the sand. "Lucien, no one is perfect. How do you know I won't fuck it up?" He ran a hand through his hair. I wished it was me doing it, touching just a part of him. I needed to see his eyes, to see what message they held. When he peered up again, I stepped forward, staring up into his eyes and offered him a small smile.

"You're so…" his soft warm hands reached up and cupped my face. He searched for the words in my eyes. "I haven't wanted someone as much as I crave you, but I am not right for you."

My heart hammered in my ribcage. "I crave you too and how do you know what's right for me?" *How on earth could he possibly know? Cassie, you need to tell him! No!*

"Cassie, you don't realize what you're suggesting. You don't know who I am. What I have done." He looked broken, torn, and I wanted to hold him.

"You don't know who I am Lucien. I am letting you in, please?" I reach up to touch his face when he doesn't back away, my heart races. His soft skin on mine had tingles shooting through me again. "Let me in?" This time I was begging. For what? I wasn't sure, but I wanted it. Whatever he would give me.

He glanced up, his eyes darkened and a wicked smirk curled his full lips. "Okay. You want this?" I nodded. "Then I am taking you home now." He laces his fingers through mine and tugs me alongside him as we race to the car.

Lucien

I couldn't talk to her all the way back to the house. There was sexual tension thick in the air driving me absolutely insane with a need for her. *Just one night that's all. You can't pull her into your darkness. She's too innocent. Too fucking sweet.* When Robert finally pulled into the driveway, I wanted to pick her up caveman style and carry her into the house. The need to possess her in ways that would make her forget about everything burned inside me. When I opened the car door, I held out my hand, she slipped hers in mine the light from her eyes shone with promise.

I dismissed Robert, and just about dragged her into the house. When the door shut, I grabbed her, pinning her to the wall. This was what I had wanted to do since the first day I saw her in the coffee shop. To have her pressed against me in such a primal way. My mouth sealed hers without asking, I licked into her sweet mouth, and groaned at the taste of her. *Fuck, she tastes like heaven.* A flavor of sweet honey and jasmine. She sucks on my bottom lip, tugging it between her teeth, and I all but come in my pants. I couldn't get enough of her. It was heady, and all I wanted was her. With a forceful roll of my hips, I show her how hard she has me, her whimper was evidence that she wanted the same.

She fumbles with the buttons of my shirt, but I can't wait. "Rip it!" I growl. Her hands grip the material and when she tugs, I am surprised at her strength, buttons pop and fly in every direction. As soon as she slides it off and her hands were on me. *Thank fuck!* Her touch lit my skin on fire. I can't explain the intoxicating sensation of how she feels, soft, gentle, but so fucking erotic. I needed to be inside her.

My hands grip her tight little ass and lift her against me. The only place I want her now is on my bed. This is where she belonged, with me, under me. The way she stared at me both turned me on and unnerved me, but made me feel like a better man. Not the dark shadow that I think of myself as. Not the evil bastard that I really am. I set her down on my bed. "Stay." I command her. She watches me move, pulling my boots and belt off, her eyes filled with a hunger that matched mine. Never in my thirty years have I wanted a woman as much as I wanted her right at that moment. I wanted every part of her. Her eyes fall on my zipper and she squirms. *Yes, darling, I will fuck you so hard and so good that you will feel me for weeks after. I promise, you will ache for me the way I ache for you.* I watch her squeeze her thighs together, and I realize she's wet. My hungry little tigress.

My eyes meet hers, while I unbutton my jeans, the zipper half way down. I can't wait to see her naked. "You sure about this?" She nods letting me know she wants this; she slips her straps of the dress off her shoulders. I drink in the sight of her in a black sheer bra. *Oh my fucking God she is perfect.* Her full tits are creamy and her nipples are peaked behind the soft material of the bra. "Fuck, you're beautiful!" I pull her up and undo her belt. As soon as the dress pools at her feet, I need to kiss her again. I tug her body against me, sealing her lips with mine.

She's so wanton with lust, rubbing her core against me. Her fingers tangle in my hair, tugging me closer to her. Like she hungers for me. Her heat is unbearable and I doubt I will last very long. Our tongues dance in an erotic tumble and I suck hers into my mouth. A soft whimper escapes her mouth, she's ready. I lay her on the bed, her bare skin on mine is incredible. I am way over dressed for this party. Without a word, I shrug my jeans off, without my eyes leaving her. Her gaze is glued to my bulge, and she looks like she's about to devour me whole. My fingers move to unhook her bra, flinging it on the floor somewhere. "Cassandra." My voice is a low growl. Her nipples are hard and I lean in, devouring them. Sucking, nibbling, tasting her. *Fuck!* My mind can't form coherent sentences at this point. I graze her sensitive buds with my teeth, and her back arches in pleasure.

I need to taste the rest of her. My mouth moves down over her belly, I kiss a soft wet trail down, noticing the goose bumps that rise up on her smooth silky skin. She's writhing up, but I need her to hold still. This would be so much easier if I had her bound to the bed. I grip her and pin her hips to the bed. I need to keep her in place, or I will lose control. A jolt of pleasure shoots to my cock when she moans my name. I am leaking, ready to be inside her. My eyes on hers, I tug her panties off. With soft feather light kisses on her thighs, I take in the sweetness of her skin. With soft kisses on her inner thighs, I tease her, not giving attention to where she needs me most. Once her panties are on the floor, I grab each ankle and kiss them. She's a fucking goddess, perfect.

My briefs find their place among the strewn clothes on the floor, she gasps when her eyes fall on my cock. I grab a condom and roll it on. Her eyes never leaving my movements. I kneel back between her thighs, my erection at her pussy. *I am so ready to ram inside you, darling.* My mouth claims her again; I trace my hand down the side of her body. I find the slick sex between her thighs and stroke her. "You're so fucking wet for me." Her whimper is more than enough to spur me on. God, she will feel amazing. "I need to be inside you, Cassandra." She raises her hips to me and I slide in slowly. It takes all my restraint not to drive into her. It's the only way to keep myself from coming too soon. She's tight, so fucking tight. Her pussy sucks me in.

"Please," she whispers, "… Mr. Verán." I need to fuck her now, this is ridiculous, and she knows what it does to me. With one hand I grip her wrists and pin them above her head. I fucking warned her. *Is she trying to make me crazy?* "Do it." Her voice is hoarse with desire. *You asked for it sweetheart. I am going to fuck you senseless until you're crying out my name. No other man will make you feel what I am about to make you feel.*

I drive into her, bottoming out inside her tight little cunt. She fits me like a fucking glove. When I hear her cry out I still inside her. I allow her a moment until she looks into my eyes with a sparkling smile. Slower now, I pull out then slide in to the hilt, giving her my cock, I want her to have every fucking inch of me. I need her to be mine, only mine. My eyes lock on hers and I hope she can see the promise in them. *You're mine now. No one else is going to have a chance with you. I will fucking own you.*

I taste her, kissing and nibbling her neck. My lips move to her mouth; her lips are bruised from my rough kisses. I bite on that plump bottom lip. When she wraps her legs around me, pulling me into her, I move faster. My orgasm is close. Pleasure runs down my spine, straight to my cock. Her teeth bite down on my shoulder, making me growl, and pleasure shoots down my spine. *You want rough baby? I can give you rough.* My relentless pounding pins her to the mattress, I pull out to the tip and drive into her so deep, knocking the wind from her with the thrust. She whimpers a plea.

"Please, please, Lucien, please?" Begging me to let her come and I don't deprive her. Her tight little body spasms as an orgasm rips through her and I can't hold back anymore. I call out her name as I slam my release into her, my body shuddering. Her face is incredible. She's so fucking beautiful when she comes. *Christ!* My gaze flits up, and I realize I have a death grip on her wrists. *Shit!* I release her and she immediately touches me, stroking me. My skin prickles in pleasure. As we catch our breath I am sated for the first time in years. I slide out of her slowly, giving her a soft kiss.

I need to get rid of this fucking condom. When I rise from the bed, I make my way to the bathroom. "Be right back, gorgeous." She looks beautiful splayed on my bed, looking thoroughly fucked. Every man's wet fucking dream. Her eyes on me, burn into my skin. In the bathroom I stare at my reflection. That was incredible. She's perfect in every way. I can't even explain what it's like being inside her. *You're so fucked, Lucien, so fucking fucked.* I splash cold water on my face, then grab a towel, drying my face.

I join her in the bedroom and offer a smile. Back in the bedroom, I slip into the bed next to her, the heat of her body ignites me from the inside out. It's like she's turned a light on inside me. If only she can light the darkness in my heart and my past. She can't find out about that. There is no way she will want me if she ever found out. My heart hurts to think I could ever hurt her in that way. "Are you okay?"

"Of course I am! Why wouldn't I be?" She turns to face me. When her fingers trace my tattoos a shiver runs through me. The gentle way she touches me, is something I am not used to, but I love it.

"I just… I don't know." I shrug. She's staring at me intently. For the first time I am unsure of myself. The need to impress her is coursing through me. "That was as wonderful as I thought it would be."

"Oh? You've thought about it?" Amusement dances in her eyes. *Fuck I slipped up!* There is no need to tell her I thought about fucking her since I first saw her, but she doesn't seem angry.

"Since the first time I saw you in the coffee shop!" Her soft body against mine, has my mind wandering, her skin feels like silk. "You do not understand how you've haunted me, my dreams, my fantasies." Honesty is the best policy; I hope she doesn't freak out. "This…" I signal to us laying naked on the bed, "… is, I can't even tell you how incredible it is." Something flickers in her eyes, but she seems adamant on not telling me.

"As wonderful as this is, I meant what I said earlier. You don't know me Lucien."

"Then enlighten me, Ms. Winters, tell me everything about you." I draw her in for a kiss, her lips are soft, pliable, and taste like strawberries. *This is a bad idea, but fuck it. I am going to hell anyway. Might as well enjoy the ride.* Kissing her was like breathing, at this point I was so far gone, I needed it to survive. Her giggle is sexy as fuck and music to my ears.

"Can we start the education when I am not so sleepy?"

"Of course gorgeous. We have a long day tomorrow and I don't think your employer would approve of you being late." When her finger traces over my hips, my cock twitches, and I am rock hard again. Just a simple touch from her and I am putty in her hands, I roll over her and tease her with my cock.

"I would have to give him something to approve of then, won't I?" Her seductive tone has me aching again. I am acting like a fucking teenager. *How can I even be hard again? She's fucking incredible.*

"I guess you should, how about right now?" Her hands travel over my back, and I lean in kissing the sweet spot behind her ear, making her back arch into me. I love the curve of her body, how she molds to me, and her begging is intoxicating.

"Lucien," her nipples pebble against my chest. "Please?"

"If you keep this up little lady, I will miss work tomorrow." I grab another condom and roll it on with lightning speed. Already the need to be inside her is causing an ache in my heart. I lower myself over her and take in the flush of her cheeks. Disbelief washes over me, I am about to take her again. "You're beautiful." I whisper in her ear. Sliding my left hand down, reaching between us, my fingers slide over her slick sex to make sure she's ready.

"Lucien," she sighs out loud as I twist my fingers inside her.

"Mmm, wet, just how I like you," my hooded gaze is dark and dangerous. Her hips rise to meet my hand. "You want me gorgeous?"

"Yes, please, Mr. Verán?" She's taunting me as only she can and I drive into her.

My teeth tug her earlobe, the pain and pleasure will shoot straight to her core, as expected her pussy tightens around me. I kneel up between her legs, never breaking our connection, lifting her knees and pushing them back, I slam into her, hitting her g spot and her eyes flutter closed. "Look at me." My voice a deep growl. She obeys my command, which has my cock throbbing inside her. I don't think I can get any harder. "Look at the man fucking you, taking you. Cassandra, you feel so fucking good around me." *So tight, so fucking tight like a glove.* "Fuck Cassandra, give it to me, I want every fucking drop. Come for me, sweetness!" I can't hold out any longer when her orgasm cinches me. Her pussy milks me and her name escapes my lips as I come inside her. Her body shudders under me and I let her legs down. With slow precision I slip out of her and roll onto my side, pulling her into me. "You will be the death of me." *She will kill me, in the best way possible.* I pull the condom off discarding it next to the bed. It will have to wait until morning, there's no way I am leaving her now.

"You are kind of wonderful." Her voice is soft as she mumbles.

"Not me, sweetness, you are. Whatever exists in our pasts we will overcome it because there's no way I am letting you go." Her light is shining like a beacon in the night. I know that whatever happened we could get through it. There's something about this girl that I can't let go of. I need her. Her eyes flutter closed and I stare at her for ages. *Why have you come into my life? I don't want to hurt you. God knows you're going to make me a better man, but Cassandra, I can't hurt you.* I stare out the patio doors from the bed and my mind is in tatters.

There is so much darkness in me, but in her, she's the opposite, filled with light and love and everything that is good. I don't deserve her, but she's chosen me. All I can do is try to be the man she thinks I am. I stroke her long hair, it's soft like silk. She is flawless, her skin smooth to the touch. I wanted tonight to end with her in my bed. I just didn't realize it would be after she's practically pulled my heart out of its cage, lit a flame inside it and then put it back. Deep down I am scared as fuck, but she's come into my life for a reason. She's like a light in my darkness. My lumiére. Sleep takes over and I dream of her. Again.

"Lucien, where are you going? Luke!" I spin around and see her, those beautiful silky brown curls. The dark brown eyes that make my body ache to be inside her. "Luke come on!" She's giggling, running along the beach. As soon as I follow her the night gets darker.

"Cassie! Cassandra, where are you going babe?" She's out of reach. Why can't I get to her? When I reach my hand out, I finally catch her. My grip on her wrist is tight, and I tug her to me. Her body flush with mine. With both hands I cup her face, and lean in to kiss her. Sparks course through my body as her soft lips touch mine. I seal her mouth, she opens up, giving me access. Her tongue dances with mine, twisting, tumbling. Her moan brings me out of the fantasy and I pull back. My eyes shoot open, I glance down at her, she's not breathing. "No! Cassie! Come back to me! Cassie! No!"

My eyes jerk open. Immediately I glance next to me, Cassie is sound asleep. She looks like an angel. An angel that I can't be with. I can't do this to her. As I slide out of bed, I make my way into the bathroom. A splash of cold water on my face wakes me up, I glance at my reflection in the mirror. The darkness in my eyes makes me shiver. *I can't do this to her. I can't bring her into my life. This was a mistake.* When we get back to LA, it ends. Back in the bedroom, I take in the beautiful girl in my bed. The sweet scent of her perfume calms me down as I slide in next to her. I tug the sheet up covering us both, and close my eyes, letting sleep take me.

Chapter Seven

Cassandra

It's Sunday morning and I open my eyes to a deafening noise. "What the—" There's a warm body next to mine when I reach over. Two of the most exquisite olive eyes I have ever seen greet me when I glance up. My smile is mirrored when Lucien's face brightens into a grin that creases his eyes.

"Good morning, sweetness," his fingertips brush my shoulder.

"Lucien," I gasped, recalling the night before.

"Yup, that's me. At least I was the last time I checked." He laughed, caressing my face. I leaned into his touch, I sighed at the electric current he sent through my body.

"Yes, smart ass! I just…" Heat flushed my cheeks. Lucien tugs me closer to him and gives me a kiss. "Was, I mean… last night…" I stumble over my words. *Just ask him! Was it a one-night thing? I mean he's your boss. You can't expect him to date you! Of course not! No, it's okay. I am fine.*

"Last night was amazing, sweetness, and it's absolutely not going to be the last." My eyes lock on his and the truth shining in his beautiful green eyes.

"Really?" I cock my head to the side.

"Why do you sound so surprised? You think I don't want to be inside you again? Because I do. So much more." He rolls onto his side, facing me. Those green eyes are staring at me intently. I watch his gaze roam my face, assessing my reaction. The delicate white sheet down moves down to my waist as his lips trail hot kisses between my breasts.

"Lucien," My back arches towards him and that incredible mouth. I breathe his name; goose bumps rise on my skin. He leaves me speechless with every movement.

"We can talk later. I have something else in mind." He rolls over me, supporting himself up on his elbows. His body hovering over mine. The heat of his bare skin on mine is intense. The crackle of electricity between us is incredible. His muscles tense, the veins on his arms bulge, and I am aching for him to be inside me again.

"I don't want to be late; my new boss is extremely demanding." I tease as he nibbles on my ear causing shivers to course through my body.

"Is he now?" His voice is a low rumble has my skin tingling. Lucien lifts his gaze, and it sears into me. His head cocks to one side and his eyes narrow, "And why would you say that Ms. Winters?"

I giggle as he rolls his hips into me, teasing me and his arousal pressing into my core. "Well, he is pretty intimidating. He said he wants to tie me to his bed." His teeth tug on my hardened nipple and I gasp at the sensations rushing through me. An electrical current shoots straight to the bundle of nerves between my thighs. "Lucien!" I cry out as he tugs on the other bud.

"Does that turn you on my lumière?" His voice dripping with desire. I recognize the French word for light, but it dissolves as his fingers find my entrance. Heated kisses flutter down my body in slow soft movements, he dips his tongue in my bellybutton and I just about come undone beneath him. "You like the notion of me tying you to my bed?" His eyes lock on mine when he laps at the heat between my thighs. My core tightens and his fingers tease me. I can't find the words to answer him so I nod. His smile is dark and so are his eyes. They're filled with yearning and desire. *Did you just give him permission to tie you to his bed? God, yes!* My legs are splayed open and I can't help bucking my hips.

His tongue slips into me while his fingers stroke my slick folds. With slow movements inside me then back out. "So beautifully wet, I could feast on you all day." He is teasing and driving me to the edge. His tongue flicks over my clit; I grip the sheets so hard I am sure I am going to rip them. "Mmmm," he moans and his warm breath blows on me. "You taste like honey, baby. So fucking sweet." A shiver wracks through my body, I am shamelessly writhing below him. "This tight little cunt is delicious." His crude words have me teetering on the edge. My eyes close as I take in the sensations he's giving me. I am so close to the release I need. That I ache for. My skin tingles, heated, like I am on fire, my core tightens around him. There is an earth shattering orgasm about to overtake me.

"Please Lucien!" I cry out loud, I need him to give me the release I yearn for. "Please?"

"Please what baby? You want to come for me?" I nod without looking at him. "This sweet little pussy will flood my tongue with juices." He continues plunging two fingers inside me, when his mouth closes down on my clit, sucking and flicking it with his tongue. My orgasm splinters through me.

"LUCIEN!" I cry out his name, my body convulsing, and bucking on the bed. His hands grip my hips holding me down as I shudder. His tongue riding out my orgasm inside me, I have never felt this good before. My breathing is erratic. Shallow, deep, fast, slow. When I finally stop shaking, he kneels up between my legs, watching me with hunger in his eyes. His lips glistening with my arousal. I watch him lick his lips and I almost come undone again. He stops, reaching for the nightstand. I shake my head. All I need is him inside me. His eyes darken at the thought of being inside me without a barrier.

"It's okay, I'm on the pill." My voice is scratchy from screaming only moments before. He moves over me then, driving into me. With a deep thrust, to the hilt he fills me, offering me what I was seeking all along. With a roll of his hips he is plunging himself into me. Like pieces of a puzzle, we fit together.

"You take away my darkness." He murmurs. His right hand gripping my wrists above my head. The brute strength of him restrains me. My body writhing under him, working to take every inch of him inside me. Everything inside me calms, I let go of my fears, my inhibitions. "You are mine now," he claims me in that moment with his body and words. When he slams into me again, he takes me higher. My eyes fall on him and his face is peaceful, but dark. "Do you understand me Cassandra? I can't be away from you, not when you make me feel like this." Lucien's voice laden with a dark lust I don't recognize. I nod. My eyes on his, and my orgasm tightens my core. I clench around him, warning him. His devilish smirk appears and his dimples tug the knot in my belly. The green eyed bad boy claiming every part of me. His lips are next to my ear. "Come for me, sweetness, give me your light." His words are my undoing as I tremble beneath him. His body tenses and is rigid as he comes inside me. An animalistic growl rumbles in his chest. We lay in comfortable silence for a few moments; my heart is pounding against my chest. *That was... I have never felt like that with anyone. How can this man make me let go like that?*

"Lucien?" He lifts his head, looking into my eyes with passion. "We may need to get up now." My voice is barely audible.

"I wish I could stay inside you all day." He plants a soft kiss on my lips, rolling over and slipping out of me. I feel empty and whimper. "Did I hurt you?" Concern etched on his handsome face. *Why does he always ask me that? After the most amazing sex ever, how could he think he hurt me?*

"No, of course not." I plant a soft kiss on his lips, then swing my legs over the bed and rise. My muscles are aching, but it's put a smile on my face. I am happy, sated, and freaked out. To fall in love at this point would be stupid. I turn to watch him get out of bed; the muscles in his back are so sexy. His ass is as sexy naked as it looks in jeans. I suppress a giggle.

"Do you like the view?" The amusement in his voice makes me blush. *How did he know I was staring at him? God, he's beautiful.*

"I am. The ocean looks incredible from your room." I tease, walking over to the patio doors.

"Yes, because that's what had your attention?" I giggle. Feeling his body behind me, he wraps an arm around my waist. "Cassandra," turning around in his embrace, I glance up into those hypnotic green eyes. "I shouldn't be with you. There's so much darkness in my life. I am bad for you. Do you even realize that?" My heart constricts at his words and the pain in his eyes.

"Lucien, please don't, I get it. One night." I step back, but he doesn't loosen his hold on me.

"No, you don't get it. I said I shouldn't be with you, but there's something that makes me ignore that fact. If this is what you want, then I'm not going anywhere." My stomach flip flops at his words. *He wants me? I do want him. Fuck, I want him so much. There's something about this green eyed man that's unbound me from my fears of the past, and now, I may just fall over that cliff with him. Ridiculously hard and fast.*

"Then I'm not going anywhere." I lean up onto tiptoes and plant a kiss on his lips. "Now go get ready. Or we will be late."

As I make my way back to my bedroom. I grab my phone from my bed and notice there are five missed calls and the same amount of text messages. All from Kenna, she is freaking out. I giggle because I realize she wants the details on my date last night. A tingle of excitement skitters down my spine when I recall last night, and this morning. I tap the call button. Two rings and she is yelling on the other end.

"OMG Where have you been??"

"I was, um…" I am not sure how to tell her. The butterflies in my stomach don't stop fluttering and I take a deep calming breath.

"Cassandra Winters! Tell me right now!" She is screaming so loud I am sure Lucien can hear her from the kitchen.

"Kenna, shh! I spent the night with Lucien." I whisper hoping he isn't at my door.

"Ahhhhhh OMG OMG OMG!! Yes!!! Was he good? OMG I am so thrilled!" I giggle into the phone listening to her. This was the exact reaction I expected, this is my best friend in the world.

"Kenna, babe. I need to go, he's making breakfast and we have work. I will call you later okay?"

"Please babe, do not call me! Spend time with that hunk you have in the kitchen.

60

OMG! Do it on the kitchen counter!"

"Goodbye Kenna." I laugh into the phone before hanging up and making my way to the kitchen. *Not a bad idea, the kitchen counter!* I giggle like a schoolgirl as I pad into the kitchen to see Lucien busy with breakfast.

Lucien

I set up the coffee machine and start breakfast. My mind drifts back to the last twenty-four hours and I am not sure what the fuck is going on. She's got me whipped. No question. The thought of her with someone else burns into me like a motherfucker. *What the fuck was I thinking marking her? Or claiming her? She's not designed to be in my world, but fuck it if I am letting her go now.* There is no way I can stay away from her. Not now. I wanted her, only her. The realization hits me, hard. *Can I give her what she needs? Is the man in my past dead and buried? Can I find my soul again?* The only thing that's clear now is that no other man should touch her. I claimed her this morning, every part of her.

My mind is all over the place when she joins me in the kitchen. "Wow, this looks amazing!" The smile she brings to my face is nothing short of shocking. I set her breakfast down on the table and grab the coffee. When I slide into the seat opposite her, I drink in her appearance.

"So much for a morning run." I mumble. She giggles at me and blushes.

"Well, we got quite a workout this morning." *My favorite type of workout darling.* Her expression is adorable. How can she be embarrassed talking about what we just did? Her innocence makes me want to rethink this, but my heart hurts at the thought of walking away from her. *Your heart? You don't have one Lucien. Remember, no love, no hearts. She's so fucking cute. That's why she makes my cock so hard. That innocence in her eyes.*

"Oh sweetness, trust me, there's plenty more where that came from." I raise my eyebrows and give her a mischievous wink. She's so sweet and innocent, my cheeky words have her choking and spluttering on her breakfast. I can't fall in love, that's out of the question, but I can certainly enjoy her. We need to get out of this house, or I will carry her back to the bedroom right now.

Once we're finished with breakfast, I clear up the table, making sure the dishes are in the dishwasher. I turn it on and turn to her. "Come on, sweetness, we have to get to work." I grab my keys and mobile from the table and we walk out to the car. My eyes rake over her and the amount of skin she's showing off today makes my possessiveness flare. Her long legs look stunning in the shorts and I recall them wrapped around my waist, pulling me into her.

Once we're in the car, I turn to her. "So, what did you want to do for dinner tonight? I can cook?"

What the actual fuck Luke? Jayce will have a good laugh at me acting like a lovesick pussy. He knows I am not the type to make dinner and buy flowers, but Cassie makes me want to do that and so much more. I am out of my comfort zone, out of control and I don't like it. The last time I was out of control, I did something so bad that I could never forgive myself. No more. Do I walk away from Cassie? Even after I know how she makes me feel? As soon as the thought hits me that I can't have her I feel sick.

"You cook?" She looks at me stunned that I offered to make her dinner. *Don't worry darling, I am as shocked at the offer as you are. This is so wrong on so many fucking levels.*

"Yes, Ms. Winters, I can cook!" I pull her to me. The ache in my body to touch her, be near her, inhale her soft sweet scent is bearing down on me.

"Well, I better take full advantage having my boss cook for me." She still sees us as employer and employee. *After the way I just fucked you darling? No way!*

I release her and turn her face to me. "Can we not be employer and employee tonight?" Not tonight at least. My eyes on hers gives too much away. She stares at me, unnerving me, like she can see my dark soul. *I wish you could fix me darling. Maybe she can? I felt it earlier.* Yes, she can. I want her to.

"Sure we can. I mean. After…" Her words are unsure. Realization hits me, this is new to her. It's new to me as well. I have no idea how to do this, but her doubt frustrates me. At that moment, next to one of the most incredible women I have ever laid eyes on, I make a choice. Even if it kills me.

"Cassandra," my index finger pulls her chin up, forcing her to look at me. "Please don't doubt this?"

Her expression shows how much she wants this; how much she wants me. "Lucien…" She breathes my name and I want to pin her down on the seat and have my wicked way with her.

My finger on her lips is warm and when she bites my finger, my cock wakes up with a ferocious throb. Fuck! I would love to see her lips wrapped around my cock. I want to fuck my cock into that sassy mouth.

"Well, we can always test your oral skills tonight." I give her a naughty wink. Her cheeks are crimson by my suggestion and I chuckle. When we get out of the car, the staff are already running around like crazy. Nothing ever gets done properly if I am not on location. As much as I love being here, my mind is stuck on the thought of Cassandra with her mouth on me. This is going to be a long fucking day. Might as well get it over with.

Cassandra

"Hey, there's my main model!" Jayce grabs me into a bear hug. He lifts me, whirling around as I clutch onto his shoulders. Lucien's icy gaze is on us, sending a cold shiver over my skin, even in the heat of Jayce's arms.

"Jayce!" Lucien's voice thunders through the crowded tent.

"Chill Luke! No need to get your boxers in a twist." He lets me down and flashes a smirk at me, giving me a cheeky wink.

"Can you attempt being professional?" Lucien and Jayce stand face to face, the air heavy with tension. Something significant must have taken place between the two. I resolve to find out what, having never seen that kind of fire in Lucien's eyes. It seems to come out particularly when he's around Jayce.

"Lucien, let's go take a look at the set." I tug him towards the water. As soon as we're out of earshot I round on him. "What's wrong with you?" He meets my gaze with the irritation clear on his handsome face. My body thrumming with annoyance and frustration.

"I don't want you near him," his body radiating anger. When I reach out and touch his hand he let's me, I draw him towards me. I lean up on my tip toes and plant a kiss on his cheek. "I am sorry Cassandra but I prefer not to share." His voice is low as he hisses in my ear.

"Luke darling!" Lucien goes rigid and pulls away from me. We both stare at the tall blonde standing glaring at our exchange. *Talk about sharing! Why does she always turn up every time we're having a moment together?*

He strolls over to her, leaving me standing with my mouth gaped in dismay. "Sasha thanks for being here." Lucien leans in kissing her on the cheek. My body ignites with jealousy and fear. This is his ex, which makes it ten times worse. I can't stand here and watch them. Without a word I stalk off towards the tent. Lucien's voice is loud when he calls to me. "Cassandra!" I ignore him. His attempt to call me annoys me further. I don't like to share either. I don't wish to be anywhere near that blonde.

I walk back into the tent and see Jayce, he's working on his laptop; I slide into the chair next to him. His blue gaze falls on me. "Jayce, you need help?" My eyes roam his arms and I spot a tattoo, it looks like Lucien's. He smiles and nods.

"Yea babe, can you arrange the images for each model? I am doing the cover shoot with blondie now, so I need to set up before the lighting changes." He grins and hands me the file with the names of the models along with their biographies. "You okay with this?"

"Yes, this is easy. I should have it finished for you by the time you're done with the shoot." Jayce leans down and gives me a bear hug.

"You're an angel! Thank you!" I give him a smile. He's a really sweet guy, but there isn't a fire inside when he holds me. Nothing like the attraction I have for Lucien. I just don't understand it. How is it even possible that I have known him all of five seconds and I am jealous? There is no reason for me to be, we're not an official couple.

Lucien

I was about to lay a kiss on Cassie's lips when the voice that sends cold ice water into my veins comes from behind me. Sasha! *Oh, for the love of God, why can't she leave me the fuck alone?* Sasha enjoys fucking up my life. Although I can't blame her, I was a dick to her, but I don't want her to fuck up this thing I have. When Cassie stormed passed us, my body shuddered with frustration. "What the fuck are you doing here?" I hiss at her, the fury in my eyes must be evident. When she doesn't answer I walk around her, but she grabs my arm. "I need to speak to you."

"What? I was with my girlfriend." The words are out of my mouth before I have time to think about it. *Girlfriend? You're a fucking goner, Verán, you've known this girl all of about six seconds and you've already laid claim to her.* I look at Sasha and I can see the hurt on her face. She always hoped that I will one day take her back, but there is no chance of that happening, ever. After our rocky past, there will never be a way to get back anything good that we shared. Actually, I don't think we ever shared anything good.

"Girlfriend, Luke? Really?" I nod. "Fine, I need you to know that I will be working on the charity now. Claudia and I have been talking, and I need to have a more active role." I run my hand through my hair in frustration. This is a bad idea, I don't want her near it, but I have no choice.

"Fine, just don't expect my help." I stalk off in search of Cassandra, leaving my past behind me as I do so. As soon as I step into the tent, I find Cassie and Jayce together, they weren't doing anything, but it bugged me. *She's fucking giggling! Are you serious?*

"Jayce, I assume you need to get started." There is no question in my voice that I want him gone. His expression is serious, with a wink at Cassie, he rises. *Fuck you, I am in charge here! She's mine.* He does it to rile me up and he's good at it, because he's known me all my life. I step up to him and our gazes lock. In my own way, I communicate to him that he needs to back off. The recognition flits across his features, he understands. The confirmation of me claiming Cassie.

"Okay Luke, I am coming. Later babe!" He's concerned, but he has no reason to be. "Let's get you in a swimsuit blondie." He pulls Sasha off to the change area and I am left with Cassie. I can tell she's angry, its rolling off her in waves.

"What the hell, Cassandra, you ran off?" I am beyond agitated now. *Why the hell would she run off? She's jealous! Seriously? Of Sasha?*

"You looked like you were busy, Lucien. I didn't want to get in the middle of—" She's mumbling and I want to shut her up. Sealing her mouth with mine, I lick into her. Her taste is addictive, and I groan into the kiss. She's so responsive to me, her lips part without any nudging. When she tugs on my hair, I realize the anger has dissipated, and replaced with fire, desire, and yearning. I need her to see that she's the only one I want right now. When I pull away, we're both breathless. My gaze locks with her mocha colored eyes; they're glistening with emotion. A dangerous mix of lust and something else.

"You drive me crazy woman! I told you, don't doubt this. Please, Cassandra?" The pleading tone of my voice is obvious, her doubts need to be erased. Even though I am doubting myself, she doesn't need to know that. Not right now.

"Lucien, she is your ex. What am I supposed to do or think? I don't like sharing either." The truth stumbles from her lips. She thinks I am a player. The jealousy is becoming on her. It makes me feel good, someone as incredible as Cassandra wants me.

"You're not sharing, trust me! Far from it!" *Darling, I wish you could see how you consume my mind.* Every fucking moment of the day, you're there, in my thoughts and in the evening you're in my fantasies and dreams. "Cassandra, I wanted you since the first day I saw you in that coffee shop." My honesty is rewarded with a smile.

"Okay, okay. I trust you, but Lucien, I need to work now." The resolve in her eyes makes me smile. *You're falling, Verán. There's no fucking way I can fall in love. She doesn't know me. I don't know her. There isn't a chance for that, but I can have fun. That's all this is, or can ever be. Fun.*

She's disarming me, one word at a time. "Fine, I am going to get coffee over there. There's an important call I need to make." I leave her to work and walk up to grab a coffee from the catering tent. The coffee is fresh and I fill a mug. I slip into the bench seat and pull out my phone. There is something I want to do before we leave here, I hit call and Robert answers on the second ring. "Mr. Verán."

"Robert, I need to set up a day with Ms. Winters on Tuesday. I want to make it special. Food, champagne, the works. Tomorrow is our last work day, and I want to do something before going back to Los Angeles."

"Yes, sir. Do you want to go to the Cove?"

"Please. Can you set it up? I don't want to leave her here alone since it's her first time on location. Can you also get the flight manifest, ready to fly out on Tuesday evening?" I finish my coffee and glance over at her. She's concentrating on the task that Jayce gave her. Her teeth bite into her thumb, and I recall this morning when she bit my finger. Instantly my cock is rock hard.

"Mr. Verán?" Robert pulls me from my dirty thoughts.

"Yes, sorry, just sort that out for me. I will let you know if there's anything else. Pick us up at 3 pm today. There are a few things I need from the store."

"Sir."

The excitement of what I have planned makes me smile, I hang up and take in the view. The ocean is sparkling under the hot sun and I watch Jayce work. He's good,

fucking brilliant to be honest. I trust him with my life, and now, since I have claimed her as mine. I trust him with Cassie. As I am about to get up my phone buzzes, fuck.
"Mother."
"Lucien, darling. How are things going?"
"Fine. What do you want?" I am in no mood for her and her fucking shit.
"I spoke to Sasha; she says you're acting like a fool. Lucien, you do realize that you need to remember your father needs you. There are certain... requirements."
"My father and I will speak about whatever he needs from me. I would like you to leave me out of your conniving shit. I am living my life the way I want to."
"Lucien, you do recall the last time you did that?" The past flashes into my mind and my blood boils. She always does this to me. I can't deal with this right now. For the first time in years I am happy. I have my girl. With a glance at her again, determination rises inside me. I will make it work with Cassie. "You know she's just after your money darling. This girl you're calling your girlfriend is nothing but a gold digger." My blood is past boiling point and I explode.
Claudia's words sting and I want to retch. Fuck this! "If you come near Cassie, I will make you pay. Do you understand me?" I spit out and she cackles.
"Lucien Verán, what would your father say to you speaking to me like that?"
"You're not my fucking mother. Leave me and Cassie the fuck alone." I hang up before she can reply. Fucking Sasha! She needs to stay the fuck away from me. If she comes near Cassie, she will live to regret it.
I grab a bagel, coffee, and walk back into the tent. She looks at me with tired eyes, and I want to hold her and make her feel better. I am not letting her go. There's not a fucking chance in hell that she is leaving my life. Ever. Without a word, I slide in next to her. I lean in and trace my tongue along the curve of her neck. Her body trembles and I smile. She's so fucking responsive. "I brought you something to eat, and a coffee." She glances at the plate and grins.
"Thank you, handsome." I am about to lean in when her phones rings and she gets up to take the call. *Who is it? Maybe she's got a boyfriend? No, she said she didn't.* I sit for a few minutes waiting for her to come back. When she doesn't I get up to find her. She's standing on the beach staring at the waves. Something is bothering her. It must be the call she received. She's upset I can tell by the way her body is trembling. I wrap her in my arms, hoping to calm her. "Who was that, baby?"
"Uhm. A friend. Kenna." Her voice is low and I don't believe her. I can read her like a book and I don't think her friend would have upset her this much. She's hiding something from me. Not that I can blame her, I mean I am hiding something from her as well. Only time will tell if our pasts will make us or break us.
We need to go shopping. I don't want to be here anymore. My need to get her alone has me nervous. These feelings are dangerous. Especially for me. Anxious to get our evening started, I tighten my hold on her. I don't want her feeling fear, anger, whatever it is. With me, she will always be happy, at least I hope so. "Come on, we need to go."
"What about the shoot?" She asks as she follows me into the tent. *Darling, that's the last fucking thing on my mind right now.* I face her and my eyes lock on hers and I give her my honest answer.
"Right now, all I want to do is take you back to the house, rip off all your clothes, lick every inch of your silky smooth skin, until my tongue dips into your sweet pussy. Then when you're writhing on my bed, or any other surface for that matter, I want to bury myself between your thighs, fuck you deep and hard, and make you come all over

65

my cock."

My voice is a low growl and her cheeks turn a bright pink. As we make our way to the car, I smirk. I love shocking her with my filthy mouth. Now, I want to make her lose control and show me that dirty girl she's hiding below that innocent exterior. Her response is priceless.

"Oh…"

Chapter eight

Lucien

We walk into the supermarket, hand in hand. It's strange to be doing something so domestic, but with her it's natural. I grab a basket as we walk down the aisles. "So, you have a choice of pasta or pasta?" I turn to her and she giggles. My famous lasagna will be on the menu tonight, it's easy and I doubt I could easily fuck it up. To be honest, I am nervous. Never having cooked a meal for any girl, this is a first for me. Something makes me think that Ms. Winters will bring a lot of firsts to my life.

"I suppose pasta would be good." She winks at me cheekily and I am tempted to bend her over the vegetable shelves and spank her ass. With the vegetables we need in the basket, I follow her down the aisle to where the pastas are shelved. "Is there a specific one you want?" She holds up two bags, facing me.

"Lasagna, sweetness. It's the flat one." I grab the box and place it in the basket. "And we need cheese." She walks ahead of me and I take in the view of her tight little ass in those tiny shorts. She looks so good, all I want to do is have her bent in front of me, holding onto her ankles. Better yet, I could have her bound, wrists to ankles. My cock springs to life. *In the supermarket? She will be the death of me.* I follow her down the aisle to the refrigerators. The cool air wafts from the dairy section.

"Gouda or cheddar?" She asks, grabbing a block of each. I walk up behind her, she's bent over the refrigerator counter and her ass is begging for a spank. I stand flush with her, my cock presses between her cheeks. A gasp escapes her lips. *She feels so good and looks even better.*

"Don't move." My voice a low growl, I glance around and note that we're alone for a second. I roll my hips against her, the friction sending pleasure all the way down my spine. The ache to be buried deep inside her tight body is taking over my brain and all the blood rushes to my crotch.

"Lucien," she breathes. I lift my hand and bring it down hard on her ass. She straightens quickly, her pupils dilated and her chest rising and falling faster than normal. "What was that for?" She whispers. I lean in, close to her ear. My chin resting on her shoulder. I am tempted to spin her around and seal her lips with mine, but I opt for teasing her instead.

"For you teasing me. I suggest you behave yourself, or I will spank you again." Her body is trembling when I reach around her, grab the cheese from her hand and place it in the basket. I step back and she spins around. Her face is one of shock and desire, but she offers a naughty smile.

"Maybe I want you to." Her words leave me speechless. I open my mouth to reply, but nothing comes out. *Perhaps she's naughtier than I thought she was. I underestimated my sweetness.*

"Well, then I can't wait for dessert tonight." A sly wink and she's blushing, I turn and walk towards the check out. As soon as we're at the till, the cashier glances at me, offering me a smile that can mean only one thing. I unpack the basket, ignoring the desire in this girl's eyes. There's only one girl I want to have look at me like that and its Cassandra.

"Is that all for you?" Her voice is sultry and her eyelashes flutter just a little too much. *Can she not see I am with Cassie?* Suddenly an arm loops through mine. *Is she staking claim to me? Does she want this?* I hope to God she does. Because slowly I am falling for this girl. *You can't fall for her Luke; it will never work.*

"Yea, thanks." I hand her my credit card and make the payment. As we walk out to the car, Cassie doesn't let go of my arm. The feeling is new to me. I haven't spent enough time with a girl in this way before. Normally its meeting at a bar, taking her home and fucking her till the early hours of the morning and calling her a cab. The whole concept of dating on the other hand, is not something I do. *How the fuck did I get into this situation? Because your cock marked and claimed her not even 24 hours ago! Yup, I am fucked.*

When we get back to the house, we unpack the groceries. The natural way we move around each other is comfortable. I am blown away at what this girl has done to me in the short time I have known her. My life is different already; it's like there is a light in the dark depths of my soul. After Sasha, I didn't think that I could ever let someone in. The past has always been my barrier. I would stop before thinking about being with a woman. Let alone a woman like Cassie. As we move through the kitchen, I brush against her on purpose. The light touches make her tremble. The responsiveness she has to me is intoxicating. There's a storm brewing between us and when it breaks there will be no reprieve from it.

"Would you like to write while I start dinner?" If I don't get her out of this kitchen soon, there will be no dinner.

"Yes, if you don't mind. I would prefer to get started with the article as soon as I can."

"Sure sweetness. I need to get changed and then start my famous pasta!" Grabbing her around the waist, I pull her against me. "And then, I know what I want for dessert!" I seal her mouth with mine in a searing kiss. My tongue pushes against her lips, she opens to me, allowing me access. She tastes so good as I lick into her. When she locks her arms around my neck, I lift her against me. Pure instinct has her legs wrapping around my waist. Our kiss becomes urgent and my cock presses against her heated core, I walk towards the wall pinning her against it. Her body arches into me and our bodies are on fire. Electricity surges through us, between us. I want to rip her clothes off, but first dinner. *See, I can be romantic. Feed her first then I get to feast on her.*

Whenever she runs her fingers through my hair, it's like I want to melt into her. We're joined, our bodies becoming one and the same. There's something truly erotic about the way she tugs me into her. Almost begging, like she needs me. My cock is straining the front of my jeans and I need her to feel me. I roll my hips into her core. Her body responds and her nipples pebble against my chest. I am about to come in my jeans if she keeps this up.

I pull away, leaving us both breathless. "We need to work... I mean I do and you should cook." Her adorable innocence tugs at my heart, she stumbles over her words, but instead of being annoyed, I find it endearing. *She's mine. All fucking mine.*

"Oh babe, I was cooking."

She pokes her tongue out, which sends my thoughts whirling, and heat shoots to my crotch. The cheeky brazen act is her attempt to tease me, and she's succeeded. "Ms.

Winters, I suggest you think twice about teasing me with your tongue. Remember, I have a tongue too, and I would love to use it on you." *God, I need to taste her tight little cunt again. I want her coming on my tongue again and again.*

As soon as I am in my bedroom, I undo the zipper of my jeans freeing my rigid erection. *Fuck, she is beautiful.* I should take a cold shower, but I want to get her dinner ready.

I decide on a pair of shorts, and nothing else. That will have her distracted. I make my way back to the living room. She's sitting on the sofa with her laptop. When her glance meets mine, she squeaks. "You're cooking in that?" Literally squeaks. I realize she's as affected by me, as I am by her.

"Yea, is that an issue?" Watching her reaction is priceless, she is chewing on her lower lip and I wonder what's going on in that beautiful mind.

She's flushed, averting her gaze. "Yea… No… I am fine." Her words are a soft mumble and I suppress a chuckle. I doubt she's fine, because I am not. There is no way I can be fine again with her.

"Stop doing that." *She needs to stop doing that with her mouth. Or biting her finger.* She doesn't notice her little quirks, but I do, so does my cock. Not meeting my gaze, she stares at her screen.

"What?" She asks innocently.

"You know what." I turn and busy myself in the kitchen. Without another glance at her, I grab the pots I need and make sure all the ingredients are on the table. My eyes dart up again, I can't stop looking at her. This is the most distracted I have ever been. She's engrossed in the article and I watch her for a while. Oblivious to anyone else there. She makes some notes on a little notebook and props the pen in her mouth. Her lips wrap around it in such an erotic way that I can't stop the groan that rumbles low in my chest. At this rate, we will never get dinner.

Once the baking tray is in the oven, I wash up. When I turn, she's standing at the table. "My God that smells wonderful, Lucien!" Her smile is bright and open; her eyes take in the left over mess in the kitchen.

"Dinner won't be too much longer. Can I get you a glass of wine, sweetness?" I grab the bottle I took out earlier and smile. Her nod is the only indication that she's listening, her eyes are raking over my abs. I pull the cork and fill two glasses. When I hand her one, I hold mine up to make a toast. "To our first working trip… And the incredible sex!" My toast earns me a glimpse of her shy sweet smile. We clink glasses and I watch her sip the dark red liquid. It stains her pink lips and I have an intense need to lick them. I need to change the subject.

"How's your story coming along, you getting work done?" My mind seems to be permanently stuck on being inside her. There are things I need to tell her tonight. I need to explain some things before we get home. Honesty is the only way this will work, but I need to take it slow. Not to overwhelm her.

"I am halfway. It won't take long to finish."

"Take another 10 minutes. I will get the table ready." She goes back to work and I need to put some clothes on. I walk into my bedroom and grab my tank top. My phone buzzes from my bed, it's Jayce.

* What happened with Sasha? She's freaking out with me *

I hit reply.

She's fucking my life up. It's over between us, she needs to come to terms with that

I can't deal with this right now. Jayce is only trying to keep the peace, I understand that, but he knows as well as I do that it's over between Sasha and me. There's no way I am going back there. I don't love her. Maybe I never did, maybe I am not capable of love. Who knows? With Cassie it's different, I feel like a man, a good man. *She will find out about what I am into and run a mile. I am not right for her, but I can't stop myself from wanting her. It's a fucked up situation, but I will enjoy it while I can. Once she leaves me, I will have to find a way to go on. How can my feelings be so strong for her?*

I make my way back to the kitchen. I grab the plates and cutlery and set up the table on the patio. Jayce's words bother me. *Sasha will be trouble.* Since I broke up with her, actually, since she left me, I haven't really met anyone that I actually want. Now that Cassie is in my life, I realize that Sasha will try her best to break us up. She's trying to ruin my life for what happened in our past and I will not let her.

I shake all thoughts of Sasha out of my mind. Tonight is about Cassie and me. I want her to give everything to me. I want her with a passion I never truly had with anyone else. *Is this the everlasting love my father tells me about? My mother still left. I don't understand.* The baking tray, along with the salad is on the table, I add two candles in the center and light them. The patio is illuminated in a soft light. It's romantic. Once the table is ready, I step back inside. She's so engrossed in her writing she doesn't notice me staring at her. *Why would a girl like her want a tarnished man like me?*

Cassandra

"Sweetness, dinner is served." I glance up and smile. The food smells incredible and I realize just how hungry I am. I shut my laptop and set it on the sofa. I grab my wine and step out onto the terrace. Outside, the night air was warm, and I watch the waves crashing in the distance. The sound of the ocean was soothing. This was such a wonderful location. I am lucky, standing here with an incredible man.

The table is all set, and the food looks amazing. "Here we are my lady," he bows pulling my chair out. His good mood is infectious, I slip into the chair and wait for him to take a seat across from me. He lit the two white candles in the center of the table. The flames danced and his eyes seemed to twinkle in the dim light. I was continually struck breathless by his beauty. *How on earth did I get so lucky?*

I grab the salad servers and dish some for myself. It's silent while we eat. I am about half way through my dinner when I glance up, and catch him watching me. I cock my head to the side and smile. "What?" I am answered with those stunning dimples as he grins. Suddenly his expression changes and he's serious.

"I..." Grabbing his glass, he takes a sip of wine before continuing. "Please, Cassie? I don't want you to run from me," he stares into my eyes, as if he is staring into my heart and soul. I stop breathing because I have no idea how to respond. "There are things you will learn about me, things that aren't pleasant." He glances away and I see the conflict inside him. *What can be worse than your demons Cassie? What on earth could a man so beautiful have done?*

"Lucien, don't—"

"Cassandra, I need to." He looks back. My heart is racing and all I want to do is hold him. I want to tell him it doesn't matter, that our history is just that, it's in the past. "My relationships have been… different. I haven't ever been with anyone I wanted to be with." I frown at him, but wait for an explanation. "My mother has an ideal for me. She needs me to be married to a particular girl. Her role in my life is to pair me up with a girl that will make sure the Verán Industries name carries on. She sets me up continually with her friends' daughters and I suppose in the past I was okay with it." He takes another sip of wine and stares me. He isn't expecting my reply, and the shock on my face must be visible. "As frustrating as it was I always obeyed." He goes silent for a moment and I don't think I want to hear anymore.

I nod, understanding what he meant. He was a successful businessman, an heir to a throne. Born into money I am certain his mother doesn't need a lowly writer to be with her son. "Lucien, I understand. When we go back, this…" I pointed between us. "It's just professional."

Anger laces his handsome face, and he shakes his head. "No! That's what I needed to explain to you." He grabs my hand, and he gives it a squeeze. "I am done attending to my mother's wishes. I need you Cassandra," his voice urgent and his eyes flash with ferocity and desire and I melt into my chair.

"Lucien." I could never be the girl his mother chose for him. A simple girl like me, with demons of my own. I couldn't do this to him.

He raises my hand and kisses my knuckles. Without another word, he rises and steps into the living room. Turning on the sound system. A deep haunting voice fills the silence and I glance up, looking at the speakers on the deck. I didn't recognize the song. "Who is this?" I ask when he joins me again.

He offers me his hands and I gratefully accept, then he pulls me to my feet. The song is so beautiful as the melody breaks the silence, he wraps his arms around my waist. Instinctively, my arms hold on to his neck. My fingers tangle through the soft hair at the base of his neck. "It's an artist called Laurel." His voice is low; his lips find the spot on my neck that sends shivers racing down my spine. He moves back, the lyrics wash over me as I look into olive eyes that hold so much emotion.

You woke me up for your blue blood
Made me come undone
Can't believe you've been here the whole time
Too nice to pass you by and I can't believe
You've been here the whole time
You made me feel again
Made me dance circles 'round the pieces of your heart.
You made me feel again

When the song ends, I pull away. I need to put some distance between us, because I can't think straight, but he pulls me back. "Was that a hint?" I smile up at him, his eyes gleaming. He gives me a non-committal shrug and I giggle. "A man of many words aren't you Mr.…" I taunt. His eyebrows shoot up promptly. "Lucien," I wink and draw out of his tender embrace.

"Oh, playing that teasing game are we?" An amused expression takes over and I don't answer, instead I turn to look at the ocean. My hands on the wooden rail of the balcony. "I can play games as well." His voice at my ear, and his hot breath on my neck. My breath hitches at his words. *Don't hurt me Lucien, please?* He stands behind me, his arms either side of me caging me in. The heat of his body is intoxicating. I need to lighten the mood after his words.

"It's not a game handsome. I never play games." I say quietly as he wraps his arms around me. The heat of his chest warming my back. His chin resting on my shoulder, I feel the stubble against my skin. I imagine how good it would be between my thighs as he goes down on me. *Fuck, I want him. I am acting like a wanton slut for a man I don't even know. A man with so many secrets, but then again, I have my own secrets too.*

"I do," he murmurs and my heart stops. "In the bedroom." He whispers in my ear and his teeth tug on my earlobe. A moan escapes my lips and I flush. His arousal pressing against my ass and I realize that we will never get to finish dinner now.

"Do you now?" I ask, as I watch the stars twinkling in the darkened sky. My voice comes out raspy. He knows he affects me.

"Ms. Winters, you have no idea." His voice is dark and dangerous, sending anticipation straight down my spine to my core. *I would like you to show me!*

"Would you care to show me?" I push back against his groin, rubbing my ass along the hard ridge of his cock. "Mr. Verán." The name is a whisper, barely audible. His hand reaches up and grips my neck. His teeth bite the skin behind my ear. I am aching and on fire. "Are you positive you are ready for me Ms. Winters?" I hear the rasp in his deep voice and the heat coils in my lower abdomen. My skin alight with desire, and I would have done anything for him right there. I haven't been so turned on before.

"Yes." I breathe. Oh God, I hope I am making the right decision. *He makes me feel so fucking incredible, I can't go back now.*

His other hand moves over my breast, pinching and tweaking my now rock hard nipple through the thin fabric of my top. Those expert fingers trace a line down to my bellybutton. My body humming with anticipation as his hand slips into the waistband of my jeans and the flimsy cotton panties. "You're so fucking wet for me, baby." I shudder when he strokes my heated entrance and teases my bundle of nerves. "Do you like me holding you down, Cassie?" I sigh into the night and my head drops back onto his shoulder. His other hand still at my neck holding me in place. I can't find words to respond, so I push back against his cock again and it twitches against my ass.

His teasing is relentless as my body trembles and my release climbs. Higher and higher from his expert touch. Slowly sliding two fingers inside me, he whispers. "You are so fucking perfect. So hot, tight and wet. Only for me." His words and his fingers sending me to the brink. He continues the exquisite torture and I am dripping on his hand. My shoulder heats from his kisses, his teeth bite my sensitive skin. It's like electricity shooting through me. I feel my orgasm about to erupt then he stops. My whimper is fueled with anguish, and pain. The ache and need to find release clouds my senses.

"Do you like teasing me, Cassandra?" He pulls his fingers out and turns me around, licking them one by one, our eyes locked. Watching him lick my arousal from his fingers has me whimpering again. I chew on my lip. I need him inside me. The only time I am whole, fixed, was when he filled me.

"I need you." I voice my thoughts and he draws me against him. His lips cover mine, kissing me roughly, while his fingers fist my hair holding me still. His dominating tongue invades my roughly. Taking control of the kiss. Our tongues dance and tangle as I taste myself on him. I couldn't get enough of him. My body responds to him in ways I never dreamed possible. I am flying and the fear of landing squeezes my heart painfully. He lifts me by my ass, I wrap my legs around him, and he carries me to the living room.

He breaks our kiss; his voice is low and raspy. "I need to be inside you." He tugs at my shorts and panties, pulling them down in one swift move. I watch him undo his shorts and slide them down. He wasn't wearing boxers and his impressive erection stands proudly. Once he's kneeling between my thighs, he grips his cock and teases me. Slow strokes against my bare pussy with the tip of his cock, I lift my hips towards him, moaning. His dark gaze is hungry, the hunter catching his prey. He looks down at me, with eyes that are black with desire. "You want me inside you, baby?" I nod. I have never been so ready in my life. My body craved him. Needed him to take me, own me, and possess me. *Where the fuck did that come from? I don't care, I want it, and I want it with him.*

He slams into me suddenly and I cry out as I come undone around him. My body shuddering violently below him from my release and he stills inside me. He watches, and waits. As I calm from my orgasm, he moves again, sliding out to the tip and driving back inside me. Filling me entirely, like he was made to be inside me.

"My lumière," his voice is gentle in my ear, contradictory to his movements as he plunges into me repeatedly. My legs lock around his waist pulling him in deeper, never wanting him to stop. I was on the verge again as I felt the heat rise inside me. He made me feel things I never thought I would again. Fixed me with his words, his touch, his kisses, and the way he made love to me, the way he fucked me. His body tensing and I knew he was close. "My lumière," he repeated the words as he tensed inside me, filling me with his release. My body convulsed as another orgasm ripped through me and I clenched around him. Holding on to him like I would disappear without him in my arms. There was something shifting between us and there was no turning back. This weekend would change our relationship, from a work related one to something entirely different. As I look up into sparkling green eyes, my heart doesn't hurt. For the first time it feels like I can breathe. *Lucien Verán was breathing life into me, into the shattered heart and soul I have hidden away for far too long.*

Lucien

I open my eyes to my phone vibrating on the nightstand, it's Monday morning, and I promised Cassie a workout. Today will be our last work day here. Tomorrow I have the surprise planned, and I am nervous. I hope she will love it. With a quick glance at her, I find she's sound asleep. We didn't go to bed till late and I don't want to wake her so early, but we are going running. I grab my briefs and tug them on. The first and most important thing is to put the coffee machine on. In the kitchen, I make sure there's chilled water in the fridge for after our run. The coffee should be ready in ten minutes, now it's time to wake my girl.

"Sweetness! Wake up, sleepy head." I lean over her, my hand stroking her cheek. Her gaze rakes over me and I see the hunger in her eyes. *None of that now, darling.*

"Good morning to you too handsome."

"Come on gorgeous, you owe me a workout." She looks adorable as she groans at the mention of a workout, but I am not letting her go that easy.

"What time is it?"

"5:45." I kneel on the bed. All I want to do is devour her.

"Okay, give me ten minutes and we can go. And you're not going like that!" She points at my boxers and naked torso.

"Why? I assumed you preferred me without my clothes on." *I want no one seeing you* naked either baby. When she sits up and I can tell she's sore from last night. *Oh baby, you will be aching when I get you in my bedroom at home.* I get off the bed and watch her.

"Yes. I do, but no one else is allowed to see you like that!" Her jealousy is refreshing, the fact that she feels it at all makes me smile. I feel exactly the same about other men looking at her.

"Ooh do I detect a hint of jealousy?" I tug on my grey pants and tie the string at my waist. Her gaze is hungry; my grin threatens to crack my face. She loves staring at me.

"No, I have nothing to be jealous about." She's still so unsure of my feelings for her. It's like she thinks that I will up and cheat on her. It's not my style. When I have a woman, she's all mine and I am all hers. "Or do I?" She pokes her tongue out at me again. That tongue of hers will get her into a lot of trouble with me. Her teasing is clear; she needs to realize that I love to tease as well and when I do, it will be until she is begging me to make her come.

"No, you do not, sweetness, at all. Trust me. And if you wish to get out of this house today, I suggest you stop poking your tongue at me."

I grab my black tank top and leave her to get ready. In the kitchen, I pour the freshly brewed coffee and wait. Normally, I love my own space, but she makes me want to spend time with her. All the time. When she walks into the kitchen, blood rushes straight to my cock. She's dressed in a tiny pair of blue running shorts, a matching sports bra, and flimsy see through tank top. She has curves for days; her breasts are natural, and her legs are shapely. Every man's wet dream, but she's all mine. I am tempted to forget the run and just take her to bed, but I promised her a workout. All I can do is hope it will calm the raging erection in my pants. "I made some coffee, drink up and then we can go." She smiles and picks up the cup. The need to avert my eyes is strong, she's so inviting, alluring.

When she's finished, I grab the keys and we head out onto the quiet road. I love being on the island, there's not very many people awake at this time of the day and I enjoy the peacefulness. We're evenly matched, and I marvel in the way she runs with such ease. Every footfall is hard, but at the same time feminine. We chat about nothing in particular. Sweat glistens on her skin and all I can think of is ripping her bra off and sucking her nipples until they peak in my mouth. Tugging her shorts off and tasting her sweet little pussy. *Stop it, Verán! How am I supposed to run with a fucking hard on?*

Once we get back to the house, I unlock the door and step inside. My muscles are aching. I love the pain. I grab two bottles from the fridge and hand her one. With a large gulp I finish mine, enjoying the cool water. When my gaze locks on her, I stare at the water on her mouth and the drops fall to her breasts. She has not looked sexier than she does now.

"What?" She asks when she glances at me, she does not understand what the fuck she does to me.

"Fuck this!" I can't stop myself anymore, grabbing her I throw her over my shoulder. Like a fucking caveman, but I don't care, I need her now.

"Lucien! What are you doing?" Spanking her ass, she yelps and I chuckle. "Put me down!" Fuck, I can't wait to see her sweet little ass pink. In my bathroom, I set her down on the counter top and proceed undressing. I grab the tank top she's wearing and shred it from her body.

"Lucien." Her breathing hikes and her pules riots in her throat. Those mocha eyes are glistening with hunger and need that I myself feel. I undo the bra restraining her tits and when they fall free, I lean forward and devour them. My mouth suckles them, just the way I know she likes it. I bite down on her nipple and she whimpers. She likes a bit of pain, and I realize she must be soaking wet. I move my mouth to her other breast and show it the same attention. She tastes too good. Like honey and sweat. Soft and feminine. I want to make sure I am the only one that she aches for.

In one quick movement I pull her shorts and panties off. Her scent is intoxicating and so fucking sexy. I seal her mouth with a kiss, her lips open for me and I lick into her. The sweetness on her tongue has my cock hard as steel. I break the kiss and head to the shower. "I want you wet and slippery."

Once I turn on the taps, I concentrate on her again. I stroke her thighs, massaging her. Just enough pressure to send tingles straight to her pussy. Her lips part and a soft moan escapes her lips. She's so fucking ready for me, but I restrain myself, it will be so much better when I finally drive into her, in the shower.

I undress and her hungry gaze is enough to tell me that she wants me. "Do you know what you do to me, sweetness?" She shakes her head hastily. This girl will be my undoing, she already is. Fear constricts my heart when I look at her, there is something close to love on her face and I can't have her love me. *Yes, I can.* Fuck. My emotions are in turmoil. The last time someone loved me, I couldn't handle it. Honesty, that's what I need to give her, but I need it from her as well. I know there is something she is hiding from me. "I just don't want to fuck this up. You need to always be honest with me okay, baby?" I am pleading with her. *Can she see it?*

Something flickers across her face and she hops off the counter and steps into the shower. *Fuck, Verán, you're making her sad. What the fuck was that though? Why is she pulling away now?* I follow her in and close the door. "Cassandra." I turn her to face me. With my index finger, I trace a slow line from her ear to her chin, lifting her face. I need eye contact. The need to see what she's feeling. I wish I could read her mind that's the only way to know for sure if she wants this. *Why can't she see I care about her? I want her for fuck sake. She needs to stop running from me, but I know as soon as she learns my secrets that's exactly what she will do.*

"I care about you, I want you. Please stop running?" Her touch is like a drug to me, quelling my fears, lighting my darkness. The ugliness that lies deep inside me. We're both standing there soaked from the warm spray, her body pressed against mine and I know she can feel I am rock hard. I lift her up, pin her against the wall and slide into her. "Your pussy is perfect, so tight, hot and slick. Just for me." My drives are slow, taking her higher, and she takes me. I want her to feel every inch of me inside her tight body. *Her pussy is amazing. Tight, warm, and mine.*

The dark need to possess her tugs at me and I grip her neck. My thrusts become urgent, pinning her back flush against the tiles. Like I did last night, I hold her in place. She accepts me like this. Her moans are raspy. I want to hear her moan all the time. For me. While I am inside her. I want to heal her, hurt her, possess her, and make her mine completely. With her earlobe between my teeth, I bite down. She flies over the edge and I feel her come around my cock. Her arousal coating me. Her body convulses and her eyes flutter closed as she rides out her orgasm. *Fuck, she's perfect.* "You are mine Cassandra, entirely mine." For the third time in the past two days I claim her, my release fills her, marking her as mine. *Taking her straight to hell with me.* This sweet innocent girl is mine. Tomorrow we go back to LA and I don't even know how I will introduce her into my world. *Will she run as I expect her to? Or will she give me a chance?*

Chapter Nine

Lucien

Tuesday had arrived too soon. I needed more time away from everyday life to make sure she will not run. This was supposed to be a one-night stand, but somehow she's got under my skin. My gaze is on the lines and patterns of the ceiling. My mind reeling with thoughts of going back to work, to everything that would threaten to ruin us. Cassie and me. For the first time in years, I have some semblance of happiness and I don't want it to be ripped away.

I glance at her, the way those soft brown curls are fanned out on the pillow, she looks like an angel. *And me?* I am the devil. Polar opposites as my father always tells me. He and my mother were the same. I wonder what he would make of Cassandra. *Would he approve?* She's not exactly high society, but that's the whole point, I want a real girl. Not some manufactured bitch who was made in a plastic surgeon's office.

I notice her eyes flutter open and I smile. Her back is smooth and her skin is glowing, I am tempted to stroke her. Mine. Every inch of her gorgeous body. All mine. I turn and plant soft kisses from her neck, moving down to her shoulder. Her eyes meet mine, as she twists around, and I am overcome by emotion. *I don't know how to do this. How can I open up to someone? To let her into my twisted desires is not something I planned.*

"Morning handsome." She glances at me over her shoulder.

"Good morning sweetness."

"Are we heading to the beach today?"

Her fingers in my hair send tingles down my spine. "Ms. Winters, do you want to get me wet?" I tease her, eliciting a giggle. *I fucking love that sound.*

"Maybe?" She rolls over, she is so beautiful. It's like looking at a painting. Pure perfection. "I don't want to leave here. It's been…" When her face falls, so does my heart. Her concerns match mine. We both realize leaving might be the end of us. Although I vow to myself I won't let that happen, I don't voice it to her. How can I? There is no way I can give her forever, but walking away is not an option.

"My lumiére, don't doubt us? Don't doubt me, please? And you promised, no running!" My voice is serious and she nods. There's something in her eyes that scares me, something she's not telling me. I can't force her to, but she needs to learn she can trust me.

"Yes, I know Lucien. I am not running. Sometimes… I have no idea why, but I get anxious."

There is only way I can answer her, to feel her body against mine, so I pull her to me. My arm bands around her, holding her. I hope that in this small gesture she can feel all my emotion pour into her.

"No need to, I want you. You are stunning, beautiful, intelligent, and I admire how you challenge me. Even though I want to spank your sexy ass when you do." I kiss her forehead. "All I want is for you to trust me. Nothing is changing when we leave here." She snuggles into the crook of my arm and her warmth on my chest calms me. My words ring in my ears, I shouldn't promise her something I am not sure about. Although, I can't help myself.

Everything tells me to stay in bed and take her again and again, but I had planned a whole day with her. I can't wait to see her face when we get there. As soon as I move, dragging myself from the bed, she whimpers. I grab my boxer briefs. "Come on beautiful, let's have breakfast. I want to enjoy the day before we fly out tonight."

Her hungry gaze burns into me and I can't help smiling. "You enjoying the view?" Her giggle is answer enough to know that our feelings of desire for each other are mutual.

"I was absolutely." She slips from the bed and pulls on my black top; it falls just below her ass. She looks absolutely fuckable.

I pull her against me, feeling her bare ass under my T-shirt. *Do we have to go out in public today?* I have a surprise planned for her, so we do, unfortunately. I would much prefer locking her inside this bedroom for the day. "God, sweetness, that tee looks so perfect on you I want to ravage you right now!" Giving her a lustful kiss, I pull away. There is a painful ache telling me to stay. "Later gorgeous, I am making us breakfast." I make for the kitchen. The most important appliance is switched on first. The coffee machine. I grab the breakfast ingredients from the fridge and get them ready.

My phone vibrates from the table, I pick it up and read the email. Then I shoot Robert a quick message to pick us up in an hour. He acknowledges and lets me know that everything will be ready. I go to find my gorgeous girl. She's in the bathroom, staring at her reflection in the mirror. I would give anything to know what she's thinking right now. "You daydreaming?" She starts at my voice and I grab my toothbrush.

"I was yes, it was fun." Her cheeks are flushed and she looks thoroughly fucked. A beautiful look on her. *I want her right here, right now.*

"I have a surprise for us today." Her eyes widen, then narrow. She doesn't like surprises, but if she wants to be with me then she will have to get used to them.

"Lucien…" I place a finger on her lips, offering her a wink. I stand behind her, our reflection in the mirror looking back at us. We look happy. I haven't been happy or content in such a long time. Without another thought, I tug the top up and over her head, taking in her beautiful naked body. I tease my fingers down her neck slowly, down her chest and over each nipple. They pebble at my touch. Her head falls back, "Open your eyes, baby. Watch me." She obeys and my cock throbs in my pants. I trace a line down either side of her belly. "Hold the counter." My voice is raspy in her ear and she trembles. I trace one hand back up. My hand grips her beautiful neck, holding her in place. Mocha eyes stare back at me, filled with desire. "Do you like when I do that?" I ask softly.

"Yes." She breathes the answer and I know she's going to take to being in my world better than I thought she would. My other hand snakes down to her smooth little pussy. My fingers stroke her slick entrance. *God, she's so wet.* I tug her earlobe between my teeth. Her eyes flutter closed.

"Open your fucking eyes." My command comes out harsher than I expect. She complies, surprising me, as I dip a finger inside her. Her moan is soft and sensual and her hips buck against my hand. She's so fucking responsive, I love it. I tighten my grip on her neck. "You see how beautiful you are?" She tries to nod, but my grip is tight. Another finger enters her and her cunt tightens. She's close. So am I. Pulling my fingers from her, a whimper escapes her lips. I bring my fingers up to her mouth and trace them over her lips. Her tongue flicks out and licks her arousal from my fingers. *Holy fuck that's hot!*

I tug my pants down, freeing my painfully hard cock. "You better hold on, because I am too fucking hard to go slow." Her eyes are wide as she watches me in the mirror. My voice is a growl that I hardly recognize. Her grip on the counter tightens and I line myself up to her heat. I grip her hips and plunge into her all the way to the base. Her gasp is loud, I still for a moment, trying to catch my breath. Fuck she feels so good. My gaze locks on hers in the mirror and I take her. Fast, deep, and hard. My hand comes down with a loud swat on her peach ass. Her yelp is sexy, and I want to do it again. I watch her body take me and it's my undoing. "Come for me Cassie!" I rasp the order and her body responds like the little submissive she is. Tightening around me. Milking me. Her body taking every drop of my come. *No love here. Sorry Cassie. I can't love you.* As soon as she's calm, I slip out of her. I know I hurt her, physically and emotionally. I took what I wanted. Made her crave me.

I finish up and walk out of the bathroom without another word. In the kitchen, I feel guilty for what I just did. I used her. For the first time in my life, I want to make it up to a girl I fucked. I start breakfast, toast, eggs, bacon, mushrooms and coffee. My mind is plagued by thoughts of what I want to and can do to her, by the time I look at the table, its stacked with too much food. It's our last morning in paradise before we face the reality. Dark thoughts swirl in my mind again and I push them away. She joins me minutes later dressed in a little cotton top with a pair of shorts. The straps of her top are thin and I notice she has her bikini underneath. *Good girl.* She slips into the chair and watches me intently. She doesn't say anything about what happened in the bathroom and neither do I. Deciding to lighten the mood, I talk about our plans for the day.

"I know you don't like surprises, but you're going to have to live with this." I wink at her and she rolls her eyes. *Darling, my sweet darling, you do not want to do that!* "I suggest you think twice about rolling your eyes in future, sweetheart." My voice is low and she gasps at my words. *Shit! I am so going to fuck this up.* We finish our breakfast in silence, but now and then, I feel her eyes on me. It's like she's trying to figure me out. Once breakfast is finished, I clear up the dishes. Robert will collect the bags later, but I want to make sure there's nothing left behind. I want to bring her here again. Just the two of us. Not for work, but for a holiday. That's if she allows me to. After what I just did to her in the bathroom, I don't know if she still trusts me.

Cassandra

After breakfast, I make my way to my room. I can't fathom what happened earlier in the bathroom. It was one of the most erotic experiences of my life, but there was something different about Lucien. It was as if something had taken over him. Maybe that's what he was trying to warn me against. *Can I handle that part of him? That darker side.* It was definitely sexy and intense. I grab my phone and text Kenna to let her know that I am leaving later today. Once I grab my purse and phone, I make my way to the door.

Robert was waiting for us when we stepped outside. I slid into the back seat and Lucien took his place next to me. "Robert, the cove please?" I saw our driver nod, and he pulled away.

"The cove?" I questioned Lucien. He nodded but didn't answer me. A naughty smirk curled his lips. His silence is infuriating; I can't stop shaking my head in annoyance. "You're so frustrating!"

"It's all worth it." He drapes his arm around me and I grin. It must be one hell of a surprise he was being so secretive this morning.

"Fine, but you should remember I hate surprises!" I shift to him, waiting for his reply. He nods and the mischievous glint in his eyes intensifies. I huff and twist to peer out of my window. Lucien places his hand on my thigh, giving it a light squeeze before running his hand higher. He stops short of the heat between my legs. I chew my lip to keep from moaning, my body reacting to him in the only way it knew how. There was no way I wanted him to see my reaction. I needed to keep calm.

"Cassandra, my surprises will always bring you pleasure, trust me." His voice is low and my heart races at the promise his words carried. *Pleasure? Mmmm, well then bring it on! Why is he so perfect? I suppose he's had practice romancing all the girls his mother hooks him up with? All the wealthy ones, the perfect statuesque ones.* I blink back the tears threatening to spill and breathe deeply. "Sweetness?" I shift to see Lucien studying me, concern etched on his handsome features. "Are you okay?"

I nod. "Yes I am. Why wouldn't I be?" I shrug nonchalantly and place my hand over his. Then I turn to face the window, watching the ocean pass by as we make our way to my surprise. It's so beautiful here. I didn't want to go back to LA, to therapy, and having to compete for Lucien's attention. When my doctor called to confirm my appointment, I couldn't bring myself to tell Lucien about it. My demeanor was making him anxious, the tension in the car was tangible. This was something I needed to deal with myself. He didn't promise me anything and I can't expect him to be with me when he had all those beautiful models wanting his attention.

"You seem… I don't know…" He trailed off, and I realized he could feel my energy. It was like we were in tune with each other. I glanced at him then and smiled. Not wanting to ruin our last day with my negative mind. With a quick shake of my head, I offer him a small smile. My hope is to reassure him. Even if it was just for now. I wanted him to smile.

"It's nothing handsome. Seriously!" I lean into the crook of his neck and kissed him, grazing my teeth over the skin, I feel him shudder. A low growl emanated from his chest and I giggled.

"Cassandra, we are going to get out of the car soon, and I wouldn't like to do that with a hard-on in my shorts." He chided me playfully. I wrapped an arm around his waist, and held him, feeling his warmth. In that moment I took in every last part of him hoping I never had to let go.

I notice when Robert pulls up to park. "Close your eyes," Lucien orders with a smile and I comply. He helps me out of the car wrapping an arm around my waist as he guides me. To have his arms around me, it's like we can't ever go wrong, there's nothing to worry about, but how he makes me feel.

"Lucien, where are we going?" I giggle. My nerves set in, but looking forward to whatever he had planned. The sand beneath my feet was warm, and I realized we were at the beach. Waves crashing and the smell of the ocean overwhelmed my senses. The sun beat down on us and I realized it would be a hot day. Lucien's chuckle is infectious, it filled my heart, and I didn't want to ever not hear it.

"You will see soon enough. Robert you can leave that there, thank you. Will you pick us up at 3:30?" It sounded like we were spending the day here wherever here was.

"Yes Mr. Verán, enjoy your day." The surrounding energy shifted when Robert left. It became electric. A prickle of excitement ran through me being alone with Lucien again. His arms wrapped around my waist and tugged me into him. My back flush against his chest. He spun us around somewhat and whispered in my ear. "Open your eyes sweetness."

As soon as I opened my eyes, it took a second for them to adjust to the light. We were in a cove.

"Lucien! It's an authentic cove!" My excitement matching that of a child at Christmas. His chuckle rumbled through his chest and vibrated through me.

"Yes sweetness a real cove." The ocean was clear as glass, and bright blue. There's a modest picnic on the beach complete with an ice bucket and champagne. This is unbelievable. How on earth did he even get all this set up in time?

"You are incredible Lucien Verán, I can't believe this. It's perfect!" His arms loosen around me and I walk over to the blanket. There are bowls of fruit, and snacks enough to feed an army. There was easily enough for six people. He rounds the blanket and sits on the opposite end as I reach for a strawberry. Sweet soft flavors have me moaning in appreciation.

"Let's have champagne." Lucien kneels opposite me. "I really am happy that you like this, I guessed you would, but of course I wasn't sure. There is still a lot to learn about your likes and dislikes." His wicked naughty smile curled his full lips and my stomach fluttered. He was so handsome. *Why on earth did such a remarkably perfect man want me? Just enjoy it Cass! Take a breath and unwind.*

"Cassie?" Lucien pulls me from my inner conversation. He hands me the glasses as he pops the cork with a flourish. The bubbles almost overflow when he pours the expensive champagne. As soon as the bottle is secure in the bucket, I hand him a glass. My apprehension about us is getting the better of me, but I vow that I will put it behind me, for today. For the first time in years, I am at ease with someone that wasn't Kenna. "A toast, Ms. Winters," sitting back I cross my legs, getting comfortable. "Thank you for returning the light back into my life, Cassandra. It's been so dark and lonely. For the first time in a while I am actually enjoying myself." I blink back tears and beam at him. It was as if he was reading my mind. My pulse raced, I didn't want to think about anything negative in this perfect moment he's given me. He just didn't know about my past. *Well Cassie, just don't mention it to him. Easy as that! You can't risk losing him. He will run if he learns about what happened!*

"Lucien, you give me way too much credit." My gaze drops and I shake my head. *Why can't he see I am not a perfect girl?* Not for him anyway. I peer up at him. His eyes narrow as he takes me in. There's an argument in his mind, which he will voice.

"You don't give yourself enough credit Cassie." His tone was urgent and his gaze intense. "Come on, let's go for a swim?" Thankful for the change of topic, I nod. With a gulp I finish my champagne and rise from the blanket. I unbutton my shorts, tugging them down and letting them pool at my feet. His intense gaze is on me as I pull my tee up and over my head. When I glance up, Lucien staring at me. His hungry eyes drink me in, slow and steady. "I think you're completely overdressed," his voice laced with desire.

"Lucien, can we spend at least one hour dressed?" I giggle and place my hands on my hips, admonishing him. My mouth waters when I watch him pull his T-shirt off and I realize I agree with him about being overdressed. This man should not own clothes. It is doing the world disservice.

"Sweetness, if you didn't distract me as much, I am certain I wouldn't mind being dressed next to you." He holds out his hand and we make our way down to the surf. The water is warm. Lucien releases my hand to run into the water. The sun beats down on his wet body and his skin glistens. I am speechless at his beauty. His tight toned body draws me in. I can't tear my gaze away from him. As I step into the water, I relish the waves crashing against me.

"Come on, sweetness!" Lucien was about as excited about this as I was. I hope he doesn't run from me. *Stop it Cass! He won't find out! Kenna won't tell him. And you shouldn't!* I walk up to him, giving him a bright smile. "You're so beautiful." His words send my heart spiraling. Without another word, our bodies are flush and his mouth seals mine with a heated kiss. His skin on mine sends electric desire coursing through my veins. My hands roam his smooth silky skin, and every touch left goose bumps in its wake. When we were so close, my mind stilled of all the insecurities and anguish. He created such calm for me. I held onto him, like my life depended on it. Somehow, I think it did.

Lucien

My eyes are glued to her movements. Her body is perfect in every way. The tiny black bikini is something we will need to talk about, it's way too revealing to wear in public. For my eyes however, it's perfect. Although, I would prefer her naked. Her gaze is hungry as she rakes her eyes over my body. She's like a hungry little tigress watching its next meal. She tempts me more than she can ever know. Her eyes are locked on my body and mine on hers.

The sexual tension between us is tangible; I need to be inside her again. She wraps her legs around my waist and I groan into the kiss. This girl has a way of making my cock hard 24/7. As soon as I pull away, she let's out a small whimper and I smile. "I think you need my hard cock inside you, don't you, sweetness?" She nods. When I reach between us, my fingers find her heated little pussy. "You're fucking dripping for me, baby." My voice is raspy, and she gives me a naughty smile. I slide two fingers inside her and watch her lips open. A soft moan escapes.

"Because that's what you do to me, Mr. Verán." Her eyes lock on mine and I am about to rip her bikini bottoms off.

"You like to tease me don't you, baby?" I continue plunging my fingers into her, feeling her arousal coat my fingers. Her head drops back, and she digs her nails into my back. *My little tiger likes it rough, and I love to make her purr.* When her heated pussy clamps down on my fingers and her orgasm rips through her body, a smirk curls my lips. *That's it sweetness, come for me. Give it to me, only me. No other man will pull your pleasure from you like I can.* When she looks back up her dark eyes are glistening and she offers me a sweet smile. "You're so fucking beautiful when you come for me."

A blush spreads across her face and I can't help planting a soft kiss on her mouth. I walk us both to the shore and lay her down on the blanket. Desire kicks in and I strip the wet bikini off her body, I take in the perfection that is my girl. Splayed open, wanton, her back arches, and my cock throbs. Her mocha eyes watch me in awe as I kneel between her thighs and place my mouth over her smooth wet cunt. My fingers slide into her in slow torturous movements, as I lap at her core, sucking her clit into my mouth. Her fingers tug on my wet hair and she holds me against her. I open her slick pink folds with my thumbs and lightly blow on her heat. When her hips rock up against my chin, I give her a salacious smile.

God, she is like a drug. I am so addicted to her. Every fucking moment of the day, I want her. "Do you want me inside you baby?" She nods so fast; she makes me dizzy. My eyes glance to the ice bucket and an idea pops into my mind. "Be still, okay." She nods again, her eyes are wide. With a small block of ice, I tease her nipples. They peak and I flick my tongue over them. Her body bows again, pressing herself against me, and my eyes lock on hers. "I said stay still." *How I wish I had rope to have her bound.* I grab another block of ice; this time I slide it down her stomach to her belly button. A whimper escapes her lips, but she doesn't move. *Good girl. Now I can reward you.*

I hover over her, my face inches from hers. My tongue licks the seam of her lips and she opens, granting me access. With one hand, I push my shorts down, enough to free my erection. With a firm grip I line up to her entrance, teasing her pussy with the tip, just enough to make her hips buck again. "Please, Lucien. Fuck me!" She cries out.

"Your wish is my command, sweetness." I plunge into her, bottoming out and her legs wrap around me. Her heels pushing against my ass. Our bodies tangle on the blanket, her arms holding onto my neck. *You will ride me sweetheart.* Before she has time to move, I circle my arm around her body, and lift her up. I sit back without breaking our connection.

"Ride my cock, baby. You're in control, but only for today." I wink and she takes her cue. Her hips move back and forth, in a slow teasing motion. She takes control and her nails rake down my chest, digging in. A deep hiss escapes my lips when the bite of pain sends pleasure to my cock. Her head drops back as she rides me, bouncing on me. Like the good girl she is, taking everything I have for her. She grips my shoulders and I lean forward and suck on her nipples. My tongue flicks over them. "Lucien…" She moans and I look up. Fuck, she looks beautiful on my cock.

"Yes, baby, take me. Take every inch of me in your tight little cunt. Look at me." She obeys and I throb, the awareness that she is letting me in pains me. Our eyes are locked in a heated stare. "You're perfect Cassie, so fucking perfect." *I need her. She needs to be mine. I want her bound to my bed while I fuck her.* The image is too much and the heat travels down my spine. "Come for me, sweetness. My lumiére, give me your pleasure." The obedience in her let's go, and she splinters apart on top of me. My release shoots into her, coating her. *Mine, all fucking mine.*

Lucien

We spent the rest of the afternoon swimming, kissing, and talking. Cassandra was easy to be with, there wasn't any awkward silences and I ached to taste her all the time. I can't begin to explain the way I feel for her. There are so many reasons I shouldn't be here, why she shouldn't be here, but I can't not have her. What worries me is her feelings, if they match mine, we're in so much shit. So many things could tear us apart as soon as we step off this plane. My phone buzzes, it's Jayce.

* You need to tell her about Sasha. Things aren't good with her *

Shit. *Why can't my past stay there?* Like I said so many factors. My gaze falls on Cassie, she's asleep. The peacefulness in her features cracks through a part of me I buried. We're about to land and all I want to do is tell the pilot to turn around and fly us back to Hawaii. I stare at the message and consider his words. This isn't my problem anymore, but he's in this predicament because of me. My stupidity from a long time ago has put my best friend in the middle of something that he didn't deserve.

* Too soon. Why? What's happened? *

Outside the clouds move below us, glimpses of flickering lights on the ground make my eyes hurt. It's still dark, but the lights of the plane light up the sky. The same way Cassie lights my life. My heart. My soul. The dark fucking soul inside me. *Fuck, I am in such deep shit right now. I need to let her go.* I look back at her sweet innocent face and my heart tightens painfully in my chest. The thought of letting her go is killing me, but how can I even begin to bring her into my life. Jayce's reply comes moments later, interrupting my thoughts.

* Sasha and Claudia. Need I say more? *

Fuck! I don't reply. As we land with a small thud, I realize I need to wake Cassie, I will deal with Jayce in the morning. "Cassie, we're here sweetness." When she opens her eyes and glances at me with a sleepy stare, I just about wrap her in my arms. *How can you want me, sweetness?* I help her out of the seat, pulling her to me. My lips devour hers and our tongues dance in an erotic sensual movement.

I lace my fingers through hers as we disembark the plane. Robert is already at the car waiting. Realization hits me suddenly. *Does she want to go home with me? Do I take her to her place? Shit!*

"I can have the car take you home if you're tired." I glance at her, hoping she asks to come home with me, but she nods and agrees to go home. My heart plummets. I mean it hits the fucking floor and I don't know how else to respond so I don't. Without another word I open the door for her and watch her slip in. Once I shut the door softly, Robert's gaze is on me. "Where are we going Sir?" I peer at him and shrug. He knows me well enough not to ask again.

My phone buzzes again, "What, Jayce?"

"Relax, I just wanted to see if you landed safely. You didn't respond to my message."

"We just landed. I will call you when I am home." I hang up before he can respond.

I slide into the car next to Cassie, and my whole body relaxes and tenses. This is what she does to me. She doesn't want to go home with me. *Why should she?* "You okay sweetness?" The need to touch her is unbearable. Instinctively I reach out and touch her thigh, it's so warm and soft, just like the rest of her. As soon as the thought invades my mind, it flits to her warm, wet pussy and my cock twitches against my zipper. *Just relax, she's obviously nervous.*

"Yes, I am always groggy when I wake up." She looks so sexy; I can see her eyes are heavy with sleep. She's exhausted. The day on the beach, had tired her out.

"You're adorable when you're tired." I wish I could tire her out more often. If she let's me.

Robert slides into the driver's seat and the words out of his mouth are like an answer to my prayers. "Mr. Verán, Summer Hills?" I glance at Cassie and she doesn't object. Before she can, I nod.

"Thank you, Robert." My eyes meet his in the rear-view mirror. He did that on purpose. I realize that my emotions for Cassie are obvious to him, he's known me for long enough to recognize how I feel about her. The only reason for that though is because I haven't ever gone to such lengths for any girl.

She must be tired; it takes a few moments to realize that we're not going to her apartment. "Where are we going?" Her mocha eyes gaze straight into mine.

"My place." Panic rises in my chest, waiting for her to refuse to go back to mine. "Unless you'd rather go home? I don't mind. Sorry Cassie, I thought—" *Verán, you need to let her decide.* I watch her reaction when she grasps my hand I visibly relax. My body was about to combust with stress that I had freaked her out.

"Lucien it's fine, I was just asking." She gives me a small smile. "I didn't realize you preferred me to come back." How in the world did she expect me to even sleep alone after the light she's brought into my life? *Why does she look so sad? I am sure I would fuck this up.*

"Sweetness, don't start that. I want you with me." Once I pull her against me, I hold on, relishing the heat of her body. She molds to me, fits so perfectly in my arms and I fit so perfectly inside her.

"I know. I'm sorry." Her voice is soft; she's worried about us again.

"Don't be, I will convince you I want you. In more ways than you imagine." I wish I could calm her fears about this. It's going to take time for her to trust me, but I will make sure she does.

"Oh Mr. Verán, I am certain you will." A naughty smile plays on her lips and my palm is twitching to spank her little ass.

"Cassandra," leaning towards her, my lips are at her ear, "that has just earned you a spanking." I am pushing her a little, testing her. When she gasps, I realize I am safe. She's not freaking out and asking Robert to stop the car or take her home. Yet. When we arrive at the house I am about ready to tie her up and pound into her so hard she's

84

breathless and screaming my name.

"Thank you, Robert, I will take the suitcases. You can pick us up tomorrow around 10?" He nods.

"Yes sir, have an excellent evening. Ms. Winters." She smiles and then takes in her surroundings as Robert makes his way to the cottage in the back. Cassie seems surprised that he lives on the property.

"He lives here?" I nod and guide her towards the door. Her constant amazement at me and things I do is all new to me. As I unlock the large entrance door, she steps inside and I take her coat. I hang it on the hook next to the door. Once I have locked up, I follow her into the living room.

"Welcome to my home, Cassie." She looks on in awe at my apartment. I don't think it's anything special, but I am sure if you're not used to living in the mansions I had to grow up in, it must be pretty spectacular. The living room is my favorite. It's open plan, with muted tones, grey, silver, black, and dark blue. Her soft touch lands on the sofa and then the mantle of the fireplace. I am tempted to give her a tour, but I should let her decide, she's not mine yet. There's one room in particular I want to show her.

"Sweetness? Would you like a tour now? Or in the morning?" She meets my gaze with a tired smile and I realize that she needs some rest.

"Tomorrow? I am exhausted." Her gaze flits to me, I nod and take her upstairs. Tonight she will sleep next to me, again.

"Well, if you're happy with sleeping next to me, I will show you to the bedroom." She smiles. I am so nervous about what she wants. Never in my life have I been unsure around a woman. This is definitely a first for me, confidence is something I don't lack. With her, I can't find it in me. She's got me under her spell.

"Yes, Lucien. Who is the one doubting now?" She asks. Her sassy mouth throws back the words I used on her. *Cheeky girl. She needs a spanking so badly. Her ass will be pink with my hand print, soon.* I can't stop the illicit thoughts running through my mind.

Another first is bringing a girl into my bedroom. This was my space. I wasn't used to sharing it with someone. She's really getting under my skin, and there's not a damn thing I can do about it. All I want to do is make her smile. I show her the bedroom and escort her to the en-suite bathroom. "Here's a toothbrush." As I hand it to her, I recognize her expression. Distrust. With my reputation, I guess I don't blame her.

"You keep toothbrushes on hand in case you bring anyone home?" Pain tugs at my heart that she has such a negative impression of me. I haven't given her a reason to wonder, but I suppose she doesn't know me. That's something I need to work on.

"No, I travel for work, Cassandra." My voice comes out clipped and harsher than I intend. I can't do this. She doesn't trust me. This is not going to work, at all. I can't be with someone who doesn't trust me, especially with my lifestyle. She can tell I am angry, my body aching to take her into the room down the hall. Bend her over and punish her for ever doubting me. Even though I enjoy things that aren't exactly vanilla, I do not cheat. I hate people who do.

"Sorry." Her gaze drops in such a submissive way, and I am overcome with lust. She opens the toothbrush and clutches the tube of toothpaste. Her voice is low and I can tell she regrets her words. *Yes, you fucking upset me, but not in the way you think darling. You've just got my dark soul wanting to play with you in ways you could never fucking imagine. The things I want to do to you, with you.*

"Cassie, I am not the playboy everyone assumes I am. I may not do things by the book, but I would never cheat on you. Ever."

85

While I watch her rinse her mouth, meeting her gaze in the mirror, my eyes plead with her. "I didn't say or think that you were. I didn't even know who you were until you introduced yourself the first day I started work." Surely she knew the company she was going to work for? Her gaze softens and I see that she's telling the truth. *Holy Shit! She didn't know me. Well, now she will know the real Lucien Verán, not the one that everyone sees or thinks they know. The rich little playboy. Or the… NO!*

"You didn't?"

"No Lucien. I told you. I mean when I first saw you at the coffee shop, I had no idea who you were." The tension evaporates from my shoulders and I feel like a weight has lifted off my shoulders.

"I want you to see, I am not a playboy. It's not in my nature. You're tired, come, I will get you a T-shirt to sleep in." I shake my head of the thoughts that pull me into my dark abyss. Pulling her into the bedroom, I grab a T-shirt and hand it to her.

"Can't I sleep in my underwear?" Her request to sleep in her underwear is a no-go.

"No," my voice final.

"Why?" She pouts, but there is no way in hell she will be sleeping if she's in her fucking underwear.

"It's very distracting and we will get no sleep." Just the thought of it has my cock raging. I walk into the bathroom and close the door, I can't stay up late tonight and she's way too fucking tempting. When I meet my reflection. I notice a difference, even though my eyes still have that dark flickering inside them. That will never change. Ever. I pull my phone out of my pocket, there's a message from Jayce.

* Dude, seriously? You get some pussy and now you're ignoring me *

He can be such a dick sometimes. He's lucky that I love him like brother or I could easily punch him. Although, Jayce could have probably killed me many times. I hit reply.

* What the fuck do you want? I just got home. We can talk tomorrow *

Once I am done in the bathroom, I pray that Cassie is under the covers, if not we will both not get any sleep tonight. Jayce hasn't replied and I don't think he will. With one last glance in the mirror, I open the bathroom door and find my sweetness in bed. She looks adorable in my too big tee, under the plush white comforter. She watches me intently, hungrily. "Do you like staring at me, Ms. Winters?"

"Always, Mr.—" Her eyes rake over me and I realize I am tempting her as much as she does me. She looks like a starving little tigress and all I want is to make her purr.

"Cassie, please?" Fuck the big meeting I have tomorrow or I would have called in sick, for both of us. "I need to relish you for tonight. Tomorrow morning…" I kissed her forehead. "That's another story."

I reach over and turn off the light. My arm bands around her waist, and I tug her into me, inhaling her sweet scent.

"Goodnight Lucien." The way she says goodnight to me is perfect. It's a soft sweet sound and I want to hear it forever. *Forever? What the fuck is wrong with me? That's not in my future.*

"Goodnight sweetness."

With my arm wrapped around her, I glance outside, taking in the view from the bedroom patio doors. The city of LA below us and I wonder how many people are with the right person. *My head is so fucked up. You're such a pussy, scared a girl will leave you? She's not just any girl!* My inner demons are wide-awake tonight. I knew they would be, as soon as I am back here, I feel them. There is so much in this town that can pull my life apart. Pull Cassie apart.

We lay in the dark, Cassie's breathing evens and I know she's fast asleep. I shift a little and when she doesn't stir, I get up and walk down the hall. When I reach the door to the room that holds my darkest desires, the dirty pleasures I ache to show Cassie, I step inside. You wouldn't know it if you looked around. There is no sign of what goes on inside. I keep it tidy, everything in it's place. Every drawer and cupboard closed and locked. The king size four-poster bed is perfectly made. The bedding a deep purple, with black cushions. The ambience of the room reveals the calm, but also the darkness. There is a small table at the glass balcony door. I picture bending Cassie over that, spanking her ass until she's begging me to fuck her.

Behind me, next to the door, is a black cabinet with five drawers, filled with toys. Opposite the bed is a long mirror. To the left of that is a walk-in closet. The only person that knows this room even exists is Jayce. The most important part of this room is the ceiling, the railing that can be pulled down, locks into place and allows me to hook the cuffs into the rings. *Fuck, Cassie would look good chained to it.* I groan, my cock is so hard I am about to explode.

I shake my head of the dirty images, turning, I walk out and shut the door quietly. Everything is quiet as I make my way to the living room. I grab a tumbler and pour a double shot of whiskey and down it in one gulp. I needed that. *No! I didn't need it, I just… What Luke? You fucking needed it and you know it. You always need it. Just like your mother. Fuck you!*

I am about to punch something; I need to get to Cassie. Without thinking I bolt up the stairs, slowing down as I reach the bedroom door. When I walk into the bedroom, she's rolled onto her back. Her flowing chestnut curls are splayed on the pillow and the comforter is below her waist. Her blue panties are so tight, so fucking inviting. *Fuck it!*

As I walk back into my play room, the darkness envelopes me and my mind is filled with images of Cassie. Splayed. Open. Wanting. Begging. I close the door gently and sit in the wingback chair overlooking the patio. *She will hate me and my tortured fucking soul. There is no chance in hell the girl sleeping next to me will ever love me.* The image of her blue panties pops into my mind and I push my black pants down. A tight grip on my throbbing erection, elicits a groan and I pump it fast and hard. The image of Cassie with my cock in her mouth runs through my mind. Those mocha eyes, those pink plump lips, I am so close. The tingle shoots down my spine and up to the head of my cock, I come, moaning Cassie's name.

Once I have cleaned myself up, I make my way back to the bedroom and slip into bed. I wrap my arm around her, close my eyes, and inhale her. She's laying on her side again, her ass pressed against me. *This will kill me.* Sleep overtakes me quickly after my little midnight gallivant.

Cassandra

I wake up to Lucien's heavy arm around my waist. The sun is beaming through the balcony door and I stare at the view. My mind is all over the place. Today is the first day back at the office and I wonder what will happen between us. Surely, he wouldn't want everyone to find out about us. If not, I had to understand. *You shouldn't worry so much! Cassie, he likes you. Why wouldn't he want the world to know? Well, his mother would not like it. I mean, his mother would be totally against us. I can sense it in my gut.*

"Are you okay sweetness?" Lucien's voice his deep with sleep and I grin. He's so sexy, he never fails to make me smile.

"I am, just savoring the view." When I roll over over, and face him, there's heat in his stare.

"I thought I was your view?" A smile curves his beautiful lips and I am desperate to kiss him. I reach up to the dimple in his cheek and caress his smooth silky skin.

"You're my favorite view, by far." I move up to kiss him. His arm tightens around my waist and pulls me in. His body is warm and solid; the muscles are taut. His tongue licks the seam of my mouth. My lips open, letting him have access to me, as soon as our tongues dance in wild abandon, my body molds to him. He tugs at my T-shirt and his hands caress my hips, up my belly and over my sensitive nipples. "Lucien." I breathe into the kiss.

"How about some breakfast, sweetness?" *What? Breakfast now? Really!*

He pulls the T-shirt over my head, but leaves my wrists bound with the material. "Lucien!"

He growls as his mouth comes down onto my breasts, licking and nipping at the soft skin. "Told you, I need breakfast." The rasp in his voice sends a jolt straight to my panties. *Ah! Breakfast sex! Yes, please!*

I chuckle at my inner conversation. His hooded eyes glance up at me as he starts down my belly. When his tongue dips into my bellybutton, I quiver. Everything he does is so exquisite. The ache and need of having him inside me is driving me crazy. "Lucien, please?" I beg shamelessly.

"Keep your hands up there okay?" He signals to my bound wrists. I nod. His mouth moves south as his fingers caress my sides. The slow torture is making me wanton with lust. My hips rock up towards his mouth and I see a smirk curve his lips.

His thumbs hook into the sides of my panties tugging them down. "I'm starving sweetness. I plan on devouring you till you scream." He growls and my slick entrance is dripping. His index finger glides over my heated pussy, teasing me. I rock my hips and I see him smirk. "Not yet gorgeous, just relax."

Relax? Seriously? His thumbs move over my smooth pussy and open me to his gaze. I watch his tongue lap at my core. "Lucien." I hiss through my teeth. My hands still bound above my head. All I want to do is grab him and pull him into me. He dips a finger inside me and I clench around him. "So fucking sexy, I need you to come on my tongue, sweetness." His order sending waves of pleasure over me, an orgasm ripping through me and I feel him smile as he licks at me.

I shut my eyes taking in the sensations of his lips and tongue. His fingers slowly ease into me teasing me open as he inserts another one. My body is shaking, writhing below him. "Lucien, please?"

He plunges his two fingers inside me. "Please what, sweetness?" I glance down to him. "Tell me what you want." His hoarse voice and hot breath on me causing my body to convulse.

"Fuck me!" I cry out as the pad of his thumbs rubs over my throbbing clit. He sits back and looks at me. The waiting is excruciating. He pushes his low slung pants down and his erection is rock solid. When the heat of his body hovers over me, his weight is on his left elbow. With his right hand, he grips his cock stroking it over my wet slit and I all but come undone. "Say it sweetness, tell me what you want?" He asks again. My eyes lock on his and I chew my lip. His eyes drift over my mouth and he smirks. The head of his erection at my slick entrance. I rock my hips up to him, but I don't beg. Not yet.

"I asked you to tell me what you fucking want?" His voice is low and dangerous. Desire tightens my core and the anticipation of him driving into me is too much.

"Fuck me, Mr. Verán." I breathe and his grin is dark. He slams into me and knocks me breathless.

"My lumière." His voice is laced with lust and hunger. My body tightens around him. He stills inside me. Watching my reaction to him. As I come down from him opening me, he continues his relentless drives in and out, as he repeats his French nickname for me. His head falls next to mine and I can't see his eyes. His voice is strained and I realize he is broken by the desire between us. I need to heal him; I crave to make him whole again. As I bring my arms down, a growl stems from his chest. "Don't." It's the first time he's not wanted me to touch him. Without arguing I move my hands back above my head. "I need this." I don't understand what he means until he plunges into me ferociously. His body tenses. My body is so far beyond turned on I have no idea if I can hold on much longer.

"Lucien." I murmur in his ear, tugging the lobe in my teeth, drawing a deeper growl from him. "Fill me, come inside me." I beg him. It's the only way I can prove to him that I want him. He slams into me repeatedly, almost violently. The deeper and harder he does, the more we both heal, although I am not sure from what. It's a dark yearning burning inside us.

"I need you to come on my dick, lumière. I want you to give it all to me." His words are my undoing as my core clenches around his erection. My release ripping through me leaving me breathless. Seconds later, his orgasm shatters him and fills me. Marking me as his.

Lucien

When Robert drops us off at the office, I walk Cassie to her desk. Every set of eyes in the office follow us in. There isn't a part of me that would have let her walk alone today. Especially after last night. It was a bad one. "You okay baby? I have to work now so I will see you at lunch?"

"Yes, I am sure I can manage sitting at my desk, Lucien." She's embarrassed. She cares what people think of her. Me on the other hand. I don't give a fuck. I lean in and give her a chaste kiss on the lips. *God, she feels so good.* When I get back to the elevators, my phone buzzes. I tug it out and see a text from Jayce.

* Claudia is in the building. *

Shit! My body is on alert. At least she doesn't know who Cassie is. I step into the elevator and hit reply.

* Thanks for the heads up. Rough night last night. *

Jayce will know what I mean. My mind was in overdrive last night. This is the first time in two years that I am allowing myself some sort of normal life. I need something to stop the riptide pulling me under. Maybe Jayce and I need a boys' night. Although all

I want to do is spend time with Cassie.

Shit. You okay? Did she see you? *

The elevator pings and I step onto the top floor. I love towering above the city. Stacy is at her desk like the good girl she is. *Fuck, she's annoying.* The only reason she runs around here is because my father and her father are such good friends. Maybe I can move her down to another floor.

"Good morning, Mr. Verán, how was your trip?" She smiles and I can't help wanting to walk right passed her. I am generally not a rude bastard, but for some reason this girl really grates me.

"Fine, thanks. Any messages?" She shakes her head. "Good. Coffee please?" I offer her a smile and walk into my office.

"Where the hell were you?" I shut the door and stare at Jayce. He's sitting on my black faux leather sofa and going through what looked like the paperwork for the meeting today.

"I was held up." As I round my desk, I power on the iMac. I am tempted to send Cassie a message, but I realize we have limited time to go over the figures for the next shoot before the stuffy board members get here. A few important emails need replying to, so I slide into my chair and start on them. "How do you know Claudia is here?" I glance up at my best friend.

"Girls in distribution." When he meets my stare, I realize exactly why he was on the fourth floor.

"Who is she?" My tone is serious, and he knows it.

"Don't get your fucking panties in a twist, I haven't fucked her. Yet." I groan. My best friend can be such a dick. A complete and utter manwhore.

"Don't fuck my staff, Jayce." The wicked glint in his eye tells me that I am talking to a brick wall.

"You're fucking your staff." I can't fault him on that.

"Yea, but I don't plan on breaking her heart." That earns me a look of surprise. Jayce narrows his eyes and I know what he's thinking. I can't help it. She's perfect. I can't just walk away, even though I know I should.

"Jesus, Luke. You're fucking serious." He gets up and walks over to my desk. When he places his hands on the mahogany, he leans in and stares me down. His ice blue glare piercing my olive green. "Oh my God, you're completely whipped. Luke, you know that you need to be careful." I nod. Really not in the mood to go through this right now. "If Claudia finds out."

"She knows. Although, she doesn't know who Cassie is, she just knows that I am seeing one of the girls I was in Hawaii with."

"Fuck Luke, you do realize Claudia isn't stupid. I mean—"

Jayce is cut off by my intercom. "Mr. Verán, the board are ready for you."

I rise from my desk and look at Jayce. "I do realize that Claudia will find out soon. Cassie is safe until after the meeting. I will tell her tonight." He stares long and hard. We have little time. He nods and we make our way through to the boardroom.

"Mr. Verán," the six board members rise and we shake hands. They're older than me, most of them my father's age. Since I took over the company from my father, they've been welcoming. Some weren't happy, but most of them had no choice but to allow the heir to the throne to sit at the head of the table.

"Gentlemen. I trust this meeting will go smoothly. I have collated the numbers with Mr. Alexander and we have all the research for the new shoot. There will be a new strategy for the marketing department. Although our print numbers are down, I think we need a revival and focus on getting the sales up. I realize we will put 5 million into this new venture, but the rewards will be triple that. The digital marketing has had a boost in sales that's the way the company is leaning."

"Mr. Verán, I am all for—" I turn my gaze to the oldest board member. The only one I knew would give me problems, he isn't one of my father's favorites either. An outside investor, Mr. Shapiro, is a friend of Claudia. At one point, I thought she was fucking him. It grates me that my father allows him on the board, but at the moment we need the financial help. Soon, I will get him out of my company, and he can crawl back into the hole he came from.

"Mr. Shapiro, I am still the CEO, the rest of the board don't have any reservations about this. We will go ahead with this vote. Can we see a show of hands on who wants to go ahead with my idea?"

The whole board, bar one, raises their hands. Jayce is obviously on board since he will work with the team, with my girl. Besides my top photographer, he is also my Marketing Director. With a degree in marketing and business management, I trust him more than I trust a shrewd old businessman that's after my father's company.

I glare at the old man and he nods. His lips in a grim line and I know I have pissed him off. I don't give a fuck. He needs to learn who is in control, and who will stay in control. I am never stepping down from this seat, so he can get over it. Or better yet, get out.

Once the rest of the agenda is covered, I glance around the table and they all seem happy enough. I dodged a fucking bullet thanks to Jayce. As soon as the conversation dwindles, I pull out my phone, and notice we've been in here for four hours. "Gentlemen." I rise and walk out, opening my email, I type Cassie an email. As I walk into my office, I am met with Claudia, sitting on my sofa. *What the fuck? Is my office just open to everyone now?*

"What do you want?"

"Is that any way to talk to your mother Lucien?" I glare at her. She's up to something and by God I will find out what it is.

"I am busy. What do you want?"

"I popped by to say hello to the new girl, you know the one that's taking over from Veronica." Her cold eyes are on me and my blood runs cold.

"What the fuck did you do?"

"Fixed a situation, Lucien. You know that you shouldn't be seeing anyone. It's not good for you and I can't deal with you going down that road again." She rises and walks to the door. Turning to look at me before she walks out. "I trust you will obey my wishes."

"Fuck you." Her devious smirk is nauseating as she closes the door behind her, all that's running through my mind is Cassie.

Cassandra

I step into the office and set up my laptop when Veronica walks down the corridor with coffee. "Cassie! So glad to see you're safe and sound. You look like you got some sun." She smiles and I nod.

"Yes, it was an incredible experience." *Sure it was! You're shagging the boss! Stop it Cassie, he's into you!* I open my laptop and log into my user account.

"Well, just a heads up Mrs. Verán is roaming around so keep your eyes open." She winks and strides into her office before I can ask. I presume its Lucien's mother. At least I hope it's his mother and not a wife he's not told me about.

I stroll into the kitchen and prepare myself a coffee. This morning's breakfast has left me deliciously sore. Lucien's peculiar mood had my thoughts whirling. Maybe he realized his mother decided on making an appearance today.

"Good morning," I twirled around at the icy voice behind me. When my gaze falls on the woman in front of me, I recognize immediately who she is. She looked highly strung, but elegant. She had long black hair that fell straight to the center of her back. Tall and petite, wearing a silver skirt suit with a delicate silk blouse. Her eyes were startling. Ice blue, nothing like Lucien's, she didn't even have his calm relaxed attitude. *So that's her. I am terrified. She's like a professor that wants me in detention forever. I can tell that we will not get along, at all. Lucien would be better off with one of the wealthy girls. I should just bow out now.*

"Good morning, Mrs. Verán." I smile. With my back straight, my shoulders back, I step towards her, offering my hand. "I am Cassandra Winters."

"Yes darling, I know who you are." Her words were clipped. My hand remained in the air for a few moments until I realize she had no intention of taking it. "I want to say one thing; my son is spoken for. He's engaged. Did he tell you that while he romanced you in Hawaii?" I was too dumbstruck to respond. "I didn't think so. Now be a decent girl and let the grown-ups play." Her face twisted into a vicious grimace reminding me of Cruella de Vil. *I swear she is a fucking bitch! Seriously? Lucien would obviously agree with her. I mean he is her son after all.* "It's okay don't feel cheap, he does this with every shoot. I didn't expect this time would be any different." She spun on her heel leaving me stunned.

The walk back to my desk was torture; like everyone's eyes landed on me. *Did they hear that? Do they know what's going on? I don't think so. I mean, surely they couldn't have found out.* I slipped into my chair and my email pinged.

From: Lucien Verán
To: Cassandra Winters
Date: June 5, 2014 - 15:35
Subject: My Girl

Ms. Winters,

I was missing you. I wanted to see if you're okay, after this morning. It was amazing waking up to you. I am smiling. And I am rock hard.

How about a late lunch?

Lucien Verán
Chief Executive Officer
Verán Publications

I was irritated, angry, and tears sprung to my eyes. After his mother's visit, I didn't want to read his loving words that held nothing but lies. My stupidity at letting someone in will once again cost me my heart. I should have just stuck to my original plan, no men. This was my fault, getting myself into a situation as bad as this. I glared at the screen, I couldn't not tell him what his mother said, but how was I meant to do it over email?

From: *Cassandra Winters*
To: *Lucien Verán*
Date: *June 5, 2014 - 16:00*
Subject: *Not Your Girl*

Mr. Verán,

I think you should email your fiancée as your mother would put it. I am nobody's girl. It was a good weekend, apparently your mother knows all about it, since you do it every year. Please refrain from emailing me again unless work related.

Cassandra Winters
Marketing & Publishing Assistant
Verán Publications

  I hit send on the email and grab my bag. The need to get out of this office was bearing over me. Before he could come down and try to lie about what his mother told me, I made it to the ground floor. I walked down the road. I needed to think, and I certainly didn't want to be inside my apartment alone. That's when I found my feet taking me to the only place that would be my refuge, the coffee shop. Once I reach the door, deliberating whether to go in or not, I am distracted by my phone. I stare at the screen and see Kenna's name. Maybe she would make me feel better, I swipe the screen.
  "Hello?"
  "Where have you been babe?" I smile, she sounds so excited.
  "Work, it's been busy." I try to lighten the tone in my voice, but I realize I can't fool her.
  "What's wrong babe?" I pick up the concern laced in her voice and I feel myself fighting back the tears. *Calm down Cass! You're in public! Do not fall apart!*
  "Nothing, what's up?" *Please drop it Kenna? Please, I can't do this here!*
  "No, not nothing! Tell me what's wrong? Is it Lucien?" Hearing his name tugs at my heart.

Chapter eleven

Lucien

As I sit down at my computer, I notice there's a reply from Cassie to my earlier email. My eyes skim the words and my heart constricts. I pick up my phone, hitting the call button on her name. Voicemail. *Fucking Claudia!* Without a second thought I race out of the office. "Take messages Stacy; I am leaving for the day."

"Yes, sir." The elevator pings as soon as I arrive at the doors, I hit tenth floor button, and it descends at a snail's pace. *Why the fuck did I not talk to Cassie before. Shit!* The doors open on the floor and I race to Cassie's office. She's gone. I try calling her again. Nothing. She must have just left.

When I reach the ground floor, I all but sprint through the reception with eyes on me. I make my way out of the building and look in every direction. *She's gone. It's over. Like fuck it is!* I run down the road towards the coffee shop. My only idea is that she would have walked that way. I know she lives close by. Only one person can help, I hit the call button, and Robert answers on the second ring. "Robert, get me Cassie's address. You have five minutes."

"Yes, Mr. Verán." Less than five minutes later her address pops up on a text message from Robert. *He's fucking incredible.*

I realize running down the street in a suit is not something you see every day, but I wish people would stop fucking staring at me. As I am about to reach the coffee shop, I spot her. She's on the phone across the road from me. My heart is pounding. *How do I approach her?* I can't go caveman on her, she will freak out. Although, I could throw her over my shoulder and spank her ass for walking away from me.

I am dumbstruck, just standing watching her. When she turns, her gaze lands on me and her face falls. The pain in her eyes rip me to pieces. *Fucking Claudia!* "Cassie!" She ignores me and carries on walking in the opposite direction. "Cassie, Goddamnit!" People are now staring at me even more. I must look like a complete lunatic. She's getting away. I have no choice, so I make a run for it. She's not fucking walking away from me. Once I reach her, with a firm grip on her shoulders, I spin her around. Her eyes are puffy and red. She's been crying.

"What Lucien?" Her voice is hard and I can see every emotion on her face. She wears her heart on her sleeve and right now, it's hurting. When I touch her face, she let's me. That's a good sign.

"Please, give me a chance to explain. Please? Cassie, you have to at least give me that?" The pain is so evident in her beautiful features. *Come on Cassie, give me a chance? I can make this right.* I realize as I think the words how much I want it. That no matter what happens I want her. She's the only thing in my life that makes sense. There is no explanation for my feelings or why they're so strong for her.

"Talk." Her voice is raspy with emotion. She is just about holding it together, so am I. With a quick nod, I scramble to find the words to make her stay.

"Look Cassie, I told you Claudia is difficult. She found out about us traveling to Hawaii from my assistant. Claudia is over protective, manipulative and evil. She will try to break us up, the malicious bitch will do anything." The venom in my words make her wince. "Please don't run, sweetness? We can get through this." I stroke her cheek with the tip of my index finger, lifting her chin, so that her eyes meet mine. The only thing I can hope is that she can see the pleading in my eyes because I have nothing else to give her right now.

Then she shakes her head, and the pain in my heart cripples me. After only a few days with her, my darkness has abated. The dreams haven't come. With her I could try to let go of my past and have a normal life. The thought of her walking away scares the shit out of me, but I have never been one to back down from a challenge. "Lucien, we only spent a weekend together. I mean. I can't. It's just painful, I have been through too much to struggle anymore. I am sorry." I wanted to pull her into my arms, to order her to stay, but she isn't mine. She never agreed to it, I can't stake a claim like that. Even though every part of me wants to claim her. "I should go."

Fuck! I am losing her! Just like that! There is no way I can do that sweetheart; you will come back to me. She walks past me and her sweet scent engulfs my senses. I stop her when our shoulders brush against each other. The visible tremble of her body is an indication my effect on her, the same as hers on me. I make her a promise, one that I will keep. No matter what. "Cassie," my lips are at her ear and I make sure she can feel every word I am saying, "I will give you as much space as you want, but I am not giving up on you. Just realize that. I fucking claimed you. You're mine." My words are harsh, dark and dangerous, but I can't let her go.

Before I walk away I inhale her scent, committing it to memory. Then I make my way down the road. I have just left a part of me on the sidewalk, along with the promise I made her. When I pull my phone from my jacket pocket, I text Robert to pick me up at the coffee shop. Once she's gone, I will go back, but I can't watch her walk away from me.

Half way down the road, I hear her call my name. "Lucien!" She's actually fucking calling me. As I spin around, I see her sprinting down the sidewalk to me. I open my arms as she jumps into them. "What's this, sweetness?" Shock radiates through me, but also something I didn't know I had. Hope. My body flush against hers. She feels so good against me I almost believe she wants me. When I pull away and look into her intense chocolate eyes.

"I need to stop running, Lucien. There are things in my past that constantly cause me to run, but I need to face things." The words she promises me there on the sidewalk make my heart skip. She wants to be with me. "I moved to LA to start again, and that's what I need to do." At that moment, I want to tell her everything, the fear of her leaving is immense, but I will give her my honesty. I am standing on the edge of a cliff, ready to fall for this girl. Hard and fast. I just hope she's ready to jump with me. My lips find hers and the breath is back in my lungs. Her mouth opens for me, accepting me, as our tongues dance in an intense erotic tumble, I taste every part of her.

She slowly slides down and when her feet touch the sidewalk, I step back and stare at her. "Good. I have a lot in my past I have to explain, but not right now. I want to take you home now." She shakes her head and I frown.

"We're going to my place. Then you need to talk." Nodding, I text Robert to come to Cassie's apartment and bring a change of clothes for me. I lace my fingers in hers and we walk side by side up the street to her apartment, hand in hand. The smile on my face is hurting my cheeks, but I can't stop it. I almost lost her, but that will not happen again. She's never leaving my side again. Ever. Just then, as if the sky knew how my heart hurt, the heaven's open on us. *Fuck sake! Are you kidding me?* She giggles and I can't help smiling as we run in the rain. This is one of the most exciting times I have ever spent with a girl. I hold onto her hand and run up the road.

When we reach her apartment and step inside, we're both dripping wet. "That was insane!" She giggles and I stare at the way her clothes cling to her curves and blood travels straight to my cock.

"I do like you all wet, Ms. Winters."

"You do? I would never have guessed, Mr. Verán." As soon as my name leaves her lips, I lift her onto the counter and undress her. My fingers fumble as I unbutton the top she is wearing, I slide it over her shoulders, it drops in a wet puddle on the floor. I unclasp her bra, and it joins the growing pile of clothes on the floor.

Her nipples harden from the chill in the air and being wet. My mouth is watering to taste her, leaning forward my mouth envelopes her hardened buds, sucking them into my mouth, biting down softly. Right now, I need to take her, be inside her and make her scream my fucking name. She tugs at my wet shirt. Her fingers move swiftly over the buttons.

"I need you, Cassie," my words are a soft moan and I don't recognize the need in my voice. "Shower?" She nods with a smile on her face. *She's letting me in, thank fuck she's agreeing.* I lift her off the counter and instinctively her legs wrap around me. We make our way to the bathroom. Setting her down, I glance at her naked body; nothing has ever been more beautiful than my girl, turned on and naked just for me. My pants and boxers are on the floor in record time. The need to be inside her is burning into me. She turns on the water and when she turns to face me again, a small gasp escapes her lips and her eyes rake over me. We step into the hot spray together. Her body is a few inches from mine, and I am already rock hard. "I will tell you everything, first, we are going to fuck." The rasp in my voice makes her shiver. She grabs the shower gel and squirts some on the sponge. I take it from her, my eyes locked on hers. She gives me a small nod, allowing me to do this is a sign, to me at least, that she trusts me.

I lather her body, with slow careful movements. This is one of my favorite things to do. Her skin is soft and smooth and I want to lick every inch of her. I rub the gel over her ass and down her legs. I can see her knees trembling at the attention I am showing her body. "Turn around sweetness," I growl. She spins around, glancing down at me. I am on my knees in front of her and from this angle, she looks incredible. My hands roam up her legs and grip her hips. She leans forward, and my tongue is on her smooth slick folds. The taste of her sweet warm pussy sends me to another place.

"Lucien, please?" My name on her lips, the moan has my cock aching to have her sheath me. Tighten around me. Milk me until every last drop of come is inside her. I continue my attention on her tight little cunt. My teeth graze her clit and her whole body convulses. "Come for me sweetness, I need to taste you." This is her undoing as she comes over my tongue. I let out a primal growl, tasting the sweet juices from her core. As soon as her honey drips from her body onto my tongue, I can't stand it anymore.

I kiss my way back up her body. My eyes locking on hers. "You're so fucking beautiful when you come."

"Lucien…"

"Slow, baby, then I will make you scream my name." My hands grip her ass, and she wraps her legs around me. I pin her against the wall, her begging edging me on. With one swift move, I slide into her. *Fucking hell, she feels good. Tight, wet, warm. So fucking perfect.* My restraint is falling away and I slam into her hard. Her nails dig into my shoulders, urging me deeper, harder and faster. *She's mine, all fucking mine.*

"Please?" She begs again as I drive my length into her and she cries out. Her head drops back against the wall; she shuts her eyes. Her lips part and a soft moan escapes, sending a shock of pleasure to my cock. There is something deep and primal about us fucking. There is nothing sweet and sensitive about this. I maintain my relentless assault plunging into her. When she digs her nails into my shoulders, I know she's close.

"Lucien." She moans loudly. My name on her lips is her claim to me. She has it. I can't deny this woman has fucking claimed me. She has no fucking idea what she's done to me, but I am hers. Every fucking inch of me.

"Cassandra, you're mine." My voice lays claim to her, again and again. The water cascading over us is like a waterfall of emotions. "Now fucking come with me!" My order sending her over the edge, she obeys me even in the throes of passion. Her pussy spasms around me, tightening around my shaft.

"Lucien!" She cries out again, her body shuddering in my hands and I hold her tight.

"My lumiére!" That's all I need to lose control and my come shoots into her heated cunt. I have just given myself to her, more than I have given anyone before. There's something about her and I am lost in emotion. *This is such a big mistake. You will hurt her Verán, that's all that you're good for.* Fuck it, I need her. Her light, her innocence, and her passion. I want her, mind, body, soul, but most of all I will claim her heart. We stare at each other for a few moments before I set her down. Her face is flushed, and she's still shaky. I hold her against me, planting a soft kiss on her head. *What the fuck have I done?*

I realize we had things to discuss, but I wanted to fuck her before we went there. A trip down memory lane is my least favorite thing to do. When I reach over and turn the water off, she steps out of the shower and grabs two towels. She wraps one around her wet body and hands me the other. *Fuck she's beautiful.* I grab the towel and offer her a small smile, wrapping it around my waist, and Cassie's face is a picture. "You look…" Her voice trails off and I can tell she's speechless after our shower.

I smirk at her. "I do?" She swats me with a hand towel and I chuckle. We walk into her bedroom, I flop onto the bed, and watch her get dressed. As soon as she's pulled a top on, the doorbell rings. "That's Robert, with my clothes."

"I will get them." As much as I want to avoid what's coming, I have to be honest with her. This will be an interesting conversation. I can't imagine what Claudia told Cassie. When she comes back to the bedroom, she smiles. "Robert says that Jayce asked for you to call him." I nod and she passes me the clothes Robert dropped off.

"Okay, I guess I didn't hear my phone over you screaming my name in there." I point to the shower as I pull up my sweats. Cassie's face turns bright red.

"Was I really that loud?" She's adorably innocent, and it makes me want to walk out the door and act like I never met her. There is so much she will have to deal with if she wants to be with me. Not to mention my penchant to tying her up and doing all sorts of dark dirty things to her. But, I am not the nice guy, I am the selfish bastard who can't let her go, so here I am. Standing in her bedroom, hoping I never have to tell her goodbye.

"Baby, I love when you're loud." I say with a cheeky wink, she's blushing again.

"Lucien! Don't be a douche!" Her face is crimson, and I can't help chuckling at her unease. "Do you want a sandwich? I am starving." I nod and she makes her way to the kitchen. As I pull my phone out of my pocket, it's thankfully still working. There are five missed calls from Jayce. I hit call.

"Luke! Where the hell were you?"

"None of your business, what's up?"

"Sasha and Claudia are having lunch at our place. I overheard them talking, apparently Cassie knows about your engagement." *Fuck! Ex-engagement!*

"Thanks Jay, I am with her now. We're going to talk."

"Call me later." As soon as I hang up, I make my way into the kitchen to find my gorgeous girl cutting the sandwiches.

Cassandra

Turning to see Lucien join me in the kitchen, I realize it's now or never. There is a lot he needs to tell me and we are not going back to anything remotely romantic until he tells me the truth. The shower was a slip on my part, but now I need the truth. I can't deal with his mother, and so called fiancée, there is no way I want to be the other woman. I pick up the plates and place them on the counter. Watching him slide into the chair, I take a deep breath. "So, we need to talk Lucien. You romancing me in the shower and fucking me till I can't stand doesn't make me forget." I glance up at him and catch him smirking. My choice words did that, but I need him to see he affects me. I can't deny it, and if I am going to put myself out there, then he should do the same.

"Till you can't stand? I like that. Can we do it again?" He chuckles when I throw a kitchen towel at him. With his hands up in surrender, his expression is suddenly serious. I dread what's coming, but I asked for this. He needs to trust me, and maybe I will be able to trust him.

"I'm serious Lucien."

"I know, babe. Let's eat and we can talk." I slip into the chair next to him, picking up my sandwich. After I take a small bite, I turn to him. My gaze falls on his mouth as I watch him devour the sandwich I had just prepared. As he finished the first half, he turned. "Cassie, I told you Claudia has a particular idea of the kind of woman I should be with. It's not the person I want to be with." When he picks up the glass of juice, taking a sip, he stalls for a moment. "I want to be with you Cassie." My heart races as he reaches for my hand. The need to touch him is overwhelming, and I slip mine in his, and the warmth envelopes me. I wasn't sure why he called her by her name, but I wanted the rest of the story before asking questions. I nodded slowly, waiting for the blow. The fiancée. He had to tell me about it.

"What about the fiancée your mother mentioned? And the annual photo shoots you go on with female staff members?" He shook his head.

"The fiancée is my ex. My mother still has it in her head we are made for each other. I would have proposed, but things happened between us. Those I will explain to you soon, for now I need you to know that I am not with Sasha in any way." I saw the anguish in his eyes. He clearly loved her. *What if he still loves her? I mean, they were about to be engaged. Surely, he wouldn't be here if he did. Why would he? Maybe he was with me to upset his mother. Cassie! Stop it! He likes you!*

I shook my head. That made little sense to me. "So you gave her the cover of your latest swimsuit edition?" He glanced up in surprise and I realized that he didn't know Jayce told me. *I was sure I mentioned it in Hawaii. Didn't I? Shit! I needed to see a doctor. The stress is getting to me again.*

"Cassie I didn't pick the models, my father did. My mother insisted he give her the cover. He listens to Claudia; she can be… persistent. She didn't realize you would come along and knock me for six." He gave me that sexy grin, dimples included. I couldn't help but return it. His smile deepened, and I found my resolve crumbling. Deep down my heart was sealed in a cage, but I wanted to release it for Lucien. I didn't think I could, not yet. There is still too much that we need to learn about each other. Too many secrets are holding us back right now, and I am scared that when it all comes crashing down, my heart will be a casualty.

"I realize there is still a lot we have to learn about each other Lucien, but I don't want surprises like that again. There is no way I can deal with it. My past has way too many potholes and I can't go back there. I was broken, I suppose in a way I still am." He nodded. The mood between us was solemn, and I detested it. He made me feel so complete I wanted us to go back to Hawaii and stay there.

"Sweetness, I never want to take you there. I want to know you, and I promise that I will never break you. The only thing I want is to be the one to fix you." He laced his fingers through mine. *Didn't he realize that he does so much more than just fix me? He makes me feel things I left buried for two long years.*

"You do, Lucien, you do so much more." There was no way I could explain it that would make sense. Maybe he thinks I am crazy, but I needed to say the words.

"And you do that for me Cassie. You've taken my darkness and given me light where there wasn't any. You, your smile, your body, I ache for you." His words broke into the cage where I held my heart, taking it from the pain and anguish I have hidden and given me something I didn't have. Hope.

"Is that why you call me your light?" I blushed; he always said it when we were in bed. Or any other place he was buried inside me. He nodded, dropping his gaze.

"Cassie, I am not a perfect guy. There are things I haven't told you about my past, and I will I… It's a lot to take in. My relationships have been forced on me, I have never cared for a girl before, the way I do for you. I don't date. Romance is something of a foreign concept to me. So, I became… The bastard. The one who caused the girls to cry because that's how I was in control. I can be rough. Aggressive. When it comes to sex, I need to dominate. My taste is darker than guys you've probably been with. When I am buried deep inside a girl, there aren't any emotions. It's just fucking." I wince at his words, but I asked. His honesty is refreshing. "Although with you, it's different. You're different. I still want to dominate the fuck out of you, and you're so responsive. You make me want to do so many things to you. Things I am sure would freak you out, but to have you kneeling for me, that would be my wildest fantasy come true." His gaze meets mine for the first time since he started talking; there is dark desire in his eyes. "I don't want to scare you, but I want you Cassandra. So many dark, erotic, and dirty thoughts run through my mind with you. When we are ready I will tell you more that's if you want to know. If you want me to leave, then I will respect your wishes."

My heart was racing at his words. His confession making me squirm. After the few times we've been together I recognized his dominance in the bedroom. "I prefer to take control; I need the girl I am with to submit to me sexually." When his eyes find mine I could see the apprehension, he was terrified of me running from the truth. "If you don't want this, I understand. Just know that I could and would never hurt you. I care about you too much. My promise is that I will always push your limits, but only to bring you pleasure. If you ever want to stop. We stop." He turned his gaze away, looking at the countertop instead. His fingers tracing the pattern on the surface. Those fingers that could bring me so much pleasure. I sat quietly for a moment, taking in the enormity of what he had just told me. I needed him, so much. He's never hurt me and I trusted he wouldn't.

"Lucien," my voice is soft, "look at me?" I plead with him. I want to say this while looking into his eyes. When he eventually turns, I offer him a small smile. "I need you." Without another thought I slide off the chair and stand between his thighs. He's wearing the pair of sweats and T-shirt he asked Robert to drop off at my place. Since his suit was soaked through. "Will you let me show you?" I murmur. He frowns, but nods. I pull him up and when he's standing, I drop to my knees in front of him and tug the sweatpants down. He's aroused, semi hard, I grasp him in my hand and gently stroke him. I glance up at him, our eyes locked in a passionate gaze. I flick my tongue over the tip, tasting his arousal, sending a shudder over his body. Without breaking eye contact, our connection, I take the first few inches of him into my mouth. I suck him in.

"Jesus, Cassie," he growls, and it spurs me on. I take him all the way into my mouth until the head hits the back of my throat. He's big, so the last few inches I pump with my hand as I swallow him. I can feel his cock twitch in my mouth. With a slow lick, I trace my tongue along the underside, feeling the veins and ridges. He grabs my hair in a tight grip and fucks my mouth earnestly. "That's it sweetness, take me deep." The rasp in his dark voice is so sexy. He thrusts in and out of my mouth as he takes control. I drop my hands, leaving the control to him. "Touch yourself, get your tight little pussy wet for me." My hands move down, between my legs and I find I am soaked. As I glance up at him, I see the light shining in him. The desire and lust that turns my core into molten lava. The pleasure I am giving him turns me on more than I ever thought possible. His eyes are dark with lust.

"You're so fucking beautiful with my cock in your mouth." His crude words sending a shiver down my spine and heat straight to my core. I suck him in further, my gag reflex subsiding for the moment as I pleasure him the way he did to me in the shower. His head drops back and primal growl emanates from his chest. The carnal way his body tenses turns me on, I love watching him lose all that control he carries. Suddenly he pulls me off him. "I need to fuck you now, hard. Bend over and hold the counter tight." His command is strained; he's barely holding it together.

I bend over and hold onto the edge of the counter. Lucien roughly pulls at my sweatpants and I hear them shred. He groans at the sight of me with no panties on, bent over in front of him. Without warning, he slams into me to the hilt. It knocks the breath from me for a few moments as he impales me on his thick hard cock. "Oh God, you're so fucking tight. This pussy will be my undoing. You will be my end and my beginning." The words a raspy whisper and filled with desire. He fists my ponytail around his hand, he tugs my head back. A bite of pain shoots through my skull, but the pleasure is incredible. "You like that baby? Do you like when I fuck you hard?"

"Yes." I hiss my reply. The coil tightens in my core and I push back onto him. We're matched as I meet him thrust for thrust. My grip on the counter tightens and my knuckles are white as I hold on. Lucien is relentless as he drives into me, pinning me against the hard surface. His cock is so deep, hitting that sweet spot that's about to push me over the edge.

"That's it, baby, milk that fucking cock. Give it to me, give me your pleasure!" His command sends me spiraling out of control and over the edge as my orgasm splinters through me. Shattering me into tiny pieces and I cry out his name.

"Lucien!" He tugs me up by my hair, my back is flush against his chest, and his heart is hammering in his chest. His lips at my ear, his teeth graze the sensitive skin on my neck as he growls.

"I love fucking you, sweetness." He slams up into me, hitting my sweet spot and I clench around him again. My knees buckle and his arm snakes around my waist holding me up, his release coating me, marking me, claiming me. "My lumiére." We stay that way for what feels like hours, my breathing is fast and my knees are shaky.

"Wow." Is all I can whisper and Lucien chuckles. As soon as he slips out of me, I feel empty. He scoops me up and walks me to the bedroom. Lucien lays me on the bed, gently. Such a contradiction to what we just did. I watch him walk into the bathroom. When he joins me, he has a warm wet cloth and softly wipes between my legs.

"Are you okay, sweetness?" I nod and smile. He always asks me that after he's taken me. It's the first time that I have been with someone as rough and dominant, but I like it. I love giving him the control.

"I am. You always ask me that and the answer will always be the same." He leans in and plants a soft kiss on my lips. His tongue licks at the seam of my lips and I grant him access. My fingers tangle in his messy, just fucked hair and I tug him to me, as I mold myself to him.

When he pulls away, I am breathless and ready for round two. He makes me insatiable. I wonder if he feels the same about me. He's said that he wants me and aches for me, but will he ever love me? It's too soon to think about that. I roll over in bed before he comes back and I feel him slip in behind me. His arm bands around my waist, pulling me into the curve of his body. "Goodnight gorgeous." He breathes in my ear and it sends shivers down my spine.

"Goodnight handsome."

Lucien

There was something about the way we fucked earlier. It was incredible. The way Cassie let me take her. I was rough, more than I have been before, but she didn't relent. She gave me her body, and that was more than I could have ever asked for. Lying in bed after our talk was good, I am calmer now. Even though Claudia won't stop, Cassie knows the truth, well most of it. There are other secrets I need to tell her, but those will have to wait.

It's just gone 2 am, and Cassie is asleep next to me. Her apartment is small, quiet, but for some reason I can't sleep. I have been staring at the ceiling for hours. There are things I need to take care of. I hope that Claudia will give up her fucking sick game of trying to ruin my life. It's not like she's my mother. I suppose that's another story.

I realize Sasha will try her luck at every turn. She's had it in for me since that night. Fuck, I was such an idiot. *You enjoyed it. You love the pain. Hurting them. When they cry and scream. Fuck off!* I can't do this anymore; this darkness is taking hold of me. Without waking Cassie, I slide out of bed, and pad to the living room. I grab my phone and call Jayce. On the second ring, he answers.

"You okay?" He's always concerned when I call him so late.

"Yes, I told Cassie about me and Sasha, not the full story, it's too soon for that." With my thumb and forefinger, I pinch the bridge of my nose. He will not like that I haven't told her everything. Although she needs the truth, I just can't bring myself to tell her and see the pain and pity in her eyes because that's all she will give me.

"Luke, I like Cassie, she's sweet, but she will not put up with you not being honest with her. I think she deserves the truth."

"Why? So you can swoop in and rescue her from me?" As soon as the words are out, I realize what a dick move it was to say that. "Look Jay, I am sorry man. I didn't mean it like that. You're the only one I would trust her with." And I do. I trust Jayce with my life and ultimately with Cassie's life. He will never hurt her; he's proven himself over and over again, since we were kids.

"I know. I wouldn't do that to you anyway. Just don't give me a reason to." His words anger me more than I would like to admit. The thought of him looking after her fills me with jealousy that can't be matched with anything I ever felt before. I nod slowly while staring out of the patio doors. It's dark out, just like my soul when I am not with her. There is no way I can be without her. "I better go. I don't want to wake her."

"You have a sexy sweet girl in bed and you're here talking to me? Seriously dude, you need to get your priorities straight." He chuckles and I can't help smiling. Jayce is ever the playboy, he's been single for too long. I keep telling him to find a girl, fall in love, but he's just like me, too much in his past doesn't allow him the pleasure.

"Yea, I am. I think I finally am. Catch you up tomorrow." I shut my phone off, place it on the table, and join my sexy girl in bed. As soon as I slip in beside her, I hear her murmur my name. I wrap her in my arms, tugging her back against my chest. Her warm supple body feels like heaven against me. I close my eyes and let sleep take over. I just hope that tonight the dreams stay away.

Cassandra

My eyes open to the sun streaming through my bedroom window. There is a warm body wrapped around me, I roll over and am met with sparkling green eyes. "Good morning sweetness." Lucien's sleepy voice made me smile. I glance at his face, its pure perfection. His gaze makes my heart thump just a little faster. He really was gorgeous. His smile, which deepened his dimples was perfect, and I couldn't help staring at this handsome man next to me.

"Good morning handsome." I smile and lean forward to kiss him. He wraps both his arms around me and pulls me into his chest. I giggle as his fingers tickled down my spine and ribs.

"I love waking up next to you." His tongue licks at my lips and I open to him. Our mouths crash into each other and the kiss grows more urgent. A low moan escapes my lips and into the kiss. *How has he turned me into an insatiable wanton slut? I am addicted to him. All he does is fuel the fire inside me.* The ache between my legs was unrelenting, and I wanted breakfast in bed, which didn't involve any food. As I pull away from him, our eyes meet. His intense gaze has me squirming.

"And I love waking up next to you. You're so warm." I smile at his expression.

"I am warm? You keep me around because you lack a radiator?" I giggle at him and nod. "Oh, really?" He rolls us over and he is above me. Lucien kneels, without breaking our gaze, grasps my wrists and holds them above my head. He pushes his thigh between my legs, and rubs against my core. I whimper at the welcome intrusion. My hips buck, and I blatantly hump his muscular thigh. "We will have to see about that, sweetness." He tightens his hold on my wrists and I tingle in anticipation of what's coming. At this rate, it will be me. Tugging my tank top up to my wrists so they're now bound by the flimsy material. "Your hands stay there; do you hear me?" I nod. "Good girl. Close your eyes." I obey his command; my body is already humming in anticipation. His hands caress my skin, from my arms down my sides. It tickles, and I am tempted to move my arms, but he told me not to. His touch is light and my body is bowing off the bed as my back arches to him. "Mmmm, you're so beautiful."

"Lucien," I breathe his name and the bed dips as he moves. His fingertips on my legs, caressing my thighs. His touch sends sparks to every nerve in my body. He then moves to my side and I feel his kisses at my knees. With a gentle yet firm grasp, he grabs both my ankles, and bends my legs at the knee. He is kneeling between my splayed thighs. The roughness of his stubble on my inner thigh makes me gasp and my hips lift off the bed.

"Please?" I beg him. He knows I need him to touch me, lick me, and fuck me.

"It's okay sweetness, I will take care of you." His words held more promise than we both realized. Then his warm mouth came down on my heated core and devoured me, licking and sucking my bare pussy. He flattened his tongue against me, lapping and laving at the arousal he was eliciting from my body. Everything he does turns me on like nothing ever did, or ever could. He slowly slid two fingers inside me, back and forth. My body clenched around him. "That's it. Come for me baby; give me your sweet honey." My body shuddered with a violent orgasm, but he didn't relent. He licked me clean, but continued to finger my tight entrance. "I want every ounce of your pleasure. Only for me. All mine. This tight little cunt is mine." I moaned, bucking my hips in rhythm with his fingers thrusting into me. "Again." His command sent me spiraling again, and another orgasm splintered through me. When my body stopped shaking, he slowly pulled his fingers from my pussy. "Open your eyes."

I did and watched him lick my arousal from his fingers. He leaned down to kiss me and I tasted myself on his lips and tongue. He suddenly plunged into me without warning. His rock hard cock filling me so deep, I almost came undone for a third time. "You are perfect." His eyes locked on mine, but his words shook me. I wasn't perfect. He didn't know that. I closed my eyes and focused on his movements instead. The way he filled my core. We fit together like puzzle pieces and I never wanted to lose this. The feeling of being completely and utterly whole again. I was so close to the edge when he uttered the words with his own release that finally sent me over as we both found release.

"You complete me." His words shattered through my heart and deep into my soul rendering me speechless.

Chapter twelve

Lucien

The past four months since the weekend we spent in Hawaii were indescribable. After the incident with Claudia telling Cassie about my alleged engagement, she seemed to stay away. I hope she accepted I was with Cassie although I don't believe that's the reason for her silence. I still haven't told Cassie about my past, the demons that lay there have been dormant since she's been sleeping next to me every night.

There were so many things still playing on my mind, but my fight with my demons and secrets seemed to disappear when I was with her. I didn't worry about things. The nightmares didn't plague me.

She's been seeing a psychiatrist, and although I fight the urge to ask her about it every day, I have given her the time she needs. I can't expect her to be forthcoming with something that's hurting her when I haven't told her everything about me. My feelings for her are strong, there are times I want to say those three words to her, but I am holding back. Is four months even time enough to really feel that for someone? Or am I kidding myself? Jayce even wondered if I had gone soft. I suppose maybe I have.

It's October and we're heading into winter, although it doesn't get as cold here as it does on the East Coast. I remember spending time in New York, not far from where Cassie lived and freezing my ass off, that is why I live in LA. "Baby." As I walk into the bedroom, I find Cassie sitting on the floor; she has her hair in a messy bun on top of her head. She's got wrapping all over the floor with ribbons, tape, scissors and she's trying to hold a corner of the wrapping down while tearing a piece of the tape from a small roll. "What are you doing?" I lean against the door and fold my arms across my chest.

"It's for Jayce." She huffs and glances up at me. She has a small piece of tape stuck to her cheek and I can't help chuckling. Jay and her have become close friends. I warned him that if ever his hands or his wandering cock zoned in on my girl, I will cut them off and feed them to him on a platter. To which he told me that I would have to catch him first. Cheeky fucker. He was a track star at university whereas I was the one in art class and learning about publishing.

"Mmm, if you spend any more time with him, I might worry about it." My gaze drifting over her. I grab my T-shirt and jeans, and make my way to the bathroom, when she calls after me.

"You should always worry, Mr. Verán." Her giggle filters to me, it's a melody I want on repeat. As I stare at my reflection, there is humor dancing in my eyes. She needs a fucking spanking for that and I want to give her one. Right now. With a tug I pull off the tank top I am wearing, I walk back into the bedroom wearing my black sweats. When she glances up, I can tell she recognizes the wicked look in my eyes. A blush spreads across her cheeks. *That's right darling, I will make that pretty little ass pink.*

"What was that, Ms. Winters?" I grasp her wrist, tugging her up. Once her body is flush with mine, I seal her mouth, licking into her sweetness. As soon as I pull away, I lift her and throw her over my shoulder and carry her to the play room. She's giggling and squealing.

"Put me down!" *You want to tease me baby, just wait and see what the teasing does.* I love doling out her punishment. She's taken to my dominance like a fish to water. It's almost as if I have eventually met my match, she challenges me enough to let me know she's no push over, but she always submits when I command her. My mind is always thinking of new fun ways to tease her, to push her out of that comfort zone, without scaring her off completely.

I set her down at the edge of the bed, spinning her to face me. Our eyes meet and I can see the challenge in those mocha eyes that seem to have a hold on me that I can't explain. There were many times I wanted to walk away. To let her get on with her life and find someone who would better suit her. I did it once, almost walked out, but the pain in my chest and my heart couldn't take being away from her.

"Turn and face the patio doors." My voice commands in a low timbre and she obeys. The sweetest submissive I have ever come across. *Mine. Always mine.* "Close your eyes." When her eyes close, I grab the soft black silk blindfold. With a small knot, I tie it around her head.

I grip her sundress and pull it up and over her head. She's dressed in just a tiny pair of pink panties and bra to match. The soft color of the material is a contrast on her beautiful tanned skin. She's spent a lot of time outdoors and on shoots these past few months and I can't help admiring the way her skin is a soft brown. Compared to most girls I have been with she's striking, beautiful and intelligent.

I groan inwardly at the way her chest is rising and falling. Her breathing is heavy and I realize she's turned on in anticipation from what I am about to do to her. I grab a set of cuffs from the chest of drawers. A small whimper escapes her mouth and I can't help smiling. *Yes, baby, you will get a spanking.*

I guide her forward to the small table at the glass doors. The sun is low on the horizon; the sky is a deep red and darkening by the minute. Placing my hand on her back between her shoulder blades, I push her down gently. Her body pliable as she bends over, I secure her wrists to the table legs on either side.

"You going to be a good girl for me today, lumiére?" She nods. *Good Girl.*

With an excruciating slow movement, I tug her panties down. The scent of her arousal is intoxicating. *Fucking hell, she's soaked already. So fucking perfect in so many ways.* Once she's stepped out of them, I stand back, and leave her for a few minutes. The anticipation has her trembling. The fear of not knowing what will happen is sending small shivers through her. I grab the crop from the walk-in closet and stride towards her. "What did you call me, Cassandra?"

"I… didn't…" Trailing the soft leather over her back, goose bumps rise over her smooth skin. *My sweet, sweet Cassie.* Her little peach ass looks so fucking good. I lift the crop and bring it down on her ass. Her moans are music to my ears.

"Cassandra, what did you call me?" My voice is raspy; she can hear the edge in my tone. I am about to crack, and I am definitely in the mood for a game right now. So if she's willing to play so am I. The teasing about Jayce and the way she says my name is driving me insane. I turn to the sound system in the room and turn on the iPod in the dock.

The acoustic guitar sound fills the room. I take a deep breath to calm the painful erection tenting my sweats. Cassie is quiet, but when I turn to her, I can see her knees trembling. The lyrics wash over us.

Never opened myself this way
Life is ours, we live it our way
All these words I don't just say
And nothing else matters

Trust I seek and I find in you
Every day for us something new
Open mind for a different view
And nothing else matters

    I walk back to Cassie; she looks incredible bent over the table. Her beautiful ass is sticking up, and she's bound, just the way I like her. It's been over a week since we've been in here and I think today it will take all my energy not to lose complete control. "Cassandra, for the last time, what did you call me?" My hand is trembling as I run the crop over her back, down her spine, sending shivers over her. I lift it again letting it come down hard on her smooth ass cheek. The soft skin turning pink. I wish it was my hand marking her, but I want her to feel the smooth leather of the crop. *She's so fucking beautiful.*
    "I… called you… Mr. Verán." She whispers and another sting on her ass has her whimpering loudly. "Luke…" Her voice is so low.
    "Quiet." My order is harsh, but she knows I am not angry. I am just so fucking turned on. My cock is a steel rod, only for her. It's taking every ounce of restraint to not fuck her hard. Until she's screaming so loud the whole of Los Angeles will know my fucking name. She struggles on the restraints, but she can't move very far. I rain down another four whacks to her ass and the small shape of the crop is pinking it. Her moans are loud now, she's soaked. I move the crop to the top of her thighs. Her gasp is knowing what I have in store for her now. As soon as the edge of the crop comes down on the apex between her thighs, she cries out my name. "Now, do you understand why you shouldn't tease me about Jayce?" She's speechless, giving me a quick nod.
    Back at the chest of drawers, I grab the small black vibrator. "My little tigress needs her punishment. You're going to purr for me aren't you, sweetness." The small whimper that escapes her lips has my cock twitching. I turn on the vibrator; the buzzing sound has her gasping. "Do you want more, Cassandra?" She nods. *Good girl.* I kneel behind her, my breath on her core makes her tug on the restraints. She can't move, but she definitely tries. "Now tell me, do you want Jayce?" She's shaking her head so furiously the table rocks. I smile. Without warning I move the tip of the vibrator over her smooth little cunt, and her body tenses. I slide it inside her in a slow measured stroke, and she tries to push back on it. When it reaches her clit, I push my tongue inside her molten core. Her honey is dripping down my tongue and the inside of her thighs. "Would you like someone else to touch you like this, lumiére?" I lap at her slick lips again.
    "No, Sir." She moans and I chuckle against her soft folds. She's a quivering mess, just the way I like her. Her body tightens around my tongue, she's close and I pull away. The quiet huff doesn't go unnoticed as I wait a beat before I push the vibrator against her clit again. Her thighs are trembling and she's begging me now. "Please, Sir, please?"
    "Please what, Cassandra? Tell me what you need?" My fingers slide over her wet little cunt; she's literally dripping into my hand. *Oh God, this is going to be so fucking good.* I

lift my hand, and rain down four whacks on her pert ass. My cock is aching to be inside her heat. I rise and push my sweats down. Once I step out of them, my body trembles at the thought of being inside her.

"Fuck me! Please, Sir." She pleads with me again, but she knows what I want to hear. I ignore the begging and carry on teasing her. Running my hand over her back, I massage her red ass cheeks. Slowly and tenderly while stroking the vibrator over her beautiful pulsing pink flesh.

"Tell me."

Two words.

One command.

She answers.

"Fuck me! Fix me! I need you Lucien! Fuck me!" Her voice is so loud it booms through the room. "Please?" Her voice drops to a small whisper. It's raspy and sexy. Not being able to stop myself anymore, I drop the vibrator, and stand behind her. With a tight grip on my cock, I slide it over her entrance.

She tries to push back against me and I slap her ass hard. "I am in charge, remember that." With a slow teasing stroke, I push inside her inch by unforgiving inch. The song reaches the chorus again, my timing is impeccable and as soon as the words wash over me. I slam into her. Deep and hard.

"Lucien!" She cries out and her cunt tightens around me, milking me for my release. *Not yet darling.* I grip her hips and hold her in place as my cock drives into her. Faster and deeper, giving her my full ten inches. I pull out and slam in, over and over again. My own release shooting down my spine. The heat of her tight pussy around my cock is too much. Her body tightens around me like a vice and I realize she's close. My sweet Cassie, she's become my dirty little submissive, letting me have my wicked way with her. She calms my demons inside.

The dark lyrics of the song resound in the room as I impale her on my cock. Faster and faster. "Come my lumiére! Fucking come with me!" I growl as she lets go. Her orgasm splintering her into tiny pieces in my hands as I fill her sweet little cunt with my release.

It takes everything to regain my composure. My pulse is skittering like a race horse. Cassie's body stops trembling after a long moment. When I slip out of her, I undo the cuffs and circle her waist with my arm. Her body flush with mine, I scoop her up and walk to the bed. She tugs off the blindfold, blinks and smiles at me. I lay her down gently and lift each wrist, kissing them softly. As I do this I need to check for any bruising, but there's none. "Are you okay, sweetness?" My eyes meet hers and she shrugs. My heart constricts with fear thinking I hurt her when she giggles.

"That was incredible. Why do you always ask me if I am okay? Seriously." Her voice is filled with amusement. I pull her against me. There is no way I can even begin explaining what happened. To tell her why, I am always so concerned with her safety, besides the things we do, my past is not something to take lightly.

Cassandra

It's almost time to head home, the day has been long and all I want to do is go home and put my feet up. Last night was another incredible experience in the play room. I shouldn't be thinking about it at work because I am already aching for Lucien.

Since the incident with Claudia, he's been attentive, romantic, and the sex is incredible. Deep down I see he still struggles with his demons. We haven't really confessed anything yet, but I realize at some point we have to get to that. There are moments when I recognize a darkness in his eyes. He's been taking it slow with me. Lucien takes me to new heights in the bedroom, the ridiculously naughty side of him is something I love, and I trust him. With my body, mind and heart. He's taken every part of me. Possesses me in ways that I have never had with anyone. He won't hurt me and I love that part of him, his darker more dominating side.

I haven't brought up my story yet, I am not ready to see the shame in his eyes. My new doctor has been incredible, and I am lucky to have found her. Dr Kessel would rather put me on my anti-depressants, but I despise them. Things have been wonderful and I haven't had any panic attacks, so, I didn't think I needed them. After what happened with my parents and my ex-fiancé, I am content for the first time in two years. Kenna arrives tomorrow, since her job was delayed, we haven't seen each other in such a long time. Lucien said we would go to the airport together. It's Friday, and I am worn out from the long week. We just finished another shoot. As tiring as being on location is, I love it. Lucien let me run with the shoots, saying I could deal with it and his belief in me gave me so much confidence. Jayce said he wouldn't work with anyone else. Although, I think he said that to piss Lucien off, he does that often.

"Sweetness?" I shift to find Lucien in my office. His voice pulling me from my thoughts. I am ready for dinner and the sofa tonight. He agreed to cook. Most of the team found out about us as soon as we got back. Lucien wasn't the most discreet. He sent me flowers, and he spent every free moment he had at my desk. It was sweet, and I loved it. I mean, of course I did! My eyes meet his beautiful green ones and I smile. He always looked so handsome.

"Hey handsome, I am almost ready. I need to send this email then we can leave." He nods.

"I will make a call," he walks off allowing me to finish up. I hit send on the email to Jayce for the shoot coming up a week from now. We are heading up to Napa Valley, I can't wait to visit the wineries up there. I shut down my laptop and slip it into my bag when my phone buzzes. *Don't answer, it's after hours!* Ignoring my inner crazy, I pick up the phone. "Cassie Winters, how can I help you?"

"You need to fuck off! Leave my man alone, or I will reveal your fucked up secrets." A voice so shrill like someone had poured ice water over me.

"Who is this?"

"I am meant to be with Lucien. You are not. You're nothing. He's merely fucking you because he's bored. Do you know that he loves me? He tells me every day." I was shaking. *Who the fuck was this? I knew no one in Lucien's life that would stake a claim like this. Not even his ex. Sasha is seeing someone now. Cassie, just hang up!*

"Look I don't care who you are, but you need to lay off me and Lucien." I hang up before she could respond. *Do I tell him?* No, I can handle this. Whoever she is, she's just trying to scare me. Nothing will separate us. I won't let it. I can't lose him now.

"You okay sweetness?" I glance up and smile.

"Yes, let's go." I wouldn't tell him about this, not yet. It would sort itself out, and I can handle it myself. I round my desk and walk into his waiting arms.

"I can't wait to get you home, tie you to the bed and lick your sweet wet little cunt till you come on my tongue." My gasp is loud at his illicit promise, and I squirm to ease the ache between my legs. He always does this, if I am sad or in a bad mood, he makes me come in the most delicious ways. He keeps me on edge until I am begging and pleading for him to take me. To fix me in the only way he can.

"Lucien, do you have to do that here?" I look around and notice that there are still people in the office. My face heats when I lock eyes with one guy that's sat right outside my office. There is no way he would have heard that, but I am still embarrassed.

Lucien pushes my door closed with a loud slam and I am flush against the wall of my office. He pins me with his hips and his hard cock presses against my stomach. I let out a whimper. His mouth crashes down on mine, and I tangle my fingers in his hair. I tug him closer, his tongue licks into me and I can't help arching my back, pressing my body into his. He reaches down, tugging the hem of my dress up running a hand up my inner thigh. A low moan rumbles in his throat when he finds my heat. I suck his tongue into my mouth, I mimic the movement as if I was sucking on his cock. His fingers stroke my core through my soft lace panties and I am climbing higher and higher. The need for release is so strong, and I almost reach it when there's a knock on the office door. *Shit!* Pulling away reluctantly, we're both breathless. I tug my dress down and run my fingers through my hair. "Give me a minute." I call out to whoever is at the door.

Lucien leans in and whispers. "I hope that made you feel better." He winks and plants a soft chaste kiss on my swollen lips. The burn of his stubble is still tingling on my chin.

"You're insufferable!" I swat his arm and he chuckles.

"But you enjoy it." I open the door and am met with sky-blue eyes. "Jayce, I… uhm… What are you doing here?" I glance between the two men, hoping that nothing sets them off again. Lucien still gets bouts of jealousy over my friendship with Jayce.

"Just wanted to drop these off. See you Monday." He hands me a folder and stalks off. There's no hiding what was going on in my office only moments ago, and it seems that it affected him more than I thought it would.

"Let's go, sweetness." Luke tugs my arm and we make our way to the elevator. As the car descends, we walk out towards Robert and the waiting car. As we pulled up to Lucien's apartment ten minutes later I realize how tired I am. We were heading to the airport early in the morning to pick Kenna up, so staying with him made sense. I couldn't wait to see my best friend.

I flop down on the sofa, staring at the wall, my mind is on the call I received earlier. "Are you sure you're okay, sweetness? You look stressed?" Lucien slips in behind me, his thighs either side of my hips. His hands softly knead my shoulders, rubbing out the knots. I turn the TV on and flip through the channels, trying to find something of interest to watch. Lucien was distracting me with his fingers and a moan escapes my lips.

"Yes, it's just been a long week." *Tell him about the phone call! No! I don't want to upset him. It will be fine.* I close my eyes savoring the pressure of his thumbs on my neck. When I move my hair over my shoulder giving him access to my stiff shoulders, his fingers work their magic on me. Another moan escapes my lips and I lean into him.

"Mmmm, I can help with that, but before we do I need to talk to you about something." His voice is soft in my ear, but there's something in his tone that has tension returning to my shoulders. My eyes shoot open and I whirl around. His tone is overly tentative. There's something wrong. As soon as my gaze finds his, my heart drops. *Oh no! What now?*

"What is it, Lucien?"

"My mother is having a charity ball on Sunday. Since, I am director of Verán

Publishing, I have to be there. So, I was hoping you would be the lady on my arm?" I giggled at his choice of words as he teased my shoulder blade with a knuckle. His gaze is soft and tender and I realize he is trying to assess my reaction to the mention of Claudia Verán. There is something about that woman that unnerves me. Even though she hasn't done anything after the failed attempt at telling me about Lucien's apparent engagement.

"Yes, who else would be your date? And why would that be an issue?" I cock my head to the side. He is hiding something; he hasn't told me the whole story. His hand now caressing my back, the next words out of his mouth send all my relaxation out the window.

"Because she's invited Sasha." I stare at him, opening my mouth and closing it again. *Cassie come on, he asked you to go with him! She will be there! I can show her he's mine! Yes! She has a boyfriend!* I will once and for all make sure his mother and his ex, realize I am not letting him go. I need to play it cool. This shouldn't be a problem, and it won't be because I will not let it get to me. No panic attacks, no stress and certainly no second thoughts about Claudia or Sasha.

"No problem," I shrug and twist my back to him so he can continue massaging me.

"That's it?" His voice is one of shock and I suppress a giggle. It's obvious he was stressed about telling me about the event, but he needs to realize that I am happy with him and nothing will change that. My nonchalance has stunned him, and I can only imagine his facial expression. I grin. Without answering the question, I settle on MTV and see one of my favorite videos come up. Always by Bon Jovi. Lucien's hands still as he leans forward. His lips graze my earlobe, sending a rush of heat over my skin.

"Want me to grow my hair like that?" He points at the guy on screen who is painting on a large white canvas, with the shoulder length dark hair and I giggle.

"Nope, I prefer your hair messy and spikey." I lean backward, into him and his warmth envelopes me. His lips find the sweet spot on my neck as he licks and nips at the skin. My core pulses with need and desire shoots through me and gathers in my panties. I love how he can turn me on with such a slight action. Reaching back, I place my hands on his thighs and stroke them.

"I am taking you upstairs now. I need to be inside you." He lifts me up and stands behind me. Unzipping my blue knee-length dress and slipping it off my shoulders. An audible growl rumbles from his chest when the dress pools at my feet. "Jesus, Cassie, did you wear that to work?" He turns me around and takes in the strapless black lace corset and matching panties. Still wearing my heels, and the lace lingerie, his expression tells me he approves.

"I did, Mr. Verán, why?" I breathe the name that will have his dark dominance surface. His eyes blaze with need and desire. My nipples pebble against the rough material of the corset.

He leans in and his breath on my ear sends shivers over my skin. "Because if I had known, I would have ordered you to my office, bent you over my desk and fucked you so hard you wouldn't be able to walk back to your desk." His voice is laced with a dark desire and the words come out as a primal growl. I squirm in front of him. Squeezing my thighs together, I know that we're heading to the play room, because the animal I have just unleashed will make me scream in the best way possible.

I drop to my knees, undoing the black leather belt and unbuttoning his pants. I tug them down his toned thighs along with his tight black briefs. He practically rips his shirt off; my eyes rake over the sculpted planes of his abs. His beautiful V muscles pointing to my reward. I lick my lips, keeping eye contact with him. He loves watching me. Fisting his cock in my hand, I stroke him in slow tortured movements and his head drops back. A deep primal growl rumbles in his chest and I can't help getting turned on from giving him pleasure. I lick him from base to tip and he growls again. "Fuck, baby."

I flick my tongue over the moisture on the tip and savor his arousal leaking out. Without breaking eye contact I suck him into my mouth, I take him as deep as I can. I love the taste of him; all I can think of, is feeling him inside me. My mouth moves up and down sucking and licking my way over the ridges and thick vein running along the bottom of his shaft. Lucien's fingers tangle in my hair, taking complete control of me. He plunges into my mouth, hitting the back of my throat. My hands grip his toned ass, as he fucks my mouth, faster and deeper. His groans are deep and when his eyes meet mine, they're black with lust.

He pulls me off his cock and lifts me up suddenly and we are now face-to-face. "I need to fuck your tight pussy. You're wet for me aren't you, sweetness?" I open my mouth to speak, but he interrupts me, sealing my mouth with his. His tongue licking into my mouth, I show his tongue the same attention I gave his cock.

Without breaking contact with my mouth as he lifts me by my ass. I wrap my legs around his taut waist as he makes his way to the play room and sets me down at the foot end of the bed. "Take off your panties, not the corset. Sit on the bed." I obey, sliding my black lace panties down my thighs; I sit on the bed and watch him. He's completely naked and I have to lick my lips. He really is impeccable and totally irresistible.

Lucien turns and his eyes lock on mine. The lust in his gaze matches my own. I need him. Nobody has ever made me ache, made me need or made me fall so deep and so hard. "Touch yourself, slowly." Without question, my fingers move between my legs. My arousal soaks my fingers. Lucien's tongue flicks out as he licks his lips, his gaze trained on my fingers. "Stop. I want you to stand, give me your hands." I stand and reach my hands out to him. He licks my fingers clean and then closes my wrists together. The lock clicks the thick soft leather cuffs, my arms bound together. "I want to see how much you can handle. Close your eyes." My eyes flutter closed, with the black silk blindfold in place, my body hums. My pulse quickens when I hear the heavy clang from above me. "What is your safe word?"

"Summer." Chewing the inside of my cheek to keep from smiling.

"Good girl."

"Thank you, Sir." I breathe the words and he groans. My body is trembling, not from fear, but from the delicious anticipation of what Lucien is planning. He moves around the room again and suddenly his heat is at my chest. Without instruction, he raises my hands and secures the leather cuffs to something and locks them in place. I am now secured with my arms above my head.

"Now, sweetness, do you like teasing me with lingerie?" His voice is at my ear and I whimper.

"Yes, Sir." I breathe.

"Mmmm," he caresses my ass, both hands moving in sensual circles. The angle of my arms allows my breasts to lift out of the corset. I wriggle at his touch. My skin is on fire where his fingertips trail, my body is humming with desire, he lifts his hand and with an abrupt swat, it comes down hard on my ass. I tug at my arms, but I am at his mercy. His hand comes down on the other cheek of my ass and I whimper again. I am thoroughly soaked. He grasps my neck and pushes his erection against my ass. The need to tease him overcomes me, I push back against him, eliciting a growl from him.

His grip on my neck tightens and I push back again. "You make me so fucking hard, sweetness." He breathes in my ear. "Do you hear me?" I nod. "When I fuck you now, it will be deep, hard, and it will be primal. You will scream so loud, when I pull your release from your soul. You will take every fucking inch of me."

My core tightens and pulses. The ache is so intense; tears roll down my cheeks. He releases my neck, the room is so quiet, but I can't hear him moving. Suddenly he's in front of me, his breath on my face. His hands on either side of my arms. With a soft trail from my elbows down my body, his touch is light, sending shivers over my skin. Goose bumps rise on every inch of my body. My moans are getting louder as I repeat his name, over, and over again. His hot breath moves down my body until he reaches my pussy. "You smell so fucking delicious." He nudges my legs apart, with his lips above my entrance he plants a soft kiss on me. I am about to come undone.

"Please, Sir?" I beg, my voice rising in desperation. I need him inside me. "I can't anymore."

"What sweetness? I am just teasing you like you tease me." The delight in his voice is evident. He loves teasing me until I am begging him to fuck me. His index finger strokes my slick folds and I whimper again. The knot in my belly is wound so tight. His tongue laps at my entrance. My legs open shamelessly as I buck my hips towards him, trying to get the pressure I need to find my release. All too soon, he stands up and moves so his body is flush with mine. His hand cupping my heated entrance, "Do you need me here, sweetness?" I nod so fast, I am dizzy. "How much do you need me?" He rips off the blindfold. My eyes fly open and I see the pleasure in his heated stare. He is enjoying this game. His other hand gripping my neck as he holds me in place. I can't move, and I don't want to.

"Please, Lucien, I need you please?" I am close to tears again from the intensity of him.

"Good." Suddenly he plunges two fingers inside me and I cry out as an earth shattering orgasm rips into me which sends me spiraling. My eyes slam shut and I see stars at the back of my eyelids. The world spins on its axis as my body shakes. "You are fucking gorgeous." His voice is hoarse. As my orgasm subsides, he pulls his fingers from my soaked core, he places his index finger at my lips, and I suck his finger into my mouth tasting myself. "My fucking dirty girl." I look into his dark green eyes as they stare into my heart. There is something distinct about him tonight, but I can't quite put my finger on it. It's like he's showing me something, him. This man has a hold on every depth of my soul and I know that he will forever be ingrained in me.

I glance down, he's naked and rock hard. "Wrap your legs around me." He orders and holds me up. I wrap my thighs around his taut waist and he slides into me all the way to the hilt of his magnificent cock. Our eyes lock and his thrusts are slow and torturous. His restraint is barely there. I am climbing again. He is incredible. All I can do to keep from coming undone is to concentrate on all the emotions he is sending through me. Fucking his love into me, in such a way it's the most intense moment we've ever shared. His left hand reaches up and twists my hard nipples. With short tweaks and tugs that send delicious jolts to my core.

"My lumiére," he slams into me faster and harder. His movements speed up and our connection is sizzling. I tighten around him, squeezing him, demanding the release that only he can give me. I realize in that very moment, I love him, and it terrifies me. He looks amazing as his body stiffens. "Come with me my lumiére. Mon Dieu tu es belle," his accent is heavy with lust and my release washes over me as he comes inside me. Our release shatters us both in unison. I scream his name so loud, I am sure the neighbors heard me. My body is shaking; Lucien holds me tight to his chest as my orgasm shudders through me.

Lucien

I stand there holding her for a moment. Not wanting to slip out of her body just yet. She feels too fucking good. This feels too fucking perfect. The way I need her is unnerving. She needs to ache for me the way I ache for her. Our two broken souls fusing into one. *This girl will break me more than I ever thought possible. She's the brightest light in my life, but she's also my darkest desire.*

"Cassie…" I want to tell her I love her, but my fear silences me. It's in her eyes. The love she has for me. You can't love me, baby. I wish I didn't love you, but I do. I want to be with you so much it's ripping me to shreds. Once you know my secrets, there won't ever be turning back. You will never be able to accept me. I know you won't. God, my heart is in my throat. I love this girl. My eyes glaze over with unshed tears, shaking my head, I try to clear the thoughts that seem to invade my mind. I can't love. I don't love. It's just lust. Four months of undeniably amazing lust. "Are you okay?"

She nods. A shy smile curls her sweet lips. I unhook the cuffs, her arms fall around my neck and I sit her on the bed. Kneeling in front of her, unlocking her wrists, kissing each one softly.

"Lucien," she stares down at me with those big chocolate eyes, my resolve crumbles and all I want to do is love her. I want to let go completely, but there's no way I can. Because losing her isn't an option, but I know it will come, eventually. I am just delaying the inevitable.

"What's wrong baby?" My heart constricts. *I hurt her. Fuck!*

"I—" The phone buzzes interrupting us. "Go, it's okay. Seriously. Go. We can talk after. Go." She smiles and I grab a pair of jeans from the chair. Once I tug them on, I glance at her again. I don't know if she's just putting on a brave face, but she shrugs nonchalantly.

"Be right back okay?" Leaning down I plant a soft kiss on her nose and run down to the door.

My phone stops ringing as soon as I get to it. With a quick glance at my missed calls, I find it's only Jayce. I will call him later. My need to get back to Cassie grows as I walk back up the staircase. I find her still sitting on the bed. "Baby? Are you okay?" I kneel at her feet and my hands on her soft smooth thighs.

"Lucien…" Her eyes shine when she meets my intense gaze. My heart is pounding in my chest. "You're incredible." I burst out laughing, letting out a breath I had no idea I was holding. The tension leaves my body and I grab her for a kiss.

"You fucking scared me baby, don't do that again. I thought I hurt you."

"Of course not. I love every… moment with you." A blush spreads across her cheeks.

"Moment?" Cocking my head to the side, I watch her intently. The intrigue and suspense of her explanation is pulling me in. The amusement in her eyes at my question is unmistakable, but she doesn't respond.

"Can we talk later? Like, when I am not sitting naked on the bed with you kneeling at my feet."

I chuckle. As I rise, I pull her into my arms, she always molds to my body like she

113

was always meant to be there. I suppose she was. My lumiére. "Are you hungry? I can make us something to eat unless you want to go out?" Her eyes are shining and the blush on her cheeks make me smile. I put that there. She looks happy, content and satisfied.

"Dinner in, with my man." Her sassy tongue is back, and she strides out of the room, butt naked. *Yes, she will be the death of me.* I make my way downstairs to the kitchen and grab my phone.

Jayce answers on the first ring. "Seriously, you need to stop with ignoring me!" He can be so fucking dramatic sometimes. I didn't answer one call.

"Yea, yea, what's up?" I slip into the chair at the counter; somehow, I know why he's calling.

"Are you going on Sunday?"

I lower my voice whispering into the phone. "Yea, you know that I have to be there." With the phone between my shoulder and ear, I grab ingredients for dinner, and set it down on the counter. Tomorrow will be a royal fuck up. I know Sasha is trying her utmost to act like she's not bothered about Cassie and me, since she's got herself a boy toy, but something doesn't feel right. Claudia on the other hand will be claws out, and I am ready for her.

"I will be there with bells on. Can't wait to see how it plays out."

"Oh yea, don't you just love drama." Jayce chuckles and I know that he is looking forward to a show down with me and Claudia. We haven't seen each other in two months and this would be the first event that Cassie and I will attend as a couple. It's official. I am in a relationship and I know that it will be an interesting evening.

CHAPTER thirteen

Cassandra

"Lucien, come on!" I am standing at the door, we were supposed to leave fifteen minutes ago and I am impatient. He does this on purpose, to frustrate me. One of my pet peeves is being late and he loves to make sure that I am fuming by the time we get in the car.

"Yes, sweetness. Don't panic, we will be there on time." He gives me a cheeky wink and a panty melting grin, dimples included and I fight off the urge to smile. I glare at him while chewing on my lip. Those green eyes fall to my lips and I can't help poking my tongue out at him. He grabs the keys, and we make our way out to the garage.

Lucien unlocks the Jeep and opens my door. I slip into the passenger seat and lock my seatbelt in place. Lucien slides into the driver's seat and starts the engine. "I am sure there's enough space for Kenna and all her suitcases. Well, let's hope so." He chuckles as he pulls out and down the driveway. I know her, she probably packed enough clothes to supply a small country. Lucien pulls out into the road and we make our way to LAX. "So, tell me about this charity of your mom's?" I ask, curiously. His body tenses at my question and I frown. "Handsome? What's wrong?"

"Nothing, can we talk about it later?" I hate when he does this. He avoided questions about his past and his family constantly. This time, I can see it's affected him more than usual.

"Why?" I twist in my seat and face him. He glances at me and averts his eyes back to the highway.

"Drop it, Cassie, we can talk later." That's the end of that, if I push it he will get angry. I am not in the mood for an argument when I am about to see my best friend. I turn to gaze out my window as he places his hand on my thigh. "Sweetness, please don't be angry, it's just going to take a lot out of me to explain it to you."

"Fine. It's okay." I don't want to talk about it anymore. It's a constant fight, like he's pushing me away and that slices my heart. Since I figured out I love him, it hurts deeper than before. As soon as he pulls into the parking area, he finds a space close to the entrance. When he cuts the engine, we both sit in silence for a few moments.

"Sweetness?" I shift and turn to him, those green eyes have my resistance vanishing. Those dimples will be the death of me. *How can he do that with one look?* I want to be angry, but I can't. Not when he's giving me a puppy dog stare. I give him a small smile.

"You frustrate me!" I respond and a smirk curves his full lips.

"Yes, but then I release the frustration." He winks and I huff at him.

"Not now!" He tugs me back and holds me in a tight embrace. I am no longer angry and he knows it. He does this all the time. The power he has over me is alarming. I find myself constantly at his mercy. It's been a month since I submitted to him. I am still learning, and Lucien loves to train me. The dominance he has over me is incredible. I never thought I would be the kind of girl that was a submissive, letting her Dom do all sorts to her, but I love it.

"Come on, sweetness, we have ten minutes." His voice is rough and his hand snakes into the waistband of my shorts. I am so glad that the front of the car is facing a wall.

"What are you doing?" I gasp as his fingers tease into my panties. He doesn't answer me, instead he slips his index finger over my clit, stroking my slick folds.

"Fuck sweetness, you're so wet for me." His teeth tug at my earlobe and I moan.

"Luke, we can't."

"Cassandra, I am in control. Remember that." His voice is rough as he pushes his finger into me. In slow strokes, he pumps in and out. I am climbing and nearing the edge.

"Lucien." I hiss between my teeth, my hips bucking up to his hand and he inserts a second finger. My body responding to him, my release about to rip into me.

"Come for me, sweetness." His words push me over and my arousal coats his finger. He holds me until I stop shuddering. As I sit up, I watch him lick his fingers. "You are my drug, baby." He winks. It is the hottest thing I have ever seen and now I want him even more. "Let's go!" He declares and gets out of the car. At my door, he opens it and helps me up on wobbly legs.

"You're such an idiot sometimes."

He laughs and I grin. The sound is low and rough, and so sexy. "That's why you love me." As soon as the words are out of his mouth, I freeze. *How does he know? We didn't mention the L word yet. I mean, I wasn't even sure if love was possible. Shit! What do I say now?* As if reading my mind, he pulls me against him. His eyes lock on mine. "I love you, sweetness." His lips brush mine softly and I melt. My heart is racing and I am dizzy.

I pull away and smile. "Well, Mr. Verán, I love you too." I giggle at his pained expression.

"You're getting a spanking for that later!" He slaps my ass playfully as we approach the entrance to the arrivals section. A tingle travels through my body at his words. Once we're in the building, we join the other families and friends, waiting on their loved ones. After what we just did in the car and the revelation of us declaring our love for each other, I am so emotional. Lucien's arm snaked around my waist, holding me against him. As we watched the people file through the doors, he leaned in and whispered. "I really do fucking love you."

My whole body ignited at those words and I glanced up. His eyes were clear green, like there was a light shining behind them and illuminating them. "And I love you too." Our moment was broken by my best friend screaming my name.

"Cassie!!" Kenna runs up and gives me a hug so tight I can just about take a breath.

"Babe, can't... breathe!" She releases me and giggles.

"Sorry babe, I am just so glad I made it. What a freaking horror!" Her eyes settle on Lucien. "And this is the boss man?" I giggle and turn to him.

"Kenna, this is Lucien," he draws her hand and brushes the top of her knuckles with a light peck. His green eyes sparkle with mischievousness.

"Very nice to finally meet you, Kenna, I have heard a lot about you." I see her blush under his intense gaze and I shake my head. No woman is safe with him around.

"Great, then you know if you hurt Cassie, I will kick you so hard in those Verán jewels," she points to his crotch, "you will forget about ever having sex again." Lucien's laugh echoes through the airport. My mouth drops open at her words.

"Kenna!" I scold her. She shrugs. I didn't expect any less from her. She can be surprisingly direct.

"Don't worry Kenna; I don't plan on making Cassie cry unless it's from pleasure." There's an assurance in his statement that dampens my panties. Again. We turn to the exit and make our way out to the car. Lucien grabs Kenna's trolley of bags and she slings an arm around my neck. When the car unlocks, I slip into the passenger seat and Kenna joins me, sliding into the bench seat at the back. I turn to her and I can see Lucien lug her bags into the trunk. "He's hot!" She hisses at me and I chuckle.

"I know!" I want to tell her he said the L word, but he slips into the driver's seat before I say anything. When I smile at him, he gives me that sexy cheeky wink, and my panties disintegrate.

Lucien

Kenna really did pack for the apocalypse. When Cassie warned me, I thought she might have been exaggerating, but she wasn't. The girls slip into the car and I see them gossiping, this will be interesting to say the least. I shake my head, trying to get all of Kenna's five suitcases into the trunk. Thankful I decided on driving the Jeep today.

I slide into the driver's seat and glance at my girl. *My girl.* She's blushing furiously, I wonder what on earth they've been talking about. Actually, on second thought, I don't think I want to know. Without another word, I start the engine. I pull out of the parking lot and get on the motorway. The girls are talking animatedly and Kenna asks about how we met, how I asked Cassie out. She loves retelling this story, about our weekend in Hawaii, although she leaves out the hot sex. Which I am actually happy about, nobody needs the personal details.

Kenna tells us about her job with a fashion house in LA, she will be staying with Cassie, even though most nights, my girl is with me. I love saying that. Yes, I am whipped, in the best fucking way possible. I glance at Cassie, she's smiling, her eyes sparkle, and she looks incredible. *I do love her.* She's a puzzle piece that completes me. I have been broken for such a long time, I didn't think I could ever be complete. Somehow Cassie does that, she makes me realize I am worthy of love and happiness. I never thought I would ever be in a relationship after Sasha, but everything is different now. I am a different person. *Get over it Verán, you'll always be that dark demented person. No, I fucking won't!* I turn on the radio, hoping to calm the voices in my head.

The girls didn't notice my discomfort. I guess Cassie knows, she's always known when something was wrong, but never asked about it. She's let go of so much and I know she's dying to ask. That's just how she is. I love her for it. More than I could ever imagine. There is so much I want to share with her, so much of me I want her to see, but it scares me to the fucking bone that she will run.

I pull into the garage and let the girls get out. I lock up and follow them up to the apartment. Since they've decided to make use of my home theatre before taking Kenna back to Cassie's, I decide to get some work done. I head to the bar and pour a whiskey. On my way up to the office, I glance into the theatre room as I pass. They've got drinks from the bar fridge and are settling in for an afternoon of giggling at girly movies.

I slide into my office chair. When I power up my laptop, and scroll through work emails. I end up working through the day. There was so much to do when you're running a company. I loved it. The responsibility that it gave me. My father entrusted his company to me, it's something I never thought I would see. After my younger years of acting like an inconsiderate child, he still loved me. Like Cassie. Although there is still so much I haven't told her, she's still here. Her patience with me is nothing short of amazing. She accepts me for who I am, not what I can give her.

When I glance at the time I realize that it was almost dinnertime. Not realizing I had been working for so long, I rise from my chair and make my way upstairs. I find the girls glued to PS I Love You. I groan inwardly. "You do realize that my screen might crack with you two watching that?" I point up to something happening on screen where the girl was crying. *Don't they all cry in these movies? Why do girls watch this shit?* I glance at Cassie and her eyes are glassy with unshed tears. My heart cracks at the thought of her ever crying. I offer her a small smile and she pats the plush leather sofa next to her.

"Shhh, baby, come sit with me?" Cassie's big doe eyes have me melting. *Fuck, totally whipped.*

We spend most of the night chatting, getting to know each other and relaxing. By 2 am, we're all yawning and ready for bed. I set Kenna up in the other spare bedroom and I take my beautiful girl to bed. As soon as we slide into bed, her eyes flutter closed and I pull her against me. Her warmth offers me the calm I need and my eyes close, hoping for the night to keep me calm. Mocha eyes pulled me into my past, haunting me like never before.

"Lucien, why are you doing this? Please, let me go! I didn't mean to upset you. We were just having a laugh, it was funny." She looks up at me with big blue eyes, they're frozen in time. Didn't she like to take risks? This is why she was here. Tied to my bed. She always enjoyed being tied up. "Luke? Baby, are you okay? Did you take those pills from Davey?" Her eyes are wide, and scared. Did she always look like that? Her body arched and I realize it was because she was bound so tight. She wanted this; she wanted me. They all want me. So now, they can have me. On my fucking terms.

"Shut up Sasha! You wanted this! That's why you're with me! You want this because you're fucking desperate to be part of my family. You want the money, the fame, and me. You're just a fucking slut!" The laugh that escapes my throat is dark, dangerous and not my own. What was that stuff I took? Shit! I can't remember. This happened the other day. Blackout. Forgetting. Delirium. I can't do this. She needs to shut the fuck up, but she doesn't. They never do.

"Luke, please?" She's begging me, I love it when she does that. Beg me. Such a fucking pathetic little slut, begging me for my cock. Just like the rest of them. I feel myself sway. What the fuck is happening? I grip onto the bedframe. She's laughing now! What the hell?

"Luke? Luke! Luke!" Cassie's voice pulls me from the darkness.

"Babe?!" My eyes fly open and I sit up abruptly. I glance at Cassie, she's kneeling on the bed next to me, staring at me. My t-shirt is stained with sweat. Images swirl through my head, those ice-blue eyes of Sasha and then the agony. *Shit!* "Are you okay?" The concern in her eyes tugs at me. She looks scared, and that's the last thing I want her to be. *That fucking nightmare! Except it's not a nightmare. It's real.*

I nod. She needs to forget this. *What the fuck did I do?* "Did I hurt you?" I reach out and she doesn't move, lacing my fingers with hers, I see her visibly relax.

"No, you just scared me. You were freaking out. Shouting. Laughing." I nod. The dreams haven't bothered me since I met her, and now, suddenly they're back. Soon, I need to tell her about them, but I am nowhere near ready for that.

"Fuck, I am sorry baby. I am just a bit stressed." With a glance at the clock on the bedside table, I see it's 3 am. I pull my t-shirt off, chucking it on the floor. Cassie, places a hand on my stomach, tracing the planes of my abs. I lay back and pull her to me. With a deep breath I inhale her scent, she smells like strawberries, planting a kiss on the top of her head, my eyes close again and I let my thoughts fill with Cassie. No dreams come after that.

The sun rays peeking through the window wakes me. As I roll over in bed, I reach out for Cassie, but her side of the bed is empty. I sit up, panic courses through my veins. *Where the fuck is she? Did I hurt her?* Her clothes are still laying on the floor. That's strange. Maybe she's downstairs. I swing my feet over the bed and grab a pair of sweatpants and a T-shirt tugging it on hastily. As soon as I open the bedroom door I am assaulted with the smell of food.

Downstairs in the kitchen, I find Cassie making breakfast, she's singing along to the music, she looks adorable. I watch her for a moment, taking in this amazing woman that's given me a chance and given me her heart. "This is how a man should wake up every morning." My voice is filled with humor. When she turns to face me, a small giggle escapes her lips.

"Is it now?"

"Absolutely, a hot girl in my kitchen making me breakfast. What more can I ask for." I stalk towards her and pin her against the counter, sealing her mouth with mine. My hips pressing into her, my cock is steel with a need to be inside her. Our tongues dance and intertwine. The kiss becomes heated until we hear Kenna clearing her throat.

"Gross guys! Get a room!" *Fuck, I forgot she's here.* I was close to taking her right here on the goddamn kitchen counter.

"We have a room; it's just as much fun in the kitchen!" I pull away from Cassie reluctantly and we're both breathless. She always leaves me that way. I am becoming soft. She's given me something I have never had or felt before, a real connection. It's scary at times. I mean, it's a situation that I never thought I could ever be in.

"Okay, kids! Who's hungry?" Cassie ever the peacemaker, hands me the plate of toast and bowl of scrambled eggs. We all pitch in to set up the table.

"What are you guys doing today?" Kenna glances between Cassie and me.

"We have a charity event; Lucien's mother is in charge of it, so her baby is required to be there." My eyes cut to Cassie and I realize she's baiting me. I sidestepped this when she asked me yesterday, but I can't do it anymore.

"Easy little lady. I am no baby!" There's only one way to explain it without having to give too much away. Don't get me wrong, it was my idea, but to have to explain to Cassie why the foundation was set up is going to the difficult part.

"Geez, that sounds…. Fun?" Kenna's grimace matches my own feelings about the event. I would rather spend the evening alone with Cassie than to be around Claudia. Or Sasha for that matter. I think about inviting Kenna, maybe it would be good having her there. Cassie seems calmer when she's here, and after tonight, I think it's going to be needed.

"You're more than welcome to join us?" I look over to my girl's best friend, I hope she agrees.

"Really? What's the charity?" She cocks her head to the side. Cassie asked me this, and I evaded her questioning. Her intense stare on me and I can't ignore it.

"Well, it's a fund to aid abuse survivors. I um…" I glance at Cassie immediately and shift my gaze to Kenna. "The charity pays for therapy for them. Help them move on I suppose." My tone is heavy with emotion, but Kenna doesn't notice. Without a doubt Cassie definitely noticed. This was it; she's going to learn about my past with Sasha.

"Sounds like a charity I would love to support, I will go. I need to find something to wear. Can Robert take me to the apartment?" Kenna rose and took her plate and I nod.

"Sure, I will call him." With that I leave the girls, grabbing my phone to call Robert, he needed to take the girls shopping. I walk up to my office and slide into the leather chair. My heart is racing after explaining that, I release a breath hoping to calm myself. This wasn't how I wanted to have Cassie find out about me. Robert answers on the second ring. "Mr. Verán."

"Robert, I need you to take the girls shopping, the event tonight requires something special. Boutique, high quality. I have a few things I need to sort out, so I can't take them."

"Certainly, sir. What time shall I be ready?"

"Give them thirty minutes."

"Perfect."

I hang up, powering up my laptop. Once my email is open, I start a new message. This is something I haven't ever needed to contact my lawyer about, but I need a confidentiality agreement. What I am going to tell Cassie tonight is classified. I fucked up a long time ago, and if for any reason she talks, my father's company is at risk. I love Cassie, but I need to protect my legacy as well. "Babe?" I glance up into the beautiful mocha eyes that seem to disarm me every time I look into them. I minimize the window. Her smile has my heart racing; I crook my finger to call her to me.

"Robert will be here in thirty to take you and Kenna shopping, take my credit card. Get something for tonight." She comes around to my desk and slides into my lap. Her soft lips brush mine in a soft kiss, my hands roam up her thigh and back. I push my tongue into her mouth and she willingly accepts me, sucking on it, eliciting a groan in my throat. *Fuck, she's good at that.* My mind is filled with thoughts of her lips wrapped around my cock as I slide it into her mouth.

"Have to go…" She mumbles into my mouth and I   smile.

"Fine, just leave me here with a hard on." A giggle escapes her lips and I give her a wink. I give her ass a slap, and she yelps and rounds my desk.

"See you later babe." She grabs the credit card from my desk and leaves me in the office. I open the email and carry on typing.

Cassandra

It was almost time to leave for the charity event. I am dressed in a long sleeveless red silk dress; the neckline was high which fell into a cowl back. A slit on the left side from the floor to my upper thigh added a sexy element to the elegant shimmer of the material. I opted for my silver stiletto pumps, which would put me almost at the same height as Lucien. I had pinned my hair into a messy bun with stray curls falling down my open back. A shiny diamond bracelet and matching earrings finished the look.

"God, Cass!" I turn and my gaze falls on my handsome man in a black Armani suit, crisp white dress shirt and a red tie that matches the color of my dress. He had a red silk handkerchief in his breast pocket. His short brown hair was styled into messy spikes. *God, this man is incredible. How on earth could he want me? Not now Cassie, he's here with you. Stop doubting.*

"What? Is this dress too much?" To say that I was nervous about seeing his mother and his ex tonight would be lying. I wanted to be the elegant woman, worthy of being with a man like him. "Do you think I should change?"

"No sweetness, that dress is incredible on you!" He pulled me into him, giving me a soft kiss on my lips. "So beautiful and so perfect." His words held a certain sadness and left me confused. We hadn't spoken about the charity after Kenna left to get ready at my apartment. I was still trying to come to terms with why it was such a sore subject to him.

"I just want to look the part, you know?"

He stepped back and stared at me. "What part?" He looked genuinely confused.

"The part of the girl that your mother would approve of." I reached out to him, but he didn't take my hand. My heart constricted at his actions and I dropped my hand back to my side.

"I don't care what my mother says!" His voice is laced with aggravation and anger. "She doesn't need to approve of you. I want you in my life Cassie." His tone was final. *Okay! Calm down.* Disbelief runs through me that he's so angry about it. I mean, I didn't want to upset him. Surely, he could see that I am nervous?

"Lucien, I was just..." I trailed off, not knowing what I was trying to say. I turn to face my reflection and watch him in the mirror. When his eyes met mine they're glassy, it's almost as if he was blinking back tears. This really was an intense subject for him. Our gazes locked in the mirror. He took a small step towards me and circled his arms around my waist. His face next to mine and the light stubble tickles my neck, sending tingles down my spine.

"Cassandra, I need you to understand one thing. My mother is not in charge of how I live my life. I will date whomever I want. She will have to accept that you're the one I want. You do not need to prove yourself to anyone, but me." A chuckle vibrates in his chest and I giggle.

"I am sure I have proven worthy of you then. Since you approve of me." I wink and he turns me around in his arms. His lips seal mine and I moan into the kiss. "Okay, then we should go." I mumble into the kiss, he nods and pulls away reluctantly. I pick up my purse and walk past him into the living room. We make our way out to the car and find Robert waiting for us. Since we still need to collect Kenna, I notice that Lucien had got Robert to drive a limo for us tonight. It's a sleek black car and as soon as I slide in the opulence of the interior leaves me speechless.

"You like?" Lucien slides in next to me and all I can do is nod. He reaches out for my hand and I lace my fingers in his. As we pull up to my apartment ten minutes later, Robert opens the door for Kenna, she slips into the seat opposite us and I notice the dress she bought earlier looks immaculate against her tanned skin. We both decided on long elegant dresses, hoping we fit into the crowd we're about to be subjected to.

As we pull up to the venue, Lucien helps me out of the car and Robert extends his hand for Kenna. As soon as we step out of the car, the press goes mental. There are shouts from either side of the red carpet, but Lucien ignores them. I hear a few shouts about who his girlfriend is and a few mention Sasha.

Lucien

I ignore the shouts about Sasha, my hand is around Cassie's waist and it pisses me off that they have the nerve to ask about my ex when there is another woman on my arm. As soon as we start walking, Jayce comes up behind us. "There's my favorite babe!" His voice cuts into me and my body locks with tension when he pulls Cassie in for a hug. I shouldn't be jealous, but I can't help it. My natural instinct is to protect her, she's mine.

"Hey, Jayce!" She giggles and returns his hug. "Don't you scrub up well!" *Is she flirting with him? This is enough!* The tension rolls off me in waves.

"Oh, you have no idea gorgeous!" He winks. He fucking winked at my girlfriend! I will kill him.

"Jayce, do you mind not pawing my girlfriend?" My voice is low and only Cassie and he heard me. Which was my intention. He cuts his gaze to me and I can't help giving him a glare to confirm that I will fucking kill him if he tries anything.

"Luke, seriously dude? I am just saying hi." Then his eyes flicker to Kenna and I realize he hadn't met her yet. Cassie takes the lead to calm the tension again.

"Jayce, meet my best friend Kenna." When Jayce takes his cue to try to seduce Kenna, I place my hand on the small of Cassie's back, and guide her down the carpet to the entrance. We stop a couple of times for the press to get a photo, but I answer no questions. As soon as we're out of earshot, she's on my case. "What's up with you and Jayce?"

"Later Cass, I can't talk about it now." As soon as I brush it off, Cassie vibrates with tension. At first, I think it's at me, then I turn and my gaze finds Claudia.

"Lucien, darling!" The ultimate socialite she walks up to us, she is dressed in an emerald green floor-length dress that sparkled. Her jewelry just about blinded me. The diamonds were so big. Her hair was pulled back so tight that she almost had no facial expression. *Enjoying spending my father's money?*

"Mother," my voice is clipped. I give her an icy peck on the cheek. "This is Cassandra, my girlfriend." I notice a spark of irritation on her otherwise expressionless face. I love causing the aggravation in her features. This is my life, and no longer yours to rule. Cassie is bristling and I lace my fingers through hers.

"Oh, I didn't realize it was a long-term thing?" Her voice is ice and I can't deal with this anymore. Not before I have had a drink.

"Mother, please?" I give her a glare, hoping she will drop it.

"Did you see Sasha is here? She's looking lovely." Without fail, she plays her card, mentioning Sasha. When the name leaves her mouth Cassie's hand goes rigid in mine. She's still so scared about my ex relationship, I have no idea why, because it's over. Forever.

"No mother, I don't really care if she is here or not. I am with Cassandra as you can see. Sasha and I are over." I grip Cassie's arm and tug her away from my mother, I am fuming. My blood is at boiling point. I need a drink. "Fuck it! She fucking riles me up so much. I am sorry about that sweetness!" When we reach the bar, I tug Cassie against me. "Kiss me." Without waiting for a reply, I crash my mouth onto hers. The sweetness of her mouth calms me more than anything ever has. When I pull away the tension eases in my muscles. "That's better."

"Lucien." She breathes my name, and it goes straight to my cock. *I would love to take you right now.* A cheeky wink has a blush spreading on her cheeks. She stares at me breathlessly.

"Do I take your breath away my love?" My perfect, beautiful girl.

"Always Lucien, you know that." She nods slowly and I can't help my heart leaping in joy.

I order us each a drink. "Sweetness." I hand Cassie a glass of wine and I take a gulp of the whiskey it burns its way down. My nerves tingle with anticipation. I am about to suggest we disappear into a room somewhere when we're interrupted by Jayce and Kenna.

Cassandra

"Babe!" I turn to Kenna and Jayce walk up to us at the bar. "Where did you disappear to?" She grabs my wine taking a small sip. All I can do is giggle and shake my head at her expression. The wine is incredible. Only the best for the elite.

"We ran into Lucien's mother." I say and her eyes dart between us. When my glance falls on Jayce and I can see his expression tells me exactly what he thinks of Mrs. Verán.

"Oh, I am sure that was pleasant," Jayce chuckles.

"Mmmm, I wouldn't go as far as pleasant." I giggle, taking my wine back from Kenna, taking a huge gulp. Jayce feels the same as I do, that makes getting through this event much more bearable. I offer him a small smile and he gives me a cheeky wink. He always does that; I realize it's just to upset Lucien. I shake my head at him.

"Guys, I am standing right here," Lucien tugs me into the crook of his arm and we all laugh. "Okay, I admit she's hard work." He winks down at me and my stomach flip-flops when he smiles, deepening his dimples. My heart races as I stare at the amazing man next to me.

"Jesus, Luke, hard work? She hates everyone that wasn't born with a silver spoon in their mouth." Jayce is suddenly serious, and the tension is tangible. It's obvious that Claudia doesn't like anyone that doesn't have a big bank account, or someone that doesn't have a title.

"No Jayce, just drop this. You of all people should be used to it." His words were harsh, and the pain flickered on Jayce's face. Something must have happened between them, something deeper than I originally thought. There is still so many secrets, but Lucien won't tell me here. I will have to wait until we're home.

"Come on Lucien, this is getting you both nowhere. Catch you guys later." I turn and smile, leaving Jayce and Kenna. Once we're out of earshot, I round on Lucien, "What the hell is wrong with you?" My gaze falls on him and the frustration in his expression is infuriating me.

"Cassie, don't do this now!" Lucien leans in and hisses in my ear. I don't want to fight and I certainly don't want to cause a scene, but he frustrates me so much.

"No, I will do this here and I will do it now. I am sick of you treating Jayce like shit because he's not a spoilt brat." I spit out the words and am immediately cringing. When I glance up at him and it looks like I have just slapped him. "I didn't—"

"No, you're right. He's not a spoilt brat. I am. Don't worry, I get it, Cassie. I told you, I am not the good guy. I am the rich overconfident bastard. You know what, I am not even her son, but she acts like that." My mouth drops open and I stare at him in shock. "Yes, Cassie, you want to know me? There, now you do. I am a bastard whose mother didn't love him enough to keep him around. Nobody likes keeping me around." He spins on his heel and walks off past the crowd and I follow him. Trying to catch up to him in these damn heels is proving impossible. All I can see is his back as he walks out of the ballroom. Once out in the hallway, I watch him duck into a room just passed the restrooms. I follow him in and find myself in a small office.

"Lucien!" Grabbing his wrist. "Just stop, please?" When he turns, the pain etched on his handsome face makes my heart stop. "Just wait, listen to me." My voice is a whisper. I want to hold him and tell him everything will be okay. That I want him in my life, I want to tell him I want him forever, but I can't. This isn't the time. It's almost as if it will never be the right time.

"Cassandra, I have a lot that you haven't yet learned about me, and yes, I haven't been open about myself. I am trying. I am not used to sharing my life with someone." He drops his gaze, and scrubs his hands over his face. All I can do is stare at the war he's having inside himself. "I have never had someone, who..." His voice trails off. This broken man in front of me needs so much love, but he keeps pushing me away. I step forward and wrap my arms around his waist, when he doesn't pull away, I realize he's calmed down.

"I know. Neither am I, you know that. I just don't like to be shut out." Tears threaten, but I blink them back. I cannot ruin my makeup. "We can talk later. Let's just enjoy the party?" His eyes flicker with mischief and I realize what's on his mind.

"Okay." He leans in and kisses me softly, licking the seam of my lips. I open to him. He licks into my mouth and I suck his tongue and flick my own over his. His hands reach down and lift me against him, walking me back, he pins me against the door. A deep growl rumbles in his chest and his erection presses against my core. He is so close; I can feel his heart racing in his chest. I pull back and take in the beautifully broken man that's stolen my heart. He's standing here, polished in his immaculate suit, only I have seen the painted body beneath. It seemed his scars ran deeper than I had thought.

"We have to get back." I whisper, although it's the last thing I want to do. He doesn't answer, instead snakes his one hand down the side of my body, finding the slit of my dress.

"Open." I obey and my legs open for him. His fingers find my soaked panties as he strokes my heat. My head drops back, and he pushes the small material of my panties to the side. "You need to be quiet okay, baby." I nod, biting my lip to keep from moaning. There are people walking past the door outside, the fact that we could get caught has my body trembling. Lucien slips two fingers into my slick folds, pumping his fingers in and out slowly. "Look at me." I open my eyes and see the desire in his mossy green eyes. His hand moves faster, taking me to the edge. "Come for me, lumiére." My body obeys as only it can and I come undone over his hand.

Lucien

Watching her come is the most incredible thing ever. I am rock hard, but we can't stay in here much longer. The speeches are supposed to start soon and I have to be there. I just couldn't stop myself, she's under my skin and inside my heart. Whenever we fight, all I want to do is hold her, fuck her and make her forget. Make the pain and agony go away. I have never truly been in love before and it scares me shitless. With a soft kiss on her lips, I pull my hand from between her legs. Her eyes are locked on mine. I lick my fingers, tasting her sweet honey. *Fucking hell, she tastes so good.*

"I suppose we better get back." I wink and she giggles.

"You're insufferable, Mr. Verán."

She whispers, her hot breath on my neck. Jesus, this will be the most difficult speech I have to live through. I would have to stand on stage with a fucking painful hard on.

"Do you like doing that, Cassie?" She turns and looks at me innocently.

"No idea what you're talking about, Sir." I have to readjust myself before we make our way back into the main ballroom. As we weave our way through the crowd, Claudia is making her way onto the stage. As long as she keeps her speech short, I can give mine and then Cassie and I can leave. That's all I want, to get out of this place. I lean in and plant a soft kiss on Cassie's lips but Claudia, starting her speech, interrupts us. Her gaze cuts to me and I see the venom in her eyes. I shiver and hold onto Cassie's hand. *This will not be good.*

"Ladies and gentleman, can I have your attention, please?" She will fuck this whole thing up I can feel it. "I would like to welcome you all to our Annual Charity Ball. All proceeds will go to our Abuse Survivors Charity. Set up in the name of my beautiful son, Lucien Verán." People applaud and turn to look at me. I give a small smile and nod. "Come up here, darling," her voice like syrup. On show for the audience. I have no choice, but to go up there. All eyes are on me, I make a public display of affection, giving Cassie a kiss on the cheek. I realize this will rile Claudia up. As soon as I am on the stage, my eyes never leave Cassie, but the next words out of my step-mother's mouth sends an icy shiver down my spine. "I also want to call up the beautiful Sasha Alexander, she and Lucien started this charity together. Since they're partners I would like them both up here." *She's calling Sasha up?! Fuck it!* My eyes immediately fall to Cassie, but she turns and runs out of the venue. I scan the crowd for Jayce, giving him a nod and watch him follow her out. There is no way I can walk out now without repercussion, so I have to let it go. My hate for Claudia is at an all-time high.

"What the fuck are you thinking?" I hiss into her ear while the crowd applaud Sasha.

"I am just protecting you from gold digging little whores. Just like that night with Sasha." Her voice is laced with venom and I feel like choking the life out of her. *What?*

The night with Sasha? Before I can say anything, the crowd are watching us again. I just hope Jayce can calm Cassie down somewhat. As soon as the crowd have calmed and Claudia continues with her speech, I give a small nod to the crowd and step off the stage. Still confused by her words, I need to figure out what she meant, but I have had enough of this shit. I need to calm down before I find Cassie.

My body is vibrating anger and I could easily kill someone. I asked Jayce to look out for her, but I have a feeling there's more to his feelings for her. In the hallway, I find Kenna. "Where is she?" I have no time to waste; I need to explain to her what the hell is going on. Taking a deep breath. I fix my gaze on Kenna, hoping she knows where my girl is.

"She's talking to Jayce. Why didn't you tell her? That's your ex isn't it?" I nod. Not in the mood to explain my love life to her right now. "Lucien, I told you don't hurt her."

"Listen, Kenna, I realize you're looking out for her, but this is what my step-mother does. She doesn't approve of Cassie, so she's going out of her way to break us up. Over my dead body will she get that right." I lose all fight when I think of Cassie walking away. It will break me. There won't be anything for me to live for. This girl has gotten into the deepest parts of me and brought light to my dark life.

"Then you need to start being honest with her. She can't go through this again. Not after..." Kenna's voice trails off. Something happened to Cassie. Fear prickles through me and I can't even imagine what she's had to endure.

"Kenna? What?"

"That's her story to tell you. You need to be completely honest that's what Cassie needs." I nod.

Cassandra

I glance around, Jayce is staring at me. My heart is racing, I take a few short breaths. *She is his partner; they obviously are working together. Closely. He didn't tell me. Why didn't he tell me?* The panic is taking over and my chest is tight. "Cassie? Can we talk?" My glance flits up into sky-blue eyes. His face is calm, and he reaches out for me. I offer a small smile and take his hand.

"Jayce." I nod staring at him, the pensive expression on his face makes me more nervous. We turn and walk towards the stairwell, I open the door and sit on the lowest one. He joins me and his calm aura envelope me. "What's up?"

"I saw you walk out after his mother acted like a fucking idiot. I wanted to see if you were okay?" When he wraps an arm around my neck, he pulls me into his arms, holding me as the tears fall down my face. *She's his partner. They have something together.*

"I will be. It was a shock to hear it. You know? I mean, I know they're over, but they work together. He doesn't even want to tell me things. Now I learn that they share something so... personal." My voice muffled by his shirt. He kisses the top of my head and I calm. I push away from him; this situation is too emotional to be in his arms. With the pads of his thumbs, he wipes my tears.

"Don't let that old hag get to you okay? You're amazing and he loves you." His words calm me further and I have no idea why Lucien is so weary of Jayce. Somehow, I know that Jayce isn't lying to me. If there was something going on between Sasha and Lucien, he would tell me. Taking a deep breath, I try to stop my hands from shaking. This is too much; Lucien needs to tell me the truth. I can't handle more surprises. He will have to open up to me sometime.

"Thanks, Jay, after my past, I find it difficult trusting anyone." His blue eyes sear into my brown ones. The sincere concern I see in his face makes me smile.

"Come on, let's get a drink." He rises from the stair and offers a hand to me. As soon as he pulls me up I am standing in front of him. He wraps an arm around my neck in a friendly gesture. We walk out to find Kenna and Lucien standing in the foyer. My body shivers at the sadness on his face. I can see he's worried, but that's not what I notice. It's the glare he's giving Jayce that has me trembling.

"Cassie! Where the fuck did you go?" He steps towards me and I can see Lucien is fuming. The anger vibrates off him. He pulls me towards him and I feel like a doll being pushed and pulled.

"I needed air, Lucien. I wasn't expecting a goddamn surprise like that." I gesture to the ballroom.

"Let me guess, Jayce was there to pick up the pieces?" He shoots daggers at Jayce who is standing beside me. This is fucking ridiculous he needs to get over himself.

"Actually Jay was the one who told me you love me and I shouldn't let it upset me," I say matter-of-factly. I challenge him to say something more as I shoot a glare at him. We stand quietly for a few moments before Lucien extends a hand to Jayce and they shake on it. I let out a breath I didn't realize I had been holding.

"I am taking you home." He pulls me along behind him and we make our way out the back to the waiting limo.

CHAPTER fifteen

Lucien

I pull Cassie behind me. We leave through the back door to avoid the paparazzi I realize will be there. As soon as we get to the alley, Robert is waiting as instructed. He opens the door for Cassie and she slips inside. "Drive till I tell you to take us home." I decided to tell her the truth tonight, but before I do it, I want to spend time with her before she knows who I really am. He gives me a small nod. I slip in next to Cassie and Robert closes the door. I can be honest with her here, the partition between the seating and the driver's section is up and Robert can't hear us.

The air in the car is filled with tension, not anger. We sit quietly for a few moments and I lace my fingers with hers. Cassie doesn't meet my gaze. She's looking out the window. This is not going well. Why can she make me feel like such an asshole by not saying a word? *Because you are an asshole, you should have told her. Not blindsided her.* I pull off my tie. It feels like a noose, ready to hang myself with. Perhaps it would be easier that way. *Jesus, Lucien, get a grip. She's still here, just give her the honesty she deserves.* "Cassie, baby, we need to talk, but can you look at me?" She turns to me and I notice the tears shimmering in her beautiful chocolate eyes.

I lean in and seal her mouth with a kiss. The urgency of our kiss is heated, her tongue fighting mine for dominance. She's never done that before and it disarms me. I thought she was angry, but the kiss tells me otherwise. Her hand trails up my thigh, she rubs my rock hard erection and I can't help groaning into the kiss. When she pulls away, I think she will tell me to take her home.

She shocks me by straddling my lap. She lifts her dress to her hips, moving back and forth, rubbing her heated core on my crotch. "Cassie…" I moan her name. The need to be inside her is tearing me apart. I am close to ripping her dress off and slamming inside her when she gives me a little smile.

"Fuck me, Lucien." Her voice is husky, and her eyes are flickering with need. I hesitate. "Please." She's begging me now and my restraint falters. *Holy shit, I need her.*

I reach between us, and unzip my pants, pulling out my cock. Her hand falls between us and she fists my hardness. My hand reaches between her spread thighs, and I tug the tiny piece of material from her and she positions herself over me. With a painfully slow movement, she slides down on me. She sheaths me to the hilt and I have to breathe to keep myself from coming to soon. *Fuck, her pussy is amazing.* "Cassie, you feel so fucking good. I will not last long." She giggles and moves her hips, back and forth. My head drops back and I grip her hips hard.

"Luke!" She cries out and moves faster. Her release is close; those luscious hips are moving faster. Not being able to control myself, I lift my hips, and slam into her, deepening our connection. Her hands on my shoulders tighten, her slick pussy clenches around me and she pulls my release from me with hers. I empty into her, she shudders and milks every drop from me. Her eyes meet mine. "I am ready to go home now." Her smile is bright and all I can do is nod.

I press the button in the panel above us and instruct Robert to take us back to the penthouse. Cassie sits back in the seat next to me. We sit in silence as Robert pulls up to the apartment a few minutes later. As soon as we're inside, Cassie walks up the stairs. I decide to give her space and pour myself a drink. The apartment is quiet, and I sit on the sofa. I need to be ready to tell her everything tonight. She may be gone tomorrow, but I have to tell her. No more lies. No more secrets. Absolute honesty.

I glance up as she walks into the living room and sits next to me. *That's a good sign right?* When I look at her my anger about Jayce surfaces, I realize this is a bad time, but I can't help myself. He will steal her from me and there's nothing I can do about it. "What Cassie? I am not apologizing for freaking out about Jayce."

"I didn't ask you to." She twists her fingers in the material of her sweatpants.

"Then what would you like me to say?"

Then comes the question I have been waiting for. "You need to tell me about this charity and why you're running it with her." The charity. Of course, she wants to know about it. The fear grips my heart, the fear that she will get up, take her bag and walk out as soon as I am finished. I stand, walking into the kitchen; I grab glasses and a bottle of wine. Once the bottle is open, I join her in the living room.

"Cassie—" I glance at her, but before I can continue, she cuts me off.

"Please?" I sit down, staring at her.

Cassandra

I lean forward and place my hand on his. I need him to open up and trust me with this. There is nothing that would tear me away from him. I try to communicate the love I have for him with a glance. The emotion between us is sizzling. I watch him close his eyes, the indecision crossing over his face. It couldn't be that bad. Why would he be so against telling me something? I mean we love each other? Nothing could change that. There isn't anything that can stop the love I have for him.

Lucien pours a glass of wine for each of us. I take a sip from mine, my eyes never leaving his handsome face. Events in life bring you to the place you were always destined to be, they also bring you to the person you're meant to be with. This is where I am supposed to be. Next to him. With Lucien Verán, my soul mate, my protector and the man that I want to spend my life with. The realization hits me, like a freight train, but I take a deep breath and calm my racing heart. He is terrified. I can see it in his eyes. Although, I realize that if I was in his position, I would be too. If we want to move forward I need to hear this.

He turns and faces me, a small smile on his lips, although it doesn't reach his eyes. The tension rolling off him in waves has my own body trembling. "After I tell you this. If you want to leave I can have Robert take you." I nod. With a gulp of wine, I close my eyes to calm the tension. "I am serious Cassandra, there is nothing holding you here. I do love you, but I understand if this is too much. If what I am about to tell you freaks you out. You can leave. I will let you go." My heart constricts and my chest tightens painfully at the thought of leaving him. *Why would he think I would leave?* When you love someone, you're in it for the good and the bad. "Lucien, I am not leaving, so just tell me." My voice is final, and he nods.

"I was young, about 21 when it started. My actions were idiotic. Stupidity reigned, but I didn't care. There were parties every weekend. Since I had the money, it was impossible to resist. That sounds like I am a spoilt brat, and I guess I was. Still am. Anyway, my father and step-mother never really cared what I did. As long as I didn't end up in the papers. Claudia Verán is my stepmother. My father married her a year after my birth mother left. I was eleven, and I grew up with her taking over as my mother, but that's not what she was. As a teenager, I rebelled by doing stupid things, being suspended from school for smoking, drinking, whatever, to get my father's attention. He spent so much time at work; all I wanted was him to see that I was hurting too. He still took me traveling, we would spend time away from Claudia, but I still missed him." He gulped his wine and continued to stare at the glass instead of meeting my eyes. I shivered at his recollection of his younger years.

"Claudia turned into the evil step mother that you see in movies. Like I said at first she didn't really care what I did. Then when I turned 20 she started telling me what to do, who to see. She used to bring these girls for me to meet. One's that she approves of. I spent most of my time out, avoiding her and her disapproving sneer. I was either at Jayce's place or whatever girl I was fucking at the time." His harsh words cause me to wince, but I didn't dare interrupt him. "When I was 25, I met Sasha. We were at some industry party. She was 22, a model working for my dad. We were both drunk, stoned, high, whatever." I sat silently watching him. At the mention of her name, my heart drops, and I have to take a large gulp of the wine he poured me. I realized she would come up, but it didn't prepare me for the ache in my chest at the mention of her name.

His hands were visibly shaking. "Claudia would set me up on these dates with girls, even though she heard I was dating Sasha. At the time, she didn't approve of Sasha, because she was a model. Claudia said that she was a bad influence on me. The only way I knew how to get through the dates was to get high. I would take whatever was on offer." He drained his glass and picked up the bottle from the table and poured a refill. "The girls, of course, were eager for me to take them home. Which I did. I didn't care. I would tie them up. Blindfold them. I started with spanking. Whipping. Caning. Anything to get my anger out. I took it out on them, some of them came back, and some didn't. When I did see Sasha, I was so angry that I would be rougher with her than any of the other girls. I guess she loved me. My mind was so fucked up at the time, I thought I loved her, but I didn't. I used her."

He glanced at me quickly. "There was something about her that made me hate being with her, but I kept going back. Being dominant appealed to me. So I found a club, a place where I could learn. That's when I met a few people, most importantly, a tutor. He taught me a lot, he was like a mentor I guess. It was the first time I was in control when I was dominating them. The scenes were mine, they would do anything I wanted. Finally, I fit in, somewhere. Sasha would go with me. She did it because she wanted to be with me. I knew she wanted a ring, my family name. That was something I could never give her. Until…" His eyes close suddenly, like he was blinking back a memory.

He stops and I can't imagine what's next. My body is vibrating with fear, anger, and frustration. Angry that Claudia put him through this, fear of what he did, and frustration that he had to live through the agony that's so clearly breaking him.

Lucien

    I had the confidentiality agreement, but I didn't ask Cassie to sign it. I trusted her with everything I had. Right now, all I want to do is get this out. This is killing me, I take a deep breath, and continue. "Sasha put up with it, she knew about the girls. Throughout that she stuck it out. Every weekend there were parties and drinking. The drugs were there too, and I started blacking out. After spending almost three years with her, she was the only one who knew. One night—" The words are strained and the lump in my throat chokes me as the words tumble from my mouth. The beginning is easier than the ending. That's the part that will ruin us, break us and I doubt we will ever be able to be put back together. Broken by desire, my dark desire.
    I take a deep breath. "One night. I tied her up. Sasha. I don't remember it. I…" I stop only to gulp my wine. Liquid courage, as they say.
    "Lucien…" Cassie breathes my name, reaching out for me. I shake my head and stand up. With my back to her, I look out of the window. I can't bring myself to look at her, to see the pity on her face. To see the disgust in her eyes. All I can do is concentrate on the glass. I hear her sharp intake of breath and I am shocking her one revelation after the other. My mind filters back, to the only memory I have of the night my life changed forever.

    "Luke, come on baby, let's play." Sasha is giggling. As usual, she's wearing nothing more than a small red pair of panties and a lace bra. She loved red, said it made her feel like the devil. After all the girls I had fucked, for some reason she always stayed. I could get pussy anywhere, a mention of my name and they would be queuing out the door. Tonight, I had taken a couple of those pills; the guy said the high is indescribable. After the half bottle of whiskey and the amount of the white powder I sniffed, I am on top of the world. This is fucking amazing. Sasha is standing in the bedroom with all the kink.
    "Fine, you want to play, we'll fucking play." My voice was a low growl. She was in for a fucking good night. I grabbed the rope and walked over to the bed. "Lay down, on your stomach." Her eyes are wide with surprise, but she complies.
    "Yes, sir." The breathy way she says the words has my cock thumping against the zipper of my jeans. My eyes rake over her on the bed. She's so tiny, it would be easy to break her with my dick. I slap her ass hard, she cries out and now she knows I am not playing around tonight. I am so fucking sick of little bitches trying to get a ring from me. She's no different.
    With a dark smile, I grab her wrists, and tie her up. Helpless and begging for my cock that's how I like them. And that's when it all went black…
    I sit up with a start. My heart is hammering, I glance around, I am sitting in the wingback chair. When I glance at the bed, Sasha is still there, tied up. Flying out of the chair, I call out to her, untying her ankles and wrists. She's not answering me. Her eyes are closed. Is she sleeping? My heart is thudding in my chest. "Fuck! Fuck!" Shaking her doesn't help either. What the fuck did I do?

    "I don't remember anything else. I guess I was so rough with her, that I hurt her. She was unconscious. I panicked and called Jayce. He helped me. Told me what a fuck up I had become. He was right. I still hated him for being right though. It was only later that day after Sasha was in ICU that I learned that she was pregnant. She had lost the baby because of me." My eyes finally fall on Cassie, she's quiet and trembling. I don't blame her. My heart is thudding against my chest and I am not sure what else to say.

That's it. My dark secret. The night that changed me. When I called Jayce that night. He helped me. I owe him everything I have, even though we don't see eye to eye, I love him like a brother. Blood bound us together. Even after that night, the only time I feel in control is when I am in the play room, the only difference is that I no longer take any drugs. I don't drink to get drunk anymore. Now more than ever I am in control. Cassandra needs to leave now. I can't have her here anymore.

"What?" Cassie's voice is so small I almost miss her question.

"She lost the baby." I gulp down the last of my wine.

"I…" Cassie sat speechless for a while. She can't be around me right now. I need to let her go. She needs space to process this, and I didn't want to influence her decision. I walk to the sofa and grab my phone. My decision to call Robert is the right thing to do. "I need you to take Ms. Winters back to her apartment. Now." He was at the door within a few minutes.

"Cassie, you should go." My statement is harsh, and I didn't meet her eyes. I couldn't, there was too much that needed to be said. She knew I loved her, but there was nothing I could offer. She didn't need a man who wanted to dominate her, she should have a man who can live in the light, not the dark. I never forgave myself for what I did that night. Even though I can't remember what the fuck it was. I don't remember how Sasha ended up unconscious, but I know I did it.

"Lucien, I want to stay."

"No. Just get out. Go." My voice was harsh, but there was no other choice. This was the right thing. For both of us. Mainly for the woman I love. Cassie got up without a word. I turned to look out the door of the balcony. To watch her leave would rip me apart. I glanced at her before she turned towards the door. She still had so much love in her eyes. *How can she love a monster?* "Goodbye." The last word I said to her as she turned and walked out of my life. My heart felt like it was being burned at the stake, shattered. I didn't know what I would do now. Breathing became impossible. I grabbed a bottle of whiskey, a glass and sat on the floor at the window where I could see Robert pull the car into the street and drive off with my soul mate. Pouring a large shot of whiskey, I downed it at once and poured another. This was the only way I would get through losing her. The love of my life. A part of me is gone. Half my heart and soul; Cassie took it with her when she walked out the door.

I forced her to leave I know that. A choice I had to make. To let her go, or to love a monster. So, I let her go. Even if in the process, it broke me more than I could have imagined. The pain in my chest was unlike anything I ever experienced. To lose someone, you care about is one thing, to let the one person who makes your very existence worth living, that is a completely different story.

Cassandra

The tears haven't stopped. I am sitting on the floor of the shower. The water scalding my skin, but how else do I numb the pain inside my heart? It's been roughly three days, at least that's what I think it has been. This has become my daily ritual. Lucien hasn't made contact since his confession. Robert dropped me at the apartment after Lucien told me everything on Sunday. I called in sick on Monday; I didn't want to be near him. Even though I hoped he might call or message me to see where I had been, but nothing. Nothing on Tuesday, Wednesday and now it's Thursday evening. I had wrapped my arms around my legs, curled under the warm spray of the shower. I thought maybe this would bring some clarity as to why Lucien would do what he did, but after three days, I am still clueless. This is how I spend my evenings, sitting in the shower, crying, the water washing my tears down the drain.

I didn't want to leave him, but he said he had to let me go. My heart hurt so much. He was my life. For the short time we spent together I fell hard, deep. My every breath is his. I had no idea what would happen between us. *Could we get through this?* He forced me away. I wanted to stay with him. There was so much we have been through. Although I haven't told him my past yet. Maybe then he wouldn't want anything to do with me anyway. I want him, even after what his past held, I loved him.

"Cass?" I twist to see Kenna standing in the doorway. "Jesus, Cass. What are you doing? You need to snap out of it." I shake my head. This is where I should be; I need to figure this out on my own. I didn't want to snap out of it. She's been putting up with me all week, I wanted to explain everything to her, but how? How was I supposed to tell her what I had learned about the man I loved? She wouldn't judge him and she would support whatever I decided. I didn't want to think about it right now.

"I don't know." My voice cracked. My body shivering now.

"Get out of the shower," Kenna pulled a towel from the rail and held it up for me. I hauled myself up from the corner of the shower and noticed my hands had now wrinkled. Once I turn off the water, I slide open the shower door and grab the towel. My body is trembling, I wrap it around me to keep warm, but the chill remains in my heart. There isn't anything that would warm me up from this. My bones were cold, and nothing I did could ever take that away. Unless I was in his arms. Kenna pulled me into a hug and held me as the tears flowed. That's why we were best friends. No words needed to be exchanged between us. She knew when to be there and when to leave me alone. "Come," tugging me into the bedroom, she sat me on the bed and turned on my radiator. Even though it was sweltering outside.

I watch her rifle through my cupboard, pulling out a pair of yoga pants and a tank top from my drawers, she handed them to me. She found a grey hoodie in my closet, which she laid on the bed and helped me get dressed. We didn't speak about what happened. It's been almost a week. I didn't tell her anything, and I realized she was worried, but I couldn't form words, let alone sentences.

I had to say something, so I swallowed and found the strength inside me. My heart was broken; shattered into fragments of the life I had with him. There are moments where I thought there was a massive hole inside me.

"He told me to leave." My throat ached. My heart hurt. The pain is visceral as well as a mental one. Her eyes found mine, and she offered me a melancholy smile. I saw the pain in her eyes. She realized I was hurting, and that meant that she hurt too.

"Let's get a drink?" I nodded. We shuffled into the living room and I sagged into the sofa. Kenna poured two shots of amber liquid into tumblers and sat next to me. She passed me a glass, and I sipped it. The whiskey burned my throat and chest as it made its way into my system.

"You don't have to explain what happened. I am here if you want to talk. We can just relax in silence and drink." I nodded again. I swallowed my whiskey. "Another?" I passed her my glass without a word. Bless her, I don't think I could be here alone. We sat like that for a long time. "Do you want music?" I shook my head. I suppose it's like living with someone who couldn't talk. Some sort of language that only me and her understood. The last time she saw me like this was a long time ago, at least, that's what it felt like. I use to sit in a corner, quiet, numb. Dead to the world.

I am not sure when she put me to bed that night, but I remember dreaming of him. Those green eyes that haunted me since the first day I saw them. That perfect smile. Those incredible dimples and his beautiful body. It was only when I learned and stole his heart that I knew he was the missing puzzle piece to my life. I guess I will always be the uncompleted picture.

Lucien

My alarm pulls me from a deep sleep. It's Thursday morning, the light was too fucking bright and my hangover told me that in the worst possible way. There was no way I would make it into the office now. The events of Sunday night played in my head, over and over again. Cassie walking out the door. The love shining in her eyes for me. *You let her go! This is on you, Verán.*

What the fuck was I supposed to do? Have her love the monster? She deserves better. There is someone out there that would care for her, someone that didn't kill his own baby. It didn't matter that I didn't know about it until after, it was still my fault. I scrub my hands over my face and feel the three-day old stubble scratching my palm. I grab my phone and call Jayce.

He doesn't even greet me, and I don't blame him. I have left him with the shit to deal with at the office. "Dude, where are you? We have a meeting in fifteen minutes?"

"I am not going to be in. Just tell them what we planned and take notes." My voice is gravelly and my throat is burning. Serves me right for finishing a bottle of whiskey. Or two, I can't remember. The banging in my head makes me think it might have been two.

"Jesus, Luke, you need to get a fucking grip. You have a company to run."

"Cassie left! Well, I told her to leave. I can't get a fucking grip!" I hear his sharp intake of breath and I realize how that sounds. He must know I told her the truth. I haven't spoken to him about why I haven't been in the office for three days, but I had to call him this morning because we had a meeting.

"She knows." It wasn't a question, but I nodded anyway. "Why did you tell her to leave?"

I shut my eyes; the throb in my head is driving me insane. This pain needs to leave me, but I did this. "She... Fuck, Jayce, she still looked at me with love in her eyes. After what I did."

"And the problem with that is? She fucking loves you man! Don't be a dick!" I know he's right, but I can't bring myself to call her. I need to give her space. Swinging my feet over the bed, I make my way to the kitchen and find painkillers in the cupboard. Turning on the coffee machine, I listen to him admonish me. I need this.

"I have to be a dick, she deserves better."

"She deserves you! Let's put it this way if she were with another man, how would you feel?" My heart tightens in my chest and I am sure that I am going to have a heart attack.

"I would want her to be happy." The words are strained and I know Jayce can hear it.

"Bullshit! You would fucking lose it." He's right. I know he is, but I can't do anything yet. She needs a few days. I will give her until Friday.

"I would. She needs time to process though. Friday, I will talk to her. Make this right. Okay?" He's silent for such a long time, I think he has hung up on me and my stupidity.

"Friday. I will cover for you. She needs you to love her, so get out of the fucking bed and shave. And for god's sake, shower! If you're not here with her tomorrow, I will find her and bring her to you myself."

I nod, realizing he can't see me, I reply with a low voice. "Thanks Jay." I hang up walk through to the living room. My apartment feels empty without her here. The silence is deafening. Turning on the speakers, I flop onto the sofa. The music plays loudly through the surround sound. It feels like every fucking song is about her. I feel like punching something. I walk back to the kitchen and pour a large mug of coffee. Back in the living room, I flop onto the sofa and power on my laptop. As my emails download, I stare at the screen, my mind is elsewhere, it's with Cassie. Shaking it off, I grab my phone.

"Mr. Verán's office, how can I help you?" Stacy's voice grates my nerves and my headache is suddenly worse.

"Stacy, I will not be in today. Please reschedule all my meetings and clear my diary for today and tomorrow? I will be back tomorrow, but there's something important I need to focus on, so I don't want any interruptions."

"Mr. Verán, I—" I don't need you answering me back, other than saying yes! "Stacy, is that understood?" My voice is cold and harsh, but I don't care.

"Yes, sir." Hanging up, I close my laptop and turn my phone off. I am not expecting a call from her, so there's no point having it on. I sit back and close my eyes. The coffee slowly easing the pounding of my headache. My hangover releasing me from the ache. I wish it were that simple to ease the ache in my chest. This girl owns me. When I think about that smile, I know she possesses me, more than I care to let on. Now I know, there is nothing I can do about it, but be with her.

I need a plan for tomorrow, maybe I can have Robert collect her at her apartment and bring her to me. I can wait at the office. Would she think that's cold? I want her to know that I miss her, but I can't message her. Would she want flowers? *Fuck, I am so deep I have no idea how to fix this.* I told her to leave, I pushed her away. What if she doesn't want me back?

CHAPTER sixteen

Lucien

Friday morning, I wake up with a new idea in mind. I would do something about my broken heart. There was only one woman I wanted and needed, and today she will be mine. I didn't give a fuck who approved or not. She wanted me even after what I told her, and today is the moment of truth. My plan was to talk to her, make her see I want her. Only one man can help with that, Robert. He would have to collect her and bring her to me. He answers on the first ring. "Mr. Verán."

"Robert, I need you to collect Cassie, bring her to the office. Be there by 08:30 am. I will wait at the office. Please escort her straight to the door."

"Yes, sir." I can hear the smile in his voice and realize he's happy for me. Since I have known him, he's treated me like a son. Now that I am actually in love and fighting for the girl, I think deep down he's proud of me. My choice of clothing is important, my charcoal Tom Ford suit, with a silver dress shirt is perfect. I am ready to sweep Cassie off her feet, and when she falls, it will be into my arms. The only place she belonged. This is it. Today is the day I get my girl back.

I pull the Aston out of the drive and pull into the early morning traffic. My heart is racing as I drive to the office, leaving Robert with the SUV to pick Cassie up. To say I wasn't nervous would be the understatement of the fucking year. I was shitting myself. She needed to take me back. There was something about this woman that had my balls in a vice and I didn't mind at all.

When I stepped into the office ten minutes later, every head turned to face me. I ignored them all and made my way to my office. "Mr. Verán, I have cleared your schedule for today, as instructed." Stacy at my heels like a fucking puppy that kept hanging on.

"Great. You can take the day off." Without another word, I step into my office and shut the door. I doubt she would listen to me; she's loyal to a fault. I sit back in my large black leather office chair and contemplate if Cassandra will actually show up.

Robert has his instruction, now to send her a message. The first one for almost a week. It's been killing me not contacting her, but she's had enough space to think. Now it's time to act.

Robert will collect you and bring you to me

I don't wait long for her reply.

Okay

No argument, just one word. *Good girl.* I face the large windows and take in the view.

The West Coast has always been my favorite place, now more than ever, because I have Cassie. Well. Not yet. Soon. I will not take no for an answer; she will take me back. I can't lose her. Although my heart is hammering so hard like it's about to break out of my chest. I take a deep calming breath.

The knock at the door startles me and I check the time. It can't be her already. *Can it?* "Mr. Verán, I have your coffee." Stacy steps into my office, placing the cup on my desk; she gives me a small smile and practically runs out again. Perhaps I am too hard on her.

Today will be a test for both Cassie and me. And I can't wait to see how well she passes it. I slip into the office chair and drink my coffee. It's not long now, and the anticipation is killing me.

Cassandra

I roll over and open my eyes. It was too bright, and I wasn't sure what day it was. *Shit! Friday!* I scrambled out of bed and picked up my phone from the nightstand. My heart stopped racing. It was only 7 am. I went into the bathroom and brushed my teeth. I looked like shit, but I felt like it too. "You're up early." I turned to face Kenna in the doorway.

"I need to get to work." Today I would take the proverbial bull by the horns and make him accept that I wanted him. I was tired of moping around like a heartbroken teenager.

"Are you sure you want to go to him?" Nope! I didn't want to see him. Yes! I did! I did want to look into those green eyes and make him listen to me. Make him see how ingrained in my heart he was. That was all the more reason to go to work. So we could talk and figure out what was going on. My plan was to walk into his office and tell him to get over the fact that he has a past because I have one too. I love him. Why can't he see that?

Back in the bedroom, I opened my closet. There was one dress I had a feeling would make this easier. Lucien has never seen me wear it, but today, her will. It was a sleeveless mid-thigh fire engine red dress. It had a zipper in the front which stopped between my breasts. I wore a black lace corset underneath and had some of the lace peeking out. My black pumps were perfect, so I slipped those on. Now I was ready to take him on. I left my curls loose down my back. Then I applied a small amount of mascara and some black eyeliner, which finished off a smoky look. Soft pink lip-gloss completed it.

"Are you trying to get him back or kill him?" Kenna giggled when she brought me coffee moments later.

"A little of both I think." I spin around, taking in my appearance in the full-length mirror. *Yes! This is it!* Kenna handed me the cup with a smile on her face. For the first time since Sunday when he told me to leave, I smiled. "I think I am ready. No, I am!" She smiles and nods.

"Good luck babe, I really fucking hope he has his head screwed on right!" My phone buzzes and I frown. There is only one person that would text me this early. My hand is trembling as I pick up my phone from the nightstand, I swipe the screen. A message from Lucien. My heart leaps into my throat.

Robert will collect you and bring you to me

"What?" Kenna peeks over my shoulder. "Oh! Well, I hope he wants to sort things out." I shrug. The text seems cold, not like the Lucien I fell in love with. Unless he's just trying to gauge my reaction and response. I hit reply.

Okay

As soon as I finish my coffee the doorbell rings. That must be Robert. "Bye babe, I will call you later." I hug Kenna. With my hand on the doorknob, I take a deep breath and open it. The SUV is waiting on the sidewalk.

"Message me and fill me in on what happens." I nod and walk to the car.

"Robert," I smile.

"Ms. Winters," he opens the door and I am half expecting Lucien to be sitting in the bench seat. When I find it empty my heart plummets.

"Where is he, Robert?" I ask as soon as he slides into the front of the car.

"He's at the office. I am supposed to escort you there." He smiles in the rear-view mirror. Checking my phone again, I read and re-read his message. I dissect the message trying to find a clue as to what mood he would be in. *What do I do if he wants nothing to do with us anymore? I mean, why would he? Unless he found out something about my past? Shit!* I should have told him myself. If he learns the truth, he wouldn't push me away. Maybe that would make him realize how perfect we are together. Two broken souls, healing each other through the dark. My Lumiére! His words repeat in my mind. *Can I show him that I can be his light?* If not, I am not sure I can go on working there, knowing we can never be.

Robert pulls into the garage of Verán Publishers and we take the elevators up. "Is he... I mean..." I glance at Robert; he will know why Lucien wants me to come to him.

"Ms. Winters, all I can say is, breathe." He offers a smile and I nod. That doesn't really help my apprehension. This is the man I love, the other half of me. We step out of the elevator on the top floor of the high-rise building. We walk to the outside of Lucien's office door, then Robert turns to me.

"This is where I leave you, Ms. Winters," Robert gives me a small nod and walks back to the elevators. I am standing outside Lucien's office door and suddenly unsure. *Do I want to go in there?* I knock, waiting for an answer. The realization of what is about to happen has my hand trembling. *Calm down Cassie, you can do this. It's will be okay!* I just need to convince him we're meant to be. *Easy as pie!*

Lucien

By the time the knock comes, I have finished my coffee and I am wringing my hands. I straighten up. I need to play it as cool as I can. Not wanting to scare her off. Robert texted me to tell me she was on the way. This was it. Show time.

"Come in." My voice is low, but she would have heard it. *Was I too abrupt? Shit, did she think I am angry?* I watch the doorknob turn and my heart races, pounding against my ribcage. When she steps inside, her eyes flicker all over the office, but not on me. When my eyes land on her though, I grip the edge of the desk so hard my knuckles turn white. *Jesus fucking Christ! That body is incredible!* She's dressed in the sexiest dress I have ever seen. It's hugging every soft curve of her body and I am instantly rock hard. She closes the door and takes in her surroundings. She's never been in my office and I realize she's trying to get a feel of my mood. I can read her like an open book.

My eyes rake over her appearance, from those black pumps, up to her eyes. I can't help letting out a strained groan. The need to bend her over my desk and fuck her into next week is strong. That's what seeing her in that dress is doing to me. It's a primal feeling that's completely taken over my brain function.

I don't move. If I stand she'll see the bulge in my pants. It's practically bursting through my zipper. Painful and hard. I remain calm, aloof almost and show no sign of why I called her here. "Sit." She doesn't say a word, but obeys me like she always does. *Good girl, Cassie. You're so fucking perfect, how could I let you walk away?* Her eyes flicker to me quickly and a blush pinks her cheeks. *Fuck, can I do this? All I want to do is bang her on the desk.* She's exquisite. Her soft skin has a shimmer, and those tits. For a moment I close my eyes and count to five. I need to calm the fuck down.

She slips into the chair across from my desk and I swallow hard. It's only when she leans forward do I notice the lace. She's fucking teasing me with the black lace corset under her dress. The emotion flickers over my gaze and she's seen it. I can't hide it anymore, my feelings for her run too deep. "I needed to see you." There's nothing else to do now, but let it play out. At that moment I let it all out. Then and there, in the office. "I spent the last few days in agony. There is no way I can be without you. I need you in my life. After what I told you, I thought letting you go would be better for you, but I can't. I am a selfish bastard. I love you." The explanation is raw, honest, one the she's been waiting for. She has to know how distraught I was without her. Her eyes meet mine and the glimmer of desire she has for me shines in those chocolate orbs. "I do Cassie, these past few days have near killed me. I don't know how to live without you." She sits back and stares at me. "Say something. Please?" She knows I need her, it's no secret, but she needed me to say it, out loud. As soon as I am done explaining, my desire goes into overdrive. I need her. To be inside her, deep, hard, and fast.

"How do I know you will not send me packing when you have a wave of guilt again?" I drop my gaze. My focus on the pen in my hands. I am nervous and she can see it, but I don't care, not anymore. "Lucien," I glance up at her and she says the words I need to hear. "I love you. I will not leave because you have a past." The only way I can show her how I feel is by making her come all over my hard cock.

"Come here," reaching out my arms to her. She stands and walks over to me. That dress is a fucking killer. I pull her into my embrace. My head resting on her hip, I inhale her scent. She's as turned on as I am.

I rise from my chair and stalk over to my door. With a click, I lock it, then I turn to her with lust in my gaze which must be evident. "I need to fix this." With the need of a crazy man I walk up to her and pull her into me. "I want you. I need you, sweetness. We can't be apart, ever." I know she can feel my erection pressing into her stomach. She will scream my name soon. I will fuck her right here and now. Not giving two fucks about who hears her. She's mine and I am hers. There is no way in hell I am losing her again.

"I can't be away from you either Lucien, but I can't live in fear that you will tell me to leave if you have a bad day." I nod. There are no words I can give her now. There is nothing, but pure unadulterated lust. So I don't answer her. Instead I seal her mouth with mine as I lift her onto the desk. Everything crashes to the floor as I swoop an arm over my desk. Lifting her dress to her luscious hips, I tug at her thong, ripping it to shreds. I am wild with lust. The zipper of my pants is down in seconds and I free my cock. My fingers find her soaked, and a low growl rumbles in my chest. I don't waste time and slam into her all the way to the base. Pressing my hand over her mouth to muffle her cries. There is something primal in my actions and she's dripping.

Our bodies locked at the hip, she feels so fucking good around me, sheathing my cock. As she tightens around me, it sends pleasure shooting down my spine. This is us, broken by desire. We will get through it; I know we can. My unrelenting drives plunge into her over and over again. Her nails rake down my back and the bite of pain is incredible as she sinks her teeth into my shoulder.

The animalistic fucking that we're doing has my orgasm close. I own her. Claiming her and fucking possessing her. She's mine. Nobody will ever make her feel like this. Her tight little cunt spasms. The idea of how much she possesses me has my balls tightening. "My lumiére! Come for me!" My command is husky, and she explodes, her body writhing below me. She clenches me inside her body. My own release shoots into her, deeper than I have ever been before. As our orgasms shake us to the core, I tell her everything I need her to know. "You're so perfect Cassie, you scare me. But now I own you. You are mine." I hold her like she is my last breath. Her body trembles in my arms, just the way it's meant to be.

"We will get through it handsome. We will." She whispers in my ear as I collapse over her. With a slow movement I pull out of her. Her face is a picture of lust, love and satisfaction. I am not sure which I should be more thankful for. I zip up my pants and help her up. Once she's straightened, I take in the mess in my office. Thank fuck I didn't drop my laptop. I can only imagine trying to explain to IT it fell off my desk.

"I guess you forgive me for being a dick?" Her giggle warms my heart.

"I suppose. A few more of these…" She gestures between the desk and us. "And I may be able to forgive anything, well… Almost anything." With her hand in mine, I lock my gaze on hers. Hoping she can see my sincerity and love.

"I don't want to lose you. No more secrets. Promise?"

"Promise." Her voice is low, and she doesn't meet my stare, but I am sure she's just nervous.

"Let me get you back to your office." With a nod, we make our way to the elevators. I escort her down to the tenth floor.

We're standing in silence, but before I leave, she whispers. "You realize that I am not wearing panties since you ripped them off." All I can do is groan loudly. If I didn't have meetings I would take her here, right now. With a long soft kiss, I stare into her eyes.

"Tonight I will punish you for that little comment." She gasps. I turn to leave after I promise to take her to dinner this evening. I have an idea and I hope she will like it.

The rest of the day goes by with meetings and more meetings. Although I feel like a new man. Cassie is mine; we will be okay. That's all that matters. When I get out of my last meeting of the day, I call her desk. As soon as she answers, my body relaxes, that's the effect she has on me. "Verán Publishers, Cassie speaking."

"Is there a beautiful brunette sitting at her desk missing her boyfriend?" *Yes, I have turned into a fucking sap.* I can only imagine what my best friend would say about this.

"Not in this department, Sir." The way that words rolls off her tongue has me groaning. "Would you like me to put you through to reception?" The amusement evident in her voice. This is what I missed, the banter, that sassy mouth.

"Ms. Winters, I suggest you think long and hard about that answer. Or I will put you across my lap." Her breathing hitches, and I bet that she's soaked.

"Now that you mention it, there is something long and hard on my mind, but it's not my answer." Lust courses through my veins at her response. She really does know how to drive me insane with desire. That's why I love her, there's no woman that has ever made me feel like this.

"Are you insinuating that I am sitting at my desk, with a hard on for you, Ms. Winters?" My voice is low and I can hear her breathing deepen. I can picture her cheeks flushed and her chest rising and falling. Her thighs squeezing together. Telltale signs that she's turned on.

"Mr. Verán, I have work to do, I suggest you stop distracting me with talk about your hard on." She's played her ace; I have to smile at her courage. She's definitely getting a spank on the ass for that.

"Fine. Robert will collect you from your apartment at 6:30. See you soon baby." I hang up and finish some work before making my way home. As soon as I step out of the shower, my phone buzzes.

What am I supposed to wear, Lucien?

I consider for a moment. It's a fairly relaxed little place on the beach. The weather has been good today, so I decided to take her to the coast.

Nothing formal. We will be near the beach. Sandals.

I grab a pair of blue Levi's and a black T-shirt. There is something about tonight that is different. Something that I am sure will change our dynamic. Cassie knows I love her, but there's a lot we need to work on. I intend to make tonight about her, and us.

With a glance at my watch I realize it's almost time. To say that I am nervous would be an understatement. I am terrified. It's going to be a make it or break it date and I don't want to disappoint her. I slide into the car and pull out of the driveway, making my way to Cassie's apartment. This is like going on your first date, hoping to make a good impression. She's expecting Robert, but this is part one of my surprise.

When I pull up to her apartment, I get out of the car and walk up to the door. Before I push the buzzer, I close my eyes for a second. No going back now. Once I buzz the apartment, I wait. As soon as the door opens, my breath stops. She looks incredible. Long wavy brown hair loose down her back. She's dressed in a flimsy light blue sundress with thin straps and a small jumper over. The color looks breathtaking on her tanned skin.

"Ms. Winters, you're looking beautiful." The smile I offer threatens to crack my face in half. Her cheeks pink with a blush and she returns my smile with hers, which lights up my world.

"Thank you, Lucien. You're not looking too bad yourself." She slips her hand into mine and we make our way to the car. I open the door for her and give her a grin that makes her blush again. There is no longer tension between us. Everything feels as it should, and all I can hope is that it's going to work out.

Cassandra

"I want to do it myself!" I giggle at Lucien. We were standing on the beach. It was almost midnight, and we decided to light lanterns and have them float into the sky. The dinner was incredible, seafood with a dry white wine. I couldn't believe just yesterday we were not talking and now, I was standing here with him. We know now we can't live without each other. It's impossible. Even though Lucien knows I am seeing a therapist. I haven't gone into too much detail yet. That will be the biggest test of our relationship. After his revelation, which to be honest shook me to the core. There is no doubt in my mind he would ever hurt me. I trust him with everything I have. We're meant to be. If we can make it through that then I guess, we could make it through anything. We will need to have a long talk; I need to find the courage to tell him about my past. "Do you want to go for a swim?" Lucien whispers in my ear.

"Yes," I spin around in his arms. As I lean up on my tip toes, my lips press against his. His hands cup my face, holding me in place. I love how he always takes control. Never in a million years did I think I would be the girl to be submissive in a relationship. Being fiercely independent, I never take orders from anyone, but that's the beauty of us. This is how it works, most women think submitting to a man is degrading themselves, when it's not. You're allowing yourself to trust on such a deep level, it's beautiful and intoxicating. By giving him my submission, I am showing him how much I love and respect him, that's the respect and love he gives me. He takes nothing from me. It's up to me to give him my trust, letting him push my boundaries, to guide me in exploring my sexuality.

"Are you joining me?" I giggle.

"Ms. Winters, I would definitely like to join you." With his index fingers he slides my dress off my shoulders. His lips find the nape of my neck. The kisses are soft, gentle, and they send shivers down my spine. "You're wearing a bikini?" I glance up at his amused expression.

"Of course Mr. Verán, I was looking forward to a swim." I wink, my dress drops to the sand and I turn to run into the water. With a glance back, I see Lucien pulling his T-shirt over his head. The water is warm and I have no trouble running into the crashing waves.

Moments later, Lucien is behind me. This was the first time in a week that I was happy. I decided this weekend would be the perfect time to tell him about my past. There was also so much more I wanted to learn about him. About his mother and step-mother. I wanted to learn everything about my amazing man.

"Come here, sweetness!" I watch him wade into the water. As soon as he's close enough, his arms wrap around me, holding me to him. I loved the heat of his rock solid body against mine. My hands tangle in his hair. When he leans in, sealing my mouth with his, I know everything in my world is perfect. His tongue licks into me, tasting me. I tug him closer, aching to feel him inside me. That sexy primal growl rumbles through his chest and I moan into the kiss. His one hand gripping my ass tight, his other hand snaking between my thighs. Stroking me through my bikini bottoms I am soaking wet, and I don't mean from the water.

"Lucien," I breathe into his neck, a shiver runs through his body. He slides two fingers inside me and takes me higher. My eyes flutter closed, the sensation of the waves and his fingers pushing me further and further to the edge. He is the only person who could make me feel this way. Soon I am clenching around his fingers as my release washes over me.

"You're beautiful when you come for me, sweetness." His voice is low and sexy and I melt into his embrace. As I stare up at him, heat pinks my cheeks. His eyes hold so much love, but deep down I can still see the pain so clearly evident from the last few days.

"Take me home?" He nods and carries me to the shore. Once we're on the sand, I pull on my dress, but the breeze has picked up and I start shivering. We run back to the car, with me carrying my shoes. Lucien helps me into the passenger seat. As soon as he starts the car he turns on the heating. My teeth are chattering, but I sit there giggling. Something has come over me and I don't know how to explain it, but I need to laugh. Lucien glances at me quickly and smiles. "I love that sound." He drove us home, to his apartment.

Lucien

When she told me to take her home from the beach, there was only one thing I could do, and that was obey her wishes. As we made our way home, Cassie was quiet, like she was contemplating something. I drove through the quiet streets. Pulling into the driveway twenty minutes later. An overwhelming need to touch her overcame me, and I placed my hand on her thigh, giving it a reassuring squeeze. I thought the dinner went really well, at least I hope it did. When I pull into the garage, the air is thick with tension, I am not sure if it's good or bad.

We make our way into the apartment and I open a bottle of wine. "Let's relax for a while." I turn on the TV, and we flop onto the sofa. Cassie sat back, snuggling into the crook of my arm. Her body fits next to mine so perfectly. I can't even imagine if she had decided she didn't want me. The thought brings an unwelcome pain and I shake my head to will it away. There's a prickle in the air and I realize something is coming, I just don't know what. Perhaps Cassie is ready to tell me about her past. As soon as the thought enters my mind, she turns to me. Her eyes glassy from unshed tears and my heart constricts.

"Lucien, can we talk?" She looks up from her glass and I am lost in her beautiful brown eyes. I can tell she's too distracted to concentrate on anything. So, I sit back and stare at her, taking in her stressed appearance. This is something that's clearly eating her up inside and I want to do anything I can to take her pain away.

"Sure sweetness, you can tell me anything. I mean you heard about my demons." She nods. Her glance falls back on the screen and I see we're actually watching highlights of this year's New York Fashion Week. It's almost as if I can see the wheels turn in her mind as she watches the screen. This is it, time for me to learn about my incredible girl. She turns to me and smiles, but it's not filled with joy, there is pain all over her beautiful face. My heart constricts and the pain in my chest is unbearable. To see her hurting is something I hate.

"Okay, I told you I have been seeing a therapist." She looks at me and I nod. "Right, so, two and a half years ago I was living with my folks, just outside New York City. I was… I was seeing my ex-fiancé, well, obviously. I mean, you know." Another deep breath fills her lungs. My chest tugs once more, learning that she was engaged to someone else. Call me selfish, but the jealousy wracks through me. "One night, I was going out with some friends to celebrate my new job. It was a girls' night. I guess at twenty-four, those were mandatory." She shuffles on the sofa, and I can tell she's scared and uncomfortable. "I'd had too many tequila shots; I couldn't drive home." Her small laugh is sad. It takes all my restraint not to hold her. "I called my fiancé to pick me up; he suggested bringing my dad to get my car. I was so stupid." When her eyes close

I want to pull her into my arms, but she doesn't let me. I can see the tears when she looks at me again. *Fuck, what happened baby?* I just want to take her pain away. She takes a mouthful of wine. Then she stares at the screen again. We watch the models take the stage. *Why are we watching this?* My head is all over the place. I can't see her in pain. This is excruciating, to see the anguish in her beautiful eyes.

"That night Kenna picked me up when she finished work." She stops suddenly, but there's a whole chunk of story missing. I frown and she's noticed. As soon as she blinks, tears stream down her cheeks. *Fuck this, I am holding you!* I pull her to me and wrap her in my embrace. She needs to get this out, I know, but having her in my arms calms me and her body relaxes slightly. She sits back suddenly, and my hands drop from her. I am helpless, there's nothing I can do to ease her pain. All I can do is listen. "I killed them. They were…" She gulps painfully. "A truck, I mean I—"

"Cassie," I reach for her, but she stops me. A slow shake of her head tells me that she needs to finish this. She needs to go on. The pain she's experiencing is ripping into me more than she realizes.

"No, I need to tell you." She glances at me and gives me a wry smile. The concern on my face is obvious. "They, didn't make it. They came to get me. They—" She closes her eyes again, and it's taking all my fucking restraint not to grab her and hold her. *Fuck Verán, this girl has gone through so much. You need to handle her with care.* My heart hurts for her. The pain of losing a parent is debilitating.

Then her words come out in a rush. "The truck driver lost control as he rounded the corner. My mother… She wanted to see me, she was in the car too. The car rolled." Cassie took a harsh deep breath, while tears flowed down her cheeks. My heart was officially in shattered pieces. She didn't just lose one, but two parents, and the man she loved. "They were taken to the hospital. They didn't make it. All three of them. I killed them. It was my fault. I was depressed for so long. To leave my apartment was difficult, so I used to sit in a corner of my bedroom just staring into nothing. Kenna left me for a while, but after two weeks, she basically slapped me into shape. She took me to Dr. Kessel, a therapist in New York. I was… They put me… I was…" Her voice came in short spurts, and I realized it was just to get it all out. "I was admitted, I mean, I spent 6 months in an institution. I am so fucked up. So broken. Nothing can ever make me whole again." She looked up at me expecting pity, but all I gave her was love. It overwhelmed her, I could tell from the expression on her face. Her tears fell, but I didn't make a move to touch her. She needed to tell me when she was ready. *How could she even want me? She has been through so much. She's so strong and I am a fuck up.* "I have these horrible attacks from time to time. I can't breathe, it hits me like a freight train and all I can do is sit in a corner. They say if you love someone too much the universe takes them from you. Maybe that was my problem. I loved them too much. I wasn't meant to be happy. I was just meant to be like this." She gestures to her face. "How can you want me? I was in a mental institution?"

Shock ran through my body, I was quiet, trying to figure out how to reply to that. *How the fuck can she think that?* I love her more now than I did twenty minutes ago. She's incredible. I waited for her to finish, but then she stood. She left me on the sofa. I took a deep breath and followed her. In the kitchen I watched her pour a large glass of water. She gulped it down and I am sure she was exhausted, dehydrated from the amount of tears she cried. I reached out for her and she started at my touch. Then I turned her around and cupped her face in my hands. Her face was beautiful, even with the tears, and puffy red eyes. She was perfect. So many emotions were tumbling through me that

I wasn't sure which one to hold onto. I decided on the one where I love this girl with everything I am.

"You're an amazing strong woman. You've been through so much and you're still here. There are no words to explain how much I love you. Let me help fix you? We're here together, we fit like pieces of a puzzle Cassie, I want to take care of you forever. Your past is gone; I don't care where you've been. Only where you're going. Let me? Please? I want to make your future better than your past." I pull her into my embrace and she let me hold her. Pain, relief, and love washes over me. She cried then, and I let her.

Moments later, I cup her face in my hands, sealing her mouth with mine in a tender kiss, her body visibly calms. "There is never a time that you should be scared to tell me anything. You're my light, the strongest, most beautiful light I have ever seen. You blind me with your strength and smile." I scoop her up and carry her to the master suite. Laying her down, in my bed, where she's meant to be. I climb in behind her and hold her to my chest. She cried some more. She sobbed, like girls do for those sappy movies they watch. All the while, I hold her. As the sobs calm and her breathing became even, I notice she'd fallen asleep with my arm around her. She looked incredible and there was nowhere else I would have her. My eyes fell closed then, and I had the best sleep I had in a week.

Chapter seventeen
Cassandra

The heat of the sun streams through the windows. When I open my eyes, I take in the beautiful view from the bed. "Good morning beautiful," I roll over to meet green eyes peering at me.

"Hi. I feel like a bus ran over me." My voice is croaky, and he smiles.

"You're cute." I groan, I don't feel cute at all. Last night was like a weight had been lifted off my shoulders when I told him about my past. The fact that he's still here is not lost on me. I can't believe he stayed. He now has a girlfriend with a crazy past. There was a small detail that I left out. I shouldn't have, but I couldn't bring myself to tell him. Not yet, we needed to get over the initial shock of everything. Or maybe he would never need to learn the ugly secret that has left me broken for so long. After his confession, this would probably hurt him way too much.

"Thank you for your honesty and letting me in Cassie, I love you." He pressed a kiss on the tip of my nose. Guilt rose in my chest. I should just tell him now. *He will never forgive you. Just let it go.*

"I love you too, Lucien. I need to call Kenna. She's probably worried." My phone has been off all night, I grab it and turn it on. There are a few messages and 2 missed calls. One is from Dr. Kessel. I will listen to her voice message later. The past is the last thing I want to think about right now. I open my messages and hit reply to Kenna's latest one.

"Yes, I have an idea. There's somewhere I want to take you today. You will love it. The arrangements have to be made first." Lucien rolls out of bed and I immediately miss his warmth. My gaze rakes in his naked toned body, the smooth tanned skin has me aching again. I can't help wanting him all the time. As soon as he's disappeared into the bathroom, I turn my attention back to my phone, and type out a reply to Kenna.

Hey babe. All okay. We spoke. Not the whole story, but most of it. See you later. xo

I push the covers down and get up. My clothes are scattered all over the room, but I find Lucien's discarded black T-shirt and tug it on. With the patio door open I step outside. My gaze falls on the Hollywood sign in the distance. There was something about being in this city, it did something, making you believe anything is possible. I realized as I stood there that I was here with Lucien. Last night was draining, and I was tired, but he didn't ask me to leave.

Moments later I hear Lucien. "Everything is ready. Our appointment is at 11 am." When I turn to face him, there is a mischievous glint in his eyes.

"Appointment?" I frown at him; he knows I hate surprises. He nods and winks at me. With a smirk, he presses his index finger and thumb together, 'zipping' his lips. Without thinking I roll my eyes at his playfulness. He has his moments where he frustrates me, but I secretly love it.

"Ms. Winters, I do not appreciate you rolling your eyes at me. I will bend you over right here on the patio and spank you." His words sending delicious tingles down my spine. That sounded like fun. *I could definitely enjoy that. Would love to have his hands on my ass right now. It would turn him on spanking me. We needed some sex! Yes!*

"Oh really? Would Mr. Verán enjoy that?" My question is soft; my voice is raspy. I used the sexiest voice I could muster. His eyes darkened, and I knew he wanted to take me. My nipples harden in the flimsy cotton material of the top. His eyes flit to my breasts and a devilish smirk curled his sensual lips.

"Ms. Winters, I don't recommend you start something now." His voice was dark and seductive. My core pulses in anticipation. I turn and lean against the railing of the balcony. My eyes fall to the bulge in the front of his sweats. It's an obvious sign of how turned on he is. His beautifully tanned torso is rock solid, the smooth dips of his abs and V muscles have me squirming.

"Why not, Mr. Verán? Can you not finish it?" My cheekiness earns me a cocky smile. The playful act of defiance has my stomach in knots of anticipation. I stare into his dark green eyes that are filled with a dark hunger I yearn for. Without another word, he stalks to me and grips my shoulders.

"Let me finish this for you. Right here." His eyes flicker to the patio where we're standing and a gasp escapes my lips. He easily spins my around. With a hand on my back he bends me over. My grip on the railing is tight because this will be hard. The first swat tingles on my ass and sends shivers over my skin. Another swat has me mewling for more. "Hold on tight, baby. Because you are going to get fucked. Very hard." His voice at my ear is low, and deliciously dark. I clutch the wood and give a slight nod. By this stage words are no longer possible.

My body is on fire. I feel him behind me. The tip of his erection pressing against my wet heat. I push back trying to force him inside me, but he chuckles. With a small step back he moves away, leaving me whimpering. The heat of his chest is on my back as he reaches around me, his fingers strum my clit and my knees almost give way. His expert touch sending me to the edge as soon as I am about to find the release I need he stops.

"Now, Ms. Winters, you rolled your eyes at me didn't you?" I nod. "That deserves punishment, and I will give it to you. Do you understand me?" I nod. "Good girl." His voice a deep growl. The heat of his breath fans over my ear, his teeth nibble the sensitive lobe, sending shock waves through me. "Tell me if you need me to stop. Okay?" I nod again.

He tugs my panties down, allowing me to step out of them. His foot nudges mine further apart. "I love when you're open and ready for me," he grunts. He strokes my slick folds again, making me moan. I mumble his name as the heat pools at my core. Again, as I feel my orgasm near, he stops. I let out a huff. "But, you rolled your eyes at me, little kitty. This is your punishment." He whispers. Stepping back, he lifts his hand, a sharp sting on my ass causes me to lift onto my toes. Left, then the right and then the center. Again, and again. My knees were wobbling, and my white knuckle grip is painful, but I don't care. I was so turned on that when Lucien's fingers stroked me again I was dripping down my inner thighs. "My sweet, sexy, wet tigress. Purr for me."

His breath on my core, is incredible, and my legs are trembling. I try to push back against him, but he's just out of reach. His tongue lightly laps at my inner thighs. "You taste so fucking good."

Suddenly he drives two fingers inside me, my orgasm shatters through my body and I tighten around his fingers. A low growl rumbles in my ears, somewhere through the haze of desire sweeping through my mind. As I am trying to catch my breath, his cock presses against my entrance. "Hold tight naughty girl. I am taking you hard and fast." He hisses in my ear, his tongue licking the shell. His lips leave feather soft kisses down my neck, leaving goose bumps in their wake. His teeth graze my shoulder as he slams into me fast and deep. My cry is loud and harsh. I don't care if the whole of LA just heard me, my lust is barreling through me. "That's my girl. So fucking tight around me. Take me lumiére, fucking take my cock."

He pulls almost all the way out and drives back in to the hilt. Reaching around me his fingers flick over my hard clit, stroking me, faster and faster. "You're so fucking tight; my cock loves being inside you, baby." He thrusts into me relentlessly, almost violently. My arms are shaking at the intensity of our movements. He teases my rock hard nipples, with his other hand, sending waves of pleasure skittering over my skin. My head drops down, I can't hold myself any longer, I moan his name repeatedly.

A second orgasm building again, tightening my pussy around his cock. "My lumiére." His voice hoarse with desire. His hand moves from my breasts and he grips my neck tight as he plunges into me. My release so close, when I clench around him, my body tenses. The connection we have isn't only physical, its emotional, deep in my heart and soul.

My eyes are shut so tight I see stars, fireworks. Nothing exists, but us in that moment. "Come sweetness, give it all to me." His order sending me crashing over the edge as I nosedive into oblivion. My body shaking uncontrollably as his release fills me. "My lumiére!" As soon as he growls in my ear, my legs give way, but Lucien holds me up against him. His hot breath still in my ear, sending shudders over my skin. "Fuck. That was…"

I nod. Unable to speak. As I come down from the euphoric high, I remember we're still out on the patio. The neighbors must have heard that. Luckily, nobody can see us from here. Lucien slips from me and scoops me up. Back inside, he places me on the bed. "Are you okay, baby?" I nod and smile.

"Yes, that was incredible. Go shower, I can't move right now." With a chuckle, he plants a soft kiss on my lips and walks off into the bathroom. My body is still shaky and all I can do is giggle.

Lucien

My mind is on the amazing sex we just had on the patio, no woman has made me lose control so much. The way her body trembles under me, and her pussy tightens around my cock. The feel of her is indescribable. As I step out of the shower, I grab a towel and make my way into the bedroom. She's already showered, dressed, and ready to go. The excitement is evident on her face. "Please tell me where we're going?" She's been asking me that all morning.

"Baby, if I tell you it won't be a surprise." I grab my jeans and a T-shirt from my walk-in closet. Her voice is muffled in reply, but her complaints don't go unnoticed. When I walk back into the bedroom, she's sitting on the bed with the sexiest pout I have ever seen. Her lips look so damn fuckable. I would love to slide my cock between them. With her warm wet mouth swallowing me. *Fuck! I need to get ready or we will never leave.*

I raise an eyebrow at her and she shrugs. "Fine, I am waiting downstairs." As she passes me, I swat her pert little ass, and I am rewarded with a sexy yelp. I chuckle at her. "Why? Am I distracting you with my naked body?" As I pull my boxer briefs up, she takes a backward glance and gives me a cheeky wink. *That girl is going to be the death of me.* I get dressed as quickly as humanly possible. Once I am downstairs, I find her sitting on the sofa, quietly flipping through channels on the flat screen. "Are you ready?" Turning the television off, she bounds from the sofa and stands at the door, waiting patiently.

In the garage I unlock the Aston. Her gaze cuts to me with awe when I click a button and the roof of the car folds and gets tucked away in the trunk. "Wow. Bringing out the big guns today are we?" She gives me a cocky smile, with her hands on her hips.

"I am just full of surprises baby; you should know that by now. Trust me, there's only one gun you need to worry about." A blush spreads across her cheeks as open the door for her.

"Lucien!" With a chuckle, I watch her slide into the leather seat. Her shorts ride up her thighs and I can't help craving to be between them. This girl has come into my life, broken down every wall, shattered every belief I had about love. Once I am in the drivers' seat, I start the engine and pull out onto the road. "She sounds almost as good as you do when you're purring."

A cheeky wink gets me a beautiful laugh from her. "Oh I purr?" I nod. "Mmm…" She doesn't reply, but places a hand on my thigh, stroking from my knee, stopping just short of my crotch.

"Cass, I need to concentrate on driving." She nods, flashing me a naughty smile.

"I realize that; I didn't do anything. Did I?" Once I change lanes, I cut a quick glance at her. Those big puppy dog eyes will be the death of me.

"No, you didn't just make my cock hard, and you didn't make me think of fucking you on the hood of my million dollar Aston Martin. No, definitely not." Her breathing hitches and I smile. *So beautifully responsive for me.* We take the scenic route, and just before we get to our destination, I pull over and blindfold Cassie. Once I am happy she can't see, I pull out onto the road and race down to the venue. The security gives me the go ahead and I find the parking number allotted to me. I lean towards her, and tug on the blindfold. "We're here."

"Are we playing in the car? Is that the big surprise?" Her giggle is soft, and she chews her plump bottom lip. She's nervous. Slowly stroking her bare thigh, using my thumb, I swipe it over the crotch of her shorts. A small moan escapes her lips and her hips buck towards me instinctively.

"Maybe we are. How would you feel about that?" I am teasing her, trying to sound as serious as possible.

"Lucien, I am all for playing games, but what are you doing? Where are we?" I sit back and chuckle. Her body relaxes and I unlock the doors.

"We're at your surprise." I get out, run around the car and open the door for her. Helping her out, I plant a soft kiss on her lips. When I see my contact coming up to greet us. "Come on darling, hold my hand." I hope she will enjoy this. I give him a quick nod and lead Cassie around to his office. He's taking us on a tour, so he needs to explain the rules and ask Cassie what she would like to see.

Cassandra

We spent the day at Universal Studios, Lucien got us an exclusive private tour. It was so exciting seeing where the shows were shot and running into some of the actors. The weather was wonderful, the day definitely lifted my spirits. I glance at the time; it was only 3 pm by the time we had finished the tour. "You ready for our late lunch sweetness?" I smiled and nodded.

He looked so handsome in his white tank and blue ripped jeans. He was wearing his Aviators, but his eyes were twinkling behind them, he laces his fingers through mine, we stroll to the car. "I am, where are we going for lunch?" Lucien opens my door; I slide into the plush leather seat.

"You should know by now, it's a surprise." He chuckles when I sulk. Once he's in the driver's seat, the engine purrs to life and he pulls out onto the road.

"You're adorable when you pout." He glances over at me and gives me a smile.

We're interrupted by Lucien's phone ringing on the hands-free holder. He presses the answer button, my skin prickles at his step-mother's voice. "Lucien, darling. Your father has taken ill, and he requires you at the house immediately." I glance over at Lucien and his face has drained of color. I place a hand on his thigh and give it a squeeze.

"What? Where is he?"

"He's here, the physician has just left. Get here as quickly as you can."
The line goes dead.

"I'm sorry baby do you mind?" With a sad smile, I nod.

"I don't mind going with you?" My question is weary, hoping he doesn't shut me out. He gives me a swift nod and makes a U-turn. I notice we're headed for the Hollywood Hills. Lucien hits the gas and we speed up the road. When we pull up to a set of black wrought-iron gates, he presses a button on a remote and the slide open. We make our way up the long paved driveway, and I take in the incredible manicured gardens. Once we've stopped outside the main entrance, I open the door and get out. I wait for Lucien to come around to my side, slipping his hand in mine, we race up to the door.

He pushes the heavy wooden door open and let's me walk inside first. The door shuts with a loud thud behind us, I hear clicking coming from the left and Claudia Verán steps into view. "Oh, you brought your friend." Her face is plastered with a scowl and I feel out of place at her remark.

"She's my girlfriend. Get over it. Where is my father?" She signals for us to follow her and we make our way up a sweeping staircase. The house is beautiful, with antiques and portraits of, I am guessing Lucien's ancestors. The house has the atmosphere of a museum. I take it all in as we make our way down the corridor. The doors are all ornate and old looking. I am sure this house has been in the family for generations. It's beautiful.

"He's weak; I think you should go in alone." She turns to us before opening the door.

"Cassandra will be at my side." Lucien tugs me behind him as we step into the bedroom.

"Father?" Lucien walks up to the bed. There is a remarkable resemblance, his father an older version of him. Mr. Verán shifts and turns to his son and I notice the unconditional love in his father's eyes. I miss my father, just being the room with both of them is an experience. They both have very dominating personalities, both being strong for the other.

"Lucien, son. I will be okay. I had a mild stroke. The doctor said I should just take time off."

"I told you, you work to hard." Lucien admonishes his father and they both chuckle. They both have the same dimples and it makes me smile.

"Who's the beautiful young lady, Lucien?" His father turns and I flush at his compliment.

"Father, this is Cassandra Winters. She's my girlfriend." He holds out a hand and I step forward.

"Hello Mr. Verán, it's a pleasure to meet you." I smile.

"Hello dear. The pleasure is mine, my son has excellent taste." He gives me a grin and I giggle. "I hope Lucien takes care of you. If he doesn't you tell me, I will sort him out for you." Lucien's head jerks to his father and I can tell he is embarrassed.

"Dad, please."

"Oh shh Luca, I am talking to your girl, not you. Winters you said?" I love the way they are with each other.

"Yes, Mr. Verán." I glance between him and Lucien, not sure why he's asking about my last name.

"My God. That's incredible. Luca, get me that box on the shelf?" We turn to an aged wooden trinket box next to the bed. Lucien grabs it and hands it to his father. I watch him unlock the antique latch. When he flips the lid, the room fills with a sweet melody and I recognize it instantly. It's a lovely classical piece by Yiruma, called River Flows in You. Lucien's father looks at me again, almost like he knows me, recognizes me. It's strange, I haven't met him before, at least I don't remember him.

"Take this Cassandra Winters. I want you to hold onto that." His father hands me a necklace, with a pendant on it. It's an antique, that much is clear, but I don't understand why he's handed it to me. The pendant itself is silver, with an intricate design, almost as if there are vines holding it together. What is more stunning is the beautiful gem, as I move it around in the light, the color changes, an icy blue and then a shimmering orange. Etched into metal are two small symbols, one a snowflake, and the other the sun. I glance up at him curiously, it's the most gorgeous piece of jewelry I have ever seen.

"Mr. Verán, this is—" My eyes flicker to Lucien and his gaze flicker at my words, I can't help smiling. "I can't possibly—"

"You can girl! I will have no debates. That is meant for you." He grins and hands Lucien something. It's an identical replica of the pendant, except his is more masculine, like a pocket watch. I am puzzled at the gift as beautiful as it is I am uncertain why he would give us these. "Cassie, our family has a rich heritage. We are from Galicia, and in Galician, Verán is translated to Summer. You and my son are polar opposites. You've been brought together, your childhood was intertwined a long time ago and now you've found each other again. So I am thrilled to see he has found you. There is a lot you—" Before he can explain what he means, we're interrupted.

"Lucien, I think it's time for you to leave, your father needs rest." Claudia strode into the room and I slipped the necklace into my purse. Lucien's dad locked the box and passed it to his son.

"Hold on to this for me son." Giving his father a slight nod, he rose and walked over to me.

"Okay dad, get some rest. I will come by tomorrow."

We said our goodbyes and made our way out to the car. Lucien asked me to hold onto the box as he opened my door. I slid into the seat and put the box on

151

my lap. I was intrigued to see what was in it, but I knew it was Lucien's decision if he wanted to show me the secrets locked inside or not.

Lucien

Cassie is the first girl to meet my father. The first girl that means something to me. I had never taken a girl to meet him before, besides Sasha. When he gave her the necklace I thought about my mother. I don't have many memories of her, but hearing my father speak so fondly of her, with so much love made my heart ache. Since the first day I saw Cassie at the coffee shop I was drawn to her. I saw a light in her that I don't think she ever knew was there. She got under my skin, inside my veins and I knew I had to have her. One way or another.

The idea of not being near her used to tug at me. Every fucking day. That's why I ended up at that coffee shop every morning. To see her. It was as if I needed her to survive, there was something so tangible between us, I couldn't let it go. I had to make her mine. As fate would have it, she stepped into my office and my heart.

I decided to make us dinner tonight. The first night I ever cooked for her was lasagna, and after everything that's happened, the need to make our situation right again. We need a fresh start, a new beginning. "Sweetness!" I called to her from the kitchen. When she joined me, I smiled. "Taste this, tell me if it's too salty?" I held a spoon up and I watched her lick the sauce, the act sent a surge of pleasure straight to my groin and I wanted her licking sauce off my hard cock.

"That's incredible! It's perfect." I smiled and nodded. Turning back to the stove, I turned it to a low heat to allow it to simmer.

"Good, now I can start the rest of dinner. Should be about twenty minutes. Do you want wine my sweetness?" She nodded and got the glasses out.

"Yes, want me to pour it?" I nod, concentrating on the food again. "Your dad is wonderful." In the corner of my eye, I watch her leaning against the sink. I know she's trying to gauge my reaction. At first I wasn't sure I wanted her to meet him just yet, but it seems that it worked out well.

"Yes, he is. He seems to be taken with you." I turn to her and smile.

"He does, I like him. Not sure what he's doing with your step-mother though. He sounds like he loved your mom very much." I still at the mention of my mother. For years I wondered the same thing, why my father married Claudia, she's just so different to how he described my mom. I turn to face Cassie, there is so much I want her to know about me. About growing up in Spain, France, and even spending time in New York. With a deep breath, I decide to tell her about what I remember.

"My mother was his first and last love. They met in Spain, on vacation. Her family lived in the US and so did my dad's. They were inseparable, at least that's what my dad tells me. I recall fragments of her." I lean back against the counter. "She always had a scent of flowers around her.

Her smile was bright, and even brighter when my father walked into the room. At least, as a child I recall seeing her face light up. After," I turn to the stove stirring the pot, "my dad became quiet, but he never neglected me. He always told me he loved me. He supported everything I wanted to do. When I rebelled from him and Claudia, I could see the hurt on his face. I didn't care at the time. It was like he tried replacing mom with her." I glance at Cassie, "I know now he didn't. He could love no one like he loved my mother. She was his lumiére." My eyes locked on hers as I said the word. She flushed, crimson and stepped towards me, wrapping her arms around my waist. She always takes my breath away when she touches me. "And you are mine." I lean down to kiss the top of her head. It's perfect, being with her.

Chapter eighteen

Lucien

"Would you like breakfast, Sir?" When she rolls over to face me, a naughty glint in her eye tells me she's been awake for a while. I pull here against me, my hand slides over her belly. Slowly dipping into the waistband of her panties, I stroke her slick entrance. *Fuck, she's so wet for me.* My finger plunges inside her warm wet pussy easily. Her tight warm body, has my cock hard and ready to drive into her. She always does this to me. I can't imagine ever not being inside her. *Mine, all mine. Forever. My lumiére.*

"Breakfast is definitely a pre-requisite before work, Ms. Winters." I roll over and pin Cassie below me. My lips find hers in a heated kiss, in less than five seconds flat this girl can bring me to my knees. Her lips part and her tongue tangles with mine in lush strokes. Her taste is addictive, there's never a moment where I don't want her, or need her. She's inside my veins, like a drug. She's crawled inside my heart, consumed my every thought, she's found the darkest parts of me and added the light I never had. Or never realized I would have again.

My hand travels down her soft skin, finding the heat between her thighs. I tease her through the material of her panties and her breathing hitches. She's always so responsive. Wet and ready. There has been nothing in my life that could give me what she does. Happiness. I need to fuck her. Now. There is always a need to connect us in a way that makes her eyes flutter, her heart rate spike and her body tighten around me.

I roll my hips into hers and a small moan gets muffled by the kiss. All I need is to do is be inside her, the ache drives me crazy. As soon as I break contact, she whimpers, sitting back, I tug her panties down. I watch as she pulls the tank top she's wearing up, before she can take it off completely, I grip it and knot it around her wrists. My own pants find the carpet in record time and I am back between her soft thighs. My cock at her entrance, teasing her. "Please Lucien?" Her begging only makes me harder, painfully so. Her pussy quivers around the tip of my cock. I slide the head in, and pull out, again and again. Her whimper makes me smile. She's ready, so fucking ready.

"Please what, baby?" I tease her again, she has to beg me for it. She has to ache for me as much as I ache for her. The need to drive deep into her is unbearable, but I need to remain in control, even though she has me so out of control all the time.

"Fuck me! Please? Fuck me hard and make me scream." Her eyes are black with lust as she wraps her legs around my waist, trying to pull me inside her. "Please?" Her soft moans and pleading have my head spinning and I slam into her, balls deep inside her sweet, tight little cunt. *Oh God she feels good! Tightest, hottest little pussy I have ever been inside.* I pull out almost all the way and drive back in.

She cries out as her head drops back. Her bound hands come down and her nails dig into my shoulder, spurring me on even more. The bite of pain makes my cock throb and harden inside her. Her heels push my ass, trying to get me deeper. My mouth finds her pebbled nipple, laving it, sucking it into my mouth. As I give attention to the other one, her pussy tightens. With a dark smirk I bite down on her nipple and she cries out my name, the most erotic sound ever. "Come for me, lumiére, give me all your pleasure." My words are her undoing as her orgasm splinters through her. I drive into her, again, as I fill her with my own release.

Our bodies still and her tight little cunt pulses around me. Her body takes everything from me, milking me. Our bodies are still intertwined as I catch my breath. "I love you baby." Planting soft kisses on her neck, sending a shiver over her skin.

"I love you too. Always."

"Always."

As soon as I slip out of her, she moans and rolls over. Her leg wrapped around me. "Baby, we need to get to work. Your boss won't appreciate you being late." I chuckle at the cute pout she gives me. Maybe she needs those lips wrapped around my cock. The image in my mind makes my cock jump.

"He will have to talk to my boyfriend, it's his fault I am late." Her fingers lightly stroke my abs. I feel the stirring of another hard on, but before she can continue, I roll out of her grasp.

"And your boyfriend has a meeting with the board today, so you have to behave." Her giggle makes me smile and I walk around the bed to the bathroom. With her hungry gaze burning a hole into my skin, I leave the bathroom door open, and turn on the spray. As soon as her arms are around me, I tug her into the shower for our second round of breakfast.

Cassandra

When we arrived at the office this morning, Lucien walked me to my office and then disappeared upstairs for his board meeting. Once I had set up my laptop and logged into my email program, I turn to the window to take in the view below. The city looks incredible from up here, and sometimes it's unreal that I am here. My mind flits back to meeting Lucien's dad, the necklace he gave me and what he said about us. Summer and Winters. Light and Dark. Although at times I am not sure who is the dark one. There are so many things in my life that would make me argue that I am. Lucien has brought love back into my life. He's brought me back from the dead, just about.

I am about to get up to make coffee when my phone buzzes. "Cassie Winters, how can I help you?"

"I told you to stay away from him, but you obviously don't listen." An icy voice sends fear racing through my veins. This is not Sasha because I have spoken to her a few times, and I would recognize her voice immediately. *Who the hell can this be?*

"Who are you? I asked you to leave Lucien and me alone!" As I am about to hang up, she says the words I have been dreading since I first started dating Lucien.

"He will learn about your dark secrets. I will make sure of it!" The line goes dead and I am staring at the receiver. *What the fuck just happened? Shit!* Lucien can't find out about the darkest part of my story. I buried it for a reason. Knowing that I should have told him the night I confessed the rest of my story tugs at me. Didn't we say honesty is the way to go? I should have listened. *He can't be angry, he should understand. I mean, I am sure he will. Won't he?* No, he won't. The dread that's hanging in my chest is making it difficult to breathe. My heart is constricting and I flop into my chair. Nothing will bring us back from this. No amount of fairytales, and no amount of pendants.

"Cassie, babe!" I glance up to see Jayce walking into my office. *Did he knock?* I must have been so deep in thought that I didn't hear the noise.

"Hey Jay, how are you?" I offer him a small smile. He closes the door behind him and turns to meet my expression. A frown creases his brow as he walks towards me.

"Are you okay? You look like you've seen a ghost." He strides closer to the desk and I can't find the words to tell him anything. "Cassie?" I sit and stare at him for a long moment before finding the strength to even think it, let alone say the words out loud.

I nod. "I…" *How the hell do I even start?* "Lucien is going to break up with me." I stare into his sky-slue eyes, worry etched on his face.

"What do you mean? Why?" Placing his hands on my desk, he leans over struggling to figure out what's got me so overwhelmed. "Cassie, princess, talk to me?"

"My past Jay, there is something I hid from him. It's something I did, if he finds out, he will never forgive me." I glance up as the tears spill from my face.

"How do you know he will find out?" He cocks his head to the side.

"I got a warning from some girl. She believes that Lucien loves her and they're meant to be together. She said she will tell him about my past." Jay looks confused.

"What did she sound like? Was this Sasha?" I shake my head; it was the only thing I was sure about. Unless she somehow gained an accent in the last few days. "Can you be sure?"

"Yes, she had a European accent, Jay." Color drains from his face, and fear rips through me. He knows something. "What?"

"Shit! There is only one person it can be. I met a girl a few years ago. When Lucien and I were at Uni. She moved from Spain, to stay with Lucien. Well, not really stay, she kind of landed here with nowhere to go. My guess is she came to win him back, but he was never interested in her. I can't remember her name. It can only be her, she was thoroughly in love with him, but he was not interested in anything long-term at the time. He told me that they were a fling and he left her. This was a long time ago why would she resurface now?" Jayce walks around the desk and pulls me up, holding me in his arms I can't believe this is happening. I will lose the man I love over some stupid jealous psycho who can't let go. Maybe I can talk to him before she has time to say anything to him. I should go up there after the meeting.

Lucien

As soon as I walk into the office Stacy is nipping at my heels. "Mr. Verán, you have an important call. The person has been calling non-stop for the past hour." I glance at the time on my wristwatch, it is only fucking 9:30 am. Who would want to even think of doing business before ten?

"Did you happen to get a name?" My annoyance for her is skyrocketing.

"No, sir. She didn't want to give me a name. Also she told me that she will keep calling back until you are in. She said it's extremely important."

When I spin on my heel, my glare falls on Stacy for the first time since I walked in this morning. Without an answer, I take a seat at my desk and open my laptop. "Fine. Get me a coffee. I have the board meeting in thirty minutes, if she doesn't call before then, it will have to wait until after."

"Mr. Verán, I sent you a reschedule, the board meeting has moved to eleven."

"Okay, get me the coffee in the meantime and put whoever it is through." With a simple nod, she leaves me to my work. With my email open, I scroll through the new messages and find the reschedule. My father wants to attend. That's strange. Other than that nothing that requires immediate attention. I am about to call Cassie when my phone buzzes. "Verán." I listen for a few moments, but nothing comes from the other side. "Listen, I have no time for games. If you don't speak then I am hanging up."

"Luca." The voice on the other end sends me spiraling. I can't even comprehend why she's calling me. "Luca, I miss you." Ice drips through my veins and I am about to hang up when the next words stop me dead in my tracks. "There is something about Cassandra you need to know." Her accent is rich, sending memories through my mind that I long since buried.

"What are you talking about? Why are you calling me?" This was my past. Something I didn't want to ever face again. There was no way I wanted to do this again. *Why didn't she just leave me alone? How many times do you have to reject someone before they take the hint?*

"I have proof your girlfriend has a secret that even you may not be able to forgive." A headache threatens as I sit back, and pinch the bridge of my nose, between my thumb and forefinger. *Jesus, I can't deal with this shit now.* "Luca?" The way she says my name still sends deep regret through me.

"What? We don't have any secrets. I need you to leave me alone. Please?" Right now, I am the one begging. I love Cassie that's all that matters. Nothing can change that.

"Check your email." Her words were final. I sat with the phone glued to my ear as my email pinged with an incoming message. My hand is steady as I open the new mail, then click on the attachment. As soon as I open it, my world rocks and free falls into a deep dark hole. My grip on the phone tightens. This can't be right. She told me everything. *Didn't she?* All I saw was rage, the anger flared inside me to an unbearable high. The darkness in my heart is now at the forefront and all I want to do is hurt her. For lying. For hiding this. I slam down the phone, and rise from the chair, stalking to my door. Swinging the office door open so fast that I hear the hinges creak. *She would not have kept something like this from me? Could she? Why? After everything I told her? This couldn't be? It had to be a mistake? Do you really believe that, Verán? She lied to my face! She didn't even fucking trust me!* My blood is simmering.

The elevator arrives as soon as I push the call button. As the car descended to the tenth floor, my blood has reached boiling point. *This can't be true. This can't be true.* I repeat the words slowly and methodically as the doors open. When I reach her office door, I swing it open. Time for the truth Ms. Winters. Jayce is in her office, standing too close. He's way too fucking close to her. *She's mine!* I can feel my anger about to explode, for many reasons. The main one was that Cassandra lied straight to my face. With no fucking guilt. *This can't be true. This can't be true. Please, baby, tell me it's not true.* I am pleading with her in my head. As soon as her eyes meet mine, I can see the shock in her expression. She's never seen me this angry before.

Cassandra

My door abruptly flies open. I glance up to meet Lucien's glare, his eyes were bitter and angry sending a shudder over me. His anger is something that was part of my worst nightmares. Those beautiful green eyes are black, in the worst sense. At his sides I saw his fists clench and release, the death stare he gives Jayce only makes me shiver more. *He knows, Cassie. There is no doubt about it. And he is here to tell you it's over. Once again you've fucked it up.*

"I need to talk to you Cassandra." Lucien's voice is cold, harsh. The man I love is no longer inside that beautiful body. This is someone else. Someone dark, dangerous, and someone filled with hate. I nod.

"I was just leaving." Jayce glances at me, the concern evident on his face. He makes his way to the door and passes Lucien, closing the door behind him.

"What's up?" I try to calm the shrill tone in my voice, but his face is severe and my heart flip-flops. There was no way I would survive this or take anymore sadness or fighting today. I realized from the thunderous look on his face, he had learned my darkest secret. It was obvious, there was nothing I could do to calm him at this stage, that much I knew. This time I just had to ride wave. Even though it would kill me, then while I drown in the pain I would watch him walk away.

"I received a call this morning. Is there something you would like to say to me Cassandra?" His voice was brisk, void of any emotion. The way he spat my name made me wince, it was an actual pain in my chest. My heart hammered in my ears and bile rose from my stomach. *He knows! Shit, shit, shit! How am I ever going to fix this? There is no fixing it, you're done.*

"Listen Lucien, there's something I didn't tell you. It's just an ugly part of my past that... I just... I told you most of it, I..." His eyes dart away. He can't even face me. I can see the disgust in his expression. It's not about me, or what I did, it's because I didn't tell him. He's angry because I didn't trust him with this. He gave me all of him, and I held back. Now, I am paying for it. This time I am paying with the love of my life. "This is difficult for me. Please look at me?" I beg him. Realization hits me that I am rambling, trying to make him see I didn't tell him because I was scared. When he shifted his green gaze on me I froze. I didn't see the man that loved me, I saw someone else.

"You preferred for me to find out from a fucking woman from my past about the woman I am sleeping with? Is that what you wanted Cassie?!" His voice roared through the office, and I winced. I felt my heart shattering at the pain, from the anger in his eyes. My head shook quickly as the tears spilled down my face. My voice and breath stolen from me in that moment. There was nothing I could do. Or say. Nothing. This was the end of everything.

"Jesus, Cassie! I had to fucking find out from someone I haven't spoken to in over 8 years, a fucking stranger to me!! Do you know how I feel? Do you fucking realize how this has torn into me!?" I was shaking now. All I wished was to crawl into a hole and never come out. "After I fucking told you what I did, you kept this from me!" He spun around, staring at the wall. It looked like he was about to punch a hole through it. In this state, I believed that he would be able to with the amount of anger in his face. His whole body vibrated with rage. The veins in his hands bulged, and he looked violent. Then suddenly, he calmed. Although the rage was still there, he turned and stalked towards me. I backed up against the window and he placed his hands on either side of my head. His angry glare fell on my face. "Look at me." The words were a blatant order, but I couldn't bring myself to move. "I said fucking look at me!" His voice boomed around me and I snapped my eyes up. When I met his black angry glare, my body shook violently as I sobbed. He dropped his voice, into a dark and dangerous hiss. "I don't want you anywhere near me! We're finished! Our relationship and you are dead to me!" With those last words ringing in my ears, he turned on his heel and strode out of my office, slamming the door behind him.

Lucien

As soon as I step out of her office, my heart felt like it had been ripped from my chest. *What the fuck have I just done? She lied. Yes. She did. Fuck.* I stalk back to the elevator and push the call button. While I wait my mind is a fucking mess. As I step into the car, my phone buzzes. "What?"

"Luke, I don't mean to—"

"Jayce, fuck, I don't even know what to say. I lost it. She lied to me." Scrubbing my hand over my face, I pressed the button for my floor.

"Dude, what the fuck is wrong with you?" I realized that Jayce was fuming. This is not a conversation I wanted to have with him right now. As the doors of the elevator closed, I left my heart on the other side, with Cassie.

The car ascends. "She lied about something Jayce. Something big. I really don't know why. I had to find out from Isabel!" I want to punch something. Grinding my teeth, my jaw tightens painfully.

"So you're just walking away?" He sounds incredulous. I don't blame him. I want to ask myself the same fucking question.

"She lied to me. If she really loved me she would have told me. I told her everything Jayce. Every fucking sordid detail about my past." The doors of the elevator slide open and I step into Stacey's reception area. I glance over at her, she looked like she was about to burst and ask me what was going on. My face must have given it away.

I hear the heavy sigh from Jayce, and my heart is as heavy. "Fine, just remember you walked away." His words slice into me, deeper than I ever thought possible and my heart thudded at the truth. I did. This is what I chose. To leave her, my love, my lumiére.

"Jay…" I whisper, stepping into my office, I shut the door with a bang.

"Yea?" He sounds weary, I don't blame him, because he knows what's coming.

"Listen, just look after her for me? Please?" I love her more than life itself, but I don't see how it was supposed to work if she was lying to me. Or just not telling me the truth. If she didn't trust me enough with something like this, then maybe she didn't love me after all.

"Always." The word hangs heavy with promise. A promise I don't want to think about. I hang up before I can say anything else. The idea of her with Jayce rips me apart. *How do you walk away from the one person that makes you whole? How the fuck do I go on living?* I will have to find a way because I can't be with someone who doesn't trust me. That is the one thing I need from the person I want to spend my life with. Trust. Such an easy thing to break, and so difficult to get back.

"Mr. Verán, there is a call for you, did you not hear me buzz?" I turn to face Stacy, there are questions all over her face. Questions I am not in the mood to answer. Not right now.

"No. Take a message. I will get back to them later. Cancel my meetings. I have something that's come up urgently." There is no way I can sit in a board meeting now. They will have to wait.

"Yes, sir." With that she leaves my office, closing the door behind her. I turn back to the window, staring at the city below me. Most days this view would bring me an insane amount of pleasure, today, it feels like a prison. She's going off to a beautiful island with

Jayce. This is shredding me inside and there is only one thing I need to do. Forget. My phone buzzing tears me from my thoughts. It's Jayce. Again.

"What?"

"You're a dumb fuck you know that!" Jesus, thank you Jayce, I figured that out. Why the fuck must he be so brutally honest?

"Jayce, I do realize that. You don't have to tell me. She needs you."

"No, Luke, she needs you. She loves you!"

"She doesn't fucking love me!" My voice echoes in the empty room. I take a deep breath, trying to calm down and apologize. "Sorry, man. Just watch her." He's quiet for a long time, I know exactly what he's thinking. There is something between them, I can tell he cares for her. It's the only reason I am asking him to watch over her. The only problem will be if he fucks her, I know he will. She's single now. So am I. As if reading my mind, he gives me an out.

"Let's go clubbing tonight?" I sit down, considering the appeal. There is none. Other than getting drunk. *Why not? You're single.* "Yea, let's do it. Robert can drive. I need to get fucked… and by that, I mean drunk, Jayce."

He didn't laugh, and I knew what he was thinking. I was thinking it to. There was no way in hell I could ever get her out of my soul, heart or mind. No matter what I do.

"Luke, it will be fine. Trust me."

"Yea. Got to go." I hang up before he gave me shit about Cassie, and the fact that I walked out on her. Looking out over the city again, I don't know how my life took a fucking nosedive. *How the fuck did this even happen? Fuck this! I am going out tonight and I will get fucking wasted.*

Lucien

It's almost midnight, and the club is filled to capacity. I am sitting in a booth with Jayce and two girls who he called over. None of them grabbed my attention. Jayce isn't drinking as much as he normally does. He drove tonight, to give me a chance to drink. I gave Robert the night off after Jayce convinced me to let him drive. I glance at each of the fake plastic faces of the girls and bile rises to my throat. They didn't hold a candle to Cassie. *Fuck her. She lied to you. Yes, but she didn't need a cake of make up to be beautiful and I love her.* As I knock back the fifth whiskey I had been nursing for almost twenty minutes, I enjoy the burn. I need another one. The effects of the liquor are taking full effect, but I am nowhere near interested in going home with either of these girls.

"Dude, can you look less like someone died?" Jayce leans in and talks into my ear. The thunderous glare his words earned him made him sit back and finish his drink.

This is my weekly ritual, every Friday night since I walked out of her office, I come here with Jayce, hoping to meet some slut who will make me forget Cassie. I haven't seen her in three weeks. Even though we work in the same building, it's almost as if we are avoiding each other on purpose. Like two planets just orbiting, missing each other. Almost a month without her. Every night, I down half a bottle of whiskey to drown her from my mind, the ache and the frustration of not being with her. It still hurts. *How the fuck can it still hurt?* She's in every part of me, like a drug in my veins. I am barely alive, not even recognizing myself.

"I need a piss." My announcement earns me a few stares as I get up and walk through the crowd of sweaty bodies, that's when my skin prickles. I feel her. My eyes roam the crowd and land on her at the bar. I watch her knock back a shot and call for another. She's drunk. *Fuck! I did this! No, I didn't, she did it. She fucking lied to me. There's no way I can ever be with her.* It's over. *Why do I care?* Without another thought I spin on my heel and make my way to the toilets. It's none of my concern what she does, it's over between us. *That's a fucking lie and you know it. You will never be rid of her.*

As soon as I walk back out of the restroom, I glance at the bar again. I can't help my eyes searching her out. It's like my heart and body have a mind of their own. My heart on the other hand is still so in tune with her. Every fiber of my being is screaming at me to go to her. *What the fuck is wrong with you Verán? She's not some fucking magic pussy.* On the other side of the bar, just out of her line of sight, I call the barman. Another whiskey is what's needed, I place my order while I watch her. She's downing shots like they will wash away her sins, I recognize it, because I am doing the same. *She could get hurt.* My inner turmoil is ripping me in two. I can't be with her, but I don't want any other man near her. She will move on, but the thought of it makes me want to kidnap her, lock her up in a room so no other man can come near her.

When she turns to the bar again, some fucking asshole steps up behind her. As soon as he leans in my whole body explodes with anger. She laughs, her head drops back and his lips are on her neck. My white knuckle grip on the squat tumbler is dangerously close to shattering it. I make my way to Jayce. "I need your help." My voice comes out as a low growl. He glances up and my expression has his immediate attention. The blonde bimbo sitting on his lap eyes me curiously.

"Hey sugar, wanna have some fun?" The bimbo tries to touch me and I turn to glare at her.

"Get the fuck away from me!" My harsh growl sends her running on four inch heels.

"What the fuck are you doing?"

I turn to face Jayce again, "Fuck off. I need your help."

"What?" Knocking back the whiskey I just ordered, I pull Jayce up by his arm.

"I need you to take Cassie home." The words are out of my mouth before I can rethink this.

"What do you mean?" He looks as confused as I am.

"She's at the bar, and really drunk. Please Jay? I can't let her get hurt." I turn to him. My gaze is pleading and I realize he's not sure if this is a good idea.

"What? More than you hurt her?" His words cut through me, he always had a way of making me realize the truth in his words. In my actions. I nod.

"Yea." I don't know if he heard me, over the loud music. A small nod is all he gives me. He leaves me standing there helpless to do anything. I watch him walk over to the bar. Cassie was swaying to the music. That fucker is still pawing her, just as Jayce reaches her, I calm. When she spins to face him, her smile lights up the room. My heart is being ripped into shreds. *I did this. This was my choice.* I order another drink, and down it in one gulp. The only thing I enjoy is the burn, I close my eyes and turn around. I make my way outside to get a cab. I didn't need to see my best friend take the girl I love home.

Out on the sidewalk, I hail a cab. Jayce has been spending a lot of time with Cassie, he says nothing has happened, I don't doubt it. I know he will tell me if it did, he likes her. It's obvious she wants him too. She deserves him, she needs someone to care for her. Too bad that can't be me. *Maybe it can? No! It can't.*

Cassandra

"Another one!" I yell over the noise. The music was pulsating through me, I needed to dull the ache inside me. I didn't want to see or hear anything that would bring back the memory of him walking out of my office door. Yes, it's been three weeks since he did, but the fucking pain won't go away. The barman pours another shot, at this stage, I am not sure what I am drinking. There's a guy talking to me, but I don't care. Turning to him I give him a small smile. When I face the barman, grabbing my drink I knock it back. I have lost count on how many of these I have had so far. A few. Maybe five. Who cares? Lucien won't care. That's the only person who matters. No. He doesn't. He ripped me apart. The pain in my chest tightens and I grab the next shot.

"Cassie!" I twirl around and glance up into sky-blue eyes. He looks incredible. Jayce offers the guy behind me a death stare. Once the stranger has backed off, he rounds on me. "What the hell are you doing?" I grasp his leather jacket, yanking him towards me. With a smile, I lean up onto my tip toes and crash my lips onto his, pressing my body against him. His hands gripping my shoulders, Jayce pulls me away and looks into my eyes. There was something he wasn't telling me, but I didn't care. I needed another shot.

"Babe!" Kenna came rushing up to me, tugging at me. I pull away and frown at her. "Come on, let's go. Please?" She stared at me, glancing at Jayce. "Hey!" Her greeting to Jay is guarded. My eyes flit between Jayce and Kenna.

"What the hell are you doing, Cass?" His cerulean gaze trained on me.

"Me? I am having fun!" I yell, the music was suddenly too loud, ignoring them both, I grab another shot and swallow it. The tension in the air is thick. Jayce isn't happy with me, but he doesn't own me. Only one man owns me. *Fuck! I need to forget about him.*

Jay turns to Kenna, his face adamant. "I am taking her home."

I turn to Kenna. "Jayce is taking me home. Ooohh!" My sing song voice earns me a sky-blue stare. She nods at him and tugs me into a tight hug, whispering in my ear.

"I love you, babe." She turns and walks off into the crowd, leaving me with Jayce, she heads for the exit. *What just happened?* I peer up and give him a smile.

"So handsome, you going to dance with me?" I smile up at Jay.

"I am taking you home!" My body sways and I grip the leather jacket. In one sudden movement, he scoops me up into his strong arms, and carries me through the club and out into the cool night air. I was too drunk at that stage to think for myself, so I let him rescue me from whatever stupid decisions I would have made. He walks over to his black Jeep and sets me down. Once the door is open, he helps me into the passenger seat and buckles me up. I giggle at his stone expression. He's definitely in a bad mood.

"Thank you." I whisper, hoping he won't regret rescuing me. When his sky-blue stare meets mine he offers me a sexy smile and shuts the door.

He slides into the driver's seat a few seconds later. "Do you want to go home? Or my place? Either way I am not leaving you alone." His voice was stern, and I giggle again. He sounds like a school teacher admonishing me for forgetting my homework. No words come out of my mouth and he shakes his head, the car is in motion and I suddenly want to puke. My eyes flutter closed, and I hope I will not throw up in his car. He senses my unease, and drives through the quiet LA streets at a slow speed, taking the turns carefully. I stare out the window and watch the lights flickering by. The city at night looks so blurry, but I think that may have been an effect from the amount of shots I had done.

"Come on, princess." Jay scoops me up and I pry my eyes open. It's almost like there are weights hanging from them. The sound of a door shutting behind him has me blinking. We're in an apartment that isn't mine. As if reading my mind, he whispers in my ear. "You're at mine. You passed out, and I didn't want you to be alone." I nod. Too tired to fight. He climbs the short staircase and we arrive in a spacious bedroom. He sets me down on the comfortable mattress, then tugs my shoes off and I let him. I fumble with the button on my jeans and slide them down. He places them on the chair in the corner of the bedroom and helps me with the covers as I slip in. The bed smells like Jayce, spicy, warm, a summer morning. It's such a calming scent. I am tired. My heart hurts.

"Jay, don't leave me?" My words are slurring and I wonder if he understood what I said. All he does is nod. "I can't do this." Words fail me, I am not sure what to say to him, but somehow I realize he understands.

"It's okay princess, close your eyes. I am here." He covers me with the soft white sheets, giving me a sexy smile. "Sleep." I nod and my eyes close.

Lucien

Once I am in the apartment, I make my way straight to the bar. I need more fucking alcohol. The cabbie looked at me like I was crazy, sitting in the parking lot until I saw Jayce walking out with Cassie in his arms. She looked so small, fragile. The pain that pierced my heart when I saw her like that was indescribable. As soon as he placed her in his car, I told the cab to drive. At my bar, I pour a triple whiskey, the burn of the liquor would numb me. With my phone in my hand, I stare at the screen, unsure of how to ask, or what to ask. Easily finding Jayce's number, I type out my message.

Is she okay?

I didn't have to wait long for his reply, it came quickly.

She's here. Sleeping. She needs to rest

I sigh, although, I am not sure if it was it from relief or anger. She was at his place, in his bed. There was nothing I could do. I didn't know if I should be happy, or completely fuck him up.

Don't you dare fucking touch her Jayce, I am warning you

Why did I still want to be with her? My body yearned for her. To tie her to my bed, slide my fingers inside her tight little cunt and savor it tightening for me. To watch her face as she came undone on my hand, on my cock. To have her body tremble under my touch. *Fuck, I really can't do this! I need to get over her.* My phone buzzes with a reply from Jayce.

She's not with you anymore. You chose this. She needs to move on some time

"Fuck you!" My shout echoes through the room and my blood is at boiling point. As I pinch the bridge of my nose, I rise off the sofa to grab another drink. Once I had refilled my glass, I flop back down on the sofa and grab my phone. Without thinking I scroll through the numbers, wanting to find someone to talk to. I hit the call button. The last person I wanted to speak to at this stage, but she might be the only person who could help me through this.

"Lucien."

"How are you?"

"Fine, how are you?" Her voice is wary and I realize why. I am silent for such a long time; her next question doesn't surprise me. "Lucien, what the fuck do you want?" This is what I need. Someone to tell me like it is and there is no one I would want to do it, but her.

"Kenna, I fucked up. I walked out."

"I know, she told me. Lucien, I don't know what to say to you." I bite down on my lower lip until the metal taste of blood fills my mouth.

"I have no idea why I called you. There are things I have done and so has Cassie, but I…" My words trailed off, I wasn't sure what I wanted to say. She would never take me back, it's been too long, I waited too long. I should have fought for her weeks ago. She's with Jayce now and there is nothing I can do to stop it. *You fucked up, Verán, as usual.*

"Luke, she's hurt right now. What you said to her. It's… You… I can't even think about this. She didn't lie to you because she doesn't love you. She lied because she does love you. Don't you see that? She was scared. Have you never been so scared of losing something you would do anything to keep it? Please can you just leave her alone? She needs to move on."

The line went dead, but the words replayed in my head. She was right, there was nothing I wouldn't do to keep Cassie. It seems she did the same. I launch my phone against the wall I watch it shatter into tiny pieces. Just like my life and my fucking heart. My soul, broken by the desire for the girl I walked out on. That part of me that will never be whole without her. There's nothing I could do now. I walked away, and she would move on. My focus should be on getting over her. Even though, she's inside me, everywhere. She's inside my veins, my heart, mind, even my dark soul. In the depths of my darkness, she's added a light. I will never get over her. Regret and guilt fill me like a poison.

Cassandra

The sun flooding through the window woke me. I reached over and grabbed a fluffy pillow, hugging it to my chest. With the pounding in my head, I am sure there was a hammer inside my brain; I didn't want to open my eyes. The scent of Jayce is everywhere, its intoxicating, I shouldn't be here, but I faintly remember not being coherent last night. There's a soft melody floating through the open door. It sounds familiar, but I can't make out the song. The sound is soothing the pounding in my head. I swing my feet over the bed and regret it at once.

This will hurt. With a small crack I open my eyes, I take in the immaculate bedroom. I have only been here once, after our office party, but it looks different. Unless it's the pounding headache. It's the first time Jayce had to carry me out of a club, I must have been far gone. I pull on his T-shirt I found laying on the foot end of the bed. My jeans are nowhere to be seen, so I guess he must have put them in the wash.

I pad to the top of the staircase. When I glance down, I can't see into the living room, but that's where the music is coming from. I stop to listen for a while, closing my eyes. When he stops playing, I sneak down the stairs and find him sitting in the living room at a black grand piano. The muscles in his back flex as his fingers stroke the ivory keys. His short black tousled hair stood in every direction. It looked like he had just gotten out of bed.

Since Lucien walked out of my office three weeks ago, I drank to numb whatever pain I felt. Kenna tried to stop me at first and later realized that I wouldn't listen, no matter what she said. She and Jay had been there every day watching me, following me. She was at the club last night and she let Jayce bring me home. I was the one in dire need of help. They weren't that close anymore, and I wondered if they had been arguing about me. I walked up to him, reaching out as he turned around to face me. His eyes were a dark blue, almost navy, it was such a contrast to his beautifully tanned skin. He was wearing a pair of worn blue Levi's and nothing else. He was so handsome, so sexy.

"Good morning, princess." He gave me one of his sexy lopsided smiles and I grinned.

"My knight in shining armor." I offered him a small curtsey.

"Always at your service," he spun around on the bench and I took in his sculpted abs. They were exquisite, but I couldn't think like that. He was Lucien's friend and my heart still hurt so much.

"So I see. You're quite the hero, bursting in and carrying me out in your arms." I giggle. His smile curves that incredible mouth and there's a familiar ache I didn't realize I had, to lean down and kiss him. *What the hell is wrong with me? Way too long without Lucien that's it! I need to talk to him. Make him see I love him. It won't work though. You need to move on Cassie. Move on.*

"Well, if I was a hero, I wouldn't be sitting here wishing I could carry you back upstairs and lay you on my bed. Slowly undress you and devour every inch of your perfect body." My breathing hitches and my pulse skitters. Heat travels from my toes all the way to my face and I am flushed. His eyes travel over my bare legs and desire tightens in my stomach. I chew my lower lip and envision Jay kissing me roughly.

"Jay—"

"I shouldn't have said that, I was just being honest." He rises and gazes down at me with hooded eyes. His body flush with mine. Heat radiating from him. I glance down at his sculpted body, reaching out I run my fingertips over his collarbone. His skin is soft, smooth and on fire.

"It's okay. I… I don't know how…" I glance up and his gaze softens. There is so much desire in his stare that it sends shivers over me. I haven't been with anyone since Luke, and it's like I can't remember what the protocol is. Like I am a virgin, unsure and nervous. *Am I ready to move on? Would Jayce be a good choice?*

"Cassie, we don't have to do anything. I was just being foolish. You love him; I have no idea why he's being such an ass about everything. It's not like he's perfect." Those cerulean eyes glance down at me and I realize what he was talking about. Lucien's past was as broken and dark as mine.

"I suppose he couldn't get over the part of mine I kept from him." Jay pulls me into his arms, holding me. I rest my head on his chest, his heart beating against my ear, its racing. *Does Jayce really want me? Is he doing this to irritate Lucien?*

"Would you tell me about it?" He steps back and cups my face in his hands. "Stay with me today, spend the day here? I will make you dinner tonight and we can talk?" His eyes plead with me. With a small smile, I nod.

"You can kidnap me today." He chuckles, the smile reaching his magnificent blue eyes. "I need to call Kenna and let her know I am still alive. I think." My headache came back with a vengeance.

"Let me get you coffee and painkillers. I guessed you would sleep in. I hope I didn't wake you?" We stroll into the kitchen and Jay hands me my purse. I pull out my phone and see two messages from Kenna. Just checking in. I realize leaving me last night was a decision she made with Jayce, and I wonder if there was an ulterior motive. *Did she know of his feelings for me?*

"No, I loved the song you were playing. What was it? I recognize the melody." I glance up before responding to my messages. He picks up a remote and presses a button. A song filters through the speakers and I recognize the song. The lyrics rip into me so deep, it feels like a knife slicing through my veins.

It was the fourth of July

You and I were, you and I were fire, fire, fireworks
That went off too soon
And I miss you in the June gloom, too
It was the fourth of July
You and I were, you and I were fire, fire, fireworks
I said I'd never miss you
But I guess you never know
May the bridges I have burned light my way back home
On the fourth of July

I'll be as honest as you let me
I miss your early morning company
If you get me
You are my favorite "what if"
You are my best "I'll never know"

    The song Luke played in the car on our trip to Hawaii. My expression must have given away my pain because Jayce walked up to my and held me. "I will play for you tonight? How about that?" I nod. The song ends and I let out a breath I didn't realize I was holding. I peer up at Jayce with a smile.
    "You trying to romance me, Mr. Alexander?" I giggle. His face holds more emotion than I am ready for right now. My throbbing headache hits me harder when I realize something. He stares at me and I know he can see the realization on my face. I didn't notice it before. When he steps back, I can see the hurt in his eyes. I didn't think about his last name before. "Jay?" I stand and step toward him. My eyes searching his face.
    "Yes, Alexander. Jayce Alexander." His voice was low, a shiver skittered across my skin when it hit me. I set my phone back on the counter. My small frame standing in front of him, staring up into those sky-blue eyes. *Holy shit! Holy shit! Holy shit! He's…? Shit!*
    "You're… I mean… You and Sasha?" I couldn't believe it, besides the blue eyes they looked nothing alike. *Were they related?*
    "She's my sister." How had I not known? How have I spent months around both him and Luke, neither of them said anything? My mind is whirling and my headache is pounding.
    "Wow, shit." I spin towards the breakfast bar, gripping the edge. My head was throbbing. Lucien dated Sasha, his best friend's sister. That makes sense. Lucien hurt Sasha. That's why him and Jay have such an uneasy relationship. That's why Lucien called Jay that night. OMG! I suppose it kind of makes sense. My hold on the counter tightens, it feels like I am about to faint.
    "Look Cass, I didn't mean to keep it from you. I never considered it would really make a difference between us. You know?" I turn to face him again. He looked so sad.
    "No, it's okay, I didn't realize. It's just a shock. Although, it doesn't change my feelings towards you." I smile at the smirk that suddenly curved his lips.
    "You have feelings for me?" He cocks his head to the side. I squirm under his intense gaze. The butterflies in my stomach decide that this is the right time to flutter.
    "You know what I mean." I pick up my phone, hitting reply, I type a message to Kenna. My decision to stay with Jayce today is easy. In my message I tell her I will see her tomorrow. The heat on my skin from Jay's gaze is difficult to ignore. I slip into

the stool. When my eyes peer up, I notice he's turned around and making coffee. My hungry eyes drink him in, his back is sexy. I admire the toned muscles moving under taut skin.

"Do you want breakfast, princess?" The earlier confession forgotten. He sets my coffee and a glass of water with some painkillers in front of me, I glance up into his eyes.

"Yes please? Only if you're joining me though?" He smiles and nods. I put the aspirin in my mouth and gulp them down with water. Hoping the painkillers take effect immediately.

"Yea, I guess I could manage food. What did you want?" He opens the fridge, pulling out eggs and bacon. I can't help gawking at how his low-slung jeans hug his hips and thighs. His tight ass filled out his Levi's perfectly. "Cass?" I glance up realizing that Jay had twisted around, I was caught staring at his jeans. The heat warms my face, flushing my cheeks and I grin.

"I don't mind, let me help you." As I hop off the stool, I take the tray of eggs from Jay. "Are we doing scrambled?" I turn to look at him and the amusement on his face. "What?"

"Just looking." His eyes darken and I wonder if he's as turned on as I am. The realization of being attracted to Jayce, being almost naked in his kitchen has me squirming.

"Looking at?" My one hand on my hip, I stare at him. Not realizing the T-shirt has now ridden up and he can see my thighs and a small glimpse of my pink cotton panties. His eyes roam my body from my chocolate brown eyes to my bare feet.

"You." His gaze burns into me and I tremble at the intensity. He shakes his head as if to clear a thought and turns around. With the cupboard open, he pulls out a frying pan and sets it down on the counter. This is the strangest time I have spent with him. The painkillers take effect and the headache eases, I am so thankful. I keep my gaze on him.

"And what precisely about me were you looking at, Jayce?" I watch him move back to the fridge, grabbing the milk.

"Just how sexy you look in my T-shirt." He turns to face me and there's a wicked smirk on his lips and I can't help smiling. He hands me a large bowl, milk and a whisk. "You do the eggs. I will do the bacon." With a cheeky wink, he turns to the stove top and busies himself with the pan, oil and bacon. I grab 4 eggs from the tray, I crack them into the bowl. We work in comfortable silence till something dawns on me.

"How did you get to me so quickly last night?" He stills and I stop whisking. "Jayce?"

He turns and gives me a sheepish smile. "I was on a kind of date, at the club." I stare at him.

"What? Kind of date? What does that even mean?"

"Not your concern. And anyway you're more important and I could see you were drunk. I didn't want you to get hurt. Or make a foolish decision you might regret later on." He's not telling me everything, but I let it go. Turning towards me, he tugs me into his embrace. The warmth of his body on mine is intense and my mind is whirling with thoughts of kissing him. His full lips look enticing and I want to bite them. "Stop it, Cassie."

My eyes meet his. "Stop what?" I give him my most innocent face, pouting for extra effect. His eyes burn into mine, his pupils dilate and his hardness is pressing into my belly.

"Cassie," his tone is low and dangerous, there is a spark between us. Over the past week it's been evident every time we're together. Now I am standing in his kitchen, wearing only a T-shirt and him only in a pair of faded ripped jeans it's like fireworks going off around us. *Can I do this? Can I be with someone other than Lucien? Yes! It's been weeks, he has had time to come to me and he hasn't. Luke chose to leave. I tried. Now it's time for me to think about myself.*

"Jay." I breathe his name; his hands cup my face. When he leans in, his warm breath fans on my face, and I shiver. His lips lightly brush on mine, its soft and sends goose bumps over my skin. Maybe this is a bad idea, but right now, I want something other than the pain in my heart.

"Cassie, tell me to stop? Because if you don't I can't promise I will be the good guy anymore. I can't deny my feelings for you. This will not be love, this will be two consenting adults, fucking. Tell me what you want?" His words have my body trembling. When I glance up into his blue eyes and I realize what I want. I want this. I nod. "Words, Cassie. I need you to tell me?"

"Yes, I want you to fuck me." I have no idea where the words came from, but I said them. With no more confirmation, he turns around and turns off the stove. When he faces me again, he grabs me by my ass, lifting me against him. Automatically my legs wrap around his taut waist, I hold on to his neck as he walks into the living room. When he sits me down on the dining table, I can't help giggling.

"On here?" I stare at him incredulously. He has has a strained look on his face.

"Cassie, I don't care where we do it." His voice low, raspy and sexy. "I want to be inside you. I want to feel you around my cock. And when you come, you going to be screaming my fucking name. I assure you of that." I gasp and the pink boy shorts I am wearing are soaked. With both hands on either side, he lifts the T-shirt, and tugs it up over my head. An audible growl escapes his lips and I grin. I lean back as he grabs my knees, pushing them open. "Fuck you're beautiful." His eyes roam over my body.

"So are you." I reach for his jeans and unbutton them. As they slide down his hips, my fingers brush the soft fabric of his Calvin Klein briefs. My hungry gaze takes in the glorious man in front of me. He is chiseled from his shoulders, arms, and chest to that beautifully sculpted V shape, pointing into his tight briefs where an impressive erection is straining the front. I scoot forward as his fingers tug at my panties, I lift my ass and he pulls them off. The material is dropped on the floor. He turns his searing gaze on me. His fingers trailing feather light touches over my bare thighs leaving goose bumps in their wake. Sending waves of pleasure straight between my legs. "I can smell you, princess. The scent of you is delicious." A smirk curls his lips. His hands move all the way up the side of my body to my now hard nipples. Tweaking and tugging them both in between his thumb and index finger, causing a whimper to escape my lips.

"Jay." I look into his eyes and they are dark with lust. The cerulean blue is now the color of the ocean at dusk. With both big strong hands, he cups my face and holds me still. I close my eyes in anticipation of his kiss when his tongue licks the seam of my lips.

"I have wanted to fuck you since I first looked into those chocolate eyes of yours, Cassie." His kiss leaves tingles on my lips. This isn't ever going to be love because my heart belongs to someone else. "But I knew you weren't available." He plants a tender kiss on my chin. "Now though, I will have you." He slowly licks at the curve of my neck, up to the soft tender spot behind my ear and I am aching to for him to be inside me. His teasing is driving me crazy. "I am going fuck you so hard, you will be feeling me next week." His teeth graze my earlobe, tugging on it gently. "And that's when we're on location. Then I will fuck you on the beach. You will scream, moan, and tremble and come, over and over again. Do you understand me Cassie?" His illicit promise tightens the knot in my belly while I squirm on the table.

My voice has abandoned me and all logical thought has vanished. I nod. His hands grip my hips; Jay kneels down in front of me pulling me closer to the edge of the table. "Lean back gorgeous." Once I am leaning back onto my elbows, I watch his tongue snake out and lick my slick entrance.

"Oh, God!" I breathe, he pushes my legs further apart and licks me in slow measured strokes. His thumbs open my folds and his tongue darts into me. "Jayce!" A strangled cry emanates from me.

"You're sweet like honey," he rasps. His hot breath on me, has my core pulsing with need. When his eyes lock on mine I see the desire burning in them. A dark smirk curling his lips and his mouth crashes back down on me and I whimper. His tongue flicks over my clit, swirling it. When he sucks the hardened nub into his mouth, my thighs tremble. I am so close to my release, "Jay, please?" I urge and he drives two fingers inside me. An orgasm rips through every nerve of my body. My arms shake under the weight of me and I am sent spiraling. He continues the unrelenting pace of his fingers plunging into me. As my orgasm subsides, he pulls his fingers from me and licks my arousal from them.

He rises and slips his briefs down, his rock hard erection standing proudly. Ripping a condom packet between his teeth, I watch him sheath himself. "Ready for me baby?" I nod, my legs wrap around his waist pulling him to me. He leans in to kiss me and I taste myself on his lips. With sudden ferocity he slams into me. My core tightens and I squeeze him inside me. "God, you're so fucking tight, Cassie!" He drives inside me, so deep I shudder.

"Fuck, yes, Jayce!" I tighten my legs around his waist, drawing him in deeper.

"Hold tight gorgeous." He lifts me by the ass and I clutch his neck, his biceps pulse. His body pinning me against the wall. He slams into me with a drive of a man possessed. "You're fucking perfect, Cassie, so fucking perfect!" Sucking my nipple in his warm wet mouth, tugging my nipple with his teeth, my core tightens around him and I realize I am in for an earth shattering orgasm. His hard cock driving into me deeper and faster, and his body tenses. "Come with me, Cassie. Let me take your pain away." His intense stare sears into me. My body clenches. "That's it, come hard!" He grunts and my release shatters through me. My head falls back against the wall and the cry that's ripped from deep in my chest shatters the silence of his home.

"Jayce!" He tenses and his release locks his body. His cock twitching inside me, sending waves of pleasure through my body. We stay like that for what feels like hours, but it is merely a few minutes. Jay holds me close to him and his sweaty body warms me. I nuzzle in his neck and take in his spicy scent. "Wow, that's some breakfast, Jayce." I giggle as he slips out of me. Once he sets me down on wobbly legs, he watches me intently.

"Well, there is more where that came from, princess." He gives me a panty dropping smile that's if I had panties on. "I think it's time for real breakfast, what do you think?" Jayce picks up the T-shirt and hands it to me. I shrug it on, then find my panties. My legs are still trembling as I walk into the kitchen.

"So did you honestly mean that?" I glance at him as I pick up the forgotten bowl of whisked egg. He turns on the stove and places the frying pan back on the heat. I watch him and realize that I like him. He's been there for me through everything, even though I care for him, I could never love him. I will never love anyone the way I loved Lucien. I suppose I did still love Lucien, even though he didn't love me.

"Mean what, princess?" His blue eyes back to normal. When he smiles there's a slight crinkle in his nose and I grin.

"What you said? About wanting me?" My voice serious now. I recall first meeting Jay, I always thought he said things to me to wind Lucien up. Now I am not so sure.

"Yes, princess. I meant every word." He takes the bowl from me and sets it down. With a small tug, he pulls me against his body. "He's a fool to let you go. I know you love him and I am tired of seeing you in pain. You need a distraction from the pain, and I will be the best damn distraction you ever had." Lucien has made it clear that we're no longer together. I have to move on at some point and if it's meant to be with Jayce, so be it. He's an amazing person. He's never hurt me and I trust him. "It's okay Cass."

"No, it's not. I want to move on. Yes, Lucien and I had something extraordinary, but it's over. I can't wallow in self pity forever." When I lift onto my toes and give him a soft kiss, I smell something burning. With a quick step back, we turn to the stove and it seems we've got super crispy bacon. I giggle as I watch Jayce as he pulls the pan from the stove. Turning to the bowl, I continue whisking the eggs.

"God woman, you're way too distracting to have in the kitchen!" He rounds on me and grabs my hips. "You undoubtedly want me to burn my house down?" I shake my head and a laugh escapes my lips. "I love when you laugh. It's a beautiful sound."

"Well, Jayce, you make me laugh." I look up at him and smile. He rewards me with a beautiful grin of his own.

"Another coffee? Because at this rate, we will never eat." He asks me amused.

"Coffee sounds good!" And just like that, my pain is at bay. For now. I will never get over Lucien, the pain of him leaving me will never abate. If I can forget the pain, even for a moment, I will try.

Lucien

Monday morning, and into the fourth week of being without her. I could lie and say it's getting easier, but I am not going to. Jayce called me last night, needless to say the conversation didn't go very well. He told me she's moved on. The words cut into me like a sharp blade, twisting in my heart. He did also tell me that she still loves me. We spoke for a long time, but I decided to let her spend time with him. *Does that make me a saint? Me walking away and letting her be happy? No.* Because she will never be happy with anyone, but me. It's all part of my plan to win her back.

I will win her back, and when I do, she will never want anyone else. The fact that he told me she mumbled my name in her sleep was evidence enough that I need a plan. That's why I was sitting in my office at 7 am on a fucking Monday morning. I sat back in my chair, the view of the city below me. My head throbbed. I spun my chair around and grabbed the phone, dialing her number before I realized what I was doing. Almost second nature. "Cassie, hello?" *What the fuck do I say?* She spent the weekend with Jayce, so why did I call her? *Hang up!* I open my mouth to speak, closing it again. *Think of the plan. Think of the plan.*

"Cassandra, I am just following up on the flight this evening. I know you and Jayce are leaving soon, and I wanted to make sure you have all the details." The excuse I give her is ridiculous, and she knows it. There is nothing that would make sense for my call. I walked out on her. Left her. Me calling her was stupid. My heart hammers in my chest, leaning back in the chair, I close my eyes. *Get a fucking grip.*

"Yes, thank you I have all the details. There is no need to check up on me. I have done this before." She hates me. I don't blame her.

"Okay." The tone of her voice sends ice straight to my heart.

"Is there anything else, Mr. Verán?" When she utters my name, my cock solidifies in my pants and all I want to do is fuck her hard. While she's bent over her desk, her tight little skirt around her hips. Those tiny fucking panties at her ankles. Me sliding into her tight heat. My fist in her long curls, tugging her head back.

Fuck! "That's all, Ms. Winters."

"Goodbye." Her voice is cold, final. I need to work harder. I want her back. As soon as I hang up, I have the need to punch something. When my door opens an audible groan escapes my lips. I recognize Stacy's perfume and I am not in the mood for her shit today. "Mr. Verán, your coffee." I glance at her placing my mug on the desk.

"Thank you, what time is that meeting?" Needing to get my mind off the girl on the tenth floor is imperative, this meeting was marked as important. I am looking forward to seeing my father again later. Perhaps he has some advice for his wayward son, to get the girl he loves back.

"It's in an hour Mr. Verán." She offers a smile, but I don't return it. I realize I am a dick, but she needs to get over it or find a new job. I glance at the time, 10:30 am. It's almost time for Cassie to leave.

"Thanks, I will be back in a moment." I rise and walk out of the office, leaving Stacy staring after me. When I push the button for the elevator, deep down I realize this is a bad idea, but I need to see her. My body has a mind of its own, I just wish it can wait for my brain to catch up. There is nothing in this world I want more than to make up with Cassie. It's something that has been on my mind for a week now, fuck, longer than that. My stubbornness and ignorance has cost me the woman I love. As soon as the elevator descends, my mind is made up. Somehow, I will win her back.

Cassandra

"What did he want?" He nods towards the phone. My eyes cut to Jayce, sitting opposite my desk. He's dressed in a blue shirt that brings out his eyes, and faded blue jeans that hug his thighs. As my gaze drinks him in, I pull my thoughts away from the call from Lucien. Right now, this is the last place I want to be. When I glance at the time, I realize we can't leave yet, as much as I want to go.

"Nothing. He's just trying to shake me with an excuse of checking if I am ready for the trip. Like I don't have a clue how to do my job." Jay leans forward, concerned is etched on his face. His worry is me going back to Lucien, but that will not happen. At least that's what I tell myself. The thing is, if my mistake could push us this far apart, how can anything bring us back together.

"He knows." Two words that could break my world, wide open. I shake my head. There isn't a chance Lucien knows about Jayce and me and this weekend. Even if he did, I don't care. Jayce seems very sure about it unless he told him?

"Frankly, I don't care, but did you tell him?" I shut down my laptop. His expression tells me he spilled the beans.

"I did, he needed to realize you've moved on. If not forever, then for now." I nod. It doesn't phase me. Actually that's a lie, it cuts me that the only reason Luke called was because Jayce told him I had moved on. That I was seeing someone else. So me being lonely and in pain is enough for him, but once I try to find some semblance of a new life, he can't handle it.

"Seriously, Jayce it doesn't matter. Whether he knows I moved on or not. He doesn't want me. It's obvious. So I will just have to move on. Forever." The words are a complete lie, I realize they are as soon as I have spoken them. He's always there, in the back of my mind. Deep inside my heart that's where he resides. He's woven into the fabric of my soul, and he can never be erased. That's where he will live forever. I slip my laptop into the bag and grab my phone. The call to Kenna is short, asking her to look after my apartment while I am gone.

Jayce sits back, the office is quiet, as he watches me. He's trying to gauge my reaction. I realize he is. Those cerulean eyes burn into me, cutting through the pain etched into my soul. He's been trying to fix me, take my pain away, and he does. There are times the pain subsides to almost a dull ache, but then there's a song, a word, a smell, and everything comes roaring back. It's like a tidal wave, knocking me off balance.

"Let's go, Alexander! I am in charge of the shoot and we need to leave." I offer him a smile and he chuckles. The deep growl in his throat tells me there's something else on his mind. He shakes his head at my cheeky words.

"You're so demanding." He gets up and fiddles with his phone.

I giggle and shoulder my bag, I round my desk and give him a peck on the cheek. "Have to be. I prefer when you're demanding though." With a cheeky wink at him as I pass to the door. He slaps my ass, and it sends tingles over my skin and heat to my core. As soon as I open the door, and step out, I slam into something solid.

My gaze flits up and I come face to face with olive green eyes. I choke on my laugh, and the guilt washes over me like a kid caught with my hand in the cookie jar. Jay's laugh stops dead and we both stare at Lucien. "What are you doing here?" I whisper, my voice is unrecognizable. The pain in my chest deepens and I can't bring myself to breathe. I realize inhaling his scent will send me into a panic attack, and I can't afford one of those now. His face gives nothing away.

"I need to speak with you, before you leave, Ms. Winters." His voice is curt and the glare he gives Jay sends chills down my spine. "Give us a moment, Jayce."

Jayce walks out and as I shut the door, he gives me a wink and I smile. Turning to face Lucien, my heart races. I haven't seen him since he told me we were through and now here he is in my office. "So…" I mumble, unsure of what to say.

Lucien

With a deep breath, I try to keep my voice even. The rage inside me is blazing and my nerves grate and it's like they're about to spontaneously combust. She can't see how much this is tearing at me; she doesn't deserve it. As soon as Jayce leaves us, the office is suddenly too small. The last time I was in here I told her it's over, the cry that ripped from her that day will forever haunt me.

"I wanted to find out how your therapy is going?" As soon as the words are out of my mouth, they stun us both. *What the fuck was that Verán? You should fucking walk out of here now!* I can't meet her eyes, I realize if I do it will completely disarm me, but I do. When I turn to face her, it sends a wave of something over me and I feel the urge to pull her into my arms

"It's wonderful, listen Lucien, I need to go. I have a flight to catch." I do need to leave. Or I will do something I will regret. With a white knuckle grip on the doorknob, realization hits me that it's just not enough time. I need more, I want to spend the week with her, but I can't.

"Be safe. Enjoy the trip. I will see you when you get back." There is no reason for me to tell her that. We are no longer together, but seeing her drunk in that club made me worry. Jay won't let anything happen to her, and that's what pisses me off even more. Once I am out of the office, I make my way to the elevator. In my office, Stacy is at my heels. With all the meetings I have today, I am grateful that work will be a distraction. Until I get home. She's leaving for the airfield and will be whisked off to a tropical island with my best friend. I need to think. "Give me a minute Stacy, please?" I close my office door. I pull out my phone, I find the number that I am dreading to call. So I send a text message instead. He will be with her, I don't want to ask him to talk about it.

* Have you fucked her? *

I don't know why I asked him. The masochist in me wants to know. Needs to know. There was something between them when I caught them in the office. I didn't wait long for a reply. That's when my phone found the wall across from my desk.

* *What do you think, Luke?* *

The office door flew open and Stacy ran inside. "Mr. Verán, are you okay?" Her eyes flitted across the room. Her gaze falling on the shattered phone on the floor, she glanced back at me.
"Get me a new phone." I turned away from her and back to my laptop.
"Yes, sir."
I did this. Fucked up the best thing that ever happened to me. Pushed her away. The thought of Jayce with her, touching her in ways that only I should be was shredding the last of my heart. *She's better off without you, Verán. You can't give her what she needs. You don't deserve her, she's too good for you. You would have hurt her. At some point your darkness would have taken over and you would have fucked it up.* The phone on my desk buzzing pulled me out of the internal debate. "What?"
"Sir, your 11:30 is here."
"Send him in."
"Um, it's a her."
"Whatever Stacy, send her in!" I barked down the phone at her. Yes, being a dick is what I do. As soon as my office door opens. I lose all brain capacity. Shock runs over my face and body. The woman standing in my doorway was an older version of Cassie, from her beautiful dark brown eyes, down to those long dark curls. This doesn't make sense. *Is this a fucking joke?*
"Mr. Verán," her voice is like silk. Smooth and soft, just like Cassie's. If I didn't know any better I would have thought that she was Cassie, playing a trick on me, what gave her away though was the wrinkles at the edges of her eyes when she smiled.
"Ms… Sorry, you've caught me at a disadvantage." I rise and walk to door, extending my hand. When she placed hers in mine, something connects. *Who the fuck was this?*
"I am Ms. Winters, the same as Cassandra." The shock on my face must have been evident. She gave me a small smile and walked into my office. When she reached the window behind my desk she stopped, staring at the view of the city below. I opened my mouth to speak, but no words came out.
She turned to face me again and smiled. Her gaze travelled over me, appraising me in a way that Cassie would. "I can see why she's so in love with you."
"I'm sorry, but you have me even more at a disadvantage here, Ms. Winters." With a swift whoosh, I close my office door, and walk towards my desk. Her relaxed professional appearance is elegant. Dressed in a dark blue skirt and white blouse, with dark blue heels, she was the picture of sophistication. I, on the other hand was a picture of complete and utter confusion.
"I do, I can see it written all over those boyishly handsome features, Mr. Verán." That was where the similarity ended. She didn't have the effect on me that my baby did. *Cassie's not your baby anymore!* When she slips into the chair across my desk, a smile brightens the serious look on her face. "Please, sit, let's get the meeting under way. I have limited time."
I have never been ordered around by a woman, but I obey her calm command. "So, how can I help you Ms. Winters?" I lean back, and recognize a flicker of fear cross her face, but as soon as it arrives, it disappears again. My senses are on high alert. I am sure

this has to do with Cassie, but what, and who is this woman?

"Cassandra is my daughter, Mr. Verán." Once again, this woman has floored me. *Mother? Her mother died! What the fuck?*

"Her mother is dead, she told me herself."

"Her adopted mother is dead, Lucien." Her gaze meets mine and my sudden wariness of this woman who is an older version of Cassie takes precedence. I am more confused now.

"She never told me she was adopted."

"Cassandra doesn't know. I would like to keep it that way." Pulling out some papers from her bag, she stands up and places them in front of me. "That is the paperwork. She was adopted when she was born. I was sixteen, with parents like mine, I was forced to give her up for adoption. Her adopted parents were told never to speak of it. This was part of the contract they signed. The only thing she has kept was my name. That was part of the agreement."

"I don't understand. If you didn't want a part of your daughter's life, why appear now? Why come to me?" I peer up and see the struggle in her eyes. There are so many emotions. Love, fear, pain.

"I need to tell you something. Something that can never leave this office."

"Look, Ms. Winters, I am not with Cassie anymore."

"You will be. I believe that, seeing the love in your eyes when you mention her name." A small smile appears on her lips.

"I have no idea what to say to you Ms. Winters. Cassie and I, we just didn't work. She... I mean—" I don't know what to tell her. My heart will always be Cassie's, there's no doubt about that. She completes me in a way that I have never known.

"You walked away didn't you?" I nod. There's nothing I can say to the love of my life's mother to make this okay. I did walk away. "Although, you still love her. You know that you belong together."

"We can't be together; Cassie doesn't trust me."

"Doesn't she?" I stare at her long and hard, then shake my head. "Then why would she tell you about the deaths she had to live through. Why would she stay with you after what happened in your past? She loves you."

"How do you know about my past?"

"My daughter's safety is my concern, Mr. Verán, I looked into you. Some things can be buried, but not hidden forever."

"Okay, but what do I do? She's moved on."

"If you really believe that, then you're not as bright as I thought you were. Nobody moves on from their soul mate. Ever." I watch as her gaze falls to the floor, there's sadness etched on her face. She's speaking from experience. This is one of the strangest meetings I have ever had. It's like talking to a ghost who knows more about my life than I do.

"How do I get her back?" A glimmer of hope sparks that maybe Cassie will take me back.

"Fight." I cock my head to the side. "Don't let her leave. Get her to see that you love her. You will find a way. Don't give up on her Lucien. She's not use to being in a relationship and sharing her past. I think you need a father's advice. Call Claude. He will help."

My father? She knows my father?

"How do—"

"You father will explain. I have to leave. Those papers are yours. Keep them. I trust you." She rises from the chair and I follow suit. "And whatever you do. Please don't tell her about me. Not yet. I am not ready to let her realize that I failed her."

"You didn't fail her."

"I did. Take care of her. Remember, you're both reeling from dark pasts. So let her in and she will let you in." I round my desk and give a small nod.

"Thank you. I will think it through, she's away now."

"Don't think for too long." I chuckle at her insistence, but she's right. I can't wait for too long. Jayce has already moved in on my girl and he won't let go.

As soon as Cassie's mom left, I called my father.

Cassandra

I look out of the window and see the clouds below us. "You thinking of him?" Jay's voice pulls me from my thoughts. I shake my head and smile. My mind was whirling with thoughts of not being in therapy for a week. After all that's taken place, I haven't missed an appointment. My new doctor was wonderful. She listened, she made observations, but never once did she want to put me on medication. Which made a difference. I hated the stuff. I glance back to Jayce and watch him. He's typing something on his phone and I wonder what it is. I doubt he's ever been in love. He looks up and his gaze meets mine. "You okay, princess?"

"Yes, why do you call me that?" I stare into his cerulean eyes.

"Because that's what you are." He says matter-of-factly, looking at me with a puzzled expression, like I should know that I am a princess. I stifle a giggle. "You don't believe me? Cassandra, you're beautiful, talented, strong, independent and intelligent. You're just…" He turns his gaze away. His eyes focus on the clouds outside the window of the private jet that's taking us to Cancun for the week. Nobody has ever suggested or looked at me the way he did. Maybe, once, a long time ago Lucien did, but he no longer does.

"I just… I have never had anyone see me the way you do. Or at least tell me. Besides—" Not being able to bring myself to say his name. I can only hope that he realizes his assumption of me is strange. Something I have never had before.

"Well, I am just being straightforward with you Cass. That's all you'll ever get from me. And let me say this while we're here and you can't run away. If ever you agree to take him back, be sure he doesn't fucking hurt you like that again. Because I will fucking kill him." His words hang in the air and I recognize the ice cold promise of his words.

"Lucien didn't hurt me. He couldn't deal with the truth. I hid something from him Jay, a loss he himself had to deal with and I understand why he's angry." My eyes find his in a stand-off and I expect the next words out of his mouth before he even says them.

"You lost a baby?" The disbelief in his tone sends me reeling, and the bile rises in my throat. I punished myself to save myself and all I did was scar everyone who cherished me. Without answering I scoot out of my seat and run to the back of the plane. Once inside the small restroom, I lock myself in. When I kneel over the toilet and heave, nothing comes out. Tears pour down my face, and I shudder.

"Cassie, open this door or I swear to God I will beat it down!" Jay was serious, and I realized he would break the door down. I grasped the latch and twisted it until it sprang free. "Shit Cassie…" his arms were around me as he held my hair back.

"I'm fine, go." I tried swatting him away, but my feeble attempts didn't work.

"No, I am not leaving you." He held me and caressed my back, gently. Calm washed over me and I sat back on my heels. Tears flowed freely down my cheeks and my sobbing almost choked me.

"I am a killer Jayce. Leave me alone." My words were strangled, my throat hurt. Jayce scooped me up and carried me to the back of the plane, opening a door which led to a bedroom.

He settled me down on the bed and brushed my hair back. My face wet with tears, but I couldn't stop them. Not being able to face him, I twisted away, staring at the window.

"Cassie, what happened?" He begged me to tell him, but I couldn't make myself repeat the horror, not right now. All I needed to do was close my eyes. A small shake of my head, and I felt the bed dip behind me. Jayce placed an arm around me. With a tug he pulled me against his body. He was a cocoon, shielding me from the outside world and the horror of my past. "Just sleep. I am here. Okay?"

I nodded. My eyes burned and so did my throat. The pain in my chest was the worst of all. There was something inside me that was broken, and there was only one person who could fix it. That one person unfortunately didn't want to fix it.

Lucien

Every time I pull up to my childhood home, it always feels like I am about to be scolded. I called my father, needing to speak to him about Cassie. She's gone for a week and I am not sure how to handle it. Well, it's not the fact that she's gone, it's the idea of her with Jayce that's killing me. Being away from her hurts, my body, mind, and soul are constantly at odds with each other. I may have walked away, but she still holds every part of me. The knowledge that her mother is still alive, shocked me to the core. I can't imagine what it would do to my sweet girl, even though we're not together at the moment, she is and will always be my girl. I fucking marked and claimed her, and I will be damned if I let her go.

Not having heard from either her or Jayce has me on edge. I grab my phone and call him. They must have landed by now, but he hasn't contacted me. "Luke."

"Where the fuck are you? Is she okay?"

"Why do you care so much? You left her. Not the other way around."

"Answer the goddamn question!"

"She's fine. She's sleeping."

"Jayce, don't touch her."

"It's a bit late for that man. She's moved on."

"Like fuck she has. She's mine. If you go near her again, I will fucking kill you and don't take that as an empty threat!" My body is vibrating with anger. She's mine. She will always be mine. I hang up before he can reply. I fucking own her, and anyone who stands in my way will be sorry. Stalking into the house, I hear my father talking to one of the servants. "Dad?"

As soon as he makes his way into the entrance, his face falls. "What's wrong?"

"What makes you think something is wrong?"

"Luke, I have known you all your life. I can see when something is wrong."

"It's Cassie, I left her."

"What?!" The alarm in his voice is apparent. Although I am not sure why he's so upset. I mean, he has only met her once before. Deep down I know she still loves me. No matter who she's fucking, my cock and my heart own her. "What do you mean? Why?" He rounds on me, but I don't answer and walk towards the office. His office has always been my favorite place, it was far away from my step mother and I could just be me.

"She lied to me. Or, not exactly told me the whole truth."

His eyes burning into my back as I stepped into his office, with him hot on my heels. As soon as I got out of the car I had the feeling I was going to get scolded.

"And you didn't lie to her as well?" I spun on my heel, my anger flaring, but I realized he was right.

When I met the reflection of my eyes in my father's I lost all fight. I almost broke down and cried. "I miss her."

"Of course you do, she's your forever. You can't be without her Luca, I told you this." I watch him slip into the large office chair that he's had since I was a kid. I remember sitting in it, spinning around and around, making myself dizzy.

"Is that why her mother was at my office today?" When his shocked expression fell on me, I realized I hit a nerve. There was something he wasn't telling me.

"What did she say?"

"No dad, it's time for you to tell me. I need to know why Cassie is under the impression her mother is dead. Why is it that Cassie happened to get the job at Verán Publishers? And why the fuck am I irrevocably and unconditionally in love with her?" I realized I was shouting but I didn't care. The need to know the truth about what is going on with me was tugging at me.

My dad sits back with deep sigh. He's going to tell me. "Lucien, do you remember the holiday we took for your thirteenth birthday? I had to attend New York Fashion week. After, we took a drive just outside the city. We stopped at a little café. There was a couple that we met with."

I nodded. That was one of the best holidays we had. I remember the amazing pancakes and syrup. They had the most delicious cupcakes. My dad spoiled me that weekend. "We had breakfast. After, we went for a long drive. Just us." He nodded and I can see he was as lost in the memory as I was. It was time away from my step mother.

"Do you remember the park we stopped at, you were playing with some kids. There was a little girl…" His voice trailed off, and I wasn't sure where he was going with it. As my memory flits back, I remember him chatting to a couple, they were friendly enough. They had a daughter, with curly brown hair and mocha eyes. *Shit!*

"Cassie…" The realization hit me like a tidal wave. When my gaze fell on him again, I saw him smiling. He nodded slowly. When he reached into his desk drawer and pulled out a photo album, he opened it to a page and turned it so I can have a look. There was a small square photo of me at thirteen and a girl, my arm around her neck. She looked younger, maybe ten. Three years. I am thirty, Cassie is twenty-seven. "But, I don't understand."

"Cassie's mom, she and I. Well. It's difficult. She asked me to keep an eye on Cassie, I always did. That trip I was supposed to go and get a contract from her adopted father. Deanna wanted me to be there to see if Cassie was doing okay. After meeting her you were alight, with something I only ever saw in myself. When we were on our way home, you said something that I will never forget son, you told me that one day you will marry her." He chuckled then and shook his head. "Since Deanna had asked me to keep an eye on her daughter, I had kept in touch with her parents. Cassie's adopted dad, he was in publishing as well, so we did some business together. When he said that Cassie wanted to work in publishing, I wanted to offer her a job. It was only until much later that I found out that they were killed in a horrific car accident. I managed to get hold of Cassie's details and invite her for the interview."

Slowly things were falling into place, but that didn't explain how I have this love for Cassie that's almost debilitating. "Luca, when you meet a girl that is meant to be with you, there is something in you that shifts. She was yours since you were thirteen. The same thing happened to me. I invited Cassie here because I wanted to see if she was your forever. The polar opposites. Summer and Winter. The fact that after seventeen years, you still love her is precedent enough." My father was Cassie's mom's first love, but why the pendants?

"I get that dad, but she was engaged before. She told me that her fiancé was killed the same night her parents were. So she didn't love me in that first moment. And mom wasn't a Winters? You loved Cassie's mom?" My eyes fell on him, I needed answers. Now more than ever.

"You were almost engaged to Sasha, you both moved through life and found your way to each other. Something I can't explain. Your mom wasn't a Winters. Cassie's mom, she was my first love. I always found Deanna, no matter what, but we couldn't be together. There were obstacles." I let out a breath I wasn't sure I was holding. *This is like a fucking soap opera.*

"Well, she's with Jayce now. She's moved on."

"Do you believe that?" I think back to the little girl with the brown curls. How did I not recognize her? It's so incredible that so many years later, she still has my complete attention.

"I remember!" Looking up, I see the smile on my father's face. I remember running after Cassie that day when we played in the park. She was giggling and teasing me about not being able to catch her. I did. After running around the park, I finally caught her. When I looked into her brown eyes, I knew that I one day I would marry her.

"You will find your way together. Why not come for dinner? This weekend." My father playing the match maker. It's a role he enjoyed playing. I nod.

"I will ask her."

When I drove away from my childhood home, I had a plan. There was hope. All I had to do was make sure Cassie wanted me back. That couldn't be too difficult. Could it?

Cassandra

"Princess, we're here." I roll over to meet big blue eyes staring down at me.

"What?" My voice is croaky. The dreams I had kept me tossing and turning, babies with olive and blue eyes. They seemed to fuse in my mind and I was exhausted.

"Come darling, we've landed in Cancun." Jayce lifted me off the bed and carried me to the main part of the plane. Once he set me on my feet, I gathered my bag, phone, and laptop. His hand found mine as we disembarked the jet.

"Ms. Winters," Robert opened the back door for me and I slipped into the bench seat. He offered me a melancholy glance, and I realized that he learned about Lucien and I. So much had happened, I didn't think about Robert. Lucien and I hadn't been together for three weeks and he must have noticed it. I decided to question him when we were alone.

"Robert, where are we staying?" I called out to him when he slid into the driver's seat. His eyes darted back to mine.

"You have the club master suite at the Ritz, Ms. Winters." His polite nod is quick, and I can tell he's non too pleased about what's happened. Then realization hits me. Lucien booked the hotel.

"And Mr Alexander?" I look at him expectantly.

"The room next to yours, Ms. Winters, likewise, a club master, with oceanfront views." His grim nod shows he is finished speaking and I nod.

"Thank you, Robert." I sit back and pull my phone from my pocket. I scroll through messages from Kenna, my doctor, and I see one last name on the list that stops my heart for a few seconds. It's from Lucien. I don't open it. My decision not to read it tugs at me, but I lock my phone, and slide it into my bag. When I cut a glance over at Jayce, I notice he's lost in the scenery and I am grateful he didn't see Lucien's name on my phone.

Robert pulls up to the Ritz and opens my door. "Ms. Winters." He gives me a curt greeting. At the trunk he helps to retrieve mine and Jayce's luggage.

"Thank you, Robert, I got it from here." Jayce grabs our suitcases and we walk towards the entrance. "Come on, princess. Let's get you to bed." I cast a brief glance to Robert and I know he overheard Jayce's comment. We step into the lobby of the hotel. An enormous crystal chandelier hangs from the high ceiling. The décor is beautiful, elegant, and the staff are immaculately dressed. I walk up to the front desk and the polished receptionist smiles.

"Hello, we should have two bookings under the Verán Publications name." She nods and turns her attention to the computer screen. A few taps on the keyboard, and she offers a glance to both Jayce and me.

"Yes, I have two rooms reserved, with sea views. They're both on the first floor."

Breakfast is from 7 am and dinner is served from 7 pm. There are also private casitas along the beach. They're charming, and you can watch the sunset from them if you're so inclined." Her gaze wanders over to Jayce. I am positive she's struggling to determine if we're together or not. Since we're in different rooms, it's evident we're not. I cast a quick glance to Jayce, but he hasn't even noticed her.

"Thank you." I snatch the keys from the desk and note the numbers. It seems they are next to each other. The concierge comes over to take our suitcases, but Jayce declines his offer.

"I got this thank you."

We walk over to the elevator and I press the call button. "This place is incredible!" I glance over at Jayce and take in his naughty smirk. "What?"

"We can have a secret tryst in one of the casitas." He winks and the prospect of what he's just proposed sends a pulse of need between my legs.

"Jayce!" He shrugs as the doors of the elevator open. We step inside and I push the button for the first floor. There is no doubt, I am still owned. One man in this world owns me, and it's not the one standing next to me right now. It's the man that's a few hundred miles away.

"I wouldn't mind taking you to my room right now and fucking you until we fall asleep." Jayce rasps and the knot in my core tightens. The doors slide open and we make our way down the hall.

"You're very sure of yourself, Jayce." He chuckles behind me. We stop outside my room and I hand Jayce's key to him. I turn to unlock my door and step inside. Without a word Jay follows me inside and sets my suitcase down on the sofa in the living room. There's a separate bedroom with en-suite bathroom.

I stare out at the view from the living room. The ocean is black, and the sky is filled with stars. The full moon hangs low and I can see the waves crashing on the beach.

"I don't recall you complaining this passed weekend." His voice at my ear sends a tingle down my spine. With my eyes closed I take in the sensation of his fingers trailing feather light touches from my shoulders down to my wrists.

"I have no idea what you're talking about." I breathe, my voice is ragged.

"You don't?" There is amusement in his voice. "Should I jog your memory?" He moves my hair over my right shoulder, exposing the side of my neck to his mouth. His lips leave heated kisses on my skin. My body is on fire and the ache between my legs increases. His other hand snakes its way over my belly, pulling me back into his rock hard body. His arousal pressing into my ass. "Anything coming back to you yet?" His teeth tug at my sensitive earlobe.

"No, not yet." My voice barely audible. Goose bumps rise on my skin and I am trembling. His left hand moves down my belly, into the waistband of the sweatpants. I whimper when his fingers find the apex between my thighs. He moves them above my panties in small circles around the bundle of nerves, aching for release. The slow stroking movements send me spiraling with need. Lust. Desire.

"What about now, princess?" His voice is dark, gravelly, and sends electricity skittering over my body. His right hand moves around to my breasts. With a rough tweak on my nipples, they pebble, pushing against the flimsy material of my tank top.

"I…" My voice trails off as his fingers push my panties aside and slide along my slick sex.

"I think your memory is coming back." He plunges to fingers inside me. I cry out as pleasure rips through me and the smile on his lips is at my cheek. "Isn't it, Cassie?"

Jayce licks the sensitive skin behind my ear. "I asked you a question, princess?" His voice controlled, dangerous, causing my knees to buckle. The prospect of him taking me rough and hard made me tingle in all the right places.

"Yes," I murmur, barely recognizing my own voice. He had me at his mercy. When he pulls his fingers from my panties, it causes me to whimper at the empty feeling. I needed him. Craved for him to take the pain away, the ache of Lucien. "Please Jayce?" I plead. He knew what I needed, there wasn't a question. Only Jayce could ease my pain, in the only way he knew how.

As soon as he turns me around, he uses his wet fingers to trace the seam of my lips. With a naughty smirk on my face, I flick my tongue out to lick them and I taste my arousal. His eyes darken as he watches me. "Please what, Cassie?" He licks his index finger, savoring me. "Do you want this?" He grasps my wrist and places my hand on his rock hard erection. I nod. Thankfully I am standing against a desk, or I may have fallen over.

He tugs my tank top, pulling it over my head. It finds a spot on the carpet next to us. With a rough tug of my sweatpants, he pulls them down and they pool at my feet. Jayce was still kneeling in front of me. "You smell so good." The desire making his voice ragged. His index finger moves my panties aside, and his tongue flicks out, lapping at my soaked entrance. I grip his shoulders and moan his name. His fists grab my panties and rip them clean off. "Open for me," I spread my legs, and Jayce licks into me, his tongue drives inside me and my knees wobble. When he rises, his mouth crashes onto mine, his tongue plunges into my mouth. When I suck his tongue into my mouth, a groan escapes his chest. I tug at his T-shirt and he breaks the kiss long enough to pull it off.

My hands fumble with the button of his jeans. He smiles into the kiss and takes over from my shaky hands. When he steps back, his eyes meet mine. "I will make you forget." His promise embraces me in a warmth I haven't felt since Lucien left. *Did I want to forget? Was it really over with Lucien? Was this it? Cassie, you love Lucien! He is your soul mate! But, he doesn't want me. Jayce does.* My inner dialogue was furious.

"I don't want to forget." The words were out of my mouth before I could think. Jayce froze, turning to me, he straightened. My eyes glance up, standing in front of me in his tight blue briefs. His solid body, sculpted abs, and beautiful v muscles sending desire coursing through me.

"Then I will take your pain away. For now." He pulls me into his arms and holds me, kissing the top of my head. "I am sorry Cassie, for taking advantage. I shouldn't have." The tension between us was palpable. I glance up at him, pulling his face to mine. His lips warmed me.

"You didn't take advantage, I did." The need to put space between us grows and I step back. "I was using you to forget about him, but I can't. You're wonderful, Jayce."

"Cassie, I care about you and if offering you a few earth shattering orgasms will make you smile, then I am your man." Our laughter echoes through the room. The smile on his face creases the edges of his cerulean eyes.

"Earth shattering? So you're willing to be my boy toy?" I ask amused at the turn this conversation has taken. It's no joke, what I am asking him, but this man in front of me is offering me a way out. I will be a fucking idiot if I don't grab it with both hands. So there, in that heated moment. I do.

"Any day, princess." Within seconds he's scooping me up in his arms, he walks into the bedroom and lays me down. "Now will you let me pleasure you?" *How can I refuse an offer like that?*

"Jayce," I mumble. He's hovering over me, leaning on his elbows. His steel erection pressing between my legs. My hips buck to meet his as I shamelessly grind myself on him. The release I need turning me into a wanton woman writhing below him.

Jayce kneels between my legs and tugs his briefs down. His impressive cock springing free. With a smirk on his lips, he grabs the foil wrapper, but I stop him. "It's okay. I'm…" My cheeks heat in embarrassment. Why? I don't know. He smiles and nods. A soft whoosh interrupts us as he drops the condom on the floor. Not wasting a moment. His eyes lock on mine as he lowers himself over me again. The head of his cock teasing me. As I reach between us and position him at my slick folds, his hips buck involuntarily.

"Tell me what you want, Cassie?"

I peer up into his eyes. "I want you to fuck my pain away." He slams into me. I cry out as the pain sends pleasure ripping through me. He pulls almost all the way out and slams back into me. My nails dig into his back, my heels pushing his toned ass, trying to draw him in deeper. My back arches as he continues to slam into me. Harder and deeper. There was never a doubt that we were making love, this was pure, dirty fucking.

His mouth on my sensitive nipples, flicking his tongue in tiny circles. He sucks one into his mouth, biting down sending jolts of pleasure through me. When he releases the one he turns his attention to the other. "You are fucking gorgeous." His hoarse whisper in my ear. "I will fuck the pleasure straight from your core." His words taking me into a pleasurable delirium. Nothing outside this room matters. My pussy clenches around him. His dirty words taking me to the edge of my release. "Let go of your pain, princess. Let go!" He growls in my ear, as an earth shattering orgasm rips from my very core, just as he promised. "That's it, more, give me more!" I cry out so loud, without a doubt the whole of Cancun heard me. He continues to roll his hips, plunging into me, riding my orgasm. Waves of pleasure wash over me, but Jayce is relentless, pulling every ounce of pleasure from me as a second orgasm shudders through me. Another two thrusts and his own release is filling me. His body tenses above me, and he slows. "Fuck me." He breathes, he's as exhausted as I am.

I open my eyes and find him watching me. "Wasn't that what we just did?" I giggle.

"Yea, I guess it was." He slips out of me slowly and I wince. "Did I hurt you?"

Shaking my head. "No, you were…" I am not sure how to describe what just happened but it was absolutely incredible. As always the pain is gone. For now.

"So were you." He gives me a swift kiss. "Can I stay the night?" He smirks.

"I expected you would." He settles back and tugs me into him. My eyes close and sleep takes me over. That night, there weren't any babies, no pain and no memories. To be honest, that night, I dreamed that Lucien came back, he asked me to marry him. Even laying in someone else's arms I couldn't stop Lucien being there. *Was I the ultimate bitch?* Maybe, but I was a woman who had found her soul mate and couldn't let go. *Have you ever loved someone so much that when they walked out the room, you felt like your breath was gone? Do you know the feeling of watching someone you love walk away and it feels like they had ripped out your heart and soul and left you gaping with pain?* Yea, now you know how it feels.

Lucien

As soon as I get home, I grab my new phone and text Cassie. We need to talk when she's back. I am giving her this week, she's working, but when she's back I am not letting her out of my sight. As soon as I have sent the message to her, I send one to Jayce.

I suggest you keep your hands off my girl. I am fighting for her.

When I sit back, a smirk slowly curving my lips. She will not let me win easily. I expect a challenge, and I don't doubt we will have a huge fight, but she will submit to me. That is one thing I will make sure of. I walk over to my bar and pour myself a double whiskey. This is cause for celebration. I will get her back. Jayce's reply comes moments later.

Maybe she doesn't want you back. Have you thought of that?

He knows better than to fuck with me. I am not in the mood for his shit. When I hit the call button, he answers on the second ring. "Luke." Him using my nickname irks me even more. My blood is at boiling point.

"Jay, what was that message about?"

"I was just saying man. If she's moved on, are you going to force her to go back to you?"

"What are you saying? She wants you?" My laugh is deep. He's toying with me; I can hear it in his voice. There's years of understanding between us.

"I am saying, you can't force her to do anything she doesn't want to." When I nod, I realize he can't see me so my reply is a low growl.

"She wants me. Look into those dark brown eyes the next time you're with her, or better yet, look into her eyes when you're touching her, when you're deep inside her and tell me she doesn't love me." He is silent for such a long time; I think the line cut out. When I hear him sigh, I realize he is still there. He knows I am right. It doesn't matter that they've fucked. That's all it was and will ever be.

"Yes, she loves you. More than you're worthy of, but let me get one thing out. If she wants me while we're here. I will give her what she wants." It's a threat. Not one to annoy me, but one to make me want to smash his face into a wall.

"The only time she will ever beg for your cock is if I tell her to and you know that will never happen, even when I am dead." I hang up before I say something I will regret. *What the fuck is wrong with Jayce? He needs to get the fuck away from my girl.* I scroll down my screen and hit the call button again.

"Mr. Verán, how can I help you?"

"Robert, I need the plane and the pilot back here tonight. I don't care how late it is."

"Yes, sir. What is the flight plan?"

"I am flying to Cancun to oversee the shoot. Change of plan."

"Yes, sir." I plan to surprise my girl. She will be mine. I can't give up. Not when the only person that's ever made me feel like this is out there. I sent Cassie two messages, but I am not surprised that she hasn't replied to me yet.

Its 3 am when I step onto the plane. The pilot wanted to wait for early morning, but the sooner I can get there, the sooner I get my girl back. Nothing would keep me away from her. Not this time. I needed to get her away from Jayce. It would not be easy to convince her that I loved her. That I wanted her back. I needed her forgiveness, and I needed to earn it. There were so many ways I wanted to earn it. The first way will be to fuck her senseless on the beach.

As soon as we're in the air, I sit back and close my eyes. I should land as soon as she's waking up. My plan is to surprise her with breakfast in bed. Actually, I think she will be breakfast. The thought of tasting her again has my cock waking up, throbbing against the confines of my zipper. She is the only woman who can affect me this way. With her or without her, she leaves me with a near constant hard on. There have been numerous meetings where my mind has wandered to her and I have had to finish the meeting early just to get back to the privacy of my office. I picture her, those beautiful chocolate eyes, that long flowing curls, that body, that's where I find calm. The thought that I will soon be with her makes me smile. Even if I have to spend a lifetime winning her back.

"Mr. Verán." I wake up to Robert staring at me.

"What are you doing here?"

"I had to pick you up, you've landed." I sit up and realize I am still in the plane. Shit, I am still groggy. Dreams of Cassie and me on the beach have my mind whirling with desire.

"Thanks, Robert." Making our way down to the car, I ask Robert to take me straight to the hotel. My body is trembling, the desire, and anguish I have lived through this month will end. Robert pulls out into the road and makes his way down to the hotel. "Is she okay, Robert?" His eyes cut to mine in the rear-view mirror and something flickers across them. I know he's hiding something from me.

"She's well, sir. Mr Alexander is… Well he's been very close with her." I can hear the warning in his voice. I need to stay calm, I walked out. It's my fault for pushing her into someone else's arms. Now it's time to right my wrong. With a slow nod, I acknowledge him. There were no words that I could find to reply to him.

Cassandra

I wake up deliciously sore. My phone is vibrating from the nightstand, but I don't remember putting it there. "It's been going crazy all morning. I told him we arrived safely. Although, I didn't mention the fucking amazing sex we had last night." My gaze flits up and falls on Jayce wearing a towel around his taut waist. Water dripping down his chiseled chest and abs. A naughty smile plays on his lips.

"Lucien?" I frown. My head is still foggy from sleep.

"No, I am Jayce, princess." His face is one of complete amusement and I poke my tongue out at him. I scoot up, grabbing my phone and swiping the screen to stop the alerts.

"Oh right, sorry I was so confused. I had earth shattering sex last night. My mind isn't all that clear." I tease him. As I glance down, I notice two messages from Lucien and three from Kenna. When I hit reply to the message from Kenna, I let her know we're safe. I don't want to open the messages from Lucien. Not right now. There was no way I was ready.

"You had earth shattering sex? Wow, what a coincidence so did I." Jayce places a mug of coffee next to me as he sits down. "We have to be on site in about an hour, it's only a ten-minute drive, so don't rush." I nod and pick up the coffee. As I take a sip, I savor the taste.

"So, I um—" I point between the two of us. Not sure how to broach the subject.

"Look, Cassie, we don't have to do this. We're adults. Last night was fun, but it doesn't have to happen again. It's cool. I meant what I said. I wanted to take your pain away. That's all." He gets up and walks into the living room and the zipper of his suitcase echoes through the room. I set my coffee on the nightstand and swing my legs over the bed I pad into the living room. Jay is tugging on his jeans when I come up behind him. My arms wrap around him and pull him into me. I run my hands over his abs, every ridge and dip. His skin is smooth and soft.

"Jayce, don't do this?" I don't know what I want from him. I don't even know what I want from myself, but I don't want lose him. He's been a constant I am not ready to let go of just yet.

When he turns around in my arms, his index finger traces a path from my ear down to my chin. He lifts my face until my eyes find his. "I am not going anywhere. Just giving you space, princess." He peppers small kisses on my lips. "Now, get ready. Or we may never leave this room, and then the boss man will have our heads!" I giggle, knowing that the boss man will most definitely have Jayce's head.

In the bathroom, I turn on the shower and step in immediately. The cool water calms my muscles, but it doesn't stop the turmoil in my head. I turn up the heat and take a deep breath. As I stand under the hot spray the knots in my neck ease. I am not sure what is going on between Jayce and me, but whatever it is I am better than I have been in weeks. The soft scent of patchouli hits my senses as I lather up.

When I turn off the water, I step out of the shower and wrap a towel around me. I make my way into the bedroom. Jay has set my suitcase on the bed. I pull out my blue linen pants and a silver halter neck top. While I rummage through the clothes I packed, my mind wanders to Lucien. I grab underwear, and dry off. Then pulling on a black thong and matching bra, I hear an audible groan behind me. I turn to Jayce standing in the doorway watching me. "Jesus, Cassie. You look so fucking good. I have to work all day knowing that's what you're wearing under your clothes?" He points at my black underwear and the hard ridge in his jeans is evident, straining against his zipper.

"Behave, Jayce and yes I will most definitely be wearing this under my clothes. Would it bother you?" I twirl around, tormenting him further. The look on his face tells me he's barely holding on to his restraint. I can't help giggling.

"Cassandra." My name, a warning on his lips. Jayce takes two long strides towards me, clutching my hips, he tugs me towards him. Our bodies flush against each other. My breath hitches and I don't think we will be on time for work. "Do you enjoy tormenting me?" Tightening his grip, he pushes his groin into me and I whimper. "I think you enjoy making me hard, don't you Cassie?" I open my mouth to speak when his lips come crashing down on mine. My fingers run through his messy brown hair and I tug him into me. Our tongues dance together; I suck on his tongue hard. His fingers are digging into my hips painfully, but the pleasure coursing through my body is undeniable. He tugs my lower lip between his teeth and I whimper at the pleasure it sends through my body.

When Jayce finally breaks the kiss, we were both breathless. "I guess I have to work with a hard-on today." He releases his grip on my hips and rearranges himself and I giggle.

"Poor Jay. Maybe if you behave I can take care of it later." I tease. He chuckles as I grab my pants and step into them. I draw the string at my waist and slip the top over my head.

"If you behave, maybe I will let you." A cheeky grin spreads on his face. He turns and leaves me in the bedroom. I grab my phone and unlock the screen and open the first message from Lucien.

Just checking if you arrived safely

I hit delete and open the second.

We need to talk when you're back

I exit out of my messages and lock my phone. There is no way I am in the mood to reply right now. With a hair tie, I pull my curls into a messy bun, and make my way into the living room. "I'm ready." He looks up, raking in my appearance and gives me an appreciative smile.

"Awesome, let's go, princess."

Lucien

When the car stops in front of the entrance to the hotel, I walk into the lobby and head straight for reception. "Good morning Sir, how may I help you?" The receptionist is perky for this early in the morning and I offer a small smile.

"Ms. Winter's room please?"

"I apologize, sir, I am not at liability to give out such information."

"I am Mr. Verán, I am paying you for the room. So either you can give me the information or I can call your supervisor and get it from him."

Worry flickers over her face and she nods. I watch her tap away on the keyboard and wait. It's like minutes are stretching into hours by the time she finds the room number.

"Here you are, Mr. Verán. This is a second key for the room."

"Thank you." I offer her a curt nod and practically run towards the elevators. As the car ascends I am suddenly unsure of what I will do. *What if she doesn't want to see me?* The doors slide open slowly and I step out into the hallway when her voice echoes down towards me. She's giggling. I find a small alcove in the hallway and watch her and Jayce come out of the same room. He's got his arm snaked around her waist and she's molded to his body. The way she is meant to be in my arms. Anger courses through me. My blood is boiling. I have never been a jealous person, but right now, I am ready to kill. They step into the elevator and the doors slide closed. I wait a minute before walking to her room.

The click of the key card in the slot is loud as it unlocks. As soon as I step into the room my senses are assaulted with her perfume. The soft scent of lavender. My gaze takes in the appearance of the room; I see two sets of suitcases. Jayce is staying in here with her. *He's going to fucking die and I will make it fucking slow, and painful.*

My heart constricts when my eyes fall on the bed, the rumpled sheets. It's been almost a month we've been apart, of course she's moved on. I mean, I don't blame her. Actually, I do. We're soul mates. I will right my mistakes, but I will do it when she's home. Right there in the midst of the disheveled hotel room I make my decision.

I leave the room and head back downstairs. There is no sign of them when I hand in the keycard to the receptionist. She gives me an odd look, but I don't entertain any questions. I will fly back today. Then I will complete my plan to get Cassie back where she belongs. In my arms and my bed.

I arrive back in LA with more than enough time to get into the office and start my preparations for when she gets back. The first thing I need is to make sure I don't have to see Jayce for at least a few months because I want to rip his balls off and making sure he bleeds to death. That will be merciful. There are so many other ways I can think of making him suffer.

When I pick up the phone, I dial the one person I realize can help me. The question is, will she? "What do you want?" Ever the friendly disposition. The knowledge that she is the only person who can help, I keep calm, and speak the words I never thought I would ever say to her.

"Kenna, I need your help?"

"What makes you think I want to or will help you?" With my thumb and index finger, I pinch the bridge of my nose. I close my eyes, picturing Cassie in Jayce's arms and I realize I have to do this.

"Because you want her happy. That's all I want. I am fighting for her. The mistake I made is something I can't live with. I need her in my life. I love her. I am drowning without her. Please Kenna?" I am begging. There was never a time I have ever begged for anything, not even as a child. This is so new to me, but if it gets me the girl I love, I will do it every day forever. "My life means nothing without her. There are things I have done that I am not proud of, but this, it's killing me."

She's silent, I realize she's mulling over my words. It's the most honest I have ever been. I have never truly been in love. Until Cassie. The love that envelopes you, holds you in a warm embrace until you can't breathe without that person near you. That's how I am without her. I can't breathe. The pain of missing her comes in waves, and I am constantly drowning, and I don't want to learn to swim. I need her back.

"Fine. What do you need?" There's a smile that curls my lips threatens to crack my face in two. She will not know what hit her. There is no way she can refuse me.

Cassandra

The day has been long, and by the time the sun is on the horizon the crew are packing up. It's so beautiful out here. This has to be one of my favorite places we have been. I stifle a yawn as I slip my laptop into the backpack and power down Jayce's laptop. It's perched on the bench next to me, so I can help with reviewing the shots. We completed most of the first day photos by 3 pm, but we had to preview the images to make certain we were happy with them.

It was a great day,
I only thought about Lucien once and that was only because someone suggested calling him about a problem with one of our suppliers. That's when I slipped into my thoughts, remembering Hawaii, how different things were then. The weekend that changed my life forever. The time that brought me to the man who will forever hold my heart.

"Hey gorgeous!" I shift to see Jayce and his newest apprentice. One of the early graduates that joined the team two weeks ago. Jayce leans down to kiss me. It's such a strange gesture, that I am surprised. We aren't dating, we both agreed, and that kiss was for a couple. For some reason I suddenly miss Lucien more than I can explain. Like a physical pain that seems to tug at me.

"Hey, I have just packed up. You need to put your camera away so we can get dinner."

"Great, I need to make a call." I turn to watch him walk out of the tent while holding the phone to his ear. "Lu—" His voice cuts off, but I am positive I heard him say Lucien's name. I wander over to the end of the tent and to eavesdrop. "Yes, she's fine." His voice drops and all I pick up are the last words before he hangs up. "Get over it." I quickly make my way back to our bags just as Jay walks back in. He packs his camera in the bag and looks up at me. "I'm ready. Let's go gorgeous." He shoulders his backpack; we make our way up to the car.

"Who was that?" I turn to him as soon as we're seated.

"Luke." His eyes don't meet mine, the tension radiating through him.

"Jayce? Why did you call Luke?" Turning his head to face me, I see resignation on his face.

"He sent me a message earlier asking about you wanting feedback on how you were doing."

"He has no right to ask you, he shouldn't even care. This was his choice." My words come out harsher than I expect and Jayce stares at me.

"He loves you Cassandra and I can see you still love him. No matter what develops between us, I realize one day you will go back to him. I just can't see you hurting." The weight of his words crash down on me with sudden ferocity.

"You don't know what I will do. I don't even know." A frown creases my eyebrows and I am so uncertain of the future I have no idea what will happen after we get back from Cancun. *Do I still love him? Would I take him back if he asked me?* If he apologized. Whatever happens I need to put me first.

"Yes, I realize that gorgeous; I mean I can see you love him." Jayce places a hand on mine giving it a comforting squeeze. All I needed, was to enjoy Cancun and not think about Lucien. At least, for now.

Robert pulled up the hotel, and we made our way up to the room. Jay followed me into mine without challenge. It was an unspoken agreement between us he was staying. "What time did you want to go for dinner? They're open till midnight." I ask as I place my bags on the sofa. When I glance at him, the thoughts in his head are obvious.

"Let's go down at 8, that gives us two hours to work up an appetite." The salacious wink he gives me has my body responding. Jayce takes two strides towards me and a shiver runs down my spine.

"What makes you think I would allow such behavior, Jayce?" Folding my arms across my chest, I see his eyes dart to my breasts. My nipples pebble under his intense gaze.

"Princess, may I remind you that you spent the whole day teasing me. Do you realize how difficult it is to take photographs with a raging hard-on?" His lips lingering over mine, his hot breath fans over my face and the anticipation is unbearable. I giggle at his words, and I realize that I am in for some delicious punishment.

"Well, it's not my fault you were ogling the models. And no I don't know because I don't have a cock." I breathe the last word and his eyes darken with lust. He stares at me with a hooded expression.

"The only model I was ogling was you. Let me show you how you tormented me today." He pulls out a soft ribbon from his jeans pocket, which I recognize as the ribbon we used on location. He grips my wrists and ties them together behind my back.

"Where did—"

"Shhhh, not another sound." He hushes me by pressing his index finger to my lips. His strong hands grip the flimsy material of my top, he shreds it from my body. I gasp at his primal behavior. *At this rate I wont have any clothes left!* The knot in my stomach tightens and my thong is soaked. Jayce grips my hair and tugs my head back. His tongue licking from the sweet spot behind my ear down my neck in a hot, wet trail which elicits a whimper from me. "I will be inside you, Cassie. And when your tight little pussy comes around my cock, you will be screaming my name."

His words are deliciously dirty. I squeeze my thighs together needing to dull the ache at my core. Jayce releases the grip on my hair and I see him move his mouth over my breasts. Pulling the cups of my black lace bra down exposing my hardened buds. He flicks his tongue over them in small circles, waves of pleasure jolt through me. I grip the wall behind me trying to steady myself.

He licks his way down my stomach, dipping his tongue into my belly button. "Jayce." I breathe his name, my voice a whisper. It sounds like an echo from the shore rather than from my lips.

"Cassandra, I said to be quiet." His voice is dark and commanding. Untying the string of my pants, he unhooks the button and they pool at my feet. A primal sound vibrates from his throat, his face in line with my soaked thong. I glance down and am nearly unraveled when I meet those deep blue eyes gazing up at me. "Are you wet for me, Cassie?" His lips curl into a wicked smirk. I nod. "Good."

In one quick move Jayce shreds my panties and tosses them with my tank top. *I seriously am going to run out of clothes with him around.* His finger strokes the slick entrance of my body. "Open for me." I spread my legs, wanton with lust, I would have done anything he demanded of me. Gripping the edge of the wall behind me to keep from toppling over. His tongue snakes between my folds and my legs give way. Jayce grips my hips holding me up against the wall. He licks his way into my quivering pussy, teasing and nibbling on my clit. I am climbing higher and higher, as his expert mouth takes me to the edge. As soon as I feel myself clench around him, he stops. I glance down and whimper.

"Jayce, please?" I am openly begging him for the release he was so close to giving me.

"I told you, I will show you what you put me through all day." As soon as my body is almost back down to earth, he feasts on me like I am his last meal. His tongue dipping into my slick folds, sucking on my throbbing clit, my arousal glistening on his lips. Taking me soaring to new heights. My head drops back against the wall and I feel the release I need, it's so close. As soon as I am about to come undone Jayce stops again. My head feels foggy with desire, and I am not sure how I am still standing. My knees are wobbly and my body is trembling with need.

He rises and our eyes lock. "Please?" I whisper.

"What, Cassie? Please, what?" His fingers stroke me, dipping into my heated pussy. Slow and steady. He's finger fucking me in such a demanding way, trying to pull my orgasm from deep inside me. "Tell me what you want?" He lifts his fingers to his mouth and licks my arousal from them. His eyes close as if savoring my taste. When our eyes meet again, he gives me a dark smile. "Tell me."

"I want you to fuck me. Take away all the pain, just fuck me now." Shamelessly begging him now, for an ounce of relief.

"Do you realize what you do to me? Today in that tiny pair of panties. All I could think about was ripping them off, spreading your legs and ramming into you until you cried out my name." His hooded gaze, the deep timbre of his voice drove me insane. His words alone could have sent me over the edge, but I was too enthralled by his grip on my hips as he pressed into me.

I nod, I wasn't sure what I was answering, but I agreed. The grate of the zipper on his jeans pulled my attention, and my gaze dropped to his impressive erection, "Now my sweet princess, I want to be inside you, taking you into delirium." My eyes flitted back up to the midnight blue gaze of Jayce's. As he pressed his rock hard body against me, he lifted my thigh angling it around his waist, as he eased into me. He let out a groan. The moan that escaped my lips was low. He filled me to the hilt in a slow deep stroke.

I wrapped my legs around his waist when he gripped my ass. My hips bucked towards him, trying to get him deeper, where I needed it. He tugged at the ribbon and my hands fell free. I gripped his neck as he relentlessly slammed into me. "You're so fucking wet and tight."

"Jayce, yes. God yes." I sunk my teeth into the muscles of his strong shoulder as my core tightened around him. Jayce hissed in my ear and I realized he was close. "All. Fucking. Day." He slammed into me with measured thrusts at each word and I tensed. The elusive orgasm shattered me as I found the release I ached for. Moments later Jayce joined me as he growled out my name at his orgasm.

That was the last time I was with him. Jayce spent the rest of the week in his room. After that night I told him I needed space. It wasn't like we were dating, but there was a spark between us. As much as I relished being with him, I loved Lucien, I still do. I mean he was part of me. He crushed me into tiny fragments of the person I was, but he also put me together. My choice came when I realized that no man would ever make me love. Lucien was my soul mate. The one man who could either break me or fix me. I didn't want to hurt Jayce, he's been wonderful, but there was never a chance for us when my heart belonged to Lucien.

The week seemed to fly by; it was Thursday, and we only had two days left on this incredible island. Only two days until I have to go back to the real world and face Lucien again. I didn't want to go back on Saturday, but I knew I had to. With the ocean crashing behind me, I take a sip of my coffee, directing my gaze at the horizon. The morning was cooler and I took a walk on the beach to clear my mind.

As soon as I pull my phone from my back pocket, and open the message from Lucien. I read it twice, before my phone rang. It's him. I push the green button. "Hello?"

"Cassandra," I hear relief flood his voice.

"Yes, Mr. Verán?" I smile inwardly, even though we aren't together, I hear the sharp intake of breath at the mention of his last name.

"Did you get my messages?" I shift to watch the tide, the light blue/green looks almost translucent.

"Yes, I did. What is it you wanted to talk to me about?" I am not in the mood for games. If he can't tell me over the phone, then I really don't want to know.

"We need to talk about us. My father has invited us to join him for dinner and since he's been ill, I wanted to make him happy. I wanted to ask if you would join me." There is sorrow in his voice which tugs at my heart. I want so much for him to tell me we should be together, that we are meant to be, just like his father said. Somehow I don't think that's what he wants to tell me though. My anger returns at the situation he dropped me in.

"So you want me to play the happy girlfriend?" I ask incredulously. *How dare he expect me to just sit and smile with his father, act like nothing happened?* A bubble of irritation rises in my chest and I am about to tell him where to shove his dinner when his answer leaves me reeling.

"No I don't want to you play the happy girlfriend. I would much prefer if you were actually my happy girlfriend, after your week with my best friend." There isn't anger in his voice, just anxiety.

"What is that supposed to mean Lucien? You can't just tell me I am dead to you and then when I have found strength to actually not drink myself into oblivion to dull the ache, you tell me you want me back!" I realize I am shouting but I don't care.

"Yes, I realize that Cass, however I don't want to do this over the phone. Can we talk when you're back? Please?" I am tempted to hang up, but deep down his request brings hope he will fill the hole he left inside me. The tears burn my eyes and I blink them away. There is nothing I can say to him. "Cassandra."

"When is the dinner?" I spin to trudge back to the tent. I need to stop this conversation. The request has my mind spinning with possibilities, some that might just break me all over again.

"It's on Sunday. You're back on Saturday, I will have Robert escort you to my penthouse."

I nod, before I step into the tent. My gaze falls on Jayce interacting with the models, the emotion is nothing close to the jealousy I had seeing Lucien with them. I want to make this work, but he will have to work at it too. "Fine. Just don't expect me to fall into your arms because you asked me to."

"I didn't expect you to and to be honest that would be boring. I will convince you that you have to take me back. No other man will ever be able to make you scream the way I do. You will be with me Cassie that's a promise. And when I have you in my arms again, I will make sure you never leave my side." He hangs up before I can reply. All I can do is stare at my phone. *He does want me back! OMG! Cassie, he loves you! No, he doesn't. He was the one who walked away, now suddenly he wants me back. There must be more to this than meets the eye. If he wants me back, then he will have to work his sexy ass off to get me.* A smile curves my lips, the prospect of having him try makes me bubble with excitement. I look forward to Mr. Verán trying to win me back. Oh, I do indeed!

Lucien

The conversation yesterday went exactly how I expected it to, the promise I made her I intend to keep. There is nothing or no one that will take her away from me again. *Don't worry my love, soon you'll be screaming my name. In pleasure. I will make you beg.* The thoughts running through my head have my cock rock hard. Thinking of bending her to my will, making her ache for my touch. To make her beg for me to give her the release that only I can give her has my mind flooded with dirty images. I look forward to Saturday when I will have her back. When I will be inside her hot little cunt. I am going to fuck her so hard, she will be mine forever.

The sweat is running down my back and I am loving it. I haven't been for a run in such a long time I only now realize how much I miss it. It's only just gone 6 am and Cassie is arriving later today. I think that's where my energy is coming from. The thought of seeing here again has my body on fire. There are a few people out and I decide to make a quick stop at our coffee shop. *Fuck Verán, you're so soppy. Get a grip of your balls man!* As soon as I step inside, instinct makes my eyes flicker to her table. When I do, I stop dead. There's a brunette sitting in the chair I am so used to seeing Cassie in, when the ghost from my past sees me her eyes light up. *What the fuck is she doing here?*

I do a double take, but there's no doubt it's her. She sits back watching my reaction to her. When the smile on her face fades, I realize she's seen my shocked expression. My blood starts at a slow simmer, as I walk up to the table, it turns to an unbearable boil. "What the fuck are you doing here?" My voice is low, the danger in it is unmistakable.

"Luca, didn't you miss me?" Gripping her hand, I pull her out of the coffee shop, earning a few strange looks from the people queuing. As soon as we're outside I pull her along the sidewalk. I stop abruptly and turn to face her. She hasn't changed. It unnerves me.

"What. The. Fuck. Are. You. Doing. Here?" I hiss in her face and she flinches. No doubt remembering the last time I told her to leave me alone.

"I… Luca."

"Don't you fucking call me that!" I pull her into the alleyway on the side of the coffee shop. "Did Claudia bring you here?" Her slight nod tells me all I need to know. "You're the one calling Cassie aren't you?" Another nod and my anger is skyrocketing. My body is vibrating with rage at this fucking game that Claudia is playing. I am over it. This ends now.

"I… She… Luca." My hand is around her neck in an instant. Cassie's face flashes in my mind, and I can't stop myself. This ghost needs to get the fuck out of my life.

"I said don't fucking call me that. You have no right!" I watch her gasp for air, but I don't care if she stops breathing. It's her fucking fault my life is such a mess. "You will leave the city and never fucking look back okay?"

When I release her neck, I watch her gulp deep breaths. The choking sounds make me smile. *Good, little bitch!* "And you tell Claudia, to leave me and Cassie the fuck alone!" Stepping onto the sidewalk, I run up the hill back to my apartment. I need to get ready. My girl will be here soon and I don't want her to find me in the state I am in right now.

When I reach my apartment, the anger has dissipated, but it's still tugging at me. I open the apartment door, and step inside. Noticing that Martha has been here. I gave her strict instructions to set up the table and make sure the place looked romantic. She's gone all out. The place has beautiful white candles set up around every flat surface. There are red rose petals strewn on the shag rug near the window. The champagne flutes are set up on the counter and I notice the bucket is ready for ice and a bottle. All I need to do is finish up the dinner when we're ready to eat. Although, there is something other than dinner I wouldn't mind devouring. Cassie. My earlier encounter with my past has drifted from my mind. I realize I need to sort it out, but I could do later. After my girl is back in my arms.

As soon as I step into the shower, I turn on the spray and revel in the heat on my skin. I close my eyes and try to calm myself, the tension in my shoulders releases and I picture brown curls, splayed on my pillow. Those mocha eyes, staring up at me as she cries out my name.

Cassandra

"So, you're going to him when we land?" Jayce looks at me earnestly. I nod, I had told him about the call and what Lucien said. "Good, I want to see you happy princess, you deserve to have that."

"Thank you for, well…" How do I say, thank you for taking my pain away with your impressive erection? *Cassie, seriously? You want to thank him for fucking you into oblivion? Well, yea!* I giggle at my inner dialogue. I stare into those sky-blue eyes; his expression is one of amusement.

"For what Cassie? Making you scream my name? It was my pleasure. Trust me, it was!" The heat on my face spreads over my cheeks, and I realize they must be crimson.

"Well, yea, I suppose, but also for being there and taking care of me." He shrugs like it was part of his job to do that. Over the past month I was a complete train wreck, but somehow Jayce seemed to pull me from the dark hole and into a rather normal version of my former self.

"Just don't let him sweet talk you into taking him back without an appropriate apology. He can be incredibly convincing." He leans forward and gives my hand a squeeze.

"Yes he can be, and I won't. I am definitely not just going to let him walk all over me. He was the one who walked away, and he said things that aren't easily forgivable. I told him that over the phone, so he needs to really go all out with his apology."

Jayce laughs, "Good, I will always be here for you princess. Remember that okay?" I nod. "Now, will you hook me up with Kenna?" I chuck a cushion at him and he chuckles. "What?"

"You're insatiable!" He nods, a thoughtful expression on his face.

"I am single; I have no one to answer to." It was true, but still something about it niggled at me. *Wouldn't it be weird if he dated Kenna? Not for me, maybe for her. I could always chat to her?* She would want all the dirty details about him. I can think about it later.

Right now, I needed to ready myself to face Lucien.

We would touch down in an hour, I peer out of the window, the sun was low on the horizon. "Jayce," I turn to him. "How long did it take for you to forgive Lucien for what he did to your sister?" I notice a glint of sadness dance in his sky-blue eyes. His gaze settles on the window as he speaks and I remain still, waiting for him to share his story.

"Two years. It was a painful time for us both. We grew up together, but I was always the kid from the wrong side of the tracks. You know?" His gaze falls on me again and I nod. "His mother," shutting his eyes as if something troubled him. "I mean stepmother, she despised me from the outset. Always telling Lucien I was bad news. When he called me that night, I wanted to kill him." He turned away again, and I assumed he would not tell me more when he astounded me and continued.

"I helped him. He was, still is my best friend. I needed him healthy. He was like my brother. I mean, he still is." A grin cracked on his handsome face and the anxiety was gone. "Once we forgave each other, it became easier, but now and then we struggle. Nothing will ever be the same, but I never walk out on my friends." His smile is genuine and the crinkle in his nose makes me giggle. He shrugs, like that made perfect sense.

"Wow, I am glad he has a friend like you. He needed it."

When we disembarked Robert was already at the car waiting. "I will talk to you later princess. Good luck!" Jayce held me for a long time. His warm embrace calmed my nerves, but only for so long. As soon as I was in the car on my way to Lucien's place they would start up again.

"Thanks, Jayce. Give Kenna a call. Maybe she wants to have dinner or something."

"Yea, maybe I will." I turn to face Robert, his face giving nothing away.

"Ms. Winters." Robert gives me a smile as he opens the door for me, I slip inside.

"Thank you Robert." He gives me a brief nod. He walks over to the driver's door and slides in, the engine purrs to life. "How is he?" His eyes glance at me in the rear-view mirror.

"He seems calm today Ms. Winters. I think he is looking forward to seeing you again." A small smile cracks on his face again and I almost gasp. Robert is always so serious, him smiling is really strange.

"Okay, thanks." I sit back and watch the city pass us by. This was it, time to fess up and come clean. If he really wants a fresh start, then we have to let go of the past and move forward together. If he doesn't, then I am not sure what I am going to do. My heart lurches at the thought.

Lucien

It's almost time, she's going to be here soon and I can't wait. The thought of having her in my arms is making my heart race. *When did you become such a pussy?* To be honest, I am scared shitless. I have to admit that. Nothing that I have ever done, could prepare me for this. There are things that have scared me before, but with Cassie the thought of never having another chance with her brings a physical pain to my chest. Something that can't be described. I need her. There's nothing more to it. She needs to be in my life.

As dark as my soul is, she's the light that makes my life worth living. Her body, her mind and her soul will be mine. I am going to own her, in every fucking way. That tight heat that milks my cock will be mine. Those gorgeous tits that I can't help devouring will be mine. Most importantly, her heart, will be all mine. The erection in my sweats is throbbing and I can't tame it. I hope she's ready to be taken. Hard and fast and in every fucking way possible, on every surface of my penthouse.

I text Robert, asking him to bring her straight to the penthouse. There is no way I could meet her there, we wouldn't get further than the backseat of my Aston, before her panties will be shred into tiny pieces and my tongue would be tasting her sweet honey.

I want her bound to the bed, she needs a whipping for fucking Jayce, and she can't deny it because I know she has. I don't care if I walked away, she shouldn't have moved on. Yes, I am being unreasonable, but that's what happens when it comes to her. I am an unreasonable bastard. That peachy little ass will be marked with my handprint. *Soon, baby. So very fucking soon.*

As soon as the car pulls up I stand at the window. When she steps out of the car my body is aching to be near her. She's brought me to my knees, the love that I have for her is all-consuming. My days are spent thinking of her, my nights spent dreaming of her. Every breath I take is because of her. I claimed her when I was thirteen years old that means she's meant to be with me. Tonight, I will make that right. In more ways than one. I wait for her in the living room. She's seen me at the window. I take a sip of the strong amber liquid, savoring the burn, before I look into those mocha eyes again.

Cassandra

Robert pulls up to the apartment and gets out to open my door. I take a deep breath and step out. When my gaze flits up, I notice the light on in the living room, I can see Lucien standing at the window with a glass of Scotch in his hand. He gives me a small wave and turns from the window.

"Ms. Winters," Robert hands me my coat and I walk up to the building. I turn back towards him and smile. With a small smile I mouth a "thank you" I turn to meet my fate.

"Cassandra," Lucien opens the door as I reach the top of the stairs. "I am glad you're here." He steps aside, allowing me access to the apartment.

"Thank you, I didn't think I would ever see this place again."

"Can I get you a drink?" I turn around and he is behind me. So close his scent washes over me and the need inside me for him ignites. Weeks of not being with him have brought me here. To the shattered man I see before me. His eyes stare into mine and I see his soul, the one he tries to convince me is full of darkness. I see right through him and I realize he sees right through me.

"Yes, please." I turn to the living room and take in the beautiful dinner setting. There are candles on every surface, their flames dancing in the dim light. Rose petals are strewn across the carpet at the window. *He's really trying.* I can't face him, yet. "You did all this?" My gaze on the window, staring at the beautiful view. The sun is setting and the lights of the city flicker to life.

"I had a bit of help." I jump at the nearness of Lucien's voice behind me. "Sorry, I…" His face looks so tired, drawn, like he hadn't slept in weeks. I turn and take the glass from his hand. When my fingers brush against his, the electric current coursing through my veins alights my desire. There is nothing this man can do to make me hate him. The love is still so tangible between us.

"It's okay, I'm just…" I am not sure what to say or do. He turns to turn on the sound system in the living room. A soft voice fills the air and I recognize the song by Jay

Sean called War. These lyrics held so much more meaning than I could have imagined. It was like he reached into my chest and gripped heart, squeezing it so tight I found it hard to breathe. I gulped the amber liquid down, wincing at the burning sensation in my chest. It's strong, but I think I need it.

Does he really know you like I know you, all the little things?
Does he really love you, like I love you, how can he compete?
If he makes me fight for you, die for you, would he do the same?
Baby this is turning into way more than a game..

Baby cause we're soldiers in a war and none of us are backing down
And I will show you victory is mine before we leave this battleground
Cause he don't wanna leave, and I don't wanna go
And I know just how this battle goes
He don't wanna leave and I don't wanna fight this kind of war

Getting kind of sick of this battle
Wish I could take it back to when I had you
I'm always thinking that I can't have you, just let him have you
It's getting kinda hard to convince you
After all the shit that we've been through
What, would you let all this happen?
You gotta choice to make it stop
It's already going too far..

"Cassie, are you okay?" Lucien grabs my elbow in concern and the electric spark that flowed between us shot through me like a hot knife gliding through butter. As much as my body wants to meld into his, I step back, looking into his green eyes and see the concern etched on his face. This is excruciating. I can't just fall into his arms; he needs to apologize. A few candles and rose petals won't make things right.

"Yes, fine. Why am I here, Lucien?" I couldn't do this anymore. It was too much being around him. I pivoted from his gaze. The need to add space between us overwhelms me, and I step back. It calms the tension in my stomach. Like a teenager on her first date I am nervous and unsure.

"I… I miss you, Cassie." His voice low, tinged with sadness.

"You were the one who walked away not me." I turn to face him. He nods, downing the rest of his whiskey, he walks over to the bar and grabs the bottle.

"Another one?" I follow him, setting the tumbler on the countertop. As I watch him, I realize his hands are trembling. *Is he as scared as I am?* The need to hold him, for him to hold me, and tell me that he wants me back is strong.

I have been and still am broken, completely and utterly shattered. The trust I gave him, letting him into my heart away when I shouldn't have. I had no choice in the matter, my heart was his before I let him in. Even when he hurt me, I realized there was nothing I could have done, because he was it for me. He was part of me. As I stand here looking at him, I know there is nothing more I can ask for, only him. "Cassandra, I want you to tell me something. I am going to look into your magical brown eyes, and I want you to tell me the truth. My feelings for you are too strong to walk away from this. You're inside me, you course through my veins like a drug. When I am not with you, I can't live. There is nothing in this world that I could ever want more than you. If I have to spend my life showing you that I will. That is a promise I am making now, and it's a promise I will keep till I stop breathing. So, now you're going to tell me everything." His gaze travels up to mine, the need in them is unbearable and I want to lay down my soul for him, right there on the bar. I open my mouth to speak, but he carries on. "And when you're done telling me. I am going to take my broken soul, the shattered pieces that I have carried with me for the past month without you," his stare is so intense I feel heat emanating from it. "And I am going to eat that sweet pussy until your back arches and your nails dig into my skin."

My breath hitches at his illicit promise. My core tightens with desire and the heat pools in my panties. He walks around the bar, his body flush with mine. As he places the glass in my hand, he leans in and whispers in my ear. "Then I am going to fuck you, hard and fast until you're screaming my name so loud the whole fucking city will hear you. After I destroy your body, with orgasm after orgasm, you're going to lay in my arms, and I will tell you how much I love you. I am going to own you. When we're done, we will do it again and again, until I have fucked every trace of any other man out of you." A soft whimper escapes my lips. *I think I may have just come!* My panties are soaked, my skin prickles with heated lust. *Holy fucking wow! Okay!!! Take me now! Do we even have to talk??* "And every time I drive into you, every time I thrust into that tight little cunt, the only person you're going to be thinking about, needing, aching for, will be me." His lips are on the shell of my ear now and my knees almost buckle. "No other man, will ever take you like I am going to. Tonight and for the rest of your life. You are mine. Do you understand me Cassandra?" I nod.

"Yes." The word comes out so soft, that I am not sure he heard me, but he steps back and watches me. We're both broken by desire for each other and I need to fix him as much as he needs me.

Lucien

I can see her visible reaction to me. A smile curves my lips, she will submit to me. Not because I ask her to, but because she loves me. She knows we are meant to be together. I have belonged to her since the beginning and she to me. Even before I realized what that meant. When she whispers her agreement, my cock jumps at the sound. Her saying yes to me is what I need, what I want.

Even though I am tempted to take her back to the bedroom, I need to make sure she's comfortable. The living room seems like the best place for that. As soon as we're on the sofa, I take a sip of the alcohol, hoping it would calm the hard on that seems to have a mind of its own around her.

My gaze is on her, waiting. She needs to talk to me, but I can't push. It must be her choice; she needs to let me in. Her body is trembling and the need to pull her into my arms, to take away whatever pain and anguish she's going through overcomes me. I am about to reach out to her when she starts talking.

"I was 23 when they…" She takes a deep breath. "After that night I wasn't myself. I partied every week. Drank myself into a coma, to take the pain away. I blamed myself for what happened." Her glance flits to the large window as she stares out at the city lights. *My girl, my baby, I need to take her pain away.* "It was three months after they were killed. There was an opening of a club in New York, some friends invited me and I didn't refuse. I wasn't sure how much I drank that night." Tears slowly fall from her eyes. "One of the girls told me I was so violently ill they almost rushed me to the ER. I had eventually passed out on a mattress in an apartment of one of the girls. The next morning, when I tried to get up, I pulled the sheet down." Her voice falters and tears are falling freely now. "There... uhm, there was blood everywhere. I..." Not being able to take it anymore, listening to her heart shatter into tiny pieces, I reached out and stroked her back. My fingertips slowly traced a line down her spine and I saw the tremble. "My fault. I didn't even know. The doctor said I had a miscarriage. The blood..." She gulped her whiskey, and I pulled her into me. I wanted her to feel my love. There wasn't anything I could do to take the memories away, so I just held her. The fact that she just trusted me enough to tell me was incredible. When I realize the amount of agony this girl, my girl, went through. I can't believe she's still sane.

"Cassie," I pull her away from me, looking into her eyes. "I am so fucking sorry for being such a fucking idiot. Thank you for trusting me." My voice is barely audible, but she heard me. With the slight nod of her head I tighten my grip around her. I can't believe she had to go through that alone. "I love you Cassie, so fucking much, I love you." The shock on her face when she pulled away to face me was evident, only then did I realize I was crying. I was broken, for her, for me, for us. "I'm so sorry I pushed you away. Now I realize I was such a fucking idiot." With my arms around her, her body molds to mine. "This is where you're meant to be. In my arms, not in Jayce's." Her body stiffens at my words. "It's okay. My fault for asking him to look out for you. I just didn't realize he would take you to his bed. It's my mistake, I pushed you away."

"Lucien." My name on her lips sends the desire coursing through my veins. No more talking. It's time to show her how much I love her. In the only way I can. I place a finger to her soft lips to silence her.

"I promised you something. Now I will deliver." When I set our glasses on the table, I rise and extend a hand to her. As soon as she slips hers into mine, I lead her upstairs to the master bedroom.

Cassandra

My body hummed in anticipation. "Stand at the end of the bed and wait for me." He walked out into the hallway and I waited. My gaze taking in the city shimmering below me. I was back where I belonged. With Lucien, this was exactly where I am meant to be. I started when he breathed on my neck. "Now my beautiful girl, I want to show you how much I missed you. Do you want to be here?" I nodded. "Answer me."

"Yes, Lucien. I don't want to be anywhere else." When he stepped in front of me his gaze seared into mine. His hands gripped my hips, pulling me into his rock hard body. Every ridge of his sculpted torso pressed into me. "Lucien." I breathed.

"Hush. You're not to speak, unless I tell you to. I have heard your story; you have heard mine. We're both still here. I am going to make up for the past month of not being inside you." He tugged at the soft tank top, pulling it up and over my head. My nipples hardened at the cool breeze on my naked skin. A sharp hiss escaped Lucien's lips when he saw that I wasn't wearing a bra. "So fucking perfect, every inch of you. Tonight I am going to savor it." His tongue flicked my one nipple, sucking it into his expert mouth. A moan escaped my lips, running my hands through his unruly spikey hair. I held him to my breast. He pulled away slowly and turned his attention to the other breast. With his tongue flicking over the pebbled bud, grazing his teeth against it, tugging gently. My body was on fire, the desire hummed between my legs, my clit throbbed and my flesh quivered with need for the man I love.

Lucien kissed his way down my belly, dipping his tongue into my bellybutton, eliciting a whimper from me. I looked down and into those incredible green eyes, they held so much promise, and love. He gripped the waistband of my shorts, tugging it down. They pooled at my feet. A deep growl vibrated in Lucien's chest. "Jesus, Cassandra. You smell like fucking heaven. I can't wait to taste that sweet honey dripping onto my tongue." His eyes flared, and my knees buckled. "Do you want me darling?"

"Yes, Lucien, please? I need you." I begged him. The slow exquisite torture was driving me insane. I just wanted him inside me. He grabbed the flimsy material of my panties and ripped it from my body.

He laid back on the soft carpet, tugging me along his body. When my pussy was positioned over his mouth, his voice rasped. "Sit on my face, baby. Open your legs for me, I want you on my tongue." His order sending delicious shivers down my spine. I lowered myself over his mouth as Lucien flicked his tongue out and teased my clit. When he flattened his tongue against my slick sex, licking me in slow measured strokes. I gripped his hair, holding him against me, savoring his mouth on me. He pulled away and looked up at me. "Did you miss me sweetness?" I nodded. "Good, because I missed you. The taste of your sweet fucking pussy on my mouth. Your skin on mine. The way your body arches into me, and the way you scream when I fuck you."

My skin was on fire, my body trembled at his words. His tongue slid into my folds and almost came undone all over his mouth. "That's it baby, I want to drink your sweet juices. This little cunt will only come for me." Two fingers suddenly plunged into me sending me crashing over the edge. As my orgasm ripped through me. I cried out, calling Lucien's name repeatedly. My knees gave way and his hands on my hips held me up. His arms held me as I came down from the incredible release. "You're so beautiful when you come for me sweetness. Go lay back on the bed." I obeyed him. Watching the man, I want forever, move between my legs. Lucien gripped my ankles, bending my knees. He hovered between my legs. I glanced down, watching him circle my clit again. Pulses of pleasure shot through me. I gripped the sheets, tugging at them as my body tensed. His movements were slow and methodical. Two fingers plunged inside me, as he crooked them up, hitting my sweet spot and I cried out. I teetered on the edge of another intense orgasm. "That's it sweetness, give me your delectable honey. Coat my face in your juices." His words were my undoing as he lapped at my entrance, licking up my arousal. My body clenching around his two smooth fingers. He kept up his unrelenting pace, and I was close to another orgasm. "Please, Luke please, I can't take anymore." A third orgasm ripped into me and my eyes rolled back. I gripped the sheets so tight, I thought I would tear them. My body convulsed as I came down from my orgasm.

Once I had finally calmed, Lucien stood up and a sexy smirk curled his lips. "Now, I am going to own you." He hovered over my boneless body, my legs splayed for him easily. "Do you want me, baby?" My eyes flitted to his hand as he gripped his rock hard erection, I watched him stroke it. It was so erotic to see. He kneeled between my legs and teased my dripping pussy with the tip. My hips rock up to meet his, inviting him. "I think my dirty girl wants me to fuck her? Doesn't she?" His teasing was relentless and I couldn't concentrate on anything but him inside me. My body tense and humming. Not believing I could need another release, so soon after having three incredible orgasms, but I don't care. All I want is him. I craved him so much, it was a physical ache.

"Please Lucien?" My delirious gaze locks on his. The desire turning his eyes black.

"Please? Tell me baby, what do you want? I want you to say it for me." Aware of what he's doing to me, his eyes glint with devilish satisfaction.

I am so turned on I am unable to form words. He wants me to beg, and I will give it to him, anything to have him inside me. "Fuck me, please Lucien. I need you inside me. Please?" My eyes are glistening with tears, not from pain, but from pure pleasure and need.

"As you wish, baby." Without warning he slams into me to the hilt. My cries echo through the room as I fist the sheets in painful pleasure. "So fucking hot and tight around my cock." When he pulls out almost all the way, and plunges in again, we find our rhythm and I am climbing. My eyes roll back in my head and my toes curl as he relentlessly drives into me. "Look at me," my eyes open and lock on his, "I want you to see who's fucking you. I want you to see who owns you." My back arches and I am about to find another release when he leans down and whispers in my ear. "I own you Cassie, heart, mind, body and soul. Your pussy, ass, body is mine." As he utters the word 'mine' my body tenses, my heated flesh clenches around him and my orgasm rips through me with such force I see stars behind my eyelids. Lucien thrusts again and again before growling his release inside me. "My lumiére, forever."

Lucien

When I look over at Cassie asleep next to me, it has my heart racing. I almost lost her, there is no way I am making that mistake again. Her breathing is even; her dark brown curls are splayed on the pillow. The sheet has slipped down and her soft skin is glowing under the light from the full moon. It's almost like she's not real. Like she's a mirage in my mind. My oasis in the desert. Every breath I take from now until my last, will be spent making her happy.

We didn't even get to the dinner I had planned. It's almost one in the morning and as tired as I am, for some reason I can't sleep. Maybe the excitement of having her back here is keeping me awake. As soon as I close my eyes, I see my past in the coffee shop. The same seat, the same table, haunting me. I need to tell Cassie. There will be no more secrets between us. My glance falls on her again, my lumiére.

I slide out of bed, and make my way downstairs and grab a glass of water. My phone on the kitchen counter buzzes, snatching me out of my thoughts of my girl. When I unlock the screen, I notice a message from an unknown number. My blood runs cold. There's a photo of me and Isabel, taken today at the coffee shop. From the angle it's taken, it looks incriminating.

Shit! My fucking step-mother will not give up until Cassie hates me. In the dark my mind whirls with ideas, ways to get her out of my life. I need to do something. There is only one person who I know will help me. Somehow, I am not sure he's talking to me at the moment. There is no other choice; asking for help is difficult, but I have to message him.

* *I know you hate me. I don't care. Help me get rid of Claudia.* *

Even though there are things that have happened between Jayce and me. There is nothing we won't do for each other. He knows that I love Cassie, and that she loves me. So I know that he will stand behind me, no matter what. When I slip onto the bar stool, I don't wait long for his reply.

When, where and how?

A smile curls my lips. There are so many thoughts in my head, I am not sure I can even go to bed now. Thinking about the beautiful girl that's laying in my bed changes my mind though. It's the first night she's back and I don't want to be without her. I need her against me. I hit reply.

Tomorrow. We can talk. I have a sweet girl to get back to.

I know that last part was unnecessary, but I had to drive it home that she's mine. He's never going to get another chance. Not even when I am dead. I know there will be a reply and he doesn't disappoint.

No worries brother. Kenna is cheering me up.

You're a slut

I chuckle, I can imagine his response. With that I shut my phone off and pad back up the stairs. When I walk back into the bedroom Cassie has rolled over onto her side and she's facing the door. I slip under the covers and wrap my arm around her waist. Her skin is warm and she fits against me perfectly as I tug her against me. Her scent invades my senses. The lavender that will always bring back the memory of running after the little girl with the brown curls in a park when I was ten. The only girl that has ever been in my heart. Closing my eyes, I can't help smiling. She's here, she's mine.

Cassandra

The sun shines into the bedroom, the rays heat my skin. There's a warm body behind me, I open my eyes and see Los Angeles through the patio doors. Last night flashes through my mind and I blush. Lucien and I made love, fucked, and spent the night in each other's arms. In his sleep at some point last night he had rolled over and was now groping my breast. My nipple puckered from the caress of his hand. As I roll over I come face to face with sparkling green eyes. "You're awake!" I giggle.

"Yes, I am. It was the first night in a month that I slept without nightmares and it's the first morning I opened my eyes without a physical ache in my chest."

His words tug at my own heart. "Lucien, I am sorry for not telling you sooner. I just—"

"Cassandra, don't. You have no reason to apologize. I was a fucking idiot for walking away. I know I hurt you. I intend spending my life making it up to you. If you would have me?" The question in his eyes made me smile. It was one apology that I would accept, no matter what.

"Mmmm, let me think about it. I just don't know Lucien." I look into those magnetic olive green eyes, amusement dancing in them. His dimples deepen with a devilish smirk.

"Oh really? Would you like me to apologize in other ways? Because Ms. Winters, I am very capable of doing just that!" He rolled above me, holding himself up on his elbows. His tongue flicked out licking the seam of my lips. With feather light kisses on my mouth, he moved to my cheek, licking the shell of my ear, sending shivers down my spine. His teeth nipping at my earlobe, tugging it gently. Instinctively I reach up, tangling my fingers in his messy hair pulling him against me.

"Lucien," I breathe as my back arches into him. His hot smooth skin against mine making me shiver. His feather light kisses down the curve of my neck has the ache between my legs throbbing and I am panting for him. This man will be my undoing.

"I just wanted to apologize properly Ms. Winters." His hot mouth finds my breast, taking the puckered nipple between his teeth, he bites down sending waves of pained pleasure straight to my heated core. When he turns his attention to the other hard bud, giving it the same attention I cry out his name. With my eyes closed and my hands fisting his hair, his finger is stroking my slick entrance. "My soaking wet girl, your hot pussy is aching for me isn't it?" Beyond words, all I can do is nod. "You want me inside you, don't you, Cassie?" I peer up and see his eyes darken. He is staring down at me under hooded eyes, I buck my hips against him. "So eager for my cock inside you aren't you, sweetness?"

"Always, Lucien." I answer him. The need inside me is unbearable. A naughty smirk on his lips makes me tingle, as he moves lower down my body. Once he's kneeling between my splayed thighs, his eyes rake over me.

"You are perfect, so fucking beautiful open for me. Hold on to the pillow above your head." I grip the pillow. "Now don't move." He leans down, licking and blowing on my belly. My back arches instinctively. I need more. The release that only Lucien can give me is building in my belly. When he blows on my wet pussy I cry out, pleading with him. The sun is higher now, streaming onto the bed, heating my skin. Lucien lowers himself over me, gripping his steel erection, teasing my entrance. "You want my cock inside you, baby?" I nod quickly.

Lucien slams into me. With a deep drive, the force pushes me up the bed. "Yes." A hiss escapes my lips. My legs tighten around his taut waist; my heated tunnel stretching to accommodate him. He slides almost all the way out and thrusts back in. I am winded, my body bowing to him. "Mr. Verán." I moan, my eyes locking on his and the desire fuels him.

He slows his movements. "When I am inside you, my darkness is illuminated by your light, baby." A soft kiss on my lips, makes me smile as he starts moving faster. I pull him closer, deeper. It's like we can't get close enough. Connected and molded into one person. "I want you to feel every fucking inch of me." He growls annunciating each word with a deep punishing thrust. My body responds by clenching around him, tensing as my orgasm builds. "Take me. Fucking give me your pleasure. Come on my cock, Cassandra." As I writhe under him, his order sending me crashing over the edge as my orgasm rips through me. My body trembles under his unrelenting drives, his body goes rigid as his own release fills me. Moments pass, and all we can do is breathe.

We lay in each other's arms until the heat of the sun becomes unbearable. "Let's get some breakfast. It's Sunday, is there something you wanted to do?"

"Could we just stay in today? I want to spend as much time with you as I can. It's been a horrid month." I reach up to touch his face. The stubble on his cheek is rough, sexy, just like everything about him. A smile on his face makes my heart soar.

"Of course we can, sweetness. Cassie, I love you. I never want you to be away from me again." With his arm wrapped around me he pulls me into him. He holds onto me like a lifeline.

"I don't want to be away from you, Lucien, ever." A naughty smirk crosses his handsome face.

"So you and Jay uh?" I punch his arm and he chuckles. "He's quite the charmer."

"He was there when you left, picking up the pieces and tried putting me back together, but I could never be whole without you. He knew it as well, Jayce told me repeatedly that he didn't see the light in my eyes anymore. I was dead inside Lucien." Tears pricked my eyes, and I blinked them away. I didn't want to cry anymore.

"I know, sweetness. I wanted you to move on. To be with someone who wasn't so broken, but I can't be without you. I am a selfish bastard; I want you all to myself. No other man can have you. Not now, not ever." His fingers stroked my cheek lightly.

"We're two broken pieces that fuse together to make a whole." With his lips sealed on mine, the kiss is heated. His tongue strokes into me, licking, tasting, and teasing. I hold onto him, his body melding into mine as if we can become one person. When Lucien pulls away a devilish smile brightens his face. "I love how I fit inside you, baby." A naughty boyish grin deepens his dimples and I stop the giggle that bubbles through me.

"Breakfast!" I slap his arm and he rolls off me reluctantly.

"Fine, be like that, but you wanted to stay in. I intend to stay inside you for most of today!" Lucien chuckles swinging his feet over the bed. I drink him in, the sexy tight ass, those powerful muscled thighs and his sculpted back made me lick my lips. I would love to devour him. "Do you like the view from over there, Ms. Winters?" He glances back at me as he tugs his boxers up over that deliciously taut ass.

"Mr. Verán you have no idea how delectable my view is." I giggle. As I slip out of bed, walking into the bathroom without a backward glance. The heat of his gaze burns my skin and sends delicious shivers over me.

Lucien

When I grab the ingredients for breakfast, I busy myself in the kitchen. I turned on the music and made my baby some breakfast. Although my mind was still on how to get rid of Isabel and Claudia. I hope Jayce has something in mind, because short of actually killing her, I really can't think of anything. I am losing my edge. As I place the pan on the cooker, and heat up the oil. The coffee is almost ready and I think I need at least one pot to myself. Cassie's heated gaze is on me, but I don't turn to her immediately. The stare raking over me makes me smile. A shiver runs down my spine and straight to my cock. This calls for a second round of breakfast.

"What a sexy chef, I am a lucky girl." Her voice is low, and full of desire. When I spin around I watch her hungry gaze travel from my messy brown hair to my chest, down to the low slung boxers I am wearing. My stare takes in the sexy little tigress standing in my kitchen. She's wearing an old T-shirt of mine and it just about covers her ass.

"I am the lucky one. And that T-shirt never looked better." I point to the white UCLA logo running across her chest. It was one of my favorite shirts when I was at university and seeing her wear it made me want to bend her over the kitchen counter and fuck her senseless.

She gives me a little twirl and my cock twitches in response. The 360-degree view causes a low growl to vibrate deep in my chest. "Well, I think I should wear your clothes more often if you love it that much." Her giggle is light and makes the topic of conversation feel like a weight lifting off my shoulders. I know I have to find a way to tell her about Isabel.

"I think you shouldn't wear clothes at all." My gaze rakes her in and settles on her bare legs. I pull the pan off the stove and stalk over to her. When I grip her hips, I pull her into me. Her body molds to mine and she submits to me. It's the sexiest thing when she let's me take her like this. I lean down and seal my mouth over hers. When I lick into her sweet mouth, tasting her, I realize I will never get enough of her. There isn't a moment I don't want her near me.

Her fingers run through my hair and she tugs me closer. She pulls me against her, our bodies becoming one. Forever will never be enough with her. In the haze of lust that courses through my veins, I remember that we need to eat. As soon as I pull away, we're both breathless. A giggle from Cassie makes me chuckle.

I turn to the counter and grab the plates. "Breakfast is ready." I announce moments later, dishing egg and bacon from the pan. She pushes up on her toes and peeks over my shoulder. I have made a full English breakfast including hash browns. Her stomach makes the cutest grumble. "Guess my love is hungry?" Turning to face her, I plant a quick kiss on the tip of her nose and she nods.

As soon as I place the loaded plates on the counter, I grab the cutlery and the coffee pot. I slip into the seat next to her and we dig in. "Can we go out later? I need a few things from the store?" Her question catches me unaware, and I glance at her and nod. We have dinner tonight, but I need to talk to her before that. In case Claudia decides to play her cards. That reminds me to call Jayce and figure out how to sort out this mess.

"Sure, my dad is expecting us at six. So that gives us time to spend the day alone before his big announcement." I pop the last bit of toast in my mouth when I notice her questioning gaze.

"Announcement?" She smiles. I nod. Not knowing what he has up his sleeve is sometimes a worry. My dad loves to make crazy decisions and drop it on us. I think it has to do with the company.

"He said that we will find out later. I have no idea what it is." Surprises rarely go well with me and he knows it. Who knows, it might be a good one, and he's filing for divorce. Now that would make my fucking week! The thought of her out of my life for good is like hearing Cassie will marry me. *What the fuck? Where did that come from?* I clear my throat and pick up the coffee pot and offer some to Cassie. "Coffee babe?" My mind is working overtime and I need it to relax. Marriage is not on the cards for me. Ever. She nods and I fill her mug.

"Breakfast was amazing, thank you handsome." With the plates stacked, I grab them and take them to the dishwasher.

"It's a pleasure my darling, so where did you want to go today?" As I walk back to the counter, I notice her still at my question. Once I have slipped into the seat next to her, I watch her reaction intently. *She's hiding something. What the fuck?*

"Just a few stores." She plants a kiss on my cheek and giggles. My stare is enough to have a blush pink her cheeks, narrowing my eyes at her, I see mischief dancing in hers.

"What are you up to angel?" Her shoulders give me a small shrug, but when she faces me, there's a fake innocence plastered on her face. The guilt, and a naughty glint give her away instantly and she now has me on alert.

"Nothing, I need to pick up a few essentials for this evening. You don't want me going like this do you?" She points to the T-shirt, turning around and lifting it enough for me to see the bottom of her ass. *That's it! You're getting fucked!* My cock tents my boxers and I rise from my seat. Once I lunge for her, a small sexy shriek escapes her lips, and she runs up the stairs, taking two at a time.

As soon as she reaches the main bedroom door, I wrap my arm around her waist, and lift her against me. When I hear her scream my name it only makes me harder. Her pulse is racing.

"You want to tease me do you, baby?" With her feet off the floor, she can't get away. I spin her around and walk into my favorite room in the house. The play room. Her tremble doesn't go unnoticed, and I can't wait to get her naked. When I set her down, our bodies are flush and my hard on is pressing against her. A faint blush pinks her cheeks and I am about to rip my favorite shirt from her body.

"Now, you relentlessly teasing me is driving me insane. I spent a month not tasting that sweet honey, from the source," my fingers reach down and slowly stroke her sex over her panties. A shudder over her whole body causes goose bumps to rise on her skin. "And it's left me, ravenous." My tongue darts out and I lick the shell of her ear. A soft whimper escapes her beautiful lips and I smile.

I pull the top up and over her head, dropping it on the floor, my gaze flits over her skin. She's bare, except for a tiny pair of pale pink panties. My cock is so hard it's painful. All I want to do is slide into her and make her scream, but I will tease her as much as she does me.

"Close your eyes Cassandra," my voice a raspy whisper in her ear, I see her tremble and shiver. Her soft pink lips open expecting a kiss, but I move back watching as she closes her eyes. I walk around her to the drawer and pull out the black silk blindfold. As soon as the soft material covers her eyes, another soft whimper escapes her. I tie it into a soft knot behind her head. "Now my darling, I want to tease you until you're begging for me to be inside you." The words are low and I make sure that my hot breath travels in a slow teasing trail over her skin. I turn her to face the bed, placing a hand between her shoulder blades forcing her to bend at the waist. "Hold onto the bedframe." I don't recognize my voice it's so thick with desire. She grips the rich dark wood of the four poster bed. I step back and admire the view, using my foot I kick hers wider. She's spread in front of me, and my God doesn't she look fucking delicious? "Mmmm, you look edible my sweetness."

I hook my thumbs on the waistband of her panties pulling them down over her hips and down her spectacular legs, they pool at her ankles. She steps out of them and I fist them. When I bring them up to my face, I inhale her beautiful sweet scent. Her sharp intake of breath tells me she knows what I just did. *Yes, Cassie, you're my drug. Every fucking scent, taste and inch of you.* Her perfect peach ass is begging for a spanking. *Who was I to deny my beautiful girl that?*

As I raise my hand, letting it down hard. The smooth soft skin pinks and my handprint marks her. Mine. All fucking mine. A second swat on her perfect ass makes her rise up on her toes. Her legs are toned and they look incredible. I reach out and stroke her smooth sex and arousal dripping from her.

"It seems my angel is enjoying this. Aren't you, sweetness?" I deliver another two stinging swats and I know she's close. Her breathing is faster; her body is trembling. I kneel between her thighs and flatten my tongue against the hot, sweet pussy that always brings me to my knees. As soon as I lap at her entrance, her body convulses, and she gushes onto my tongue. *Fuck she tastes good!* "Your pussy tastes like fucking honey. Give me every drop sweetness." Another wave of pleasure, travels over her and I drink in every drop she's giving me. My cock is so hard it might snap off. I have never been so fucking turned on, ever.

"I want you on my cock." Once I drop my boxers I grip my steel erection. In slow strokes I tease the slick folds of her cunt. She's so fucking wet that the tip of my cock is glistening with her sweet juices. With just the tip, I ease inside her. The need to ram into her is strong, but I bite back. In a slow movement, I take her inch by inch. She pushes her ass back onto me, but I step back. I am teasing her just like she teases me.

She wants it fast and hard, but I wont give in, even if I am killing myself in the process. I want her begging and pleading. A smirk curls my lips because I don't have to wait long when she whines. "Lucien…" She tries pushing back onto me again, gripping her hips, I hold her still and a loud mewl comes from her. I slide into her again, inch by inch and pull back out again.

"I want you to say it. Tell me what you want, sweetness?" My voice is laced with desire.

"Fuck my pussy, hard and fast and deep!" When she screams her demands I grip her hips harder, knowing I am marking her, bruising her.

"As you wish baby." I drive in deep, bottoming out inside her and she cries out my name as her second orgasm rips into her. *That's it baby, it's my fucking name that you will scream forever!* I don't relent my thrusts; I want to pull pleasure straight from her soul. Another orgasm is close and I want it. Her body shakes violently under my grasp as a third release takes hold of her. My fingers dig into her soft skin, there must be pain biting into her, but what is pleasure without a bit of pain? I am unaware of anything, but plunging my cock deep into her tight heated pussy. "I love having your tight pussy milk me like that, baby."

Her heated tunnel clenches again, and she cries out, cutting through my lust filled delirium and I slam into her, deeper than I have ever been. "My turn to fill you." I growl, and my orgasm tightens my balls. My hand fisted in her long brown hair, pulling her up so her back flush with my chest, my hot come fills her. My voice a husky growl, "My lumiére!"

Cassandra

I slipped on the lingerie I bought on our earlier shopping trip. The excitement bubbled inside me; I was never really a fan of corsets, but this was beautiful. Black lace with sparkling rhinestones made it shimmer like stars in the night sky. The sweetheart neckline dipped low between my breasts and it was finished with a stunning lace-up back. The matching panties were sheer lace; it was soft against my skin. I pulled up the thigh-high stockings and clipped the garters to them.

The floor length sleeveless ivory dress looked incredible against my tanned skin. My long brown hair flowed in effortless curls to the middle of my back. I stepped into my silver four-inch heels. The beautiful diamond necklace and earrings that Lucien gave me earlier sparkled in the dim light. I took the pendant that Lucien's father gave me and had it fastened onto a matching bracelet which adorned my wrist. The beautifully woven silver of vines holding the sun and the snowflake. The polar opposites, summer and winter. Verán and Winters. I smiled, making my way down the staircase to the living room.

Lucien was standing on the patio, dressed in a black tux with a black dress shirt. I walked up to him, wrapping my arms around his taut body. "Mi amore," turning around in my arms, he pressed a soft kiss on my mouth. When he pulled away, I stepped back.

"Do you like my dress?" His eyes raked over my body appreciatively.

"You are beautiful sweetness, however, I would love to slip it off you." His lips curved into a devilish smile. The olive green in his eyes flickered with mischievousness.

"Lucien, we have to leave soon, or we will be late." I giggled and stepped back into the living room. Just then Lucien's phone rang.

"Might be my dad. Or not." He frowned, swiping the screen. "Jayce," he listened for a few minutes. As he spins around, his eyes meet mine. "What?" His eyes sparkled with ferocity and I shivered, whatever Jayce was telling him was not good. "I will sort it out. Thanks man." With that he hung up. "Come on, sweetness, we need to talk before we get there." He walked over to the sofa and I followed. Something was wrong, and the tension was rolling off him in waves.

"What was that? Are you okay?" I sat down next to him and placed a hand on his thigh. When he covered mine with his, he gave my hand a squeeze.

"My step-mother, she's invited someone to the dinner. Jayce called to warn me before we walked in together." With his index finger and thumb, he pinched the bridge of his nose, as if in pain. I waited for him to continue, my heart hammering in my chest. This has to be bad, or he wouldn't be so angry. "The girl's name is Isabel. This is something from my past that doesn't seem to want to go away, I knew her a long time ago. She was the one who kept calling you at the office." When his green eyes met mine, I could see the anguish so evident in them. My heart plummeted. *Why would she be here?* It made little sense.

"Was this Claudia's doing?" Her name left a foul taste in my mouth. Lucien nodded quickly and my blood ran cold. *Why the fuck can't she leave us alone?* "It's okay babe, we're together, nothing will come between us." I reach out to him, lacing my fingers through his. "Let's go."

"I just didn't want you to walk in there, and—"

"Luke, it's okay. You told me. There's nothing that will take me away from you again." I make him a promise I intend to keep. He rises from the sofa, pulling me with him. His fingers grip my hips, tugging me against his body. Every hard ridge of him burns into me.

"I love you Ms. Winters." His dimples peek out when he flashes me a panty melting smile. *Was he always going to have this effect on me?*

"And I love you, Mr. Verán." No sooner has the words left my mouth, do his lips come crashing down on mine. His tongue plunges into me, licking inside me, tasting me. I moan into the kiss as it becomes more urgent. In the back of my mind, I know we have to leave, but right now, all I want to do is spend the night indoors. With my hands on his chest I push back slowly. His teeth tug my bottom lip and I can't help squeezing my thighs together. With the pad of his thumb, he slowly swipes over my lips. I am tempted to bite his finger, but I know that will ensue more kissing. "Lucien, you're mine and I am yours. Don't worry." He smiles and nods and we make our way outside.

Lucien

Robert was waiting at the car for us. He opened the door with a quick nod to Cassie, "Ms. Winters," a small smile cracks on his face which leaves me shocked. He's normally so serious. She offered him one of her sweet smiles and my heart swelled with pride to have such a beautiful woman on my arm.

"Thank you Robert." Slipping into the bench seat, I watch her curves as she slides over and I can't help myself wanting her. It's a constant ache I have, and she's the only one who can satisfy me. Her smile, her eyes, her body. Her face is priceless when she sees the bottle of champagne chilling on ice. I glance at her as I join her, giving a smile. "What's this for?" Her question is guarded, she hates surprises, but I can't help myself. I needed to celebrate the fact that she's with me again.

"We're celebrating, sweetness. I finally have the woman I love and I need to make sure she knows just how much she means to me." I lift the bottle and pop the cork. Her giggle is like music to my ears and I want to make sure she spends her life smiling and laughing.

"Grab the glasses for me please, baby?" The two flutes on the shelf are sparkling in the light of the limo. Cassie grabs them and holds them up for me. I fill each of them with the clear bubbly liquid. I place the bottle back in the ice bucket, grabbing my glass, I touch it lightly to hers. "To you coming back to me. My lumiére, my love, my sweetness, my angel. I am so glad you're back in my life, my arms and most importantly in my bed." Giving her a cheeky wink, I notice her cheeks pink. She looks so fucking beautiful. "And you look breathtaking love, I can't explain how much you take me by surprise everyday."

"Lucien, you are the one who has taken me by surprise. You've broken me, but you've also fixed me. I am finally whole." I tug her into the crook of my arm, holding her close and inhaling her scent. That sweet lavender scent of Cassie that I can never tire of.

By the time we arrive at my childhood home, I am relaxed and happy. Deep down, I realize something is off when I see two other cars in the drive. Jayce mentioned that Claudia has something up her sleeve. My mind needs to stay focused, I need to be alert for her. Tonight I am not in the mood to deal with her shit.

I let Robert open Cassie's door, when she rounds the car, I lace my fingers in hers and we make our way to the large door that may hold all my secrets just beyond. As soon as we reach the door it opens with a soft whoosh and we are greeted by Greta, she's been with the family for years and I remember how she used to make the best peanut butter and jam sandwiches.

"Mr. Verán, your father is in his study. He would like to see you and Ms. Winters." She gave a quick curtsey, and I smiled, she always does that. I use to tell her not to do that, I wasn't her boss, but she never listened. The staff always showed the utmost respect.

"Thank you Greta." My hand fell possessively on Cassie's lower back. I guide her through the foyer and we make our way towards the right, the study has double doors of beautiful mahogany. The gold doorknob sparkles, I twist it and allow Cassie to step through first.

Claudia wasn't around, but I am sure she's sitting in front of her cauldron somewhere cooking up some fucking shit to throw at me at the dinner table. "Son." My dad gets up and makes his way towards us. He is looking a lot better than the last time we saw him. He glances at Cassie and his smile brightens.

"The gorgeous, Cassandra," he leans in and gives her a kiss on the cheek, and pulls her into a tight embrace. When he steps back he takes in her appearance and I can tell he is as floored by her as I am on a daily basis, "You look beautiful!"

He turns his stare to me and pulls me into a warm embrace. There's something different about him, I can't quite put my finger on it. "Come you two, we have lots to talk about. Sit." He points to two ornate wingback chairs opposite his desk.

I let Cassie slip into the closest one, the slit on her dress glides open and my eyes rake in her smooth skin. *Fuck! Did she have to wear that dress?* Before I sit, I need to readjust the front of my pants I notice her stifling a giggle. *Oooh, you will pay for that little one, with a nice handprint on your peachy ass!* I cut a glance over to my father, thankfully he missed the exchange. I mouth "later" to her, watching her eyes widen in shock.

"Okay, I wanted to talk to you both, since you're both an integral part of Verán Publishing. After much consideration, I will retire. I wanted you both here, since I see my son is very much in love with you, Cassandra," he gives us both a bright smile, like it was the best news he's heard in a long time.

I don't answer, the shock is written over my face and I am speechless. "Lucien, you are to take over from me. The next 3 months will be busy, many late nights, but I think you both will handle it with grace. Cassie, you needed to be here because I want you to handle the publishing house while I get Lucien up to speed on the rest of the holdings." His words slowly sink in and I am left in utter disbelief.

My gaze flits to Cassie who is as shocked as I am. She lifts her hand to her mouth when I notice the bracelet on her wrist. Dad notices it as well. "It looks perfect on you, ma chérie." He says with a smile.

"Thank you, Mr. Verán, but is this a good idea? I mean, I have no idea how to run a business." Her words drift into my mind, I realize she would do an incredible job. She shouldn't question herself.

"Dad, I… This is…"

"Cassandra, hush child, you will be perfect. Lucien, I want to go back home for a while. To see the family. So I need you to look after everything here. Can you do that?" The tone in his voice says that he isn't asking permission but rather telling me. A small nod confirms that I will take over Verán Industries, this pushes me to be the youngest billionaire, in the country.

"I don't know what to say dad," this is out of my depth. I mean running the publishing company is one thing, but the holdings? His gaze meets mine, there's something else he's not telling me. Something deep down tugs at my heart and my concern is for his health. The doctor said he needed rest. Maybe this is why he is now taking the time off.

"Say yes, you and Cassandra together will be a formidable force." He stares at me and I nod. I could never deny my father. "Good! Now, there is another thing I need to speak with you about. Your step-mother and I are getting a divorce. I can't live this life anymore, she will fight for half of everything, but thankfully there is a prenuptial agreement in place that will stop her from even trying." My heart speeds up at the news; this is what I was thinking about earlier. A divorce. She will not like this one bit. "With that said, let's get to dinner. Oh, and Cassandra, I am glad you're back with Lucien." His voice is amused, and Cassie's face is a picture to be hold.

Cassandra

I stare at this man, my mouth agape. *How did he know? Lucien didn't mention that he told his father!*

He chuckles at my shocked expression. "I could see it in his face when he was here this past week. I lost my love, once, I recognized the emptiness I had in my eyes, in his. Then I forced him to tell me what happened." We all stand, and Mr. Verán walks around his desk, making his way to the door as I glance at Lucien. The tingles travel down my spine when he places his hand on my lower back.

We hear voices in the dining room, Claudia, Sasha and a young brunette are laughing as we walk in. Her eyes fall on me and they chill when her gaze turns icy. "Lucien, darling. So good to see you. You've brought a friend? I thought this was a family dinner?" She turns to Lucien's dad, and his reply stuns me and the rest of the room.

"Cassandra is family. Now can we have dinner?" He spins on his heel and walks over to his seat. We all stare at him dumbfounded as he slips into the chair at the head of the table.

"Lucien, Cassandra, I hope you're both well." Sasha steps up to greet us. She plants a quick kiss on Lucien's cheek and turns to me. Her smile seems genuine and I return it. She leans in for a quick hug and I am once again stumped, I didn't think she liked me. "My brother told me you're back with Luke, I am happy for you." She whispers in my ear and straightens.

"Thanks." My voice barely audible.

"Cassandra, this is Isabel. She has known Lucien for years." Claudia's icy voice sends chills over my skin. I glance at the girl. That's her. This is the girl who's been threatening me. I smile and nod. There is so much venom on my tongue, but I bite back. I will not lower myself to their level.

Lucien ignores them, helping me into the empty seat next to him and takes his seat. He places his hand protectively on my thigh. The slit in my dress falls open and his thumb massages circles over my heated skin. I can't help squeezing my thighs together to dull the ache that he's suddenly produced. I glance up at him and the knowing smirk on his face is obvious. He knows what he does to me. I so much want him to move his hand higher, to calm the tingles his touch is sending through me. My brain is foggy with desire, I reach for my glass and take a small sip of water, hoping it will cool me down.

"So, Lucien, I want to talk to you and Sash about the charity. Since you're both named partners on it I would like to step down. Your father has mentioned going to Spain, and I would have to accompany him." She glances over at Lucien's father and I see his face still, amusement in his eyes. He hasn't told her yet that much is obvious.

"Mother, I doubt I would be capable of handling something like that. I am sure Sasha would be more than happy to do it. To be honest, I think it's time I step down." Reaching for his wine glass he brings it to his mouth and takes a long sip. His tongue flicks out and wets his lips and I bite back a moan.

"Claudia, I think Lucien will be kept busy with the Verán Industries, I told you I am retiring. He will need to put all his focus on there. I have spoken to both him and Cassandra. She will help Lucien with Verán Publishers."

"What?!" Her perfect façade slips as she glares at her husband. The staff enter bringing in our dinner, interrupting her spewing obscenities. Roasted lamb with grilled asparagus, a dark onion gravy and crispy roast potatoes with mint sauce was served. We sat and ate in silence. Lucien stole glances at me whenever I drank my wine, his gaze fixed on my mouth. A naughty glint in his eye told me exactly what he was thinking. I could feel the ice of Isabel's gaze. It took everything inside me to ignore her. The fact that I was sitting here with Lucien was testament enough she had no claim on him. He was mine now, and forever.

The rest of dinner was much the same, after the blow Mr. Verán delivered, Claudia was silent. I think she was plotting revenge, her sneer was evident, and I was thankful for Lucien being next to me.

With the plates cleared away, Mr. Verán requested coffees to be brought out.

"Dad, I want to show Cassie the rest of the house and gardens." As he pushes his chair out, Lucien offers me his hand. I slip mine into his.

"Good idea, I need a minute with Claudia." His gaze cuts to her, and I realize what he means. This is definitely not going to be a quiet evening. "Don't be too long, I want to chat to you before you leave." Sasha, Isabel and Claudia are wrapped up in a conversation about mink coats when we walk through to the foyer and up the sweeping staircase.

"Where are we going? I thought you said the gardens?" I turn to Lucien, his eyes have darkened and his hooded gaze sends spirals of pleasure to my core.

He leans in and whispers. "I need to be inside you. Do you realize I have been rock hard all fucking night?" The desire dripping from his words have my brand new panties wet. He tugs me into a bedroom that looks like a teenage boy's room, he pins me against the wall and seals his mouth on mine. I whimper into the kiss and arch my body to his. His erection poking into my belly and I am aching to have him inside me. His hand slips the material of my dress aside, opening the slit to gain access to my moist entrance. The lace of my panties are suddenly ripped away with a quick tug and I gasp.

"Those were new!" I gasp and he winks. Lucien shoves them into his pocket and finds my slick folds, plunging a finger inside me, I bite back a moan.

"Fuck, you're so wet, Cassie." His groan is loud and I stifle a giggle.

"Shhh." I whisper.

"I don't fucking care." My hands come down and I tug at his pants and zipper, freeing his impressive erection. He is rock hard in my hand as I slowly stroke him up and down. "Put me inside you." He growls and I wrap a leg around his taut waist.

He lifts my dress, making sure not to rip it as he grabs my ass. My legs lock around his waist I position him at my heated sex and he drives inside me in one swift move. This will be hard and fast, and I love every second. "That's it baby, open up and take me." His thrusts are relentless and I am climbing into a state of delirium that only he can take me to. I tighten my grip on his neck, my back is flush against the wall as he fucks me deep and hard. "Give me your pleasure Cassie, come for me, lumiére!" His words a hiss between his teeth as my release shatters me. My body tenses and I tighten around him. With another final long hard thrust Lucien growls his release deep inside me.

Lucien

"Cassandra," I glance up when my office door opens. Cassie walks into my office with a devilish smirk on her lips. We haven't spent a lot of time together recently, with me taking over the company, I have been so busy. She had taken so well to running Verán Publishers and the pride I have for her was incredible. "What have I done to deserve this beautiful surprise?"

"Mr. Verán, I think you need a quick lunch break." My name on her lips, and the fact that I haven't been with her in a few days has my cock twitching in my pants already. She twists the lock on my office door, steps further into the office and rounds my desk. Perching on the edge. My eyes rake over her appearance. She's dressed in a black knee-length skirt and powder blue spaghetti strap top with black pumps. The most difficult thing I have to do everyday is leave her in bed. I watch her push up further onto the desk and I realize exactly what she has planned.

I roll my chair back, and she positions herself between my legs. My cock is straining to be let loose and slide inside her, but this is for her. "Open for me." I demand with a low growl and she's squirming already. With my hands on either of her thighs I push her skirt up. When I see the stockings and garters my cock pulses against my zipper. I almost come in my pants. Grinding my teeth to keep calm, I sit back and watch her. She complies and spreads her legs, I slide my hands up her thighs slowly. As soon as I reach her moist panties my lust kicks in and I give her a smirk that has her gasping. "Did my dirty girl come in here to tease me? Cassandra, did you come here to get fucked?" My words are crude, and she whimpers. Nodding.

"Tell me."

"Yes, Sir. I want you to make me come." Her words are a low whisper that shoots to my groin. I press my hands on the inside of her thighs and splay her open. The tiny satin panties she's wearing are soaked and I can smell her arousal. *Fuck me, she's beautiful!* I lean forward and I hear her breath hitch. *That's it baby, you will do more than gasp when I am done with you.* I push the flimsy material to the side and flatten my tongue over her bare pussy. *God she tastes amazing; fuck I can't get enough of her.* My eyes lock on hers, "God, I missed you baby," flicking my tongue over her little clit, sending a spasm through her body.

    I slide a finger inside her warm tight cunt, licking in slow measured strokes. "This what you wanted baby?" I whisper up to her and see her nod. When I add a second finger, her heated tunnel tightens around me. She's close, but I am moving so slow that I keep her on the edge. I want her to beg. I fucking need her to beg. *Come on baby, beg me to fuck you. Please? Because I am going out of my mind!* "I do love tasting you, baby."

    "Please, Luke, please I need you. I fucking need you." Her words are like music to my ears. *That's my girl, begging for my cock inside her. I fucking own you baby.* I rise and pull my fingers from her core. My gaze locked on hers, I licking her sweet honey. "Jesus, Lucien. Please?!" Desperation drips from her words. Unbuckling my pants, I pull out my cock. The strain on my zipper was killing me.

    When I lean over I plant a soft kiss on her lips, her tongue darts out and I suck on it. When I pull back, I grip the tiny thong and rip it from her body. "Take off your top, I want to see your tits." My words are raspy, this will not be romantic, I am going to fuck her. Hard. When the soft material drops to the floor so does my jaw. She's wearing a tight black corset the seems to push her breasts up and I just about come from the sight. "Fuck, Cassandra!" The words come out as a growl. *This is most definitely going to be a hard fuck. I guarantee it!*

    Cassie reaches down and slowly strokes me. "Put me inside you baby, now!" My words come out harsher than I expect, but she's got me so fucking hard it hurts. Once I am positioned at her entrance, all my thoughts disappear, all that matters right now, me, my lumiére and how hard I am about to fuck her. She's so fucking ready I am about to lose it completely. "Hold on tight, this will be fast and hard."

    "I was counting on it. I need you." Her moans are more than enough to spur me on and I drive in to the hilt. I watch her bite down on her bottom lip to keep from alerting everyone outside my office to what I am having for lunch. Once I am inside her, I move faster, deeper, and harder. Thrusting into her. She's pinned below me against the mahogany. I grip her hips and plunge inside her wet heat. Deep measured strokes as we both climb into the abyss of our passion.

    Her grip on the desk is tight, her knuckles are turning white. My hold on her hips will leave bruises, but I can't stop myself from the orgasm that's so close. Her pussy tightens and clenches around me sending lust through every inch of my body. "That's my lumiére, come on my hard cock baby." My release shoots down my spine and straight to my balls. Cassie's tight little pussy squeezes around me again and I slam into her with my release as she comes around my cock. Her body convulses under me, and I hold her. I ride out her orgasm until she stills and her eyes meet mine.

    "I love you, baby." My whisper is low, and I collapse on top of her, holding her against me. When I feather soft kisses on her lips, down her neck, and nibble her ear, it awards me a soft giggle.

    "I love you too. Now, I need to get back to work." I groan in agony of having to move. Wishing I could spend the whole afternoon inside her. We straighten up, I reach out and help Cassie to her feet. She's adorable and beautiful and I can't get enough of her. I place a soft kiss on her lips and walk with her to the door of the office. "Later, Verán." She giggles, opening the door and shutting it on my shocked expression. *That woman will be the death of me.* When I walk to my desk, I can't help smiling. The picture in my mind of her on my desk will forever be etched in my mind. *Now how the fuck am I going to concentrate on work for the rest of the afternoon?*

Cassandra

When I get back to my office, Jayce is sitting in the plush armchair. "Alexander, what are you doing in my office?"

"I need you darling!" He chuckles when I slap him on the bicep. "Just kidding, we need to go over the details for winter shoot coming up and I wanted to know when you're free." As I round my desk, I slip into the comfortable black leather chair and glance into intense blue eyes. Jayce had been amazing when Lucien and I broke up and since we're back together, Jayce hadn't moved on as he said he would.

"Let me have a look, probably tomorrow afternoon? I am not in the management meeting so you can come down then."

"Perfect. So, how's Luke?" His gaze is expectant and I am not sure if he wants good or bad news, somehow it's unlikely he wants me to tell him we're happy.

"He's fine, trying to make up for everything. It's been difficult, things are still tense sometimes, but we're getting there." When my gaze meets his I see a flicker in his sky-blue eyes. They remind me of a clear blue ocean, on a tropical island, my cheeks flush when I recall our time in Cancun.

"Cass?" Jayce pulls me from my dirty thoughts.

"Yes? Sorry, I am exhausted."

"It's okay, I need to go. See you tomorrow." He rounds my desk and tugs me into a hug. The soft material of his grey hoodie smells like him. "You're amazing, remember that." He plants a quick kiss on my forehead and leaves without another word. *What the hell was that?*

A knock on my door startles me from the peculiar visit from Jayce. "Come in." I call out. As the door opens, I peer up to see my assistant, who Luke's dad so graciously hired for me.

"Ms. Winters, this package arrived for you about ten minutes ago. I didn't want to interrupt Mr. Alexander's visit." When I offer him a smile and nod, he steps further into the office.

"Thank you Paul, it's not a problem. Leave it on the table, I will have a look at it later. Can you please make sure my diary is clear tomorrow afternoon I have a meeting with Mr Alexander at 2:30 pm, send him the request as well? Also please get me a black coffee?" With a small nod, he wanders off down the corridor. As soon as I hit send on an email, I rise and round my desk. The silver envelope is sealed, and I tear it open. I wonder if Lucien bought me a gift. He didn't mention it earlier, not that I gave him an opportunity to. When I slide out the card, I turn it over, there's an elegant script on the one side. Not recognizing the handwriting, I frown. That's strange. Luke didn't mention he's working late.

Meet me in my office at 6 pm. I have a surprise. Love you baby.

Just before six, I shut down my computer and grab my bag. With the envelope in hand, I make my way out of the office. The floor is so quiet, everyone has left for the day and I can't wait to get home. When I push the call button, I don't have to wait for the elevator, and step inside as soon as the car stops on my floor. Still finding it strange that Luke delivered an envelope, rather than calling me. I step out onto the top floor and make my way to his office. The door is slightly ajar when I walk up to it. As soon as my hand grips the handle I hear voices. "Luca, please. I love you. I always have!" A girl's voice cuts through the silence. My heart unravels and shatters slowly and suddenly it's too difficult to breathe. *What the fuck is going on? That's the voice of the girl who's been harassing me! Isabel!*

As soon as I push the door open I come face to face with green eyes. My gaze flits down to his hands on her hips. She's stroking his chest. There's no doubt about what is going on. Their faces are so close I am sure he was about to kiss her.

"Cassie!" Spinning on my heel, I run towards the elevator and push the button for the car to take me away. "Baby!" As soon as he reaches me I step into the waiting car. I can't do this. Lucien stops the elevator with his hand and the doors slide open. "Please? I was telling her to leave. Believe me, please?"

"Let me go." Those were the only words I could utter. My breath had stopped, and I knew that if he put his hands on me I would waiver, but he was about to kiss another woman. "Just let me go."

Those were the last words I uttered, and he stepped back as the doors slid closed, to my heart and my soul. The only person that I have ever given everything to and now it was gone.

Lucien

As soon as I walk back into the office, I glare at Isabel's face. "Do you even fucking realize what you just did!?" I am shouting, but I don't give a fuck. The woman of my dreams, the love of my life just walked out the door, or into an elevator and asked me to let her go. *What the fuck was I meant to do now?*

"She will forgive you Luca. Trust me." My glare cuts to her again and I round on her. My hand is on her neck suddenly and I have her pinned against the wall. Her breath is short as she struggles, but I don't care. The pain she's just put me through is more than I can even fucking imagine and no one will come out of this alive. Not her or Claudia!

"Trust you!? Are you fucking crazy? Get the fuck out of my life. Vous me dégoûtez putain!" Her eyes are as big as dinner plates at the words I have just spat at her. When I release my hold on her neck, I see the surprise on her face. She didn't know what I am capable of, but she better fucking learn quickly. Nothing, I swear on my fucking life, nothing will take Cassie from me!

As soon as Isabel is out of my sight I call Robert. I need him to source the original contact between Claudia and Isabel. I need proof and I need to take it to Cassie. She won't take me back now, but once I can prove nothing happened, I know she will see it my way. At least, I fucking hope she does.

"Robert, I need you to pull records."

"Yes sir, I can have Daniel on that. Who's?"

"Claudia. Isabel" I hear his sharp intake of breath and I know what he's thinking before he even says anything. My heart constricts at her expression as those goddamn doors closed.

"Mr. Verán."

"Robert please?"

"Yes, sir."

Once I hang up, I slide into my office chair. The memory of her sitting here only a few hours ago is burnt into my mind. *How the fuck does life fuck you so hard? Fuck!* I slam my hand on the desk in frustration. *This is the fucking point isn't it?* I mean. *Isn't this why people fall in love? To feel the pain and anguish. No, they fall in love to feel the happiness!* I unlock my phone and call Jayce; he will know what to do. The fact that he knows how to make my girl happy angers me so much, but deep down I know he's probably the only one who can get through to her. Voicemail. I leave a message for him to call me urgently, mentioning Isabel and Claudia. He hates them as much as I do. I close my eyes, trying to think of some way to make her come back to me. She needs to know what happened. The truth. Not what she saw. My eyes snap open as my phone rings, thinking it's Jayce, I slide the answer screen. It's the hospital. Immediately my mind is on Cassie. "Mr. Verán?" The question has my blood running cold. *Please don't let Cassie be hurt!*

"Yes, this is Lucien Verán," I listen for a few moments before shock cuts in. The news shocks me into panic. "I will be right there." There is only one person I need right now, scrolling down to her number, I hit the call button. Her voice calms me, even though she's angry. "What, Lucien?"

"My father. Hospital." Those are the only words I can mumble.

"Pick me up." My heart fills with more love for this woman than I thought was possible. As angry as she is with me, she's willing to be by my side. I don't know what's wrong with my father, but I sure as hell don't want to find out without her next to me.

I call Robert to bring the car immediately, quickly filling him in. As I make my way down to the reception, I step onto the sidewalk and out to the car. My mind is all over the place. I only need Cassie.

Cassandra

When we stepped out of the elevator, my gaze falls on Claudia, she was talking to a doctor. "What's going on?" Lucien's voice clipped, he hated her with a vengeance. Frankly, I do not blame him.

"Lucien, this is Dr Shaw, he has done a few tests. He came out to give me the results." Her eyes fell on me and the chill in her glare was ice on my skin.

"Doctor," offering his hand to the older man. The doctor gave a small smile and told us that Lucien's father was in a critical condition. He had suffered another stroke, more serious than the first. They had to operate due to bleeding directly on the brain. The problem however was that his heart wasn't strong enough to fight through the after effects. They cannot give any more information until he wakes up. It could be a few hours or two days. My heart leaped into my throat and I couldn't think, my mind whirling with worry. When the doctor walked away, Lucien turned on Claudia, "What the fuck happened? He was fine!" Her sneer was undeniable.

"Lucien, please. Don't cause a scene. Nothing happened." She dropped her voice and stalked towards the small room reserved for family. Once the door closed behind us, she sat down in one of the armchairs and crossed one leg over the other like she was posing for a photograph. Ever the cold hearted bitch I realized she was.

"Claudia, I am not in the mood for fucking games. You need to tell me what the fuck happened with my father!" Lucien's voice grew an octave and boomed in the tiny room. His grip on my hand was tightening, and the anger vibrating through him, flowing into me. Like we were connected in more than just a physical sense. As angry as I was with him for what I witnessed in his office, this was something even I couldn't deny him. I had to be by his side through this. I owed him that much. After, I don't think I can promise him anything more. The thought of that constricted my heart painfully, and I took a deep breath.

"Lucien, you need to sit down. We need to talk about your father's will and final wishes. His condition is serious." When she glanced up I recognized the calculating stare, all she cared about was the money and what she would get if anything happened to Lucien's father. My blood ran cold.

"Fuck you!" Lucien spat the words, spinning around, he tugged me out of the room, slamming the door behind him. Everything he was feeling, I did too, the pain, the anger, and the love for his father.

"Lucien," my voice a low murmur.

"Not now." He pulled me along, I had no choice but to follow, his grip on my hand was so tight the blood flow had stopped going to my fingers. He tugged me into an empty room, closing the door, he pinned me against it. "Give me your light baby, please." He sounded so broken, torn, and so desperate. The electricity between us whirled, the air in the room thick with emotion. His voice raspy, I recognized the pain etched on his beautiful face. Realizing what he needed, the only way I could take his pain away. With my hand on his erection, I squeezed, and stroked him over the soft material of his pants. When his eyes closed, a low growl vibrated deep in his throat. "Fuck this, I need to be inside you." His hands tugged my sweats and panties down in a swift move, allowing me to step out of them. When he rose, his mouth came down over mine, sealing my lips with his. Opening my mouth, his tongue licked into me.

His hands were on my hips in a painful vice grip. My body flush against the door with the full weight of his body pinning me in place. His hips rolled into mine, and his arousal pressed against my core. His one hand found my slick sex. He stroked me, plunging two fingers inside me deep and fast, my body tightened around them. The rasp of his zipper echoed in the quiet room and suddenly his fingers were replaced by his rock hard cock. My body filled to the brink as he slammed inside me. He fucked the emotion into me and through me. His pain, my pain. Our anger colliding as our bodies molded into one. He drove into me violently.

My gaze locked on his and the pain slipped from his eyes. "My lumiére, I love you so fucking much." His raspy whisper sending me over the edge. My teeth bit down on his shoulder to keep from screaming. He thrust into me one more time, growling out his release. As we caught our breath, he lowered his forehead onto mine and planted a soft kiss on my lips. We stayed like that for a few moments as we both came down from the intense orgasm that shattered us both.

He pulled out of me and I winced. The emptiness was unwelcome. "Shit, I am sorry baby. I didn't mean to hurt you."

"You didn't, Lucien." cupping his face in my hands I placed a kiss on his lips.

"Do you mind staying here? I can have Robert take you home?" There was no way I would leave him when he was going through so much turmoil. I shook my head. "I need to talk to you about what happened at the office. Claudia has been trying to break us up for months and Isabel is part of it. I need you to trust me please baby?" He pleaded with me and I realized I had walked in on something I didn't have the whole story about. He needed to explain, but not now, not here. After his father goes home, then we can talk.

With a small smile, I nodded, I wasn't leaving. This is where I belong, with the man I love. "I want to be with you Lucien, please don't send me away?" With his arms banding around my waist, he pulled me into his arms. As he held me I felt the tension in his body calm. The anguish he is going through is something I understand, the stress of losing your father, a parent. It's something nobody can ever imagine until it happens to them. I remember losing my own father, blaming myself for years, that love is something you could never get back. Ever.

"Never baby. Never."

We stepped out of the room into the hallway, walking towards the room where his father was laying in ICU. I can't believe this is happening. "Luke!" We both turned to Jayce. His eyes faltered for a second at our linked hands, but he seemed to recover quickly.

"Jayce, what are you doing here?" They shook hands, tugging each other in for a quick hug. Jayce's eyes fell on me and he pulled me into a hug. Once he released me, and stepped back, the flicker of emotion in his eyes was noticeable. I realized he still had feelings for me, even though he denied it.

"I heard about your dad from Sash, Claudia called her about something and mentioned it." A frown creased his brows, something seemed strange about this.

"Why would she be calling your sister?" Lucien voicing the question I was too scared to ask.

"I don't know man; she's been on at Sasha for weeks now. Like they're fucking BFF's or something." Walking to the coffee machine, I release Lucien's hand for the first time since we arrived. I grabbed a mug and filled it with coffee, listening to the boys.

"I don't like it Jayce, I don't fucking trust Claudia. She's up to something. I can feel it and with Isabel in the picture, something's not right." My body shivered with cold fear that Claudia somehow had something to do with Luke's father being in hospital.

"Mr. Verán, can we talk?" We all turned to come face to face with the doctor.

"Yes, whatever you want to say can be said in front of my brother and my girlfriend." Lucien reached for my hand. Jayce placed a hand on Luke's shoulder. The doctor nodded.

"Please follow me." He turned, and we made our way down the corridor to a small office. When the doctor closed the door, fear ran through my veins. This could not be good news. Deep down in my gut fear took hold, and it didn't let go. Lucien pulled me onto his lap and Jayce took the other chair opposite the dark wood desk. "Mr. Verán, your father isn't well. I am afraid the tests show that the stroke your father suffered was more severe than we thought. He had suffered a heart attack prior to the stroke. We have to guess that's what brought on the stroke. He must have been under a large amount of stress before the incident. Do you know if he was working? Or if there was something that could have upset him to the point of causing something so severe?"

I glance down at Lucien and my eyes flit to Jayce, we were all on the same page. This had to do with Claudia, the company was doing well, and Lucien was working with his father, they were happy and enjoying spending time together, so work wasn't the cause. The tension rolled through Luke's body like an electric current.

"My father was definitely not stressed at work. There is one thing that would have been playing on his mind and that is a pending divorce which he filed for recently. Other than that, there wasn't anything out of the ordinary that could have caused this. What do we do now doctor?"

"We wait. I am afraid I can't do much more. We will stop the medication that has kept him sedated and wait for him to pull through. Then we can decide if surgery is an option. He will need a pacemaker, but we need him to wake up of his own volition."

"And how long will that take?" Lucien's voice is strained. It's clear he wants to leave this room and most probably kill Claudia. I glance at Jayce and he is as on edge as Lucien.

"If he pulls through, it should be in about twenty-four to forty-eight hours." The doctor placed his hands on the desk, holding on to a folder I guess was Mr. Verán's.

"I would appreciate this to stay in this room, please doctor. My step-mother need not know any of this, not right now." The doctor nods and rises from his chair. I follow suit and Lucien grabs my hand. His stare is on the doctor and he offers a small smile. "Thank you, doctor."

Once we step out of the room, Lucien and Jayce stare at each other. "I told you man, this stinks of Claudia." We turn and make our way to the reception desk, we round the corner and find Sasha and Claudia whispering to each other. As soon as we close in on them, they straighten.

"Luke, are you okay babe?" Sasha grabs Lucien into a tight hug and bile rises in my throat.

"Lucien, Sasha was worried about you. She needed to spend time with you. So I told her to come and support you." Claudia's tone was icy cold, when her gaze landed on me, I shivered.

"I have my girlfriend here, Sasha, so you don't have to worry about me." As Lucien steps back, the look on his face is of complete disgust.

"Lucien, there is no need to be so rude."

"You're not my fucking mother, so stay out of my life." Lucien's grip on my hand releases and he storms off down the corridor leaving us all standing there. I turn to follow him when Jayce grabs my arm.

"Can we talk?" I nod. Watching Sasha and Claudia disappear into the family room. "Luke told me you walked out." His voice was low, but it sent shivers over my body.

"How do you know?" He pulls me into the stairwell, and carries on explaining.

"The girl that you caught Luke with, that's Isabel. She's Luke's ex from a long time ago. I overheard my sister and Claudia on a call and it sounded like they're planning on getting the company from Luke by breaking you and him up. I can't tell Lucien because he isn't thinking straight at the moment. Sasha hates Luke, for the past, but also that he didn't want her back. His guilt ate him up for so long when she couldn't forgive him. It's understandable, but she hasn't been the innocent one here either. I think—" My phone buzzing startles me and I jump. I tug it from my pocket and Lucien's name flashes across the screen.

"Hello?"

"Where the fuck did you go? The doctor just called me."

"I am coming." I glance at Jayce, giving me a nod he waits till I make it back to Lucien before making an appearance himself. "What's happened?"

As soon as I find Lucien he tugs my hand and pulls me down the hallway. When he spins to me again the heartbreak in his eyes rips my heart open. I swallow a lump in my throat when I realize what must have happened. *No, no, please no!! I can't. Lucien can't! Shit!*

"He's not making progress, they're keeping an eye on him, but the doctor doesn't sound positive." I pull him into my arms and hold him. "Please don't leave me baby." His words are strangled and I realize he's trying not to lose control of his emotions. I glance up and my eyes lock on bright sky-blue eyes.

"I am not leaving you, Lucien. Stop thinking it." Jayce stares at me and turns to walk away. Leaving us standing there embracing. I need to tell Luke about what Jayce said, but I know this is not the time or the place. We need to be prepared for whatever Claudia has planned. I will have to talk to him later.

Lucien

There is so much going through my mind right now. I need to talk to Jayce, there's something that Claudia has planned and I will be damned if she will win this fight. There was never a time I thought I could hate, but right now, when Claudia is near me, I do. It's inside me like a poison running through my veins. She's tried taking Cassie away from me and now my father, but she will not win.

The hours pass as we wait. What's killing me is the waiting. Not knowing if my father will wake up or not. "Luke." I turn to see Jayce walking towards me. Cassie went to grab two coffees, and I think that's why he's here. There's something in his eyes when he looks at her and I realize it's because of their time together which must have meant a lot more than he's letting on.

    It's not his fault. I walked away, letting her go. After a month apart, she moved on. Even though it was with my best friend, it was my fault. "Jayce, what's up?"

    "I spoke to Daniel and Robert; they have phone records. Claudia had contacted Isabel when Cassie first started at Verán publishers. Although they're not sure why."

    "I do. Claudia wants something. Although I do not understand what it could be." I have a million ideas passing through my mind, but none of them make sense.

    "There's something else."

    I glance up to see a guilty expression on his face. "What?" This can't be good.

    "I overheard my sister and Claudia a couple of days ago. They didn't realize that I was home, but, they were talking about Verán Industries. Claudia wants ownership. Although I have no idea how she would get it since you're already running it. I mean—"

    "Shit. If something happens to my father. The will." My eyes cut to his and I realize something that Claudia said earlier. "She mentioned my father's will and last requests. There must be something in there, but what? I mean he's always left everything to me. He told me so before I even finished school."

    "I can get Daniel to do some research into it. Robert is downstairs." I nod. Jayce can handle this; I need to find Claudia. When Cassie returns with our coffees, I take in her appearance. She's tired, we both haven't slept. "Come on baby, let's go sit down. You need to sleep."

    I grab the coffee from her, but she shakes her head. "No, I am fine. This is where I need to stay, with you." With my arm around her we make our way to the small family room. There's a sofa in here. I slip into the one corner and pull her into the crook of my arm. "Sorry I walked out. I thought you were—"

    "It's okay. I know."

    "No Luke, I should have trusted you."

    "Baby. If you don't stop, I will be forced to spank you." Her sharp intake of breath makes me smile. "Now just relax. We're here together."

    "Yes, Sir." Her voice is a low whisper and if I wasn't listening I would have missed it, but it still has the effect that she was eliciting. I have to take a large gulp of coffee to calm myself. My phone buzzes interrupting my thoughts. I unlock the screen and see a message from Jayce.

* All sorted. Will get news to you asap *

    Cassie lays her head on my lap and I lean back and close my eyes. Sleep comes easily, but the dreams haunt every moment.

    "Luca! Come here!" Isabel is running through lavender fields. We're on our family holiday in France. I met Isabel at the guesthouse where we were staying. Her mother and father owned it and were old family friends of my parents. As I run up to her, I wrap my arms around her. She's lovely, but for some reason I can't say the things she wants me to say. I am only sixteen, she talks of love and I don't.

    "Luca, what are you doing?" Her voice is shrill and grates at my nerves. My eyes dart around, I am back in my dorm. I am at University. On my bed is Isabel. What the fuck is she doing here? Bound to my bed with ropes. She wanted this, came here asking for me. I know she's looking for the boy who she remembered from that summer. He no longer exists darling. "What the fuck are you doing here Isabel?"

My voice is harsh and I see her flinch at my anger.

"I missed you Luca. I love you."

"Fuck love. It doesn't exist. I don't love you! Don't you remember?" My legs on either side of her, I see the fear in her eyes. Good, you should be scared. "I never wanted you, don't you get that?" Tears form in her eyes. I love seeing her cry. All these fucking bitches want me, but they're just never going to be the One. The girl with the mocha eyes and the curls. I don't know her; I can't remember her name. My mind is filled with messed up images, it's too much. I lean over and snort the last bit of white powder, letting the effects take over me. That's better. "Now, you came here for what? Me? That stupid little boy you remember is gone!"

I start at the sound of the doctor's voice. *Shit, those dreams again!* "Mr. Verán. You can see your father now." I nod and watch him leave. When I glance down at my girl my heart rate calms. Cassie was always the one. Even though we both didn't realize it. The girl with the mocha eyes and the curls. Jayce is awake when my eyes lock with his I realize he knows what was in my dreams. "Did you hear?"

"Yea, you had that dream again. You need to let it go man."

"It's difficult. Cassie changes me. Deep down there's still something that's bothering me."

"Give it time. Just don't hurt Cassie again."

"Fuck you, Jayce."

"Fuck you too, Luke. I care about her." His words are sincere. I realize he does, and it makes me angry. Even though he is the only person I would trust her with.

I keep my voice low. "You do. I can see it. You don't love her though." It isn't a question, it's a warning. He isn't allowed to love her. My eyes lock on his and I know without him saying it that he does.

Cassandra

"Baby." I am woken up by Lucien's hand stroking my hair. "The doctor said we can go inside and see my dad." I sit up slowly, groggy from the terrible night sleep. I had some strange dreams, but Lucien doesn't look like he's had any rest. He leans in giving me a loving kiss. "Do you want a coffee?" I nod and smile. When I reach up I groan as I try to smooth my hair that feels like a bird's nest. As soon as Lucien walks out the door, I sit up properly.

"Good morning gorgeous." I start at the sound of Jay's voice.

"Jayce. Shit, I didn't realize you were here." He cocks his head to the side, amusement in his blue eyes. His gaze rakes down my body and back up to my hair.

"You look beautiful, so does your hair." I groan. Not believing a word he says.

"Jayce, please don't—"

"I know, just stating a fact." He holds up his hands in defense.

"What fact?" I turn to see Lucien at the door with my coffee.

"That her hair doesn't look like a bird's nest." My eyes flicker to Jayce, willing him to not say the other so called fact that I looked beautiful.

"No, baby, it doesn't. You are gorgeous always." Lucien slides into the chair next to me.

"That's my cue. Catch you both later. I need to get myself some caffeine." Jayce leaves us, closing the door behind him. I watch the door close, but I can't bring myself to calm. There is something bothering him and but I have no idea what it is. I just want to help him.

"What was that about?" I glance at Lucien and he shakes his head. The most frustrating thing about the man I love was that he loved to hide things from me. As much as it frustrated me I couldn't get him out of it. "Luke?" I sip my coffee, staring at him, willing him to tell me.

"Jayce reckons that Claudia is trying to get her grimy hands on my father's company. I don't doubt it. Also there's this whole fiasco with Sasha, I mean she's moved on. So have I. There is nothing between us." His gaze falls on me and I can just about bring myself to say what I need to.

"Except for the charity and the fact that she was your first love?" As soon as the words are out of my mouth I want to swallow them back in.

"She and I have nothing in common, there is nothing between us. My future is with you Cassie!" His words are adamant and they make me smile. Even in this sad time the love that burns in his eyes makes me feel like a princess. My thoughts drift to Jayce's words. *Princess. That's what you are.*

"Okay Luke. I am still sleepy." With his heated stare on me, I raise my cup and drink my coffee. He smiles and turns his attention to his phone and I watch him tap a message to Robert. When his green gaze meets mine again, he smiles.

"And you're adorable. Ready to go see my dad?" I nod. When he laces his fingers through mine, we make our way towards his dad's room. Before we step inside, I give him a reassuring smile.

"Let's go." Luke's hand on the doorknob twists it. As soon as we're inside, the site takes my breath away. I hated hospitals. All my life. As a child refusing to walk into any hospital, the pain and despair in the air always tugged at me. Mr. Verán is still unconscious, I let Lucien go to him and wait in the seat at the foot of the bed. My heart is in tatters watching the man I love try to talk to his father, who might not be able to hear him. Memories of my own father come to mind, and I am forced to blink back tears.

I sit back and close my eyes, listening to Lucien's calm voice as he talks to his father. A jarring noise causes me to jump up from the chair. The monitors are beeping and I see the terror on Lucien's face. Suddenly the room is full of doctors and Lucien is pulled aside by one of the nurses. "Let them do their job, Mr. Verán, please can you wait outside?" We step outside and I curl myself into the crook of his arm. Doctors and nurses are frantically shouting at each other and I am not sure what all the medical terms mean, but when I hear the words 'not looking good' my stomach plummets.

"Cassie," Lucien's voice is so low, I almost miss the fact that he just said something over the commotion coming from his father's room. The empty corridor is filled with the click clack of heels. We turn to see Claudia rushing towards us.

"What is going on? Did you upset your father?" Her accusation slicing into my heart and anger is radiating through Lucien's body. He leans into her face so close I think he is going to head-butt her.

His words laced with hatred, "Get the fuck out of my face!" He spits the words at her, but instead of stepping back she gives him an evil smirk.

"I am your father's wife. I will not be spoken to in such a manner. You better watch yourself boy." Spinning on her heel she struts down the hallway and I step in front of Lucien.

"Luke, she's not worth it, look at me." I cup his face in my hands, making him meet my stare. "She's not worth it." I repeat the words and his arms wrap around me. His demeanor visibly calming.

"I have no idea what I would do without you baby." Resting my head against his chest, I can hear the beat of his heart and I smile. As long as I have his arms around me, we can get through anything.

"I am always here. It will be okay. I love you, Lucien Verán." His body shivers at the mention of his name on my lips. We lean against the wall waiting for any news from the hospital room where doctors are working. When the door flies open, we both glance up at the Dr Shaw, he pulls off his mask. The moments tick by before he speaks and our world stops. Cold fear grips me.

When Lucien crumples to the floor against the wall, pulling me with him, all I can do is hold him. My heart constricts and my chest tightens. I understand exactly what the love of my life is going through at this moment. Our world has just crashed around us.

Lucien

I don't remember getting home. When I look up, my eyes fall on Cassie in the kitchen, everything is too surreal. It's November, almost Christmas and I have just lost my father. As soon as I my gaze locks on Cassandra my fears calm. She's my family now. I have to make her happy. It's what he would have wanted. When I rise from the sofa, I walk upstairs into the bedroom and out onto the patio. I inhale a deep breath as I take in the view of the city. The place I grew up. My father loved taking me up onto the hills and telling me stories about growing up in France and Spain. The two places where my legacy lies.

One day I want to take Cassie there. The sun is setting low on the horizon and the sky is taking on an unusual glow, purples, pinks and deep orange. "How am I meant to go on without you? I can't run the company alone. Dad, you were my guide." I whisper into the wind. My heart is so heavy with emotion, I need my baby. Tonight I want to take her to my play room and get lost in her. "I love you, dad."

"Luke?" Her tentative voice behind me, pulls me from my pain. She's heard me. I don't care, sharing my heartache and pain with her is part of being in a relationship.

"Baby, come here." When her footfalls on the carpet come closer, the warmth and love radiating from her make the ache in my chest ease. Out on the patio, she circles her arms around my waist, and I am calmer already. She has an incredible effect on me. "I want to try something tonight. In the play room."

"Okay." Turning to face her, she's nervous. I can tell by the look on her face. With a reassuring soft kiss on her forehead, I hold her body flush with mine. She molds to me in a way that shows how we fit together like perfect pieces of a puzzle. That's the reason I can never be apart from her. I would be broken, beyond repair.

"Don't be scared, I need to feel you. Lose myself in you."

She leans back and looks up at me with those beautiful chocolate eyes. "I'm not scared. I know you won't hurt me, Luke. I trust you." Rising up on her toes, she places a soft kiss on my lips and my cock hardens at the thoughts of what I want to do to her tonight. "Do you want to eat?" Her question is innocent enough, but there are deliciously dirty things running through my mind.

"Yes," lifting her over my shoulder, I walk straight into the play room and set her down. "Get undressed, leave your panties on. Everything else on the floor." My voice taking on an authoritative tone and the anticipation is etched on her face. "I want you kneeling, legs spread and your hands on your thighs. Eyes on the floor."

"I thought—"

"Did I ask you to talk?" It's harsh, but the tremble that courses over her body is evidence that she's turned on by my dominant nature.

"No, Sir." Her whisper sends blood straight to my cock and all I can think of is fucking her. Hard. Until she's coming over my cock, while screaming my name. Her submission, letting me take her is what I need right now. I open the drawer and grab what I need. I turn to face her, she's in presentation position and she looks incredible. He soft hands are flat on her smooth thighs. Her head dipped and her eyes are on the floor. She's kneeling for me and those beautiful legs are spread.

"Close your eyes." She obeys and I tie the blindfold around her head. When it's secure with a knot, I watch her for a few moments. She's only wearing a pair of panties and looks good enough to eat. I grasp her hand and pull her up, guiding her onto the bed, letting her lay flat on her back. I grab the blood red rope and which will have her bound to my mercy. "What's your safe word baby?"

"Summer."

"Good, remember that." When both her ankles are secure, I move and tie her wrists to the bedposts, taking in the beautiful sight of my girl, spread before me on the black satin sheet. She is at my mercy. Only for me. Forever. I grab a blade, lifting the material at her hip, I slit the tiny pair of panties she's wearing. Once the other side is slit, I pull them out from under her. She's now completely naked.

The rise and fall of her chest is the only sign that she's nervous. Her nipples have pebbled and I am dying to lick and suck them into my mouth. I pick up the feather which I retrieved from the drawer and trail it across her skin. The movements are slow, light and leave goose bumps in their wake. From her feet, up her beautiful legs, just missing her sweet bare pussy. When I reach the sensitive spot below her breasts, her nipples harden even more. A low whimper escapes her soft plump lips. Her breasts are heaving with every breath. *I need to suck them. Fucking beautiful.* Her moans are getting louder and my cock is getting harder. With the tip of the feather, I trace a trail from her neck, and I bring it all the way back down between her legs.

"Luke…"

"Shhhh lumiére."

I step back, watching her writhe on the bed. "Luke."

"Shhh, baby. I'm here." I turn on the small vibrator and her breathing hitches. When I sit on the bed her head turns as the bed dips. "I will not hurt you. Just breathe and enjoy the sensations. They will overwhelm you, but you will enjoy every moment. Because when I fuck your tight pussy, you will come harder than you've ever come before." I tease her lips; the soft vibration sending tingles over her mouth. When I move it lower, down the nape of her neck, her breathing hitches. I reach her nipples and her hips buck off the bed. "Still baby, don't move."

The teasing must be driving her crazy, tonight she will never forget. Every emotion and every sensation will be magnified right now. Once I have teased her nipples I move the small pink vibrator down her stomach and over her mound. She's trying so hard not to move. "Good girl. Just relax."

When it touches her sensitive clit, it sends a pulse through her and she cries out. Just like I wanted her to. I take it off again. "You're not coming so soon lumiére." She huffs and I stifle a chuckle. "My sweet, Cassie. Always so eager for me." Time for the another sensation to send her reeling. I rise from the bed and grab the matches and strike one. She stills on the bed, not sure of what I am doing. I light the red candle on the nightstand and place the burnt out match next to it. "Do you trust me, lumiére?" She gives me a small nod. "Good girl." I sit on the bed next to her and trace feather light touches over her soft skin. Goose bumps rise in the wake of my touch. *Perfect, now you're ready*. I reach for the candle and when the hot wax drips over the rise of her breasts, her nipples pebble further.

"Luke!" Her cry is a plea, of pleasure rather than pain, the fine line between the two is ever present, but her body bucking to the sensation is testament that she's close to the edge. I watch the cooling wax on her skin. Goose bumps prickle on her smooth silky skin. When I pick up the remote control, I press play on the sound system, the slow melodic piano of Hurricane by Thirty Seconds to Mars starts.

"My gorgeous girl." I reach for the candle again, and drip wax down her soft stomach, stopping at the top of her bare little cunt. Its glistening with her arousal and I am aching to slide into her. "You like that, lumiére?"

"Yes, Sir."

I place the candle back on the night stand, the next few days will be difficult for both of us. Tonight I need to savor her. My lips pepper soft kisses on her nipples, feather light. Teasing. "Still, lumiére, keep still." As the song progresses, her breathing hastens and I see the pulse in her neck quicken. I pick up the crop and rise from the bed.

"Luke, please?"

"What do you need, baby?"

"I want..." She quietens, and I am worried I have hurt her. "you."

"Do you need to use your safe word?" She shakes her head in a quick movement. "Then what, Cassie?" The frustration in my voice is evident. I need to keep calm.

"Fuck me." Her voice is low as the song starts again.

I bring the crop down on her belly and her back arches. *Fuck she's beautiful.* I bring the crop down for a second time and her moans increase in volume. "Luke please?" Stroking the soft leather tip across her nipples, she gasps. The beautiful sight of her back arching off the bed is the most erotic thing I have ever seen. The pleasure on her face is making my control waiver.

"Soon my lumiére. You're so fucking beautiful."

This is insane, I need to be inside her. I drop the crop, and undo my pants, tugging my shirt off. I stand at the end of the bed, dropping my boxer briefs. When kneel between her spread legs, I plant soft kisses on her smooth skin, from her knees, up her thighs. Inhaling the sweet musky scent of her arousal. I flatten my tongue, and lap at her bare little cunt. "Oh God!" Her voice is raspy with desire when she cries out.

"Fuck your pussy tastes good, baby!" My voice a low growl. The lyrics wash over us as I feast on her. Sucking her clit into my mouth as she bucks and trembles under me. I slide two fingers inside her tight wet core. She's so hot inside, as her desire climbs, her pussy clenches around my fingers. Her orgasm is so close and I want her to come on my tongue, to taste those delectable juices. Fuck, I want to drink her in everyday of my life. My fingers set a relentless pace as plunge into her. "Come for me. Now." When I curl them, touching a sensitive spot inside her, it pushes her over the edge as she screams out her release.

No matter how many times that you told me you wanted to leave
No matter how many breaths that you took you still couldn't breathe
No matter how many nights did you lie wide awake to the sound of the poison rain

I need to be inside her, right now. Sliding up her body, I grip my steel shaft, it's so hard. I tease her entrance with the head of my cock. "Is my dirty little sub ready for my cock?"

"Yes!" She hisses through her clenched teeth. With one unrelenting drive I slam into her. "Fuck!!" Her cries magnify the lust inside me. The need to make her feel everything that I feel. All my emotions pour from me, into her. The anger, pain, anguish, and ultimately the pleasure. When the song reaches a crescendo, my body drives harder into her. Her hips buck up into me, accepting me, taking me.

No matter how many deaths that I die, I will never forget
No matter how many lives that I live, I will never regret
There is a fire inside of this heart and a riot about to explode into flames

I thrust into her, deeper and faster. "You're my love. My lumiére. I love you Cassie." I lower my body over hers, planting soft kisses on her lips and neck. My teeth nip at the sensitive spot behind her ear. I love how her body writhes under mine while my cock is buried deep inside her.
"Oh God, Luke!"
"Don't come baby, wait for me."

Oh, the quiet silences defines our misery
The riot inside keeps trying to visit me
No matter how we try, it's too much history
Too many bad notes playing in our symphony

My relentless pace pins her to the bed. She needs to see me; those chocolate eyes need to look into mine. I reach up and pull the blindfold off. Our gazes lock, the lust between us is palpable. She sucks in her bottom lip, biting down hard. I can't stop, there is no way I can slow down either. My release surging through me and I fuck her faster and faster. She closes her eyes and I growl. "Open your fucking eyes. Look at me!" She snaps her gaze up. Our eyes lock in a heated stare.

Do you really want me?
Do you really want me dead, or alive to torture for my sins?
Do you really want?
Do you really want me?
Do you really want me dead, or alive to live a lie?

"Come for me lumiére. Give me your light!" Both our bodies tense and her cunt clenches and tightens around me. Milking me for every drop of my seed. Her cries echo through the room as I call out her name. We still as we come down from that intense scene. I have never played out a scene like that before. Intense, but filled with real love, and emotion. Cassandra draws out my darkness, and instead of it being a danger to her, she revels in controlling it. She owns every part of me. When I look into her eyes, there is nothing I can't do or feel or be. "Fuck." I can't muster up anything else, but that one word. Nothing in the world can ever prepare me for sex with Cassie. As I slip out of her, I see her wince. "Did I hurt you?"

"No. You didn't…" A shy smile plays on her lips. I undo the ropes and flutter soft kisses on her ankles. When I inspect her making sure she isn't bruised from the strain, showing the same care for her wrists. As I flop onto the bed, I pull her into me. Spooning against her soft body.

"Are you okay baby? I wasn't too rough." Cassie rolls over to face me. She plants a chaste kiss on my lips. Her eyes are filled with something. *Love? Excitement? Desire?*

"That was incredible." A shy giggle erupts from her throat and I smile. My arms tighten around her, holding her so close she can feel my heart beat in my chest.

"My gorgeous girl."

"Yes, Sir." I groan in pain at her words. "What's wrong?" The concern in her voice is evident and I can only chuckle. She's so unaware of the effect she has on me.

"You make me hard when you say that." Another giggle, as we close our eyes. Pulling the soft satin sheet over us as sleep takes over.

Cassandra

I sat in the office staring into nothing. My mind whirled with the pain Lucien was going through. The funeral would be in a few days; all the arrangements were made. We were still both in shock, this situation was too surreal. The only good thing to come from this was that Lucien had not pushed me away. Quite the opposite, he had pulled me closer. He spent every waking moment with me. This being the exception when he had to be the powerful CEO. Since his father passing the board had to have meetings to decide on what the best way forward was. Lucien was named acting CEO until the annual meeting which was taking place in February. They would then vote, with the shareholders and only then would he become the official CEO. Since we were in November now, we had time to get all the paperwork to prove that Lucien knew the business better than any of the other directors vying for the role. Also, his dad was training him to take over once he had retired, which made Luke the obvious choice. There was no question about it.

I sat back and spun my chair to face the window. My office overlooked a beautiful park and in the distance the ocean looked angry in the glum grey light of the day. Rain fell in heavy sheets, and I shivered. "Cassie," I spun around to see Jayce. He looked exhausted, being Luke's best friend, he had been there through the whole ordeal. Dressed in a pair of familiar looking ripped Levi's and a grey hoodie, he stepped into my office and offered a small smile.

"Jay, what's up?" I made to get up when he shook his head.

"Don't, I need to show you something." He placed a folder on my desk. When I pick it up, I glance at him. The list is full of phone numbers I don't recognize, but there are photo's in the folder too.

"Fuck!" My eyes snap up to Jayce, his face confirms my suspicion. "We have to tell Luke. This could be something that might hinder him getting CEO. That bitch is going to try to take the company from him." I slam the folder shut, unable to bring myself to look at it anymore. The photo's show that Claudia was meeting with the Verán family lawyer not long before Luke's dad fell ill. This is evidence she must have had something to do with it. *Why else would she be meeting with the lawyer?* This is spiraling out of control.

"It's up to you Cass, he will lose it when he sees this. Is that a good idea before the meeting? It's only a few months away, but he needs to keep his wits about him." Jayce makes sense, but Luke needs to see this. He's up against this and he can't be alone. Next week will be the reading of the will and if Claudia had anything to do with it, I am sure she's got Mr. Verán to give her something. Anything. A feeling that something bad will happen takes hold of me, and I can't shake it.

"You're right Jayce, I don't want him blindsided."

"Who is blindsided?" Jayce spins around and my eyes dart to the door to find Lucien standing there with a quizzical look on his face. As he steps inside his eyes immediately fall to my desk and zero in on the folder. "What's that?" I glance down and pick up the manila folder. My eyes flit to Jayce as I hand it to Luke.

"Jayce brought it. There's been meetings between your family lawyer and Claudia." The temperature in the office is Arctic. Luke is radiating anger.

"She's fucking responsible. Who got this?" He turned on Jayce.

"The team we set up a few days ago. It's legit, Luke."

"I need to call him to find out what the hell she was doing there. Jesus Christ, this fucking woman is a bitch. Cass, baby, I am going up to my office, pack up here. We need to leave in an hour, I need to go to the house and get a few things from my dad's study." I nod. There wasn't a chance I could argue that I had work to do. "Jayce, can you come by my place later? We need to talk about what we will do. And if your sister is involved. I am not sparing anybody if they're working together. I have had enough shit to deal with." Lucien's eyes flit between me and Jayce, guilt tugs at my heart and mind.

"Yea, anything you need Luke." When Lucien closes my office door, I glance up at Jayce and I see the concern in his eyes, sky-blue shining with emotion. "I better go; I guess I will see you later?"

"Yes, I will be there." I offer a small smile. Watching him close my door, I pick up my phone and call Kenna. I needed her to be there tonight. There will be way too much tension.

"Cass, babe! How are you?"

"I am okay; are you busy tonight?"

"Unfortunately, yes. I have a late night we have an important show this weekend so I need to work. Why what do you need?"

I slump into my chair, trying to find the words.

"Well it looks like Claudia was meeting with Luke's dad's lawyer. Jayce and Luke will be at his apartment later and there is no question Luke wants me there."

"Ouch. Um, I will try to finish early, but I can't promise anything babe. I am sorry. Just stand between them, they both love you so they can't hurt you." The fact that she's trying to make light of the conversation makes me smile, but then her words sink in. She's right, Jayce looks at me the same way Lucien does.

"Kenna, that's not even a tiny bit funny." I admonish her. "Can't you distract Jayce? I mean he's really hot, and good in bed."

She chuckles on the other end of the line and I realize she's considering it when her reply isn't immediate. "I do think he's rather sexy. Maybe. Let me have a think about it. Good in bed you say?"

I nod. "Yes." I giggle at her gasp.

"I am sure I can tear him away for a while, a day, maybe more. How good? Does his cock hit the right spot? Like earth shattering?"

"Kenna!" She didn't have a filter sometimes, and that's why I love her.

"Ugh fine, don't tell me. I will find out for myself." Her giggle is obvious even though she's trying to hide it. "I better go; these idiots have no idea how to drape material. Call me later, Cass."

"I will. Don't work too hard."

"Not a chance in hell." She laughs and I hang up.

Lucien

I hit send on my last email and sit back, this will be a difficult time. The only thing keeping me sane as I prepare for my father's funeral was spending time with Cassie. The knock on my office door pulls me out of my thoughts. "Come in."

"Mr. Verán." Robert steps into my office. He walks around the office, and I watch him with confusion. With my head cocked to the side, I stare at him.

"Robert—" He silences me with a stare. I stand up, following Robert to the small bookshelf at the corner of the office. He points to the shelf and I see exactly what he's showing me. They can hear everything in the office. I should have known. So Claudia knows that Cassie's mom is alive. *Shit!* This will be a disaster if Claudia tells Cassie, I need to talk to her, explain everything.

I mouth, "follow me" to Robert and we make our way into the en suite bathroom. Once I have opened the tap and closed the door, I turn. "Robert, I need to get Cassie home."

"Yes sir, I will take her, but with the agreement in place with the lawyer, you need to make sure Claudia knows that you're sticking to it." The paperwork that's laying on my desk from the lawyer, states I need to be single to be named CEO. This is ridiculous. I can't lose Cassie. The worst part is the clause added by the bitch trying to take my father's company. It's a threat to everything I worked so hard to build, that once I am named CEO I am to marry Isabel.

"We need to find the original papers. Please, Robert."

"We will sir, trust me." I nod. Once we're back in the main office, Robert leaves and I stare out of the window. My mind is whirling with thoughts of everything they've heard so far.

I can't believe I have to do this. I hope she doesn't hate me. The pain my heart rips into me, leaving me breathless. This is more than I can bear right now. Cassie may never let me forget this. Robert will explain it. I know he will, but will she be able to stand by me through this? As soon as my office door opens, I realize it's show time. My back is to the door, but I can smell her perfume from where I am standing. The sweet scent of her lavender perfume fills my office.

"Luke?" I turn to face her, hoping she can see the pain that is so clearly etched on my face. I need her to see into my soul for the first time I am opening myself to her. "What's wrong?" Her voice trembles and I need to hold her.

"We have a problem." In two strides I am in front of her tugging her into my embrace. Her heart is racing, and I hope she can feel mine. "I love you so much darling. So much." My whisper is a plea for her to understand, if not now, once she walks out of the office.

She pushes back against me, when our eyes lock, I try to tell her how much I love her with a glance. "What is wrong? You left my office a few minutes ago." I can't meet her intense stare. The air is thick and I can't find the words to tell her what I need to. "Is it me? You can't deal with the fact I was with Jayce? It wasn't anything Luke. I love you. You're my soul mate, my other half."

"Cassie, stop." My tone comes out harsher than I expect. She doesn't understand, but I can't mess this up. I need Cassie safe. That's the only thing that matters.

"No, I will not stop. Do you not want me because I moved on when you pushed me away? You've done this before Luke. I am sorry about everything." Tears spill from her eyes and it takes all my fucking restraint to not pull her into me and hold her. "Lucien, you can't push me away, you said you love me. I was there when your father died Luke!" I grip her hips, my stare imploring her to understand. I mouth the word 'please', but she shakes her head.

"Cassandra, you need to go home. Robert will escort you." I lean in and whisper in her ear. "I don't want you alone right now. There will be a member of the team watching your apartment." Her pulse thrums against my lips. Before I lose control, I step away, with my back towards her. I take a deep steady breath. Cassie drops her bags on the chair and suddenly she's behind me. Her hand on my shoulder almost breaks all my resolve. She rounds on me, looking into my face. Steeling myself to her intense gaze, I need to keep emotion from showing. This needs to sound as real as possible.

"Does this have to do with the past? I told you all my secrets Luke." Her voice is so soft. I can barely hear her. I need her to leave, or this plan will not work. If they're listening, which I am sure they are, they need to hear that I am leaving Cassie. The bug is picking up every word. Before my resolve crumbles, I tell her to go.

"Cassandra, I suggest you leave now. I can't do this anymore. It's best that you forget about me. I can't give you what you want." As soon as the words leave my mouth, I turn to her, my eyes never meeting hers. I hope to God that she can see I am lying. My eyes rake over her face, the realization in her features calms me somewhat and I offer a small nod.

Cassandra

Under any other circumstances I would have believed his words, but at that exact moment I realized he was lying. The reason I knew that was because he wouldn't meet my gaze, not once. Lucien has never lied to me. He always looked into my eyes when he spoke. It made little sense for him to push me away after the last few days. This was a complete contradiction. I held on to the hope he wasn't looking at me because he was lying. I challenged him on it.

"You're lying, you don't even believe the shit you're spewing, so I suggest you look into my eyes and tell me that. If you can do that, then I will leave, and when I walk out, I will never come back." When he turns again my heart constricts. Sure I have just blown it when he shakes his head. He places a finger on my lips to silence me. Cocking my head to the side, I fix him with a questioning glare.

"Cassandra, like I said, you need to leave. Don't make this harder on yourself." A frown creases my brow, and he offers me a small smile. Turning to the desk he picks up a piece of paper and his fountain pen. In his neat script he writes the words *'Will explain later, trust me.'*

Those green eyes that disarm me every time finally lock on mine, he's hurting as much as I am. There is a flicker of pain in his eyes and I recognize a mix of emotion. When he reaches out, my anger fades, and he tugs me into his arms again, holding me close he plants a silent kiss on my head. A knock at the door startles me and Lucien steps back. "Come in."

"Mr. Verán, the car is ready to escort Ms. Winters back to her apartment." Something passes between the two men and now I am confused and intrigued. Robert needs to explain what's going on, or I might explode.

"Thank you Robert, she's ready. Goodbye, Cassandra." His eyes don't meet mine and his words hold nothing, no emotion. I turn to retrieve my bags from the chair and walk towards Robert. When my backward glance falls on the man I love, I realize that there is something wrong and I need to be strong. My decision is made when I see tears brim in his beautiful eyes. He's playing a game, but I will have the last word.

"Don't you dare come near me again." I spit the words at him and I can see his heart shattering into tiny pieces. The pain on his face makes me falter, and he shakes his head.

"Ms. Winters, we need to leave." Robert's voice pulls my gaze from the man I love and I follow him to the elevator. As soon as we step into the car and it descends, I round on Robert. I don't care if he works for Lucien. He will tell me what the hell is going on.

"What the fuck just happened?" His trained gaze falls on me and he shifts.

"Mr. Verán spoke with the lawyer. There is a clause in place to take the company from him. Certain conditions have been added to the new paperwork, that Lucien is to marry Isabel. We realize that this is Claudia's doing, since we know that she met with the lawyer on numerous occasions. The original will and testament is missing. We need to locate it before next week when the new one that the lawyer has, is read. We can push the reading out to January if we need more time, but there is another condition in place that Lucien has to be a single man before being named as CEO, if he is not, the role will fall to his step-mother. She will then retain control of Verán Industries." When Robert finishes the elevator has stopped at the basement parking and I am reeling. This was her plan all along, she wants me out of the picture, I still don't understand why she hates me so much.

"But, what was that in the office, why didn't he tell me?"

"The office is bugged. We need to play along for now. If they figure out we know, they might force our hand and push up the timeline. Lucien will lose control of his father's company. I will now escort you to the apartment, you will use the back entrance and wait for him there. Please do not leave at the front, there might be people watching the building." Robert opens the door and I slip inside. My head hurts and so does my heart.

I pull out my phone and see a message from Luke.

Most difficult thing I ever did. See you soon baby. Robert will explain. Love you forever

My heart soars and I realize that it was all an act. The only problem is, he was too convincing and even though I know he didn't mean it, my heart was still in shreds.

Robert pulls up to the apartment moments later and helps me into the apartment. It's so quiet and cold without Lucien here. My mind replaying what happened at the office. The first place I stop is the bar, grabbing a glass and pouring a whiskey, I down it in a quick gulp. The burn intensifies all the way down and I pour a second shot.

I hear the garage door opening and closing. Luke is home. I slip into the chair and wait, the two shots of whiskey I had, have my body buzzing in frustration and sadness at this whole situation we are forced into. "Baby?" His voice echoes through the penthouse.

"In here." I slip off the stool and walk towards the entrance. Luke scoops me in his arms

"I am so sorry, I had no time to warn you. It was the most devastating thing I have ever had to do. I am so fucking sorry baby." He seals my mouth with his and the pain and anguish wash away. His tongue licks along the seam of my lips, requesting entry and I give it to him. When my mouth opens, I tease his tongue with mine, earning the sexy growl I want. My fingers tangle in his messy hair, holding him against me, savoring him. His fingers stroke my spine, placing a hand at the small of my back, he presses my body into him. His arousal is evident as it pushes against my stomach.

Lucien breaks the kiss and stares into my eyes. "I need a drink and we need to sort this out." He rounds the bar, grabs a tumbler and pours a generous amount of whiskey for himself, then fills my glass. "Let's go to the living room gorgeous."

Once we're seated on the sofa, I cross my legs under me and face him. "So what happened?"

"Well, I spoke to the lawyer. He's got the paperwork in place for my step-mother to gain control of Verán Industries if I don't comply. I am supposed to be single the months leading up to the board meeting that will name me as CEO. Then," the gulp he takes of his whiskey makes me shudder, I know this is the worst part. "There is a clause, that I have to marry Isabel. If I don't Claudia will gain control of the company and be named CEO." His gaze falls on me again. "I know my father had a will drawn up which had none of this shit in it. So I need to find it. I have got Robert and his team working on it. Until they can find it, I basically need to appear single. The office is bugged that's why I had to say those things to you. I meant none of it."

"I see." Knocking back the whiskey, it burns on its way down and I am breathless for a moment. My thoughts are filled with what Luke has just told me. Why would anyone do this?

"Baby, I am not letting you go, we will just have to be discreet. Just until Robert can find the original will, I doubt it will take that long, but, I need you to know I am not letting you go ever." Lucien pulls me to him. He lifts me allowing me to straddle him. I cup his face in my hands and lean down, placing a kiss on his lips. His hands stroke my back in slow circles, calming me. My top is soon tugged from my pants and finds its way onto the floor. A low growl rumbles in his chest when he sees my sheer black lace bra. My nipples pebble against the soft fabric. With the pads of his thumbs, he teases them, tugging them gently, sending delicious waves of pleasure straight to my core. My head drops back, I close my eyes and a small whimper escapes my lips when his mouth comes down on them sucking them through the fabric into his warm mouth. "Luke, I need you, please?" I whisper. His fingers deftly unclasp my bra; he drops it on the floor along with my top.

"Stand, baby." I stand in front of him, his fingers undo the zipper of my pants and tugs them down. A wicked smirk curls his lips when he sees my sheer thong. "God, you're fucking beautiful." His thumbs grip my panties, and he shreds them from my body. He strokes my slick sex with the pad of his thumb. "I need you baby, I want to be inside you." I glance down into his green eyes and nod.

His fingers unbutton his shirt quickly, and he shrugs it off. He rises and his body is flush with mine. I hear his zipper and the shuffle of material. I can't tear my eyes away from his. Without looking, I reach out, and feel his hard cock, gripping it in my fist, stroking him up and down. His eyes darken with lust and I smile. "Hold on baby." He rasps. My hands grip his shoulders, his hands grab my ass, lifting me against him and I wrap my legs around his taut waist.

He turns and walks up the staircase into the bedroom, laying me on the bed, he kisses his way down my body. His hands press my inner thighs open, splaying me to his hungry gaze. I glance down and see his eyes shining with lust. His thumbs open my slick folds and his tongue is at my core. I watch his tongue laving me, his lips are glistening.

I am so turned on. "I love when you're open for me and so fucking wet." His words are laced with primal hunger. I cry out when his tongue slides into me, taunting my wet pussy. He continues his assault on me as my release coats his probing tongue. "Mmmm, like fucking honey." His voice is hoarse as he licks every drop I have to give him. "I love tasting your cunt, baby." He releases my thighs and sits back watching me with a hooded gaze.

"You want this baby?" His hand grasping his rigid erection is one of the most erotic things I have ever seen and words fail me. I watch him stroke it, and I buck my hips as an invitation to him. A deep chuckle rumbles in his chest and I watch his glistening lips curl into a sexy smirk. His lips glistening with my arousal has my body trembling.

"I need you, Mr. Verán." My voice a whisper.

"On your hands and knees." I roll over and kneel in front of him. Suddenly Lucien drives into me, and I cry out. Filled with the man who fits in me like no one else can or does. He stills inside me, allowing me to get used to the feel of him. "Look at me." Turning my gaze back, our eyes lock and I arch my back. His hips roll into me, pushing him deeper. When he slides almost all the way out, I whimper. He slams back in leaving me breathless.

"I love you, Lucien." My words falter when he drives in hitting the spot inside me that has my core tightening and I clench around him. His grip on my hips tighten.

"I love you, baby, I always will." He moves slower, the torturous movements keep me on edge and I need to find my release. I push back against him. "Slow baby. I love having you on my cock." His slow unrelenting drives are taking me to the precipice and I need to jump.

He reaches around, gripping my neck, and pulls me up against him. My back is flush with his chest. When his teeth tug at ear, my core tightens again, and he growls in response. "Come for me lumiére, give me your light." His growl in my ear shatters me as my orgasm surges through my body. Lucien stills inside me, but his grip doesn't relent. "Now, you're going to cum again, with me again."

His thrusts start again and this time they're fast and I know he's close. Placing soft wet kisses on my neck, his lips find the sweet spot behind my ear and he sucks my sensitive skin into his mouth. My back arches again, this time another orgasm is just out of my reach. "My lumiére, mine. Forever." He slams into me, "Come for me." He grunts as his body tenses behind me, my heated pussy tightens and my body spasms again as another orgasm splinters me and Lucien's hot release fills me. Nothing could have pulled us apart, the connection was tangible. The love I had for this man was dangerous, dark and all consuming.

In the quiet of the room, we lay in each other's arms. "Cassie, I am never letting you go. I want you to trust me. Saying those things to you ripped my soul apart. My love for you is all consuming." *Can he read my mind?* Our legs are intertwined and my head is on his chest, I hear the steady rhythm of his heart. I trace the tattoo that covers half his bicep, a large dragon. The intricate design is beautiful.

"I trust you with my heart and soul." Kissing the top of my head, his fingers stroke my arm and I shiver. I trace the lines of his sculpted body. He is so delicious. The toned muscles of his chest and stomach, smooth tanned skin. I dip my finger in the ridges of his v muscles, his breath hitches as I hit a spot on his v line that is particularly sensitive. "Are you ticklish, Mr. Verán?" I ask playfully. When I sit up and lean forward tracing the same spot with my tongue and his gaze becomes dark and dangerous. The mossy green shines with a mischievous glint.

"Ms. Winters, may I remind you, that you shouldn't tease me, there will be consequences." His playful smile is back and I giggle. Kneeling at his stomach, I trace my tongue along the ridges of his abs. My eyes lock on his and I see them darken. His erection hardening in response to my mouth, close, but just not where he needs it.

"I enjoy the consequences so much, Mr. Verán," smiling up at him as my tongue flicks over the tip of his cock. His arousal on my tongue, and I savor the taste. I grasp him in my hand and stroke him from base to tip, as I suck him into my mouth.

"Jesus, Cassie," his head drops back onto the pillow and his eyes close. He reaches down and his hands tangle in my hair, gripping and tugging, moving me deeper onto his cock. I swallow him till the tip of him hits the back of my throat. "Fuck, your mouth is amazing. Just like that baby, suck me deep. Take my cock into your throat, baby." His dirty words spur me on and I move faster, my need growing and I am soaked from pleasuring him. "Shit, Cassie, yes. I am close, if you don't want me to come you need to stop." He warns me, but I want to taste him. The ache inside me calls for him to fill my mouth with his come. A grunt of satisfaction emanates from him and he curses his release into my throat, "Fuck." I feel his hot seed coating my mouth and I swallow every drop. "My God woman, you will kill me." When he looks up at me again I notice the green has returned to normal and he has a sated smile on his lips.

As soon as I sit back we hear the elevator ping. "Fuck sake!" Groaning Lucien rises and plants a soft warm kiss on my lips. "You're a goddess." Tugging his briefs on, I giggle as he tries to rearrange himself inside the tight confines of the material. I get up and grab a pair of sweats, tugging them on along with a t-shirt. Lucien takes in my appearance and frowning that I am not wearing underwear.

"Luke!" Jayce is in the living room.

"Be right out!" Lucien winks. When his eyes widen and he whispers. "Your clothes are in the living room." He turns and makes for the door, rushing downstairs. The thought of Jayce sitting on the sofa where my bra and top are laying has a heated flush burning my cheeks. When Luke runs back into the bedroom carrying my clothes I release a sigh of relief. "He was at the bar." Smirking he leans in to kiss me again. "Meet us in the living room when you're properly dressed." Handing me a bra I notice that the T-shirt leaves little to the imagination.

"Yes, Sir." His eyes darken and a tingle shoots through me, heading straight for my core.

"You would do well to remember that baby." A playful swat on my ass has me quivering in all the right places as Luke leaves me in the bedroom.

Lucien

As soon as I leave Cassie in the bedroom I miss her. I find my best friend at my bar. "Jayce, did you find anything?" When he's eyes cut to mine, I know there's something in the paperwork he has that could get me out of this shit with Claudia.

"There's info here. Robert and Daniel dropped it off at the office. I was working late, but haven't went through it yet. Thought you would like to have the honor." I watch him pour another shot for himself, and raise an eyebrow.

"And that?" I gesture to him knocking back the whiskey like its water.

"Long day man."

"Why? Kenna not putting out?" I chuckle, but his stare is hard. *What the fuck?*

"Cassie upstairs?" His voice is strained. I nod. Then I see it. He still has feelings for her. *Well too fucking bad because she's mine.* I grab the bottle, pouring myself three fingers, picking up the folder and making my way into the living room. When I get comfortable on the sofa, I open the manila folder and spread the papers over the coffee table. "I'm sorry man." As my gaze falls on him, I see his expression.

"Don't mention it. Shit happens. She's taken."

"I know. There's no way I would come between you. Just don't hurt her again." My glare cuts to him and I fix him with a hard stare. I sit upright and wait for him to say more. When he doesn't, I sit back.

"Why do you think I would hurt her? She's mine, Jayce. I claimed her a long time ago." A small shrug tugs his shoulders and he drops it. I decid to let it go because I know it will turn into an argument. When I pick up the papers I have laid on the table, nothing more is said. We read through the information in silence. That's what we're like. A few words, everything in the gestures. He's looking out for Cassie, but with me, he needs to know he doesn't have to. My phone buzzes from my pocket, puling it out I see a message from an unknown number.

* *The old will isn't gone. I have a copy. We need to talk. Ms. W* *

My body is on high alert, and my heart is racing. Cassie's mother asked me not to tell her she's alive, but I can't keep something like this from her. She deserves to know the truth. Lies almost broke us apart last time. I glance at Jayce, but he's too absorbed in whatever he's reading to notice my dilemma. *Shit! What am I meant to do? I need that will.* One meeting. That's it. Then I can tell Cassie. I hit reply.

* *When and where?* *

"Fuck!" I am pulled from my thoughts by Jayce cursing so loud it echoes through the large room.

"What?" He hands me the sheet of paper and my eyes fall on the paragraph with the name of the one person who hates me more than anything. His sister. That fucking bitch, Sasha Alexander is definitely working with Claudia. *Why would she want me to marry someone else if she still wants me back?* None of this makes fucking sense. I am about to round on him when Cassie walks in looking incredible with my T-shirt and a pair of tight yoga pants. They're too tight, the curves of her legs and ass look incredible. It doesn't go unnoticed to me that Jayce's eyes drink her in a little too closely.

Cassandra

When I join the boys in the living room, they're both poring over documents. "Hey Jayce," when he glances up I notice him take in every inch of my appearance. *Well Cassie, this isn't awkward at all. I mean both the men who want you in the same room. What more could you want!*

"Cassie," he flashes me his panty dropping smile. *I wish Kenna was here right now.* I flop onto the sofa next to Lucien and glance at the paperwork he's looking through. They've got phone records and emails, everything pointing to Claudia, Isabel, and Sasha, but nothing incriminating enough. Nothing giving us a sign of where the original documents are.

"This is fucking insane. Why is your sister doing this?!" When Lucien chucks the papers back on the table, he turns and the frustration is evident on his face. "Baby, do you mind getting us a drink?" I shake my head and rise from the sofa, grabbing the two empty tumblers. Once I am at the bar, I grab the whiskey, pouring a double measure in each glass. My glance falls on the boys and there seems to be tension between them so thick, you could cut it with a knife. I was waiting for this. When I get back to the living room the air is thick.

"It's your sister Jay!" Luke hisses and I realize it's something to do with Sasha. I place the glasses on the table and sink back into the cushions of the sofa. "This is ridiculous, why the fuck is she doing this? I don't love her. She has to get over me not wanting her!" Luke's words are spat out with pure disgust and something flickers in Jayce's eyes. This is his sister. I realize it must hurt hearing someone talk like that about your family.

"Luke, I can't explain why my sister is doing this. I don't know. She knows you don't want her, it's obvious. It's been years since she's even talked about you." Jayce downs the whiskey in one gulp and rises. "I need to go." He walks up to the chair, grabbing his hoodie, he shrugs it on. "Cassie, have a good day. Luke." He walks out to the door. Before he can open it and walk out, I run up to him, I can't explain why but I needed to see if he was okay.

"Jayce, he's just tense. I mean he didn't mean to—"

"Cass, princess. Don't make excuses for him and you have no reason to look after me. It's my job to look after you remember. I will be okay." He offers me a cheeky wink and steps out, shutting the door behind him. The door closes, and his intense blue is gone.

Turning back to the living room I sink back into the cushions and glance at Lucien. "He loves you, I can see it." His voice is low. This will come up at some point, it might as well be now.

"He cares about me Luke, we're friends. There's nothing—"

"Cassandra, please don't, he loves you." When he fixes me with a stare, I can see the anguish marring his handsome face. *What does he want me to say?* I mean I love him. *Why can't he see that?* I am here with him. There is no one else I can or want to be with, Lucien is my forever, and he doesn't want to accept it.

"Well that's too fucking bad Lucien, because guess what, I am in love with you. And if you can't get that into your head then I have no fucking idea what else to say to you." I make to get up when he grabs my wrist, tugging me down. Before I have time to think, he is hovering over me and my body responds to him in the only way it always does. The heat knots in my stomach, travelling to the bundle of nerves between my thighs. The need for him never calms and I know it never will.

"Cassandra, do you think talking to me like that is respectful?" His stare is so intense, I tremble and a small whimper escapes my lips.

"No, Mr. Verán." The devilish smirk on his face deepens the dimples on his cheeks.

"And what pray tell do you think I should do to make you respect me, Ms. Winters?" His voice drops to a raspy whisper, his lips on my neck. My pulse skittering across his lips as they curl into a smile.

"I don't know, Mr. Verán, what would you like to do to me?" My voice a soft whisper.

"Right now, I would like to take you across my lap and mark that soft smooth ass of yours with my hand." The lust in his voice sends shivers over my body. My body squirming below him now, and his rigid erection is pushing into my stomach. With a smooth roll of his hips, he makes me fully aware of his cock. "See what you do to me, Cassandra?" I nod. "I asked you a question and I expect an answer." The rasp of his voice in my ear, and his teeth tugging at the lobe makes the butterflies in my stomach flutter.

"Yes, Sir." As soon as the word leaves my mouth, he shifts back and his hooded gaze meets mine. The wicked smile on his mouth shows the approval of me using the word.

"Come, I think you need to be shown exactly what happens when you talk to me like that." He stands before me, reaching his hand out and I slip mine in his. I can't help giggling when he tugs me up the stairs to the play room. "Get undressed. Leave your panties on." There is nowhere else I would rather be, giving him all of me, my body, heart and soul. This is what I want. As soon as the words leave his beautiful mouth, I obey the order. My fingers tug on my yoga pants and I slide them down, watching them pool at my ankles. I step out of them and place them on the small chair in the corner of the room. The T-shirt and bra joins them. I turn to face him, waiting on my next instruction. "Lay down, on your back. Close your eyes." He's standing at the chest of drawers that hold secrets I can only imagine, and some I can't. I crawl onto the large four poster bed and lay down. My eyes flutter closed in anticipation.

"Lift your head. And not a squeak from you." I lift my head and give a small nod. The soft fabric of the blindfold covers my eyes. Once it's secured Lucien rests my head back on the soft pillow. He continues to tie my ankles to the bedposts with the softest fabric I have ever felt. "Are you okay, baby?" I nod. "Good. What's your safe word?"

"Summer." A hint of a smile on my lips, the English translation of Lucien's last name.

"Good girl." The amusement in his voice is evident and I giggle. "Shh, baby."

The room goes quiet for a few moments and I wonder if he's left, but then shuffle of material grabs my attention. I realize he must have taken his top off. Then the rasp of the zipper of his jeans fills the room. The shuffle again and I am sure he's now naked. When the faint scratch of a match sounds, my senses are on high alert. I smell the lavender immediately. Then I recall the candles on the chest of drawers. The last time we played like this I came so hard. A soft thud of a heavy candle on the nightstand has me turning my head towards the sound.

"I want to watch you, baby. Touch yourself." I small gasp escapes my lips at his request. "Now." I run my hands over breasts, down my stomach. My compliancy has Lucien groaning in approval, my legs are spread and I know his gaze is raking over my body. The heat of it sizzles on my skin, goose bumps rise over every inch of my body. The intensity of me laying splayed for him makes me squirm.

My hand slips into my panties, I stroke myself. My fingers flick over the bundle of nerves throbbing under my touch. "That's it baby." I feel the cold blade against my hot skin as Lucien slices my panties from my body and I moan. His words fuel my confidence, I slide a finger into my heated pussy. His groan is low and sexy; his restraint is impeccable. "Fuck you're beautiful." My release tightens in my belly. "Stop." His command is dark and sexy, and I obey.

The bed shifts and there's a sound to my right. Lucien unties my ankles. "Turn over, on your hands and knees." I kneel on the bed, holding myself up on shaky arms. My body humming in anticipation. I was so close earlier. Lucien moves and then the soft leather of a paddle traces over my skin, its flat and feels big against my back. He traces a line along my spine. As he moves it down to my ass, goose bumps rise in its wake.

"Now, tell me Cassandra, do you like disrespecting me?"

"No, Sir." My voice is barely audible. My senses are on high alert and my core is dripping with desire. The paddle leaves my ass and I wait for it. The sting comes hard and my toes curl. My breathing hitches and the tingle left on my ass is indescribable.

"How many would you like, Cassandra?" His voice is low and as he growls my name, the ache of desire coils tighter. My blood is racing through my body, and I shiver.

"I don't know, sir."

"Six would suffice. Can you handle that?" I nod. Unable to speak because I know it would be a whisper. A swat comes down hard and I whimper and squeak. "Count." His voice is demanding, sexy, and guttural.

"One."

A second.

"Two." I whimper, but it's loud enough to keep him going.

Then a third.

"Three." I am sure I am having an out of body experience. Never have I ever been so turned on, the heat on my ass is stinging, but my body is thrumming with ache and need.

The fourth one stings and the knot in my stomach is wound so tight. My arms are shaking, and I don't think I can hold myself up for much longer. "Four." The fifth has my eyes rolling back in my head and I am close to the edge. So damn close and I know I can't come without his permission. "Five." I don't recognize my voice.

"Last one, are you ready baby?" My nod is quick.

The sixth one comes down, nipping at my exposed core and I cry out as my release shreds into me. He drops the paddle with a thud. The scent of the lavender candle somehow calms me. It wasn't meant to be dripped on me like last time. The room is filled with a euphoric mix of sex, lust and lavender.

He kneels behind me now. Something cold drips on my tingling ass and his hands massage the soothing cream into my heated skin. "You're such a good girl, Cassie. You look so beautiful, your skin marked with my paddle."

"Thank you, Sir." His hands are firm but his touch is gentle. The soothing cream eases the tingling. When his hand dips between my thighs I gasp. His finger stroking from my pussy up to my puckered hole. His touch has me wriggling against him. I push my ass back trying to get his fingers inside me.

"You look so fucking gorgeous wriggling for me." He leans down and whispers in my ear, "You're so fucking perfect Cassie, so wet and needy for me. Aren't you dirty girl?"

"Yesssss." A hiss escapes my lips and my legs open to him, hoping he will take me now.

"So eager, I can smell you, Cassandra. That sweet honey dripping from your cunt is intoxicating." His rude words never fail to make me gasp and I chew on my lip. The head of his cock is teasing my pussy and I push against him, but he moves back, keeping me on the edge. The teasing slow strokes up and down my bare lips sends me spiraling. He moves away and I whimper, and shamelessly spread my legs further hoping to entice him. When his mouth seals my entrance, I cry out pushing back, chasing my release that is just out of my reach. "Come for me." His tongue laps and flicks at my core, as he plunges two fingers inside me, and a sudden orgasm shatters me. My arms are shaking and I am struggling to hold myself up. A blinding white light explodes behind my eyelids as my pulse soars. His tongue rides out my orgasm as he savors the flavor of my arousal. "Do you want my cock inside your tight little cunt?"

"Please, Lucien? Please, yes, fuck me?" I beg him. I need him more than I need my next breath. The bed dips and he has left me again. Lucien pulls the blindfold off and I blink in the sudden brightness of the room. "Get up, baby." His voice is strained. When I move the sting on my ass is still present. I slip my hand in his offered one and we walk over to a chair near the full length mirror. Lucien sits down and pulls me to him. "Now, will you disrespect me again, Cassandra?"

"No, Sir." His smile is devilish. The dimples and his sparkling eyes are ever present making my pulse race. "Sit on me baby." He turns me around as I straddle him, my back to his chest. I can see us in the mirror, watching him slide inside me is erotic.

"You're so fucking tight; I love being inside you." When he moves his hips, I moan. His grip on my hips is vice-like, he moves me up and down slowly. He's so deep, stretching me open wide. I am so full. Nothing comes close to what he's making me feel. "Touch yourself, baby. I want to watch." My hand moves down between my legs where we're joined and I strum the pulsing bundle of nerves, bringing myself closer to another intense release. My head falls back and my eyes close in pleasure.

"Open your eyes. Watch. I want you to see me inside you." I bring my head back up and our eyes lock, his hooded gaze darkens, the green of his eyes are black with lust. "Come for me, my lumiére, give everything to me." Laying claim to my body, heart, mind and soul, Lucien stills inside me as my core clenches around him. "That's it baby, every fucking part of you, I own." My orgasm tightens every muscle of my body as is shreds me. I am at breaking point as tears roll down my cheeks, from the pure intense pleasure. He drives in again, with a growl as his own release fills me with warmth. He watches every second of my release with a satisfied smile on his lips. When our breathing returns to normal, his voice is laced with concern. "Are you okay baby? I didn't hurt you did I?" I smile at his reflection in the mirror completely sated.

"No, not even one bit. That was…" I can't form a coherent sentence that will explain what I am feeling for him right now. The thought of what's hanging over our heads brings me crashing down and more tears slip from my eyes.

"Cassie? Baby, what's wrong?" He slips from me and I wince. I hate not having him inside my body. When he scoops me up, he carries me to the bed and lays me down gently. Our bodies so close, it's like we're one person. Our connection is so deep; I believe nothing will tear us apart, but deep down the fear still haunts me. Tears fall now, and he wipes my cheeks with the pads of his thumbs and pulls me into his embrace. The gentle thump of his heart lulls me and I take a deep breath.

"This situation, it's so fucked up. I am hiding here because of some stupid fucking clause on a piece of paper." When I glance up at him, I see the anguish on his face.

"I love you, we will find a way past this. That is my vow to you. There will never be a day where we are apart again." His promise makes my heart flutter. I just hope that things will work out.

Cassandra

"Jayce, please can you get this for me?" I turn and am met with big blue eyes staring up at me in amusement. "Stop being a douche! Help me!" It's two weeks to Christmas, and I have spent most of my time at my apartment. The lawyer has given Lucien the paperwork and, they have postponed the reading of the last will and testament to early January. Since the holidays are here, we've been sneaking time with each other. It's been a week since that incredible day we spent in the play room and I am aching for Lucien in so many ways. I crave him with such a deep intensity, it hurts, and it kills me not seeing him.

"Okay, okay. What time is Luke supposed to get here?" His playfulness disappearing.

"He said he would come after a late meeting with Robert and the team. I am not sure how he will feel seeing you here. You guys have to seriously stop fighting."

"Well, it's difficult since we're both so hot headed." I spin to face him when my footing slips and I fall back. Jayce's arms reach out and he catches me bridal style. Just then my patio door opens and I glance into green eyes that turn me into a burning ball of need. I scramble out of Jayce's embrace, mumbling a thank you. I make my way to Luke. His steely glare is trained behind me, directly at Jayce and I realize this could go either way. I need to calm him down. "Luke, baby. Look at me." I cup his face and pull him to me. Leaning up on my tip toes, I planted a kiss on his lips. The tension releases from his body and he wraps his arms around my waist, and tugs me into him. "What are you doing here? You said you would be late." I mumble into his shirt.

"I left the office early. The meeting was postponed, and I needed to see you." We step inside and Jayce offers a hand to Luke. "Alexander. Can you for one moment keep your hands off her?" The tone of his voice is dangerous and I shiver.

"She fell, Luke. What did you want me to do, drop her?" I tug on Lucien's hand. *Cassie, you need to get them to relax. It's like a battle of fucking testosterone in here.*

"If you both would like to be left alone, I can leave, but this will not work if you're both going to be stubborn. Luke, I love you. Jayce knows that. Just come and sit down. I will get you a drink." He nods and flops into the sofa.

"So what happened? Is there any news about the missing will?" I place a drink in front of Luke and hand one to Jayce. As the door swings open we all turn to Kenna.

"Hey guys, sorry if I interrupted your little ménage à trois." She giggles and I cringe at her choice of words, fixing her with a glare. She and Jayce have been on and off seeing each other. "What? Oh, there was an envelope in the mailbox." I shake my head and grab the mail from her. She's always been one to say what's on her mind. I rip open the silver envelope which looks like an invitation. My eyes skim over the card and bile rises into my throat.

If you don't go away, everyone will know what a murderer you really are. You have until midnight of the Verán Industries Christmas Ball to leave.

I am shaking like a leaf. Kenna grabs the card from me and her eyes immediately dart from Luke to Jayce. They're at my side in an instant.

"Kenna what the fuck does it say?" Lucien's voice is demanding as he gently strokes my arm. She hands him the square silver card, once he's read it, Luke stiffens beside me. "Fuck, this is ridiculous!" Pulling his phone from his pocket, I watch his fingers fly over the keys. He holds the phone to his ear, pacing back and forth. "Robert, I need you at Cassie's apartment. ASAP."

He hangs up and pulls me into an embrace so tight that squeezes the breath out of me. "This is my fucking fault. I am so sorry baby." I try to shake my head, but he's holding me too tight, and I can't move. Jayce and Kenna fall silent and leave us, heading into the kitchen. The sound of glasses clinking filters into the living room and I hope they're pouring me a large one. God knows I need it right now.

"Luke, I can't do this. Maybe if I left for a while. I am not strong enough to do this." My eyes cut up to him, a million emotions run over his face, but pain is the most evident of them all.

"Me losing you is not an option, Cassie. I am not giving up. Let's just wait till Robert gets here?" I nod and lay my head back on his chest. The only thing that is even remotely calming me right now is his heartbeat.

"Guys, I have an idea, Kenna is coming with me. We will be back in a while." I nod. Jayce and Kenna make a hasty retreat. I am not sure what they're up to, but knowing Kenna it can't be good. She's always had my back and this must have got to her. She knows that my past was difficult, and this could be a potential step back from my healing process.

"I wonder where they went." Lucien releases his tight hold on me and I pick up the squat tumbler. I take a big gulp of the alcohol. It burns its way down.

"Jayce said he might get information from Sasha. I highly doubt it though since she's working with Claudia. I need to get into the house, but the bitch hasn't left." My mind clouds and a thought pops into my mind. Luke will not like it, but I think it may work.

"What if I went to her?" When his eyes meet mine, the answer is no. The idea was bad, but there was no other way. I didn't see another way out of this.

"No fucking way! There is no way I am letting you go near her!" His phone buzzes interrupting the conversation. "Verán," he listens and motions for me to open the door. As soon as I do, Robert walks in He has two men with him. One I recognize, but the other one is a stranger to me. They looked like they could kill someone with a mere glance.

"Ms. Winters." Robert gives me a small nod and I smile. Actually, it might have been more of a grimace. "Mr. Verán, we're at your disposal, you know Daniel. This is Brax. How can we help?" His glance flitted to me.

"Cassandra will stay. She can answer any questions about the envelope. She's the target. Besides myself, which isn't important. I need her safe." The man called Brax glances at me, and I feel uncomfortable under his scrutinizing gaze. "This was delivered today." Lucien hands the envelope to Robert and they huddle around it. Robert glances at me and I can see the emotion in his face. For the first time since I met this man the concern is written in his features.

"Ms. Winters, can I speak with you?" Robert ushers me aside and Lucien gives me a small nod. He trusts Robert with his life, so I trust him too. "Is this about the incident when you were younger? After your parents… accident?" His consideration for my feelings as he speaks makes me warm to him. He always seems so serious, his gentle side is refreshing. I smile and nod.

"Yes, I am not sure how they found out about it, but this is the second time I have received a note, other than the calls I have been getting." His eyes grow in surprise.

"Where did they contact you?"

"At the office."

"Not your personal cellphone?" I shake my head.

"This is kids play, I promise you that my team will figure this out, Ms. Winters." With a slight nod, Robert and two other men leave, with the note. Suddenly the apartment looks sparse without their large looming frames.

"Baby?" I turn and my gaze falls onto green eyes that are filled with concern. "Are you okay?"

Not being able to meet his intense stare, I walk into the kitchen to turn on the kettle. "Cup?" He nods and leans against the counter watching me.

"Baby, come stay with me?" I spin around and stare at him. He knows we're not even meant to be talking to each other, now he wants me to live with him?

"No, Lucien, you could lose your father's company. I will not be the cause of it."

"Nobody will find you there, we can get Robert to help with a decoy if you're worried about that. I don't want you here, sweetness. And that's final." With his serious expression, it will be impossible to argue with him. Why is it that a man ordering me around makes me want to jump him?

"Can I stay here till Saturday?" It's three days and he might not agree, but I am letting him control this and he should allow me a few days. "Kenna will be here and Saturday we can have the decoy set up and it would make more sense." A slow smirk curls his lips and I frown. "What?"

"You're adorable when you ramble. That's fine, I will get everything in place and then you're coming home with me. Even if I have to throw you over my shoulder." There is a playful jilt to his voice and I giggle.

"Don't be such a Neanderthal!" I admonish, handing him the mug of coffee. A mischievous glint in his eyes warns me that he has taken that as a challenge.

"You have no idea Ms. Winters. I intend spending my life showing you though." When I glance at him, I see a serious expression on his handsome face. We've never spoken about marriage or our future. My heart leaps into my throat and I try to swallow it the emotion that have taken hold.

"Lucien, let's try to get through the next two months, then we can discuss what the future holds." I sip my coffee hoping it would steady my trembling hands.

"There's nothing to discuss Cassandra, I want you in my life." He shrugs and turns to the living room, leaving me in the kitchen reeling, and smiling at his words.

"Lucien you can't just say something like that and walk away. What do you plan to do, drag me to your cave and tie me up so I can't leave?" His eyes darken at my words and I flush at the hungry look he's giving me.

"Well, I would love to tie you up, but trust me, you wouldn't want to leave once I am done with you, sweetness. I would have you writhing on my bed, your body trembling like a leaf in a storm. Make no mistake, that you will beg to stay. You've not complained so far." Giving me a panty dropping smile with his dimples teasing their way onto his cheeks, he flops onto the sofa. Needless to say that I am left standing in shock at his words, with an ache pulsing between my thighs. I am about to retort when the door flies open and Jayce and Kenna come tumbling in. They're both giggling and when we turn our attention to them I notice Kenna's face is flushed. Somehow I doubt it's the cold weather outside.

"Luke, we need to go. There wasn't anything at Sasha's place, but I have another idea. I need your help." Lucien nods. Kenna drags Jayce off into the kitchen.

"Baby, I will call you later." Lucien pulls me into an embrace. When his lips touch mine, the world feels like it will be okay. Our kiss deepens as his tongue dances with mine, and I press my body against his. We won't see each other for at least another three days and I feel like a part of me will walk out that door with him. When he pulls away, I am left breathless from his words and his lips. "Three days!" His stare is adamant. I don't have a choice.

"Okay, I said three days and I will be there." I glance into his green eyes.

When he leans in and whispers, "Good, then I am tying you up and you're never leaving." A naughty glint flickers in his eyes and heat pools in my panties.

"Come on dude!" We turn to Jayce and Kenna. They look like they've been up to something I would rather not know about. Her face is about the same color as a tomato.

Lucien

"So what was the big plan?" I turn to Jayce as soon as we're in his black Jeep. He pulls out into the evening traffic before answering me.

"I thought about something, it's perfect, it will work out perfectly." His eyes cutting a quick glance to me, I stare at him incredulously.

"What? And you didn't tell us?"

"Just listen. You need to let Cassie see Claudia. She's counting on it. There's an ultimatum on the cards, Claudia is going to have to tell Cass exactly what it is. She doesn't know that we know. Right?" I nod. None of it is making much sense right now and I hope to God he has a point.

"So, let her play into our plan. By giving Cass that ultimatum is proof enough that Claudia knows she's on a deadline. Maybe Cassie can get her to spill where the original documents are. If not, Robert will find the paperwork. Then on the evening of the ball, you call her out, in front of everyone. We just need the evidence." His eyes are ablaze with excitement and I can tell he's thought this through even though we don't have a leg to stand on.

"What if it doesn't work?" I remember the message from Cassie's mother. As soon as I am home I need to call her and set up a time to meet. She said she has a copy of the will. *How?* Nothing that my father said in past conversation comes to mind.

"It will, just trust me." Jayce pulls up to my apartment, before I get out of the car, I cut a glance at Jayce. I trust him. He's my best friend, I am just shit scared this is going to blow up in our faces.

"I do. You know that." He nods, but there is still an underlying tension between us. One we need to sort out at some point. Tonight though. I can't. Making my way inside, I grab my phone and find the number I saved under a random contact.

Your daughter needs you. Can you meet me tomorrow?

I don't wait long for her reply.

I know. Tomorrow midday. Santa Monica Pier.

It's a long way from the office which is why I reply that I will see her there. I need to sort this out. Something still doesn't add up. *Why would she have a copy of my father's will?* I make my way to my bedroom, pulling off my shirt and pants. Grabbing my sweats, I pull them on, contemplating a run, but I am drained. Exhausted. This shit needs to end. I need my girl here and I can't even do that. I want her here, I need her kneeling in front of me with her lips around my cock. *Fuck it! I need her now.*
Maybe I should go to her? No. I can't risk it. I need to relax. She's with Kenna, at least I know she's safe. As soon as I walk back to the living room, I make my way to the bar, grabbing a glass I pour a whiskey. I flop down on my sofa, and turn on the sound system. Flicking through my play lists, as soon as I hear the song I want, I sit back.

Look at me
I'm not the man I used to be
When she smiles at me
I live the light I used to see

There she goes and I know
On my own, I'm not whole
Can't believe, she can't see
That she's taken the best part of me

I'm half a man with half a heart
With nothing left to tear apart
Half of me is walking 'round
The other half is on the ground
She mends me

I picture her, as always, she haunts every part of my mind, heart and soul. *How am I meant to live without her?* I can't think that way. We will get through this. Some way. If Cassandra's mother has the information I need, and if the lawyer will accept it, this will be over soon. This plan of Jay's better work. I hope he's right, because if I have to lose my father's company to be with her then so be it. But there is no way I am going down without a fight. That bitch, Claudia, will regret the day she walked into my life. I will make sure of it.
Fuck this, I can't do it, I need to speak to my girl.

Cassandra

Once Jayce and Lucien left, I round on Kenna. "You need to tell me what's going on." Her giggle confirms it. "You and Jayce?" She nods.
"I hope it will not be weird for you?"
"No, it won't. Jayce and I were just a fling. Nothing serious. The fact that he's

moved on is good. As long as you're happy. I need to go pack, Luke wants me to move in with him until this shit is sorted." I turn to my room, with Kenna hot on my heels.

"You're moving in?" She screeches. I nod, as I pull my suitcase from the closet. As soon as I set it on the bed, I unzip it. When I glance over at Kenna, I can see she's dying to ask me something.

"What?" I stop what I am doing and face her. Crossing my arms over my chest, I realize it's a sign of defense, but I don't feel like discussing Luke and me right now. Things are not ideal, but it's not like I am moving in permanently, he's just trying to keep me safe.

"Moving in is a big step and after everything that's happened babe, are you sure you want to?" When I flop on the bed, I lay back and stare at the ceiling.

"I do Kenna. Losing him again is not an option for me. We need to be together forever. There is no way I can live without him." I turn to face her and I see her smile. She always understands me before I even understand myself.

"Babe, I realize that, I just want you to be happy and he makes you happy, I can see it in your eyes. The way he looks at you is something I have never had." She's quiet as she stares at me. I know she's trying to assess my feelings. "He's your one isn't he?" I nod, tears threaten to spill, but I blink them back. *I am in love. He is the man I want to spend my forever with. I can't imagine my life without him. You're happy Cassie, roll with it!*

"He is, there's something inside him that fixes me. And I think I do the same to him. When we're apart it's like I am ripped in half. You know?" I glance at her, but she doesn't understand, she's never been in love. I remember even when we were younger, she always enjoyed being free, single. Like Jayce.

"Then go for it. I spent too much time sitting by and waiting for you to start finding love again, you're like my sister and I don't want to see you hurt again. Although, I don't think he will hurt you. He seems too fucking obsessed with you. Broken by desire, fixed by love. Now that sounds like a love song." I roll my eyes and we giggle. When my eyes meet hers, she smiles and I can see she's happy for me.

"Right, and you're so happy I am broken?"

"Nope, happy he fixed you, even if it was with his cock." I gasp at her brazen words and launch a pillow at her head. "Hey! I was only stating the obvious." We explode into fits of giggles.

"You're crazy you know that!" Sitting up, I stare at the empty suitcase. I realize nothing can prepare me for moving in with Lucien.

"That's why we're friends, we understand each other. Come we will have a few drinks. I think a girls' night is needed." She jumps up and stands in the doorway. Her questioning gaze on me.

"Fine, you pour the wine, I will pack. We can drink in here." I giggle when she gives me an incredulous smirk. "What?"

"You are so in love aren't you?" I smile and nod. "Finally! Took you long enough. Now it's time for wine!" Kenna leaves me to pack. My phone buzzes next to me, grabbing it I swipe the screen and see a message from Lucien.

* I miss you already. Wish you were here, what are you doing? *

I hit reply.

* I am packing actually, my boyfriend asked me to move in with him *

Turning to my closet, I grab a few pairs of sweats, tops and a few outfits for work. I wonder if he will forbid me to go to work as well. Shaking my head at the dominating man who's stolen my heart. My suitcase is almost full when my phone buzzes again.

Really? He's a lucky bastard. I hope you're packing sexy lingerie

I giggle and hit reply. "Are you two sexting?" When I spin around Kenna is watching me with a shrewd stare and I blush. "OMG you two definitely need an island to yourselves." Her laugh is infectious and I poke my tongue at her.

"Don't be jealous." I retort.

"Yea, I wonder if Jayce is up for a session of text teasing." She looks thoughtful and smirks.

"Ugh, Kenna, TMI babe, please?" This is something I missed, time with my best friend. "I missed you, babe, sorry I have been so wrapped up in Luke." Turning to her, I grab her in a tight embrace.

"Seriously, Cass, I am just glad to see you're getting some and it's made you less of a grumpy bitch." I know she's teasing, but I swat her arm. "Hey! You were grumpy. You do realize that if you don't get any you turn into a devil woman."

"So do you. Just by the way." She hands me a glass, and I take a gulp of wine, when my phone buzzes again.

Sweetness? Did you get lost in your lingerie drawer?

Giggling at his message, I hit reply.

No, I was talking to Kenna. And I will think about including lingerie in my packing

"Okay, so tell me. Do you think Luke will ever propose?" My gaze shoots up and I frown. Do I want him to? Yes, I do. I really want that with him, to share forever with him, but does he want it to?

"To be honest, I have no idea. I mean, he's been through so much. It's also very soon. We've only been together for a few months, well technically, we broke up for two months in between. I mean—"

"Don't make excuses, I can see you want it Cass." Lucien's next message interrupts us.

Lingerie is optional. I prefer you naked, tied up, and blindfolded anyway. There is nothing I want more than to wake up next to you.

I can't help the blush on my face from his text. "There is no doubt that I want it Kenna." The words leave my mouth as I stare at his message. I do want to wake up next to him, forever. "This… I don't even know what to call it, I mean it seems like every time we make progress we get pushed back and it's exhausting." Kenna flops onto the bed next to my full suitcase. Before she answers my phone rings. "Hello?"

"I wondered if you had forgotten about me already." Lucien's tone is playful and I smile.

"With a glass of wine and my best friend, the only thing missing is you." I glance at

Kenna and she's making gagging noises.

"Tell Kenna to behave. Doesn't she have Jayce to go flirt with?" I giggle.

"Luke says you should go and flirt with Jay." Her head drops back and she laughs out loud.

"Tell him not to order me around, if he's stealing you I deserve a few days." Before I can relay her message Luke answers.

"Okay, okay. I will call you later. Message me when you're in bed. Okay babe?"

"Yes. I will. Chat later."

"I love you."

"And I love you." I hang up before he can respond because I know we will end up on the phone for another hour. Not that I mind, but I need time with Kenna.

"You two, are seriously whipped. It's adorable." She holds up her empty glass, beckoning me to finish mine. Gulping the last of the chilled Chardonnay, I hand my glass to her.

"Are you trying to get me drunk?"

"Nope, just tipsy enough to tell me all about Jayce." I follow her to the living room.

"What do you want to know about him?"

"Well, you know him better than I do. What is he like?"

"Is this a test? You want to see if I have feelings for him?" Crossing my arms over my chest, I watch her reaction and it's obvious that is what she's up to. I don't blame her. She turns and nods. "Okay, well, he's sweet, he can be very romantic, and he's definitely good in bed." The words leave my lips and I grin. I have to be honest and that was it. I couldn't deny the fact that he definitely was an amazing lover.

"See, was that so hard? It's not weird, so stop acting like it is." Handing me the topped up glass, she winks and I relax. "Now, let's talk about you and Luke, if you're living together surely it's a lot more serious than you're letting on?"

I nod, "I guess so, I mean things are all kinds of fucked up right now." I grab the remote and press play. My Luke play list starts and I smile. I created it when we first met, it's kind of like my mixed tape. I turn back to Kenna. "When he found out I didn't tell him about my miscarriage he totally flipped. I understand why. There is a lot we needed to learn about each other. We're both completely fucking broken, Kenna. His past is almost as dark as mine if not more." My eyes glaze over from staring at the floor. I can't meet her eyes. There are so many things I can't tell her about him.

"Cass, do you trust him? I mean, that he won't hurt you. Physically."

"No! He wouldn't! I trust him with all I have. Yes, he is a lot more than I am use to. There is something in his control, his dominance that I love. He fills an empty space inside me that no one else ever could, like I am whole again. It's like he takes those shattered fragments of me and glues them together." I smile at the way my heart pounds when he's near. My body instinctively aches for him in ways I have never known, but that's for my mind only.

"So he's the whips and chains kind of guy?" My gaze flits up to her and my eyes are as wide as dinner plates. "Oh come off it, I am not a virgin!" I giggle and my thoughts drift to Luke and the play room. "Okay, get your mind out of the gutter, I know you're thinking about his cock." Sometimes Kenna can be so direct, I am blushing from being caught.

"Shhh! Do you have to be so vulgar?"

"It's the truth!"

"I know," fits of giggles ensue and soon it feels like old times. I am happy, despite everything that's going on right now, life seems to be okay. This time it's Kenna's phone that buzzes, as soon as she opens the message there's a smile on her face that makes it obvious who it is. "Call him! I am going to head to bed." Getting up I give her a hug and head to the kitchen. I fill the kettle, and turn it on. My mind is wrapped up in images of Lucien and me. The thought of marrying him has now been ingrained in my head and I can't help, but imagine it. If only we could get past these threats. A cup of chai tea is what I need, and a call to my sexy domineering man. Who knew I would want someone that loved tying me to his bed, pouring hot wax on my body. The thought of those moments have my nipples pebbled and I can't help the heat between my thighs.

When I make my way to my bedroom with my tea, I close the door. I set the suitcase on the floor, I change into my shorts and tank top. Sliding into bed, I pick up my phone. Luke's number is first, and I hit dial.

"Sweetness, I thought you would never call."

"Mr. Verán, I was wondering what you were doing?"

"I am sitting in my office, working on some documents for my meeting tomorrow. What are you doing baby?"

"I am laying on my bed." Taking a sip of the warm tea soothes my nerves. I haven't ever really spoken to Luke for any amount of time like this, we're normally together, and hearing his deep raspy voice makes me miss him more.

"The perfect place for you, bed. Tell me what you're wearing?" He's definitely not thinking about paperwork at the moment.

"I am wearing a pair of shorts and a tank top, Mr. Verán." I giggle when I hear his sharp intake of breath and I know there is no way in hell I won't get a spanking for teasing him.

"What's under those shorts, sweetness?" Heat prickles over my skin and heat flushes my cheeks.

"Nothing." My answer is barely audible and I hear his breathing become harsher and heavier on the other end of the line. Grabbing the remote next to my bed, I turn on the sound system and the voices of Little Mix, the song Secret Love Song fills the quiet of the dimly lit bedroom.

"Cassandra, you do realize what you've just done to me?" Lucien's voice is low and the growl that follow his words tell me exactly what he means and my body hums with desire.

"No, why don't you tell me?" My voice is low.

"You've made my cock rock hard. What do you intend doing about it, Cassandra?" Electricity shoots through me. My nipples are hard against the soft cotton of my tank top and I imagine Lucien's expert mouth teasing me.

"Would you like me on my knees in front of you, Sir? My mouth open ready to take you into my throat? To swallow every inch of you." I blush furiously at my brazen words, I have always been shy about talking dirty, but Lucien makes me do things that take me from my comfort zone into unknown amazing places.

A deep growl from him tells me that he would very much like me on my knees in front of him. "You're such a dirty girl for me, Cassandra. Put your hand inside your shorts. Stroke that sweet bare cunt for me." I whimper as I obey his order and find myself slick. "Is my girl wet?"

"Mmhmmm." Words fail me as my eyes flutter closed and I imagine Lucien stroking me.

"Good, I have my cock in my hand. I wish I was sliding into that beautiful dirty mouth of yours." A moan escapes my lips and I slide my fingers inside my heated core. "Are you fingering your tight pussy for me, Cassandra?"

"Yes, Sir." My whisper a soft moan.

"I love your sounds. They're so beautiful, just like you my sweetness. I want to slide into your tight heat so badly right now. I want to bend you over my desk, rip off those tiny shorts. I bet they're soaked with honey, aren't they, Cassandra?" His words have my body shuddering, so close to the edge.

"Lucien…"

"Yes, baby, that's it, feel my hard cock fucking you deep. Come for me, Cassandra." His words send me to my release. My body trembling as waves of pleasure rip through me. He's quiet for a while as I ride out my orgasm. "Fuck it. I can't do this. Don't go to sleep."

Without another word I hear the line go dead. I open my eyes and I realize he's hung up on me. *What the fuck? That was so freaking strange!* I get up and make my way to the bathroom. My legs are still shaky from the orgasm. I brush my teeth and take in my appearance in the mirror. My cheeks are flushed and a giggle escapes, I can't believe I just did that. Butterflies flip flop in my stomach.

When I walk into the bedroom, I slip under the covers and grab my phone. No message from Luke. I wonder what happened to him. He said not to go to sleep, but what am I supposed to do? He just left me like that. I hear muffled voices in the living room and suddenly my door flies open. With a startled gasp I glance into Lucien's olive green eyes. "Luke!"

He closes the door, and steps into the room. His body is over me in seconds. "I needed to be inside you." Before I have a chance to respond his mouth is over mine, sealing it with a deep luscious kiss and I moan, arching my body into him. Our tongues tangle and I suck his into my mouth, tasting him, sweet and spicy and so damn good. Just Lucien. His fingers dance across my collarbone and up to my neck, teasing feather light touches to the spot behind my ear and my body hums with pleasure. "You made me rock hard, sweetness. I couldn't not be inside you." He says when he finally pulls away.

"So you decided to drive to my apartment at… What is it? Midnight?" I giggle at the incredulous look on his face.

"Did you expect me to sleep with a hard on?" His teeth tug on my earlobe sending sweet shivers down my spine, goose bumps rise over my skin and I whimper, pressing myself into him again. "I needed that hot tight pussy to sheath me, then I want to come inside you deep and hard." The rasp in his voice turns me into a mess of molten lava.

"Please Luke?" His eyes meet mine and a sexy smile curves his lips. He kneels up on the bed, pulling his T-shirt off and I glance down, noticing the straining bulge behind his zipper.

"Yes, Cassandra, this is what I had to sit with all the way to your apartment." He answers my question without me asking. Lucien pushes up off the bed, he unzips his jeans and tugs them down along with his boxer briefs. His impressive erection is standing proud and I can't wait to have him inside me. He leans over to tug my shorts down my thighs, licking his lips when he takes in my bare pussy.

"You look good enough to eat, but that's for later, right now I want to fuck you." In an instant Lucien is hovering over me and his cock is at my core, teasing me relentlessly. My hips raise to meet his, he plunges into me deep and hard, leaving me breathless.

254

"Fuck, your pussy is so tight sweetness!"

My legs lock around Lucien's taut waist. I pull him into me. My back arches. With every deep drive into me, I whimper. My core clenches around him. "That's my gorgeous girl. Come for me lumiére, I want to own you, possess you." His teeth graze my neck as my release renders me speechless. My heated tunnel cinches around him and I writhe below the only man who could ever make me whole. Lucien stills inside me and watches with a look of adoration in his eyes. "You are fucking beautiful when you're under me, coming on my cock." His movements are slow and steady, making me climb higher and higher.

"I love you Lucien." My words are strangled.

"I love you my lumiére." He moves inside me faster and deeper. "I want you forever." His words crash over me as he slams into me. He drives in to the hilt, sending me to the edge of another earth shattering orgasm. My thighs tighten around his waist when suddenly he rolls over without losing contact between us. "I want to watch you." His grip on my hips are vice like. I move on top of him, feeling him hit a spot inside me that sends pulses through me. His hooded gaze looks hungry and my hips move faster. "That's my girl, ride my fucking cock." His crude words making my body tremble, our gazes lock on each other and his cock twitches and thickens inside me. He fills me perfectly. I smile down at him, scratching my nails over the sculpted planes of his chest and abs. A growl low in his chest ignites the heat in my body as our orgasms come crashing down in unison. "My lumiére!" I collapse on top of him, his arms wrap around me and I can hear his racing heart.

Lucien

As soon as I walk into the office, Stacy is at my heels. I have meetings upon meetings. A headache already threatening, and the day hasn't even started. "Block out my morning, I have an important meeting at midday, I need time cleared before and after to get back to the office. Get the car ready."

"Yes, sir. Can I get you a coffee?"

"No. Call Mr. Alexander and have him come up here." She nods and leaves me to my morning conference call with the board members. So far they've been happy with me running the company. It's confirmed I will take over Verán Industries. Now to get rid of Claudia. Robert has since taken the bug out of the office and his team have swept the rest of the area and found another two which they disposed of. Now that I am free to talk without worry of them hearing anything, it's easier to be in the office.

As soon as I hang up the call, Jayce enters my office. "Hey man, what's up?"

"I have a meeting at midday. I will get us what we need. It's in Santa Monica and you need to keep an eye on Cassie. I will be back late. Maybe take her to lunch or something?"

I glance up at him and notice the confusion on his face. "You're asking me to take your girlfriend to lunch?" He gives me a shit eating grin and I am ready to punch him.

"Jayce, don't fuck with me. I am not in the mood."

"Just kidding brother, what's crawled up your ass?"

"I want this shit over now. My future needs to start now. Cassie and me need to move forward." He nods. The last time Jayce Alexander fell in love was a long time ago. She was a blonde bombshell in college. They were inseparable until her folks moved them to another state and she changed schools.

"I know man. I can take care of her. Just get back here. We need to figure out what we're going to do, the deadline is getting closer."

"Yes, that's the reason for my meeting today. There is a source, a reliable one, who can give me what I need." Glancing at my wristwatch. "I need to get going. When I get back, we should have something we can use." I make my way to reception and out to the waiting car. With a text to Cassie, letting her know I am out till late afternoon, I slide into the bench seat. Tonight I will have to tell her I met with her mother. This is not something I can keep from her. To say that I am nervous about telling her is an understatement. Her reaction could go either way. *Will she be able to forgive me for keeping it from her for this long?*

As the car speeds towards Santa Monica pier, I know my father and Cassie's mom have a past, but that didn't explain the will. My dad had been in contact with her adopted parents, but something wasn't adding up here. When Robert pulls into the parking lot, I get out and take in my surroundings. Since it's a weekday it's quiet, which is what I was banking on, no interruptions. "Robert, wait here. This shouldn't take long. At least, I don't think it will." With a swift nod, I make my way to the end of the pier.

When I reach the end, I find her standing there. Dressed in a pair of jeans and a blue jumper, she looks so much like Cassie it's remarkable. "Ms. Winters." She turns and offers me a smile, the same one that always brightens Cassie's face.

"Luca. Please call me Deanna." Her use of my nickname that so few people know stuns me and its evident when she looks away, staring out at the water. She shakes her head, deep in thought. "I am sorry to hear your father passed away. Claude Verán was a special man."

"You knew my father." It's not a question, but she nods. "He told me he loved you." She doesn't reply, but motions for me to follow her off the pier and onto the beach. We're walking towards the main promenade when she finally starts speaking.

"Did he give you the pendant? For Cassie?"

"Yes, well he gave it to her before he..." I can't bring myself to say it.

"Okay, well... Did he tell you the history behind it?" She stops and turns, there is something in her expression I can't place, but she looks so forlorn. Her dark eyes remind me of my girl. I shrug, I don't know too much about it apart from what my father told Cassie and me at the house that day.

"Not much. He said that it was made for him and his soul mate. I always figured it was my mom." When Deanna's gaze falls on me, her eyes were alight with something, secrets. I hated secrets. Always there, just waiting to threaten my relationship with Cassie.

"I met your father when I was sixteen. He was only a year older. My family had taken me to the south of France, on holiday. The summer had moved too fast for our liking." She stopped to watch the waves crashing before carrying on with her story. "We fell in love. There was nothing I could do, after the summer, I was going back to school and your father was coming back to LA."

"Wait, you and my father didn't..." I groaned in frustration. *Please don't tell me what I think she's telling me.* Because I feel a migraine threaten.

"No, no," amusement on her face made me chuckle. "We were in love, too young for marriage, or... anything else. There was a jeweler down the road where we were staying who made the pendant for Claude. He paid with his allowance. Bought it for me. If you read the back of the pendant there's a poem your father wrote engraved on it." I don't remember a poem. I make a mental note to take a careful look at it when I get home.

"Are mine and hers the same?" She cuts a glance at me and smiles.

"Yes, they're meant to be two halves of a whole. Summer and Winter."

"If you were so in love, why did you not seek each other out once you finished school?"

"Your father had married your mother, and you were on the way. I wasn't going to interfere, we stayed friends. We always would, I knew that. After she left, I found him, but Claudia had wormed her way into his life. She was adamant she was pregnant and your father, being the good man married her. When she told him a couple of months later that she lost the baby he was furious, hence this..." She pulled out a folder, handing it to me. Before I opened it I knew exactly what it was. "It should get you the company and null any claim that Claudia has on any of your father's assets. I hope they will accept the copy. The original, I am not sure what Claudia would have done with it."

"But—"

"Your father was an intriguing man, with many secrets, but he loved you more than life itself." When she places a hand on my shoulder, I felt love in her touch. A mother's love. Something I have never had and my breath caught. Something still tugged at me though.

"Why did you not find Cassie or try and talk to her?" As soon as the words are out of my mouth, I want to stuff them back. The hurt in her eyes tells me she didn't leave because she wanted to, she left because she was forced to and that made me sad. Not only for her, but for the love of my life.

"I was young Luca. After your father left, I was devastated. I went on to date an older boy. Cassie's father. He… He left me. My parents told me I had to give my baby away." Deanna swipes a tear from her face.

"But, my father said he saw Cassie as a child." Once again it's a statement not a question, but she nods.

"We kept in touch, I told him I had the baby, named her Cassandra. He promised me he would watch over her. A silent guardian, I suppose you could say. That's when you met her, you were both so young. Do you remember that day?"

"I do. Apparently that was the day I told my dad I was going to marry her." I chuckle and she cuts a glance at me.

"Do you want to?" Her face is serious and for the first time in a long time I realize I do. There's no question about it. I don't want anyone else in my life.

"Yes, I do." She nods and smiles.

"I am happy that our families will finally be one. Keep an invitation for me." She hands me a small black velvet box. "Your father has a jewel box, a vintage one. There are two letters in there. One for you and one for Cassie. When you're both ready, I want you to read them. I have to go now."

"Wait… Why is Claudia so adamant to destroy our relationship?" She stares at me for a long time, and I wonder if she will answer me.

"Claudia is jealous; she always has been. She shattered my relationship with your father. Now she's trying to do it to you and Cassie. You see, Luca, she has a daughter. One she believes should be running Verán Industries with you." I frown, Claudia never mentioned a daughter.

"Daughter?"

She nods a quick assent. "Yes, Isabel." The words send ice through me. I remember Isabel from a long time ago, her parents ran a bed & breakfast. Her mother wasn't Claudia. As if reading my mind, Deanna carries on. "Claudia is Isabel's mother. Her sister and husband ran a holiday home where Isabel spent her vacations." I nod, everything is falling into place. "Read the letter's when you're ready, Luca. I must go now."

"How will I know we're ready?"

"Oh, Luca, you will in here." She places her hand flat on my chest, right where my heart is. "Trust me." She gives me a conspiratorial wink and walks off into the crowd. I glance down and open the box she handed me, inside is the most beautiful ring I have ever seen. A platinum band with a princess cut diamond surrounded by smaller intricate rose colored diamonds. And as I stand there on the beach, I know what my plan is.

When I reach the car, Robert gives me an inquiring stare, but I am still in shock. Cassie's mother has given me so much to think about. To find out about my father, and his life is something I can never thank her enough for. I open the folder and I want to sing. Inside is an original copy of the will my father had written up and signed. *This is it!* We can do this. "Robert. Have the team meet at my office, I have it."

"Sir." That's all acknowledgement I need. I glance up and I can see the smile in his eyes. "Cassandra's mother?" I nod.

"Wait. How did you know?" Our eyes meet in the rear-view mirror briefly.

"Sir, you do realize I have been driving you around for most of your life?" My nod confirms this, and he continues to explain. "I met your father when you were only nine years old. I have known Ms. Winters for a long time. Although I didn't realize she may have had a copy of your father's last will and testament."

"And you didn't tell me?"

"You didn't ask." I chuckle. He always had a smart ass answer for everything.

Cassandra

The office was too quiet, an anxious feeling knotted my stomach. I needed to work late, but this was eerie. Last night Lucien spent the night and there was something different about him. Something shifted between us. I know he's been stressed about our situation, but that's not it. We had connected on such a deep level, my soul with his. Whenever he touched me, it was like he was touching something inside me long forgotten. His kisses last night heated me in a way that scorched deeper than I thought was possible. This man owned every part of me and there was no walking away now. It was all Kenna's fault for putting the idea of marriage in my head. I wasn't ready for it, and neither was he. Surely I was reading too much into it. My office phone interrupts my thoughts. I had a sinking suspicion of who it could be, but I am no longer hiding. When I glance at the time, I notice it's almost 7 pm. I pick up the phone with a shaky hand. "Cassandra Winters, hello." My voice sounds low, nervous.

"Ms. Winters. I trust you are well?" Claudia's voice is smooth and sends an icy shiver through my body, sliding down my spine. Her dislike for me hits me as if she were in the room, choking me.

"Yes." Grabbing my mobile, I text Lucien an SOS.

"Good. My call is to discuss you leaving Verán Publishers, and subsequently leaving LA. I have certain requirements for my son, and you're not one of them. You need a new job which I will gladly help you with. There are numerous publishing companies in New York, it's time for you to go back home, Cassandra. Time for you to face your demons you so easily forgot about."

"I forgot nothing Claudia, and I don't intend running away from a bully." Her cackle over the phone is loud and unladylike, especially with the persona she avidly portrays.

"I understand my son has already kicked you to the curb. So, at the Verán Industries Christmas ball next week, he will make a public announcement about his engagement to Isabel. You can stay, witness it, when midnight strikes you will leave Los Angeles, for good. Those aren't suggestions Ms. Winters, those are orders." Immediately the line goes dead. I am left sitting with nothing but ice coursing through my veins. *What did she mean engagement? Lucien didn't tell me anything about the progress he's made. Cassie, you need to heed the warning. No! I am not running away from him, or her for that matter. I am not a fucking child! I need to stay and fight for the man I love!*

My office door flies open, my gaze flits up to blazing green eyes. *I should just get my*

door taken down. "What happened?" I frown at him. *How did he get here so fast?*
"Were you upstairs?"
"Yes, I was working late. Robert and his team had something for me to check out. What did she say to you? Why are you still here? Alone?" He rounds my desk, perching on the edge and I watch the concern flicker over his handsome features in the dim light.
"I am not alone, clearly. And I was working. Even if I had gone home I would be alone, Kenna had an assignment to work on." I roll back in my chair and try to get some distance between me and Lucien, I can't think straight when he's this close and I need to talk to him about Claudia. "She said you were announcing an engagement at the Christmas ball. She told me I had until midnight in LA, after the ball I am meant to leave, back to New York, she will help me find a job." I turn to face the night sky. It's darker than normal because it's winter. Matching my mood more than I am letting on, and it frustrates me that she has this effect on me.
"Baby, you know that she is trying to make you angry. She's trying to scare you off and I don't want her to. I am not getting engaged. Look at me Cassandra!" When I turn, the pain in my chest at the idea of him being with anyone but me leaves me breathless.
"There's nothing we can do Luke; she's will win this. We're never going to find your father's original will. It's just gone. You will marry Isabel." I blink and the tears spill, not able to stop them anymore. I love this man more than I have ever loved anyone before. He's taken my soul. Owns every part of me, I can't be complete without him.
"She will not win, fuck it, Cassie! I am not losing you. I will give up my father's company before I lose you! Trust me. I have a plan. The details need to be ironed out, but I need your trust." My gaze falls on him and I nod.
"You're not giving up what your father built. Not for me. Luke, I am not worth it." Lucien, grabs me by the shoulders, his eyes blazing with intensity.
"You are worth everything to me! I wish you can see that. My life is not complete without you. I can rebuild the company, but I can't rebuild us. Give me a chance?"
I nod again. "Fine, but I can't have my heart broken again Luke. I can't be without you either. It seems like the universe is against us. Every time we find each other something comes into play and forces us apart." The ache in my chest rips into me, more than I ever thought possible. If Lucien and I were ever apart now, I wouldn't survive. He's become my anchor in the rough sea that we're wading through. After the hurt of losing my parents and my ex fiancé, the pain that I may have to walk away from Lucien, ignites the agony.
"Not this time sweetness, remember what my father said. We are destined to be together. Summer and Winter, polar opposites." I giggle through my tears. I never took him to believe in that fairytale stuff, but hearing the words from his mouth makes me smile. "Is something funny, Cassie?" His tone light and playful as I cuddle into his embrace.
"Definitely not, Mr. Verán."
"Do not even tease me right now, Cassandra," his tone is serious, but I hear a drip of lust and smile to myself. The fact that this man can still be affected by something so minor is beyond me.
"Why? Will there be consequences?" I giggle.
"As always and you will be screaming when I am done with you!" Gasping at his words, I glance up and see the devilish smirk on his lips. His dimples are deep and I am so tempted to run my fingers over them. "I need to go baby. Will you please pack up? I

will have Robert take you home. I don't want you here alone." He leans toward me and plants a quick kiss on my forehead, then he flops into one of the armchairs in my office. Powering off my laptop, I slide it into my bag. Moments later I shoulder my bag and round the desk, making sure I have everything.

"So, will you be visiting me again tonight?"

"I would love to darling, but I have a few things I need to finish. The Christmas ball is next week; we have time. You will stay with me, Robert will escort you to work and back. If she's intelligent enough to have eyes on you, we can set up a decoy, somehow I doubt she's that bright. I plan to make an announcement on that night. And it wont be an engagement to Isabel that you can be sure of." My heart soars, but then sinks. *Did you want him to propose to you? Do you think he would? Not so soon after everything that's happened between us. No, I shouldn't let myself get that serious. I mean, what do you think Cassie, he's just going to give you a ring? Yes! He will, we're just not ready yet.* "Baby?" I peer into Lucien's green orbs and the concern flashes in them. There is no way I can tell him that I want a ring, or what I was thinking about.

"Yes, yea, sure. Okay, let's go."

"Were you even listening?"

"Yes."

"Don't lie to me, Cassie."

"My mind is just all over the place. Sorry handsome."

"It will be okay baby, I promise. I will make it okay." Lucien laces his fingers through mine and we walk to the elevator. When it pings open Robert is inside waiting for me.

"Home safe darling. I will call you tonight, be ready." His words sending shivers down my spine. I can only imagine what he has in mind.

Lucien

I make my way back up to the office. The team are sitting at the conference table. I didn't tell Cassie about the paperwork yet. I want her safe. She will find out soon enough. I have a plan and I want nothing messing it up, mainly, I don't want Cassie in any danger. "Team. Robert had to escort Ms. Winters home. I will officiate the meeting. This is the paperwork we need. I want surveillance on both Sasha Alexander and Claudia Verán. I need more information on Isabel, apparently she is Claudia's daughter."

Daniel rakes over the information and passes it on to the rest of the team. I brief them on how the evening will play out at the event. When they've left, I sit back in my chair thinking over what Cassie's mom told me. My dad never mentioned being with anyone other than my mom. I guess it makes sense. It was before I was born. My phone pulls me from my thoughts. "What's up Jayce?"

"I am on my way up to you now. Did you talk to the guys yet?"

"Yea. Come up and I will explain."

I tug at my tie; it feels like a noose around my neck. Undoing it, I throw it on the desk. I text Cassie to let her know I will call her later. Jayce walks in and gives me a smirk of satisfaction. He drops a phone on the desk with a thud and I stare at him. "What's this?"

"Sasha's phone."

"What? How did you get this?"

"I have my ways, check the latest message thread." I unlock the screen and open the messages' app. There's a long conversation between her and Claudia and a few from Isabel. The plan they had, was for my proposal to Isabel to take place the night of the ball which we had found out a few days ago. There's something else though. My gaze darts up to Jayce. So Sasha wants the publishing company and Claudia promised her that. From the last message to Claudia, my heart stops. Isabel is fucking deranged. She's going to hurt Cassie.

"Is this?" He nods, there's a dangerous expression on his face. His feelings for Cassie run deep. "I need to get to Cassie, she can't be alone. Is Robert with her?" I can't remember if I told him to stay with her. *Fuck, my mind is so fragmented.*

"He's there, I checked when I found the messages. Go. I will see you both later, I need to get the phone back." Not giving it a second thought, I grab my phone and laptop, shoving it in my briefcase. Jayce and I leave the office and make our way to the elevators, stepping in and pressing the call button. "Do you need a ride?"

"I have the Aston here." The doors open when we reach the basement and we walk to our respective cars. Before I get in, Jayce calls out to me.

"Take care of her." I nod. Once I am in the car, I tear out of the garage and speed down the quiet streets to my girl.

Cassandra

I unlock the door of my apartment. Robert enters first and I follow close behind him. He does a quick sweep of the place. When it's clear he nods and leaves letting me know he will be in the car just outside. I need a hot shower and I need time to think about everything that Lucien said. He's adamant we can make this work, but I don't see how it's possible without his father's will. I make my way into the bathroom, turn on the shower and strip. Once inside, and I am under the hot spray, my muscles ease with the tension that had turned me into a bundle of knots. I can't imagine living my life without Lucien, I want to fight for our relationship. With my eyes closed, I try and calm my thoughts. I enjoy the water beating down on my back and shoulders, easing the tension.

If he proposes there is no doubt of what my answer would be. *Stop it Cassie! Just relax, let things fall into place, the way they're meant to do. Just let Lucien ask you when he's ready.* The problem is will he ever be ready. I know he said he wants a forever with me. My doubts cloud my thoughts, they always do.

After everything I have been through, it's normal. Instinctively my hand goes to my belly. My gaze falls and my gut wrenches at the thought of what I did. What I could have had, but deep down I know that I was too young, too fucked up to ever consider keeping a baby. Adoption would have been the best option for me. To a home where he or she could be loved. When I blink tears get washed away with the spray of the shower. Almost as if they won't stop. I stand there wallowing in the pain that grips my heart as the water runs cold. I need Luke so much right now.

When the water is ice cold, I realize I need to get out of the shower. I turn off the taps, and grab my towel. My reflection in the steamy mirror is foreign, gone is that happy girl I saw not so long ago in Hawaii. So much has happened in the months I have been with Luke. We broke up once, I slept with his best friend twice, and now we're here, being threatened by his step-mother, where he could be engaged to someone else in a few days' time. The worst part was his father passing away. The funeral was so difficult, because Luke and I had to be apart, I couldn't even console him.

Next week is Christmas and the only thing I want to do is spend the day with people I love. I think we should have dinner at Luke's. That is if his plan works. We could invite Kenna and Jayce. As soon as I walk back into my bedroom, my phone buzzes from the nightstand. "Hello handsome."

"Took you long enough in that shower." His voice one of amusement and frustration. My fears evaporate and the pain leaves when I hear his voice. How can one person turn your life around with just a few words. The pieces of me slowly mend with just the sound of his voice. With his touch he surrounds me in safety, and when he is inside me I am complete. Then it dawns on me what he said.

"How did you—"

"Because I am behind you." I spin around, and sure enough Lucien is standing there dressed in a pair of faded blue jeans and a grey T-shirt. He steps towards me and tugs at the towel. "You look lovely flushed and dressed in a towel, but it's that shocked expression I find so alluring."

"But," I sputter, how did he even get in the apartment.

"Baby, just accept that I am in your bedroom and I need you." Goose bumps rise over my skin and my nipples pebble at the icy breeze and Lucien's lustful gaze.

I grab at my towel again, wrapping it around me and flopping onto the bed. "Stop being so god damn confident." I am not sure why I am frustrated, but I am. When he slides onto the bed next to me, I can't help breathing in his intoxicating scent. It smells of spice and Lucien. It's his smell, inexplicably him.

"I thought you liked me being over confident, and I missed you. You need to trust my love for you and only you. Forever. Now will you drop the towel?" A suppressed giggle escapes my lips and I glance at him. My gaze drinks in his appearance and I point to his clothes.

"You first, handsome." In one swift move, Lucien pulls his T-shirt up and over his head. I drink in the perfect planes of his chest and abs. They never fail to make me gasp, but it's when he stands up, drops his jeans and boxer briefs, I lose my train of thought. I take in the exquisitely sculpted man and I am instantly aching with a need so strong, all I can do is stand up and drop my towel.

"I could look at you forever, sweetness." Lucien's hungry gaze travels over me, sending a shiver of excitement over my skin. He leans in, his hot breath on my face and I savor it. Our bodies are flush and his rigid erection presses against my stomach. *How can I ache for him all the time?* My body responds and I wrap my arms around his neck, pulling him into me.

"And I you Lucien."

Lucien

We're laying in bed, my arm wrapped around her. My heart is racing and I wonder if she can hear it. It's time to come clean, I have to tell her. "Baby." I whisper in the darkness and I hope she's asleep. *Why?* Because I am scared shitless that she will leave me when I tell her that her mother is alive and I hid it from her. I stopped at home before coming to see her, so I have the box with me. The letters her mother mentioned were in there. Along with a few photographs. One of Cassie and me on the first day I ever saw her. The day I knew she would one day be my wife, even though I was young, she had affected me. It's a strange feeling.

"Mmmm..." She's so adorable when she's sleepy.

"Can we talk?"

"Luke, you just near killed me with amazing sex. And you want to talk now?" Her giggle echoes through the bedroom and I chuckle.

"I didn't kill you, you're still talking. Are you ready for another round? I know I am." Giving her a cheeky wink. I roll my hips and her low murmur is evidence that she can feel my cock, it's rock hard again.

"Luke. You're insatiable."

"And you my darling are gorgeous." When Cassie rolls over, I can see her mocha eyes sparkling with amusement.

"What did you want to talk about?"

I reach over and turn on the light. The lamp on the night stand offers a soft glow in the room. I scoot up in bed and reach for the box, I left on my side of the bed. Unlatching it, I pull out two envelopes. I haven't read mine yet, but it's time. Time for me and Cassie to finally put out past to rest and move forward. The ball is next week, and I want to show her I have moved on from my past, only because she is in my life. As much as she thinks I own her, she owns me, heart, mind, body and soul. There is nothing in this life, or the next that I wouldn't do for her. To see her smile is the only thing that pulls me from the demons of my past, propelling me into the future, with her.

"What's that?" I hand her one, and I keep the one addressed to me.

"It's our history. The path that lead us here and why we are in this bed, together. There are things we need to know. There are things you need an explanation for." I glance at her. My nerves are taking over and I am not sure if this was a good idea.

"Our past?" I hand her two old photographs. Her eyes rake over them and her stare pins me. There is shock in her expression, but in her eyes is something I didn't think I would see. Love. "This... It's... But how?"

"Do you remember that day?" Cassie smiles and I can see she remembers it as clearly as I do. "Well, my father reminded me, when you were... Onsite at the last photo shoot. He reminded me of that day." I place my hand on hers, the electricity shooting straight to my cock. *Fuck, Verán, get a hold of yourself.* My hunger for her never goes away. "That day I told my father I would marry you one day." The words come out as a rushed whoosh and her eyes cut to me.

"You..."

"Cassie, I just want you to know, I love you. No matter what's in that letter." I point to the faded envelope on her lap and sit back.

"What do you mean? What is it?" She rips the flap open and pulls it out. I follow suit and open mine. We sit in silence for a long while and her body is trembling next to me. I snake my arm around her shoulders and pull her into the crook of my arm. When I glance at my letter again, the pain in my heart leaves me breathless. My father will never see me marry Cassie, never meet our grandkids.

"My mother? She's alive. But..."

"Cassie..."

"Luke, please take me to her? Tell me about her? What is she like?" My breath lets out in a heavy whoosh. She's not angry. There must have been a damn good explanation in that letter to have kept her calm. "You met her didn't you. This letter says that she's alive. Did you see her?" I nod, still not sure if she's going to lose it or not. "Luke."

"Cassie. When all this is over I will contact her and we can meet with her. There are things she told me. About Claudia. This shit needs to be put to an end. We will sort this out. Trust me." I look deep into those chocolate eyes and I can see that she trusts me.

"Okay, then I want to meet her. I need to see her face and hear her voice." I nod. Then I remember the pendant. When I got home earlier I forgot mine on my nightstand.

"Do you have that pendant my father gave you?"

She nods and leans over, opening the top drawer of the chest next to her side of the bed. As soon as she hands me the pendant, I turn it over and read the back. It's the poem. The poem is perfect, describing our relationship perfectly.

My light in the dark,
Pieces fit like a puzzle,
Twin flames, Soul mates,
My lumiére, forever

"This is what your mother mentioned when I saw her last." I hand the pendant to her. Her eyes dart to mine and she gives me that soft sweet smile that makes my heart soar.

"Tell me everything. This is incredible, she's out there. I am not alone. Why didn't she find me?" Whatever was in that letter was my saving grace, because I was expecting more shouting and a little less smiling. I tug her into the crook of my arm, and start the story. Reveling at how she fits against me so perfectly.

"You're never alone when you have me, baby. I promise you that you will never want for anything. When we met, I wasn't the guy that would give you forever. Now, after these seven months with you, I can't imagine my life without you in it." She blinks back tears, but deep down I know they're happy ones. This is the girl who took a playboy, only out for a one-night stand, and she's changed my outlook on life. On love. On forever.

We laid in bed for the rest of the night talking. I told her about her mother and she told me about things she remembers about me. About the day we first met as children.

Dear Luca,

My son, I am so proud of you and the man you've become. I always have been and I always will be. There were secrets I kept from you, but I kept them because you needed to find your own way. Now that you're grown and you've found love, I want you to trust and be happy. You deserve that and so much more. Keep in your heart the knowledge that wherever I am, I will forever watch down on you.

No matter what is happening you will always find your solace in your lumiére. There are times that may seem like the world is against you, but Luca, you need to be strong. There is a lot that will stand in your way, through life, and through being with the one person who makes you whole.

I have taught you from a young age to fight, for your dreams, your beliefs, and for what you want. When you find a love as pure as yours there will be no dissuading it. Nothing can prepare you for losing her, so don't give up. I made that mistake. I may be an old man, and you may think this is an old sob story, but I am speaking from experience.

There will always be that one person that can pull your heart from the darkest cave and shine a light on it so bright you are blinded. When you're broken, when those pieces you've been ripped into don't fit anymore, she's the only one who will be able to put you back together. The same goes for you. She will need you to be hers as much as you need her.

I am not there now, to see you get married. To see my grandchildren grow up, but I know in my heart that you will be an incredible father. Alongside her, you both will be the perfect parents and I know that you will make me proud. More than you have done already.

As much as I have given you grief about your love life you will find happiness, somehow I think as you sit there reading this, she is in your arms already. Remember, life isn't easy, neither is love, that's why you need appreciate everything that you have. I always wanted the very best for you. Take each day as it comes, but also, love, laugh, don't ever give up, and never let her out the door without saying "I love you".

If you're ever in doubt, ask yourself three questions:

Is her smile the one that lights your darkness?
When you're with her, do you feel like the world is full of possibilities?
When you're on your death bed, is her face the last thing you want to see?

No, I am not being morbid, I am being honest. If you answered yes to those three questions, then you have your answer. Then you know you've found your lumiére.

Forever
Dad x

CHAPTER twenty-nine

Lucien

I open my eyes with Cassie's arm draped around me, and can't help smiling. We fell asleep as the sun was coming up over the horizon. The ball will be where all this shit ends. What I have planned will shock everyone. For the first time in days, weeks and maybe even months my hope that Cassie and I would get a break will not go to waste. Something good will happen, and I would make sure of it.

"Morning handsome." Her sweet smile makes my heart swell.

"I love waking up to you, baby." I pull her in for a kiss, needing to feel her warmth. We have three days and then this will all be over. I pull away and lock my gaze with hers. "This will work out. I can promise you that in three days this shit will be gone." The ball will be on Tuesday evening. Only two days before Christmas, and what an explosive day that will be.

"So, you want me at the ball?" She rolls over and looks at me. *Why would she even ask me that?* Of course she has to be there. I wouldn't want her anywhere else.

"You have to be there. With my plan, it will only work if my girl is there." This girl has taken my life, my heart and mind, turned it upside down and all I want to do is be with her. After last night, there is so much that we have already overcome, and if her mom and my dad really believe in us, there has to be some truth in it. I wanted her for so long, wanted to own her, possess her and now I have her, there is no way I am letting her go.

"I always trust you Luke." Her fingers brush the hard planes of my body, dipping into the deep ridges of my abs. Her touch is like an electric current which shoots straight to my cock. She trails a gentle line down the chiseled V that's pointing to the soft white sheet covering my hips. It's taking all my restraint not to pin her to the bed and fuck her senseless.

"Cassie." The warning in my voice has her trembling, I hope she knows what she's doing, and what will happen. She ignores my warning and trails the other side of my V line. Goose bumps rise on my skin and the sheet is tenting with my erection. Her hand travels lower, beneath the sheet, finding my rigid cock. "Fuck, baby." My voice is a low rumble, and she fists my cock in slow measured strokes.

I close my eyes and my head falls back, the sensation of her hand on me is too much. My hips move at their own volition. Thrusting into her hand. I move faster, my orgasm fast approaching. The need to be inside her overtakes me. As if reading my mind, she pulls the sheet down. I watch her kneel up on the bed. She looks so beautiful, her hair has that just fucked look and her cheeks are flushed. "Baby."

"Shhh, I want you." She straddles my hips and lowers herself on me slowly. Her tight little pussy is so hot, wet and I almost come just from the heat of her sheathing me. I watch her move back and forth, slowly. Her nails raking down my chest and abs, sending shivers down my spine. She's moving at a teasing pace, but this is too much for me. I grip her hips, holding her in place, I plunge into her. Deep strokes into her heat. Her head falls back and her beautiful tits bounce with every thrust. I know it won't take long to find my release.

"Look at me." My voice is strained, and she meets my heated stare, her body tightens around me. She's close and so am I. Her eyes are locked on mine and it's like we're the same person. I need to feel her come around me. "I love your hot pussy on my cock." She trembles and I know it's because of my dirty words. "Come for me lumiére, milk my fucking cock." My command is laced with heat and her body obeys, just like it should. Because I own her.

An orgasm splinters through her rendering her speechless. I join my girl moments later growling my own release inside her. She collapses on my chest. We lay there holding onto each other. Our hearts are racing, in time with the other. Connected. She's mine. I am hers. Heart, body, mind, and soul. My forever.

Cassandra

The morning after learning my mother was alive, Luke promised that everything would be okay, I trust him with my life and my heart. The fact that he met my mother still astounded me. Work has been so busy today and I haven't seen Luke. He told me not to worry and that everything would be okay. Tomorrow we have the Christmas ball. I need to get something to wear. This calls for a shopping trip. There is only one person to call, Kenna. I should have done this over the weekend, but Luke and I hardly left the bed.

"Babe!"

"Hey Ken, I wanted to find out if you're up for shopping later?"

"I am there babe, I love shopping! What are we getting?"

"Dresses. For the ball tomorrow night. I have to be there." As soon as the words leave my mouth, my heart constricts. Luke promised his plan would work, but there is still a fear he would have to leave me. "And there's something I need to tell you. About my mother."

"Your mother? What do you mean babe?"

A knock at my door interrupts us. "I have to go. Meet me at midday? Outside the office?"

"Sure." I hang up. "Come in."

Jayce steps inside dressed in black pants and a blue dress shirt that make his eyes pop. He looks so handsome. "Hey princess, how are you doing?"

"Good, just made a date with Kenna to go shopping. I need a dress for tomorrow night. To be honest, I am not sure I want to go."

"You have to be there. It's important that you're there." He rounds my desk, reaching out both hands to me, he pulls me up. Our bodies are too close, and I can't bring myself to glance up at him. Jayce places his index finger on my chin and tilts my head up so I am facing him. His sky blue gaze is caring, and he gives me a small smile. "Be my date?"

"Jayce, I can't—"

"Princess, you can. Luke and you aren't supposed to go together. The plan will work. The car will pick you up at 6 pm." When he leans in my breath hitches. "I promise, Luke and you will be together."

I nod, stepping back. Turning to face the window, I take a deep breath. "Jayce, I can't go as your date. Luke will not be happy."

"We have to keep up the ruse, until the speeches. Cassie…" His touch is gentle on my shoulder. I glance back at him and give him a small smile. "Trust me?" What is it with the men in my life asking me to trust them? They are both clearly in on this, but I can't doubt them. I know they won't hurt me.

"I do."

"Good. Then you will be ready at six." I watch him walk out the office. This is something that has to happen, I have to accept that, but going with Jayce. I don't know.

Lucien

I pick up my phone, and call Cassie's extension. "Hello lover." Her term of endearment makes me chuckle. To have this woman on my arm forever will be the best decision I ever made.

"Hey gorgeous, what are you up to for lunch?"

"I am going shopping with Kenna. I need a dress for the ball tomorrow. What color is your tie going to be?" I frown at the question.

"I think red; you remember the dark red one?"

"Yes, I remember it. Can we talk later handsome? Need to finish up so I can meet Kenna."

"Sure baby." Once I hang up, I call Robert. "Tell Daniel where Cassie and Kenna go shopping. I need to get there before they do." My mind has something naughty to surprise her with. As soon as I think about it a smirk curls my lips, grabbing my jacket, I slip it on, and make my way out of the office. In the reception area, I find Robert's assistant waiting for me. "Where are we going?" He opens the door for me and before I slide in, he tells me which designer boutique we're headed to.

"Gucci, sir." I nod, perfect. This is something I have never done before. All the sales assistants remember me there, so the little surprise will be easy to set up. When she sees me walk in, her expression will be worth it. The car pulls into the traffic and we make our down to Rodeo Drive and I feel anxious. I pull out my phone, I text Kenna my plan. Her reply is immediate. This will be fun. Daniel stops outside the store, and I get out, leaving my jacket.

"Give me an hour?" He smiles and nods. As soon as he's pulled away I walk into the store. It's quiet, and the assistant is setting up the dresses in the back. When she sees me, a smile lights her face. *Here we go again.*

"Good afternoon, sir. How can I help?"

"Two ladies will visit the store and I need you to set up a private room for them. The one is my girlfriend and there is a dress I want in the dressing room." She nods and smiles.

"Follow me." We walk to the back of the store, up the stairs and I see she has two private dressing rooms available. I point out the one I want and she reserves it. "Now which dress is it you had your eye one?" Making a beeline for the deep crimson dress I know will fit those exquisite curves like a glove.

"This is the dress I want in there. Another thing, I want to surprise her when she arrives. Can you help?" She beams at me and nods. Once I have given the details, I walk out of the store, crossing the road walking into Tom Ford, I could see as soon as Robert pulled up.

I didn't have to wait long. Robert pulled up, the girls got out, and he walked them to the door. When they had disappeared inside the store, I made my way back across the road. "Mr. Verán, everything is set up for tomorrow night. Mr. Alexander, has the information and the box."

"Perfect. This will be good. Thank you, Robert." He gives me a smile and gets back into the car, no doubt off to find parking. When I step into the store, the assistant that helped me earlier, smiles and nods. Taking the stairs calmly, the knot in my stomach is anything but calm. The girls are talking and giggling. When I get to the top of the stairs, I wait and listen.

"I am going to try this red one on, it's incredible." Cassie sounds excited at my choice of dress. *That's good darling, because you won't be wearing for very long.* When I hear the click of the lock, I step into the waiting area. Kenna glances at me and smiles. She's dressed in a beautiful black and silver evening dress. I am sure Jayce will be dying to take it off her when he sees it.

"Thanks Kenna." I whisper as she makes her way downstairs.

"Have fun." She gives me a sly wink and disappears. I knock on the dressing room door.

"Hang on, Ken. This zipper is stuck. I need your help." The lock clicks and I push the door open. When Cassie's eyes lock on mine in the mirror she gasps. "What are you—"

"Shhh." As much I want to see the dress on her, I want to see her out of it a lot more. I slide the soft silk over her shoulders and the dress pools at her feet. She's standing in front of me in her hot pink bra and a pair of matching panties. Closing the door behind me, I twist the lock, and help her step out of the dress. "I needed to see you."

"Well, I was at the office this morning." She giggles, watching me hang the dress I had already paid for against the hook.

"This is the dress you will wear tomorrow night. It's paid for already."

"Luke, you couldn't have known I wanted that dress?"

"I did. Because I liked it." A cheeky wink has her shaking her head, and her cheeks pink. I lean forward brushing her lips with mine. "Now, I want to fuck you, right here." Gripping her hips, I spin her around. We're both looking in the mirror, and I tease the bra straps over her shoulders, unhooking it. I drop it on the floor.

Her panties follow soon enough, and I have my girl, standing in front of me in nothing, but her black heels. *God, those heels look fucking good.* "Hold onto the mirror." She leans forward and places both hands flat against the mirror. Her dark eyes are glistening and so is her pussy.

I use feather light touches to skim over her body, not missing an inch of her silky skin. My touch has goose bumps rising in their wake. Her nipples pebble and a soft moan escapes her lips. Lust shoots down my spine and into my cock. Her eyes flutter closed. "Open them." Our gazes lock as my hand dips between her legs. Her knees are wobbly and I can tell she's as turned on as I am. "Do you want me here, baby?"

"Yesssss." Her hiss is low and sexy. My fingers glide over her smooth wet lips. She opens her legs wider, allowing me access to her heated core. With my other hand, I pinch and tweak her nipples until she's squirming against me. I push two fingers inside her, and her body tightens around them, tightening in the lush way she always makes me come.

"Good girl. So fucking ready for me, anywhere, anytime." She nods. When I pull my fingers from her sopping little cunt, I move them to her mouth. I coat her lips with her sweet arousal. Like the bad girl I know she is, she sucks my fingers into her mouth and I almost come in my pants. *Fuck she's so hot.* "Enough." I whisper in her ear. Within seconds my zipper is down and my cock is out. I tease her and slide the head over her pussy. "Is this what you crave?" Sliding just the tip in, her whimper answers my question.

Her hands are flat against the mirror and she slides her ass back against me, trying to fuck me into her. I lift my hand and bring it down on her ass in a loud swat. When I glance at her, I see her teeth chewing her plump bottom lip to keep from screaming. My body leans over her, and I bite her earlobe, tugging it with my teeth. Her body vibrates under me, she's about to come. "Fuck my cock, baby. Take what you need." I position myself at her hot entrance and watch in awe as my girl moves back and forth. Faster and faster. Her body finds its rhythm and I glance at her in the mirror. She's lost in delirium and she looks fucking beautiful.

Suddenly she shudders and her pussy grips me. The desire and my own release shoots up my spine and into my balls. I grip her hips and hold her against me as close as she can get. I want every inch of my cock to be inside her. Her orgasm shatters her as she comes over me. My orgasm sends me reeling as I empty myself deep inside her.

"Luke." My name a whisper on her lips and I can't help smiling. "That was…"

"It was my, sweetness." A smile curls her lips and I slide out of her. I plant a soft kiss on her back. Helping her get dressed, we tidy up the dressing room. Daniel has already picked Kenna up and taken her home. Now I need to spend time with my love.

"So I am getting the red dress then?" I nod. When we make our way downstairs, the assistant packs the garment into one of their opulent bags and I pay for the shoes that Cassie had chosen before I interrupted, as well as Kenna's dress and shoes. "You didn't have to get Kenna's."

"I did. You both should be there. Both of you will look incredible. Too bad, Jayce is walking in with both of you." Robert is waiting outside, opening the door for my girl, I can't help, but check out her sexy ass when she slides into the seat.

"Mr. Verán, are you going back to the office?" I glance at Cassie, and she gives me a small shrug.

"Take us home, Robert?" He nods. Once he's in the driver's seat, he starts the engine and pulls out onto the busy Rodeo Drive. I lace my fingers in Cassie's and offer her a small smile. "That dress is perfect on you."

"I hope so, I didn't get to see it, since you took it off before I had a chance to put it on." Her cheeks flush, but I can see she enjoyed our little impromptu fuck.

"I didn't hear you complaining, Ms. Winters." I lean in and whisper in her ear. Inhaling the soft scent of lavender and sex on her skin. "If I remember correctly, you whimpered and moaned, begging me to fuck you." I keep my voice low and my hot breath sends a shiver over her, and her grip on my hand tightens.

"Luke, can you wait till we get home?" Her voice was raspy, and I was ready for round two. I chuckled and sat back. Her squirming in her seat is evidence enough that she's ready too.

Lucien

My alarm woke us early on Tuesday morning. I tug Cassie into the curve of my body, feeling her push back against me, my arousal grows. "Good morning, sweetness." Today is the ball and the end of this shit storm. I can't believe everything is coming to a head today. There are so many things that could go wrong, but I am not thinking about it. I need to stay positive, our plan will work.

"Good morning handsome." She rolls over and her brow furrows. "Why do you look so worried?" Mocha eyes glance up at me and I can't help smiling. When I lean in, I plant a soft kiss on her nose.

"Today is important. I want everything to go according to plan."

"It will. We can't keep this charade up. And I need to be with you." I nod.

"Cass, baby, I need to talk to you about something." My heart is racing, this is a big step for me, and I am not sure she will say yes.

"What?" I can see the worry in her eyes and her brow creases further. She's so cute when she's stressed. There is something I am burning to ask her. Now is a perfect time to do it.

"Well, I was just thinking…" I trail feather light touches down her arm. My heart is hammering in my chest. I have never been so nervous. Why I am stalling, I don't know. I should just ask her. This is something I never realized I wanted, but with her. I do.

"What Luke?! You're freaking me out!" She scoots up, and the sheet falls, leaving me face to face with her beautiful breasts. Distracted by her nipples, I almost forget what I am about to say. I know I am completely and hopelessly in love with this girl.

"Will you move in with me?" I look up at her expectantly. A blush spreads across her cheeks. My heart is in my throat while she watches me. *Why isn't she saying anything? Shit! She is going to say no. Fuck, it's too soon.* "Look, Cassie, I mean. We don't—"

"Yes, Luke. I will move in with you." She giggles when she realizes she had me freaking out.

"You little minx! That right there earned you a spanking!" She plants a chaste kiss on my lips, swings her feet over the bed and I watch her pad out the bedroom. *Where the fuck is she going?*

I get up and walk out of the bedroom. "Cassie?" As soon as I pass the guest room, I glance inside and find it empty. Walking over to the play room, I notice the door is cracked. "Baby?" When I push it open, a low growl rumbles in my chest and a smile cracks on my face. *Fuck me, she's perfect.* The scene in front of me is like a dream come true. Cassie, kneeling at the foot of the bed. Wearing a pair of white lace panties and nothing else. Her hair is tied back into a ponytail, her hands are behind her back, pushing her perfect tits out and her legs are spread. She's in a presentation pose and my cock wakes up. She is so perfect. I can't believe I have such a beautiful girl.

"Baby, do you need me inside that tight little pussy?" My voice takes on a low timbre and I know this turns her on. Her eyes don't leave the floor and I smile.

"Yes, Sir." Her voice is low, respectful and shy.

"Did you tease me when I asked you to move in with me?" I am now standing in front of her, my legs are in view of her gaze.

"Yes, Sir."

"Look at me." Her eyes flit up, there's a hint of naughtiness in her expression. She knows this is driving me insane with need. The need to fuck her so hard. I offer her my hand, which she gratefully accepts. She rises gracefully and I notice her body is trembling. "Are you scared?"

"No, Sir." She breathes. Her lips are soft and pink, and I seal them with mine. My tongue licks the seam of her lips, requesting entrance. She opens for me and I lick into her mouth, tasting her, savoring her essence. *My girl.* I am overcome with desire for her. Never in my life, have I ever wanted to punish, savor, and fuck anyone the way I do right now. When I pull away, her lips are swollen and sexy. With the pad of my thumb, I swipe it slowly over her mouth. Her eyes are on fire. She opens her sweet mouth, taking my thumb in, sucking in at a slow pace. Such a tease. I groan in agony. My cock needs to be inside her. "Stop." Her mouth pops off my finger and I push her to her knees. Taking her cue, she hooks her fingers in the waistband of my briefs and tugs them off. She fists my steel erection, pumping it up and down. Her beautiful mocha eyes looking up at me.

I watch her in astonishment as she takes me in her mouth, deeper until the crown hits the back of her throat. Expecting her to pull back, she further astounds me by taking me deeper. A soft gagging sound in her throat has my head dropping back, her throat tightens around the head of my cock and I almost come in her mouth. *Jesus fucking Christ, she's going to kill me!!*

"Stop, Cassie, I am going to come." I warn her, but she smiles, at least, she tries to smile. She doesn't move, she keeps sucking, licking and swallowing my cock. Deep in her throat, when she lets out an appreciative moan, I can't hold back anymore. "Fuck, baby, I am coming!" I roar, but she keeps up her relentless pace. My release spilling into her warm wet mouth and she swallows every drop. When she finally pops her mouth off my cock, she looks up at me with a satisfied smile on her face. "Baby, that was…" I have no words.

"It was." She giggles and I can't help smiling. *My girl.*

"Get up. I owe you big time for that." She shakes her head and I frown.

"Later. it's time for breakfast and then we have work." I take her hand and pull her to the bed. Letting her sit down, I stare into her eyes.

"Lay back. That's an order." Her eyes go wide, but she complies. When she's comfortable, I take her panties and tug them down her legs. As soon as they hit the floor, I turn and take in the incredible sight. The most beautiful woman I have ever seen. Naked for me, I push her legs open. She's beautifully splayed in front of me and I can't help licking my lips. I kneel with my head between her thighs and place soft kisses from her knees to the inside of her left thigh. Then I move to her right leg and do exactly the same. She's trembling below me already.

My eyes meet hers as I flatten my tongue, and I lap at her entrance. Cassie cries out. Fisting my hair, she tugs and pulls me closer to her. I suck her clit into my mouth as I slide a finger inside her heated little pussy. *Fuck she's so tight.* "You're so wet baby, you taste so good." She glances up and our eyes lock. Desire is etched on her face. I know she needs the release, but I can't help keeping her on edge, just for a little longer. Her heated cunt tightens around my finger and her legs are shaking.

"Please, Sir, may I come?" It's the first time she's begged and called me sir, and I am suddenly rock hard again. Pulling my finger from her dripping cunt, I lick her arousal from my finger. Kneeling between her legs, I slide into her easily. She tightens around me. Her legs wrap around my waist so tight I can't breathe.

"Hold on, baby girl." Her arms lock around my neck, and I lift her. Walking over to the wall, I pin her against it. I drive into her faster, deeper, and harder. My grip on her hips tightens, I lift her off my cock, then slam her back down. When her head drops back, and she cries out her release, I feel mine not far behind. "Fuck you feel incredible, lumiére." I slam into her again and my orgasm erupts from me, filling her, marking her, making her mine.

Cassandra

This morning was incredible. It replayed in my mind most of the day. Being with Luke has been a whirlwind, a roller coaster, but I loved every moment, stolen or not. My office is quiet and I think back to the stranger in the coffee shop. Never in my life did I think I would be sitting here, with him as my boyfriend. The final step was moving in together it was huge, but I couldn't deny him that. After he asked me this morning, the only thing I wanted to do to show him I accept his offer was to completely submit to him. To give him me. He owns me, every part of me, and as scary as that may sound to anyone, it makes perfect sense to me. My life has taken on a path of love, trust, and happiness. *Who knew?*

A knock at my door interrupts my thoughts. "Come in." I spin around in my chair, and my whole body freezes when I come face to face with Claudia Verán.

"Cassandra, I came to say goodbye. I trust you to remember your time is limited." I know I have to play along, Luke told me he has a plan, so I fix her with a glare.

"Claudia, I don't need reminding. Now if you'll excuse me, I have work to do." With the hope she will just turn and leave me alone, I glance down at my desk. No such luck, she steps further into the office, but I don't flinch when she leans on my desk.

"Your fucking mother, came into my life to fuck it up. Well, you will not do that to my daughter. Goodbye, Ms. Winters. I hope New York treats you well." Her words are dripping with venom and I shiver. The sweet smile I plaster on my face is as fake as hers. I rise from my chair, rounding my desk, I step up to her, my face inches from hers.

"I said, I have work to do. Get. The. Fuck. Out. Of. My. Office." Grabbing a scissor from my desk, I point it at her. Not sure where the courage came from, maybe it was her insulting my mother, but I was trembling with anger. Her face was a picture before she turned and walked out, slamming the door behind her. A deep breath I was holding whooshes from my lungs, and I slump against my desk. *Fucking hell, Cassie, where did that come from? I can't believe I did that. She riles me up so much. Fuck!*

Turning back to my desk, I flop down into my chair. Checking the time. It's almost three. Not long now. I need to pack up and go have my hair done. Jayce is picking me up at six, from Luke's apartment. This is all such a fuck up. There's no time to waste, I pick up the landline and call Kenna.

"Hey, babe! What's up?"

"I am leaving work in thirty minutes to get my hair done. Are you coming to Luke's? Or is Jayce picking you up at the apartment?"

"He said he's picking me up at 5:45, so I am guessing I will see you later."

"Listen K, there's something I need to tell you." I sit back, calming my nerves. I am not sure if she will be happy.

"What babe?"

"I am moving in with Luke… Full time." Her screech on the other end of the line says she's excited. "So, I wanted to know if you want my apartment?" And another screech has me shaking my head. I laugh at her shouting. Her colleagues must wonder what on earth is going on.

"That's so fucking awesome babe!! Yes! I want the apartment. You do not understand how happy I am for you." She's giggling now.

"Okay, okay. I will see you later." I hang up and power off my laptop. Making my way out to the elevator, I take one last look around. I may or may not be back here tomorrow. It all depended on what happens tonight.

Lucien

"Is there anything else, Mr. Verán?" Stacy got up.

"No, that's all. You can finish up and go get ready for this evening." She nodded and rose from the seat opposite my desk.

"Thank you, sir. Would it be okay if I brought my boyfriend this evening?"

"Yes, sure, that shouldn't be a problem." Her smile brightened her whole face. I didn't even realize she had a boyfriend. Not that I gave her much time.

"Thank you." She turned and walked out of the office. My phone buzzed with an unknown number and I knew who it was.

"Deanna."

"Luca. How are you?" I could tell she was smiling. There was so much that was happening tonight. I wished she could be there. *Maybe she could?*

"I am well. The plan is in place for tonight. Would you like to be there? I mean, you helped. So, please say yes?" She sighed, and I knew she was contemplating my request. I would like her to be there for Cassie, but I wanted her to see Claudia get shoved out of the company.

"Are you sure?"

"Yes, please?"

"Okay. I will be there." I smiled. This will be an incredible evening. I wanted nothing more than Claudia out of my fucking life. I said my goodbyes to Deanna and hung up. When I powered off my computer, I had a smile on my face. I pulled on my jacket and made my out of the office. Everyone had left already. The ball was one of the most famous of industry parties and this was the first year without my father. I knew I needed to be strong, this was not a time to break down over this. The elevator was waiting on the top floor and I stepped in, pushing the basement button. The car descended and my mind was reeling with all that was planned for tonight.

I text message buzzed on my phone, as soon as I saw it was from Cassie, I unlocked the screen. My smile couldn't be bigger when I read it.

* At the hair salon. See you at home, Sir *

She really was incredible. I wonder what I did to get so lucky. Hitting reply immediately.

Well baby, I am on my way home now. See you soon

In the garage, I slid into my Aston, the engine purred to life and I made my way home. There was a time when I thought I would be a bachelor forever, but having Cassie live with me makes my heart soar. *Fuck, Verán you're a sappy idiot. I wanted to spend my life, with her, next to her, inside her. Feeling her body underneath me, writhing in pleasure. When she whimpers in the pained pleasure, I can give her. Shit, now I have a fucking hard on.*

Pulling into my garage, I make my way upstairs. The penthouse already feels different. In the bedroom there is a stack of suitcases, Robert must have brought Cassie's clothes from her old apartment. There is nothing that can distract me from what I am about to do tonight. I walk into the bathroom, I turn on the shower, and step into the hot spray. The fact that I asked Cassie's mom will be one surprise for my baby, but there's another surprise. A much bigger one. Let's just hope she likes it? *If she doesn't, I'm screwed.*

By the time I get out of the shower and enter the room, Cassie is sitting on a stool at the dressing table. Her makeup and hair are done, and she looks like she's about to step onto a catwalk. "Baby, my God, you're beautiful." She giggles and turns to face me. When she stands I take in the whole ensemble. She's wearing a deep red and black corset. The tiny matching thong leaves very little to the imagination, and I am picturing tearing it off with my teeth.

"Do you like?" She smiles, twirling in front of me. Her soft silky skin is glowing in the dim light and I lick my lips. I am utterly speechless. I nod when she looks at me again. "Has the cat got your tongue?" She walks up to me and smiles. Her body flush with mine, she leans up on her tiptoes and whispers in my ear. "Sir." My towel tents in 0.5 seconds flat. I can see this being a problem tonight.

"Cassandra, baby. We don't have time. Tonight, though, you will pay for that."

"I look forward to it." She strides past me and grabs the hanger with her red dress draped over it. I get ready, thinking of my plan to distract myself from my fucking hard on.

Cassandra

I slip my dress on. The soft material is beautiful. A rich alluring crimson, that has a slight shimmer. "Please help me with the zipper, handsome?" I turn to Luke, who's fascinated with my movements. I have to chuckle, he looks like a man swept away, and I have done nothing. He strides up behind me and I feel his fingertips brush my skin. The slow movement of the zipper and the heat of his touch ignites me skin. By the time Lucien steps back my whole body is on fire. I glance in the mirror. It's perfect. The mermaid sweetheart neckline with spaghetti straps is exquisite. A tight fit that hugs all my curves. It's simple, elegant and makes me feel like a princess. My hair is pinned in a messy updo with stray curls framing my face and neck. With the diamond earrings the Luke gave me, the outfit is perfect.

"I got you a present, baby." I turn to face Lucien, who is dressed in a black Tom Ford suit, a white crisp dress shirt and a deep crimson tie that matches my dress perfectly. His messy spikes are standing in all directions and I am breathless. He looks unbelievable and I wonder how a man like him could ever want an average girl like me.

"Why? What is it? I don't need more gifts." A smile on his face makes me curious.

"It's a special one. Go stand at the mirror." I turn and make my way to the mirror. He steps up behind me and brings his arms over my head, he's holding a diamond choker with the pendant hanging form a clasp in the center.

"Oh my God, Luke. This is way too much!" I gasp when he's hooked the clasp behind my neck.

"It's never enough. This is my way of promising you forever baby. Think of it as a sign of ownership. You are mine. Collared. Owned. Every part of you." I spin around and lock my arms around his neck. My eyes gaze into his, those green eyes that can have me melting with one glance.

"All of me," I whisper. A smile curls his lips and his dimples deepen. His eyes twinkle with mischief and I know he's thinking about something naughty.

"Forever." The words from his lips sends shivers over my body. He's promising me forever. *I wonder if he will ever want to get married?* I can't think about that now. The doorbell interrupts the moment and the earlier tension is back. I know he was nervous about the outcome of tonight, so was I. "You better get going baby." Giving me a soft kiss, he walks me to the door. Jayce is waiting in the living room, dressed in a silver Calvin Klein suit with a black shirt, the first few buttons of his shirt are undone. He's hair is in a messy state, just like his best friend's. They both look like they stepped off the pages of GQ magazine.

"Cassie, my God." Jayce's eyes rake over me and I suddenly feel self-conscious.

"Thank you?" I giggle and he shakes his head.

"Come on princess. We need to get going." I nod and we all walk to the door. Luke leans down and gives me a soft kiss.

"It will all be over soon. See you there. I love you forever."

"I love you too. Forever." I turn to walk out the door and my heart feels heavy. Leaving Lucien here while I head off to the party makes me anxious. I slip into the limo; Jayce immediately hands me a glass of champagne. Thankful for the liquid courage, I take a small sip and sit back.

"Don't worry so much Cass, it will work out. Luke won't lose you." I nod and smile, but somehow I can't bring myself to say anything.

Lucien

The most difficult thing was watching her get in the car. I should be the one sitting in there with her. As soon as I grab the documents, I make sure everything is in the folder. Robert is waiting at the car when I get there. I hand to him the folder that holds my future. Down the driveway, I notice two other cars parked in my driveway. Daniel is driving one and Brax is in the other. The two men that had helped Robert finalize tonight's details.

Our three cars pull out onto the road and we make our way down to the hotel where the event is being held. There will be press swarming outside the venue; they will have a field day with this. When we arrive, the two other cars pass by, parking at the back so they are not seen by the press.

As soon as I step out of the car, they descend like vultures. Questions about my father, Cassie, Sasha, anything they could get their hands on. I stop for a few photos, but I answer none of their questions. When I get to the entrance, I notice Jayce, Kenna and Cassie are already here. They're near the bar, but I can't go to her. My body yearning to be with her. Close to her. "Luke darling." Turning to face Claudia, I don't make any move to greet her. My glare is enough to put her off asking me anything.

She gives me a smirk and I notice Isabel is behind her. Perfect, the mother and daughter can be chucked out later. Together. You will soon get what's coming to you. The only thing you deserve. Nothing. "Luca." Isabel's voice cuts through my thoughts and I glance at her.

"What?"

"Would you like to dance?" I laugh so hard that a few people around us look in my direction.

"Like fuck." I stalk away from both women and make a beeline for the bar. The barman is at my service in an instant. "Laphroaig, 12yr, three fingers." He turns to pour the drink, as soon as he places it on the bar I down it in one swallow and order another.

"Dude, slow down." I turn to look at Jayce, the two girls have him flanked and I can't deal with Cassie standing next to him. She should be next to me.

"Cassandra, would you care to dance?" She nods. I gulp my second whiskey down and feel the burn. My hand falls on her lower back and the electric current shoots up my arm as I guide her to the dance floor. The song changes, it's one I recognize the voice of Jon McLaughlin, the song is called Before You. I couldn't have picked a better song for us to dance to.

I feel like somebody else
I don't recognize myself
Staring into the mirror
Smiling ear to ear

It's funny how all this time
I thought I was alive
Now I see things clearer
Smiling ear to ear

And now
Screaming at the top of my lungs
Finally I found someone
Never knew what love could do
Before you

And I am opening my eyes
For the very first time
I never knew what love could do
Before you

"I love you," I whisper. A blush pinks her cheeks and the only thing I can do is smile. As the song ends, I realize I have to step away before I kiss her. It's time for the speeches, and I see Robert at the side of the platform they set up as a stage. He has everything I need. Glancing at the exit, I notice Daniel, he's standing in front of Deanna. Everything is perfect. "Trust me." Cassie nods and I leave her in the center of the dance floor. Jayce and Kenna flank her and I step onto the podium.

"Good evening ladies and gentlemen. Firstly, I need to welcome you all to the Annual Verán Industries Christmas Ball. As all of you know, this is our way of thanking the staff for their hard work, commitment, and ultimately support. There is one person, however, that isn't with us tonight. The most important of all." The festive decorations that trimmed the room felt wrong without my dad here. Brax brings the easel with my father's portrait on it. Placing is just behind me. This is for you, dad. "My father, Claude Verán started this business from the ground up. He worked hard all his life, but he never once neglected me. He taught me so much, ever since I can recall, he was constantly showing me new things, making me aware of the world. When I wanted to take over Verán Publishers, he supported me. He also told me to fight for what I want, and what I love. As you all know, he had decided to retire and I would have taken over the holdings from him. When he…" I faltered, and my eyes fell on Cassie, her smile gave me the strength to carry on.

"When he passed away, I thought my life was over. Things were difficult, dark, but I found a light. My father taught me a very important lesson not long before he passed. He taught me that true love is for a lifetime, not for a moment." My eyes cut to where Daniel was standing, and I saw Deanna, she was smiling. "I thank him now, for teaching me to appreciate when you find that one special person, to never let her go. I will be eternally grateful to him for that. Now, I want to tell you about my true love. I first saw her when I was thirteen. She bewitched me, and since that day, we were connected. And with my father playing matchmaker, he brought us together." Everyone chuckled, but I had everyone's attention. Claudia walked up to me then and her voice was a low hiss. She was seething with anger. it took all my strength not to laugh in her face.

"What the fuck are you doing? You will lose the company." Ignoring her, I continued.

"Life has been full of ups and downs, and I never expected I would actually say these words. But because of this extraordinary girl, I am saying them now." I make my way off the podium, I strode straight to Cassie, everyone formed a circle around us. I dropped to my knee. "Cassandra Winters, you're my love, my life, and my lumiére, the light in my future that can never be dulled. No matter who tries. Fate brought you to me, a long time ago. Destiny brought you back now. So, in saying that. I need you to spend the rest of your life with me." I pulled the little black box from my pocket and snapped it open. Her expression was priceless, just like I knew it would be. "Will you be my forever, Cassie?" My heart was hammering so hard, threatening to burst through my chest. I peered up into those mocha eyes and she nodded, with tears spilling down her face. I slipped the ring on her finger and rose. Pulling her into an embrace. With applause all around us. I couldn't help but grin.

When the commotion alerted people to turn around, I stepped backward and looked at Claudia and Isabel being ushered out by the police. People gasped watching the spectacle unfold behind them. I lifted the mic and finished my speech. "Each of you will receive an email once I finish my speech to explain what has happened with Claudia Verán, who will be stripped of the Verán name. She is no longer part of this family. Now, after all that drama, let's enjoy the evening." I placed the mic back on the podium, to applause all around. The DJ started the music then. Taking my baby in my arms, we swayed to the music.

"So soon-to-be Mrs Verán, when would you like to marry me?" She giggled, a melody that was music to my ears. My lumiére.

"Well, Mr. Verán. I guess we should have our wedding in June, in Hawaii." It will be our one-year anniversary. It was perfect. Cassie was perfect. I couldn't have asked for anything more. Thank you, dad. You've given me a gift I could never have known I wanted. Now I have it. I will never let it go.

Epilogue

Cassandra

"Cassie come on, you're going to be late!" I whirl around to see Kenna and my mother, they're both dressed in exquisite knee-length dresses. Kenna's soft blush pink, strapless satin dress, fit her perfectly. The black chiffon bow ties in the front and she's barefoot. Since we decided to get married on the beach, I requested that no one wear shoes. My mom looked incredible. Her dress was longer, stopping just below the knee in an incredible ivory color, with a cap sleeve and intricate beaded detail.

I didn't believe when Luke told me she was just an older version of me, but she is. Since the night of the ball, we've spent so much time together, and she's been a support throughout the wedding planning too. She loves Luke accepting him as her son, well, he pretty much is now.

"Yes, I am just about ready. Do I look okay?" I turn to face them and they both stare at me. "What?" I am freaking out. My heart is racing and my palms are sweaty.

"You look amazing, super hot!" Kenna, forever the one to speak her mind. I can't help the laugh that echoes through the modest room.

"Kenna, please help me with my necklace?" It was the diamond choker that Lucien gave me the night of the ball. The pendant hung in the center, on a small white gold ring. Collared. Owned. His. A blush spread across my cheeks at the thought of what that means.

"Cassie, darling, you are so beautiful. Lucien will not know what hit him." I smiled. Giving my mom a hug. I couldn't cry now. My makeup would be ruined. So I stepped back and looked at both the ladies in my life that loved me more than life. "We're going to be outside. You have ten minutes." I nod and offer a smile.

"I will be right there, Kenna. Is Jayce ready?"

"Yes, darling, everything is ready. Don't be too late." She offers me a small wink and they close the door behind them.

When I am alone, I glance at the mirror. My white dress is long, the train at the back is soft chiffon and the silk of the dress hugs my curves. The plunging neckline stops just below my breasts. It's sleeveless with a high back. I sit on the small stool and open the letter Lucien gave me last year. The one from my mother. Today is my wedding day, and it couldn't be more perfect. With people I love most in the world, I never felt happier. I pull out the folded page and take a deep breath.

Dear Cassandra,

If you're reading this, that means you've found the love of your life. The one who makes your heart soar. I had to leave you at an awfully young age. My life is filled with past mistakes, and regrets, but you were the only thing that was perfect in every way. I hope one day to meet you, to know the extraordinary woman you are.

I had you when I was sixteen that didn't bode well with my parents. So the most difficult thing I did was giving you up for adoption. It ripped my heart out and I had never felt a worse pain. I cried every night, knowing I couldn't be with you, as you grew up to be the beautiful woman you are today. The family you stayed with kept one promise for me, to give you your proper name Winters. They were good people, and I knew they would look after you, give you the love you deserved.

When you're older, I will come back and I will find you. Your forgiveness for leaving is all I will ever want. I hope you understand that my love for you has lifted me through the bleakest moments in my life. You have a guardian angel, in the form of Claude Verán, my first and only love. We could never be together, but I pray that you and your love will be.

I can't give you advice on love, since I could never be with the one person who made me whole. What I can tell you though, is that when you find him, don't ever walk away. We're all on this earth, twin flames, soul mates, and when you find the one who fits you completely, you will know. That sacred bond between two people is unrelenting, you will find each other throughout your lifetime, but you will only find forever with each other when the time is right.

In this envelope is a ring, a wedding band you will place on your soul mate's finger, when you say your vows. Take care of him, I know he will do the same for you.

Cassie, darling, I love you, and I will never leave you again, my sweet baby.

*All my love,
Mom*

    I fold up the letter and pack it back into the suitcase. There's a knock at the door, smoothing my dress, I turn and call out. "Come in, Jayce."
    It swings open and Jayce walks in, tentatively. He looks incredible, dressed in a white pair of slacks and blue shirt. The sleeves rolled up to his elbows and the first four buttons undone. "Princess, now isn't that a fitting name? You're perfect, exactly like one." He gives me a cheeky wink and I can't help giggling.
    "Thank you for doing this Jayce."
    "I wouldn't have it any other way." Pulling me into a tight embrace, he plants a chaste kiss on my head. "Come on, you can't keep my best friend waiting." We make our way out to the beach. My mom and Kenna walk down the aisle. The set up is perfect. There are white rose petals everywhere. Two pillars with beautiful white drapery on either side of the entrance to the aisle draped with pink roses. Luke catches my eyes and my breath hitches.
    "Wow." I gasp. He is dressed in a white shirt, sleeves rolled up to his elbows, the top buttons undone, against his tanned skin, it looks incredible. He's also wearing white slacks, and his spiky hair is standing in every direction. Those green eyes that had me hypnotized since the first day I saw them glint in the sunshine. "Don't let me fall, Jayce." I glance up into eyes the color of the sky.
    "Never. Come on Mrs. Verán, let's do this." No sooner had the words left his mouth, when the song I chose for this day started playing. Ella Henderson sings Yours

as I make my way down the aisle. Lucien's gaze rakes over me and I see the love in his eyes. I blink back the tears and I take a deep breath. "Just breathe, you'll be fine." Jayce whispers and gives my hand a squeeze.

Lucien

Fuck me, my girl is perfect. She looks like a princess. I can't take my eyes off her as she walks down the aisle towards me. My heart is racing. Robert grips my shoulder giving it a reassuring squeeze. He's been a rock since my father passed away, and I am proud that he is here. When Cassie reaches me, Jayce steps back and gives me a nod.

I offer her my hand, a smirk and I am rewarded with a radiant smile, her eyes are glistening with tears. I hope to God they're happy tears! "You look incredible, Mrs. Verán," I whisper in her ear. Her body trembles and I have to grin. She's always so responsive.

"Thank you, Mr. Verán." Her whisper sends a jolt of desire to my crotch. *Is she trying to kill me already? We haven't said I do yet.* I chuckle and we turn towards the officiate.

"Ladies and gentleman, we are gathered here today, to celebrate the coming together of Mr. Lucien Verán and Ms. Cassandra Winters. If anyone here who disagrees that these two people shouldn't be married, speak now or forever hold your peace." The crowd is silent, and he gives a small nod. "Well, let's get this union under way."

My thoughts wander as he rambles on, explaining the importance of love, support, being there for each other through good and bad. We wrote our own vows and I hope I don't fuck this up by forgetting mine. My palms are sweaty. *Is it normal to be so nervous? Shit, she's beautiful.* I sneak glances at my bride, I am like the luckiest bastard alive. She's amazing, and I can't imagine my life without her.

A year ago, I never pictured myself standing at an altar, with a woman about to say I do. She's wearing her necklace and I can't get my mind out of the gutter. I want you in just that choker and a pair of heels, baby. Kneeling for me. I let out a small groan and Cassie's gaze flits to me. She narrows her eyes and I can only shrug.

A naughty smile curls her lips and she knows what is in my thoughts. "Do you have the rings?" I am pulled back to the present and nod. Turning to Robert and Jayce standing to my right. Jayce steps forward and hands me the platinum wedding band.

We turn to face each other. *This is it Verán!* "Cassie, there was never a time in my life I believed I was capable of marriage. You know that my life hasn't always been perfect. With all your beauty and love, radiating from your eyes, you brought me to a place of happiness. I knew that you completed me the moment we touched. You've taken my broken soul and mended it, with your light. We have overcome obstacles that no couple should face, but we're still here. Stronger. I promise you, from this day forward I will support, love, and cherish you with everything I am. You are my lumiére and I never want that light to fade. I love you. With all of me. Forever." I lean in a whisper in her ear. "Mine." When the ring is on her finger, I see the tears spill on her soft pink cheeks. With the pads of my thumbs, I wipe away her tears. *Jesus, Verán, you've really gone soft. Fuck off! I love her.*

"Your turn Ms. Winters."

She nods and takes a deep breath. "Luca," her use of my childhood nickname sends me reeling, tears threaten in my eyes. "You're a formidable force, since you've walked into my life, I have found myself again. The person that I had hidden away. Even though I didn't think I could love, you broke down my walls and shattered my defenses. You took my broken soul and with your constant love, fixed me in a way that I thought was lost forever. You've taken me from the torn woman I was and made me whole. You're my missing puzzle piece. I promise, to support you, love you and cherish you with everything I am. I love you. With all of me. Forever." She leans up on her tiptoes and whispers in my ear. "Yours." As soon as the band slips on my ring finger, we stare at each other for what feels like hours.

"And now I pronounce you, husband and wife. You may kiss the bride." I cup her face in my hands and seal her mouth with mine. "I present to you, Mr. & Mrs. Verán." The guests whoop and applaud, but nothing can tear me away from kissing my wife.

For those who know me, you will know how much music means to me. I had so many songs on this playlist. Songs that inspired me and also songs that made the characters come alive in my head.

Angel – The Weeknd
Laurel – Blue Blood
Jay Sean - War
Thirty Seconds to Mars – Hurricane
Metallica – Nothing Else Matters
Marc Anthony – She Mends Me
Ella Henderson – Yours
Jon McLaughlin – Before You
Thomas Rhett – Die A Happy Man
Fall Out Boy – Fourth of July

Why is this the most difficult part to write? This second novel was a labor of love, pain, sweat, tears, and nights of agony (seriously!). Many late nights, too much coffee, and a few sneaky glasses of wine, went into this. It's been an incredible journey, an eye opening road that I am so happy to have traveled, and continue to wander on. When I got to the end of this, my word count was 171000 words, a lot of hard work, but I am very proud of this story. I hope you will love Lucien as much as I do. There might be a book for Jayce, we will have to see how popular those blue eyes are with you.

First and foremost, I need to thank someone special. Even though I am a complete pain in the ass, he puts up with me disappearing into my cave for months on end to write. My best friend and partner. He who shall not be named, but is an unwavering support to me through my craziness. (And he buys me wine when I need it!). Thank you! Love always.

Miriam, where do I even start? My stories wouldn't be readable without you. Your meticulous attention to detail is incredible. I know you've been busy with your own goals while I wrote this, but you still took time out of your schedule to sit down and proof for me. That means the world to me. You are the other half of me. Your support, love, and encouragement, have brought me through times where I wanted to give up. Thank you a million times over!! You are special sweetheart. I love you twinnie!

I want to thank my incredible "Research Team", without you there wouldn't be a book fit for reading. Dee and Kaz, you both really have no idea how much you mean to me. I can't thank you enough. There were times that I doubted this and your continued support, love, and understanding have kicked my ass through until I finally hit the 'Publish' button. And for that, I will be eternally grateful. The laughs we shared and to those hilarious comments about exploding underwear, I know you gave me grief for that, but I know you loved every moment.

A special shout out to two special friends I met through Instagram - Emma (Emmbooks) and Simmy (booksareverything), you've both been incredible. Making me laugh at all the abuse I receive from you both. Thank you for Beta reading this and for the feedback. It's been a pleasure getting to know you both, and a MASSIVE thank you for blogging, posting and reviewing for me. And for those awesome edits! Your support is definitely appreciated more than you can imagine.

To the awesome lady (also on Instagram) that I got to know while in the process of writing this story, Selin (uncoloredthoughts) you are incredibly beautiful, inside and out. You never fail to make me laugh. Thank you for your continued support. So glad I met you darling!

To all the amazing authors on Instagram, who support by sharing my pics, cover reveals, teasers, thank you a million times over. I am so proud to have met all of you incredible ladies. Thank you! <3

The readers, I don't even know where to start, thank you for buying the books. Thank you for supporting my dream, if it wasn't for you I wouldn't be here, doing something I love. I hope that you enjoy this book as much as I enjoyed writing it. Find me on social media, leave reviews, message me, connect! I love hearing from each and every one of you. This is much my book as it is yours. Please leave a review, on Goodreads and Amazon, it really makes a huge difference!

Much Love! xo

Dani René is a freelance graphic designer and indie author. She started writing in January 2015 and after a few fan fiction stories, she decided that her first novel Ace of Harts needed to be published. On a daily basis she has a few hundred characters, storylines, and ideas floating around in her mind. If she isn't on Pinterest or Instagram looking for her next muse, you can find her on Twitter or Facebook.

When she's writing, hiding in her cave, she's happiest. If you can't find her sitting behind her MacBook writing about hot alpha males, she's probably drinking coffee at a little coffee shop, or wine tasting one of the few hundred wine farms in her home city of Cape Town, in South Africa.

She also has an addiction to reading and reviewing books, TV series, music, tattoos, chocolate, and ice cream. Always looking for a new book to get lost in, Dani's favorite authors include - M Never, Meghan March, M Andrews, BB Reid, Whitney D, EL James, Sylvia Day, Sierra Simone, K Webster, and that's just to name a few!

Keep an eye out for other titles by Dani René

Ace of Harts (Available now on Amazon and iBooks)
Between Love and Fire (Coming mid 2016)
Within Me (Dark Secrets Book #1) (Coming soon)
Without You (Dark Secrets Book #2) (Coming soon)

Why don't you find me on social media to keep up with news about my upcoming books?

Follow me on Amazon:
amazon.com/author/danirene

Find me on Facebook:
https://www.facebook.com/DaniReneAuthor

Follow me on Twitter:
http://twitter.com/DaniReneAuthor

Find me on Pinterest
https://www.pinterest.com/DaniReneAuthor/

Find me on Instagram:
http://www.instagram.com/danireneauthor

Visit my website and subscribe to my blog:
http://www.authordanirene.com/

Printed in Great Britain
by Amazon